MW00769483

# YEAR'S BEST
# WEIRD FICTION

## VOLUME ONE

UNDERTOW
PUBLICATIONS

## Also by Laird Barron

The Imago Sequence & Other Stories
Occultation
The Light is the Darkness
The Croning
The Beautiful Thing That Awaits Us All

## Also by Michael Kelly

Songs From Dead Singers
Scratching the Surface
Ouroboros
Apparitions
Undertow & Other Laments
Chilling Tales: Evil Did I Dwell, Lewd I Did Live
Chilling Tales: In Words, Alas, Drown I
Shadows & Tall Trees

# YEAR'S BEST
# WEIRD FICTION

## VOLUME ONE

### GUEST EDITOR
### LAIRD BARRON

### SERIES EDITOR
### MICHAEL KELLY

UNDERTOW
PUBLICATIONS

AN IMPRINT OF

**First Edition**

Year's Best Weird Fiction, Vol. 1 copyright © 2014 by Laird Barron &
Michael Kelly
Cover artwork copyright © 2014 Santiago Caruso
Cover design copyright © 2014 Vince Haig
Interior design, typesetting, layout © 2014 Samantha Beiko & Michael Kelly

Foreword © 2014 Michael Kelly
Introduction © 2014 Laird Barron
"The Nineteenth Step" © 2013 Simon Strantzas
"Swim Wants to Know If It's As Bad As Swim Thinks" © 2013 Paul Tremblay
"Dr. Blood and the Ultra Fabulous Glitter Squadron" © 2013 A.C. Wise
"Year of the Rat" © 2013 Chen Qiufan
"Olimpia's Ghost" © Sofia Samatar
"Furnace" © Livia Llewellyn
"Shall I Whisper to You of Moonlight, of Sorrow, of Pieces of Us?" © 2013
Damien Angelica Walters
"Bor Urus" © 2013 John Langan
"A Quest of Dream" © 2013 W.H. Pugmire
"The Krakatoan" © 2013 Maria Dahvana Headley
"The Girl in the Blue Coat" © 2013 Anna Taborska
"(he) Dreams of Lovecraftian Horror" © 2013 Joseph S. Pulver Sr.
"In Limbo" © 2013 Jeffrey Thomas
"A Cavern of Redbrick" © 2013 Richard Gavin
"Eyes Exchange Bank" © 2013 Scott Nicolay
"Fox into Lady" © 2013 Anne-Sylvie Salzman
"Like Feather, Like Bone" © 2013 Kristi DeMeester
"A Terror" © 2013 Jeffrey Ford
"Success" © 2013 Michael Blumlein
"Moonstruck" © 2013 Karin Tidbeck
"The Key to Your Heart Is Made of Brass" © 2013 John R. Fultz
"No Breather in the World But Thee" © 2013 Jeff VanderMeer

ISBN: 978-0-9813177-5-5

Printed in Canada

# TABLE OF CONTENTS

# Michael Kelly

## FOREWORD

**Michael Kelly** *is the editor of* Shadows & Tall Trees. *His fiction has appeared in* Black Static, The Mammoth Book of Best New Horror, Weird Fiction Review, *and others. As editor he's been a finalist for the* Shirley Jackson Award, *and the* British Fantasy Society Award.

Welcome to the inaugural volume of the Year's Best Weird Fiction.

What is weird fiction?

The simple answer is that it is speculative in nature, chiefly derived from pulp fiction in the early 20th century, whose remit includes ghost stories, the strange and macabre, the supernatural, fantasy, myth, philosophical ontology, ambiguity, and featuring a helping of the outré. Weird fiction, at its best, is an intersecting of themes and ideas that explore and subvert the laws of Nature. It counts among its proponents older and newer writers alike: Robert Aickman, Laird Barron, Charles Beaumont, Ambrose Bierce, Octavia Butler, Ray Bradbury, Angela Carter, Neil Gaiman, Shirley Jackson, Kathe Koja, John Langan, Thomas Ligotti, Kelly Link, H. P. Lovecraft, and many others.

Weird fiction is not specifically horror or fantasy. And weird fiction is not new. It has always been present. That's because it isn't a genre, as such. This makes the prospect of defining weird fiction difficult, and perhaps ill advised. Weird fiction is a mode of literature that is present in other genres. Weird tales were penned long before publishers codified and attached genre labels to fiction. You can find weird fiction in literary journals, in horror magazines, fantasy and science fiction periodicals, and various other genre and non-genre journals and anthologies that are welcoming to speculative fiction of the fantastique.

# YEAR'S BEST WEIRD FICTION

There's been renewed interest in weird fiction, spurred by the likes of Jeffrey Ford, Elizabeth Hand, Margo Lanagan, China Mieville, Reggie Oliver, Jeff VanderMeer, and Kaaron Warren, (to name a few), and by the publication of anthologies such as American Fantastic Tales, Black Water, Black Wings, The New Weird, The Uncanny, Strange Tales; and journals such as Black Static, ChiZine, Shadows & Tall Trees, and Weird Fiction Review.

Weird fiction is here to stay. Once the purview of esoteric readers, it is enjoying wider popularity. Throughout its storied history there has not been a dedicated volume of the year's best weird writing. There are a host of authors penning weird and strange tales that defy easy categorization. Tales that slip through genre cracks. A yearly anthology of the best of these writings was, in my estimation, long overdue.

Each volume of the *Year's Best Weird Fiction* will feature a different guest editor. This, I believe, gives the series a fresh and unique quality, as each editor will leave their indelible aesthetic on the book. After all, the weird, perhaps more so than any other mode of literature, invites fresh perspectives and is open to multiple interpretations. What's weird for you isn't necessarily what's weird for me. Thus, the possibilities are exciting, and each volume will ring with a distinct voice.

My short list for who I wanted to edit the inaugural volume of the *Year's Best Weird Fiction* was really short. It had one name: Laird Barron. Barron is, in my estimation, (along with Caitlin R. Kiernan, and Ramsey Campbell), a current master of the weird mode. And he's a student of the weird. His knowledge of both the past masters and the current up-and-comers made him the ideal candidate to helm this first volume. He is a sharp and inimitable critic, and a unique and powerful writer and editor. So, I was extremely pleased that Laird agreed to edit the inaugural edition. As you will soon note, it is a remarkably diverse, eclectic, and potent collection of tales.

Laird, it must be said, is a true professional. I couldn't have asked for a more gracious and patient co-editor. It was a joy working with him to shape this volume. I owe him a debt of thanks.

It should be noted that I had initially planned on writing a summation of the year in weird fiction. While I did read upwards of 3,000 stories for this volume, there were several publishers who, despite several entreaties from me, did not respond to requests for material for consideration in the book. Thus, I felt a summation of the year, as lofty and admirable as that would have been, would feel incomplete.

I sincerely hope that this inaugural edition is successful enough to warrant a second and subsequent volumes. Already, even before publication, we are getting push back from buyers who are ill-informed about the long and fine tradition of the weird tale. We are, dear reader, at your mercy. I'm confident you will enjoy this initial offering, and hope you will consider it an annual "must buy."

Finally, thank you to all the backers of the crowd-sourcing campaign. Truly, we could not have done this without you. You now hold the fruits of our labor in your hands. You did good! Thank you!

So, without further ado … welcome to the weird!

—Michael Kelly
Pickering, Canada
June 23, 2014

# Laird Barron

## We Are For the Weird

**Laird Barron** *is the author of several books, including* The Croning, Occultation, *and* The Beautiful Thing That Awaits Us All. *His work has also appeared in many magazines and anthologies. An expatriate Alaskan, Barron currently resides in Upstate New York.*

Morbid and fatally-curious primates that we are, we are for the weird.

Telling ghost stories was popular during my youth in Alaska. Whenever my family and friends gathered around the campfire, and as the shadows lengthened and the hour grew late, inevitably someone would begin a round robin tournament of eerie tales. My grandmother occasionally spoke about a fateful Thanksgiving, back in the late 1940s. While the assembled relatives kibitzed, she went down into the cellar to fetch a jar of preserves. The cellar wasn't much more than a pit reinforced by rotting timbers. Raw earth lay exposed where Grandpa hadn't gotten around to finishing the retaining wall. That hole in the ground was always cold, always damp, and dark, utterly dark but for the light from the kitchen that cast a feeble glow on the moldering shelves.

As the story goes, Grandma reached for a jar and at the moment the cellar door slammed shut. She started up the steps, feeling her way in the pitch blackness. A hand, cold as meat from the locker, clamped around her ankle. She began screaming. Of course, within moments, family members flung open the door and came to her aid. As the kitchen entrance was the only way into or out of the cellar, no one took her story seriously. They attributed her claims of being accosted by a lurker beneath the stairs to panic and claustrophobia. Within a few minutes her ankle swelled and bruised into a recognizable pattern of black and blue fingerprints. Cue the Theremin.

Doubtless there was a rational explanation, but Grandma never forgot that night, and neither did my mother, who retold the account on numerous occasions. It became something of a family legend that persisted for decades. Such is the power of the unknown upon our imaginations. Humans are pathologically obsessive creatures. We like bright things, such as fire and blood. We fear the dark. We invented cautionary tales to enhance our species' survival rate, but also because we're enraptured by questions of mortality and have been since one of our ancestors split his neighbor's skull with a rock, since the shrieks of carrion birds and the moan of wind through night-cliffs caused us to wonder if the animating force of meat could manifest as spirits of vengeance or suffering. We don't know, can't know, so we tell stories to give shape to the black chaos that surrounds our specks of light, our tiny islands of stability.

We are for the weird; its presence is ubiquitous in pop culture. Look at the folklore generated by its manifestation in the physical world: The Mary Celeste. Ourang Medan. Phineas Gage. Edgar Cayce. Judge Crater. MKULTRA. Cattle Mutilations. Satanic Murders. Hollow Earth. Little People. Poltergeists. Doppelgangers. Stigmata. Cult of the Comet. Campfire ghost stories. This stuff may well be imprinted on our DNA. Given our fascination with paranormal phenomena and unsolved mysteries, I am perplexed that it has taken this long to conclude there's a need for a year's best weird amidst similar catalogues of fantasy, science fiction, and horror.

Someone recently asked me what I consider the greatest weird tale of them all and I said, "The Willows" by Algernon Blackwood. But that's from my limited perspective and it's not entirely true. There are too many shades of weird, too many striations, and too many layers in the fossil record of this particular literary vein to proclaim "greatest" or "best" with any authority. I can only point and say, "Well, I like that a lot. It surprised me. It filled me with a sense of unease. I looked at the world differently, more suspiciously, after I read it."

Years of life on the range in Alaska biases me toward the starker, darker aspects of fantastic literature. I gravitate toward the cold and the violent, the notion that sentient life is fragile, impermanent, and possessed of a fragmentary piece of the big picture at best. Brutal wilderness-scapes and ominous pastorals make me happy. The darker side of the weird is where it's at-- the seam that intersects with the sinister styling of Edgar Allan Poe, Algernon Blackwood, Shirley Jackson, and Robert Aickman.

Blackwood's story is precisely the kind of work that resonates with my own experiences. The story is simple. Two men traveling along a remote stretch of river share an inconclusive encounter with an ineffable force. In a handful of pages Blackwood transforms the bucolic and mundane countryside into a hostile and alien environment. Not unlike another quintessentially weird tale, Carroll's *Alice's Adventures in Wonderland,* Blackwood's "The Willows" sends the reader down the rabbit hole with expert finesse. Quietly, relentlessly, and inevitably, the facade of normalcy is stripped to reveal a sliver of the raw universe.

The protagonist and his companion make guesses as to the provenance of the malign presence, or presences, within the river and the willows. But they cannot apprehend its nature, for it is beyond their reckoning. All they know is that for them, true north is no longer true. They have glimpsed something much larger than themselves, and it is frightening. Frightening because it is inexplicable and also because man is an animal not far removed from the cave. The human brain for all its adaptability doesn't react well when its reliance upon a codified set of assumptions is challenged. Held in thrall by this immense and apparently malevolent entity, the travelers are reduced to the most primitive roots of our species. The men cower and speculate, even broach the notion of supplication via human sacrifice. Same as it ever was—we venture into terra incognita in trousers and shoes instead of animal pelts, bearing machined knives and compasses instead of flint spearheads and relying upon the direction of the setting sun for navigation. The unreasoning fear of the dark and the unknown, of the other and of *othering* effects, remains lodged in the heart of modern Homo sapiens. Blackwood's story speaks to that deeper part of us like an animal handler coaxing some wild beast from its den, and it has done so for many decades.

Of course, the weird informs a great deal of genre literature, especially pulp era material. Take a closer look at the John Carter series by Edgar Rice Burroughs, or Robert E. Howard's Conan saga and you'll find yourself in as similarly strange territory as the poor bastards caught on Blackwood's nightmare vision of the Danube. It's simply that Burroughs and Howard hew from a radically different narrative angle. John Carter and Conan meet the weird and the ineffable head-on with a bloodthirsty gusto. Anything can be hacked with an ax or a sword or dominated by the will of a strong man.

Burroughs work exemplifies the Sir Arthur C. Clarke maxim that any sufficiently advanced technology would be indistinguishable from magic. In Burroughs' John Carter series, Barsoom (Mars) habitability is maintained by ancient machinery, its inhabitants fight wars in the name of old traditions and older gods aboard vessels equipped with anti-gravity devices. He gives a bizarre and baroque pageant of sensory excess—alien customs, alien mores, and aliens, all of it a hair's breadth from good old Terran reality, a madman's counterfactual odyssey.

# We Are For the Weird

Howard gave us Conan, a Wildman from the north whose freebooting journey across Hyboria is equal to Carter's in its expression of the baroque and the alien. Lizard-loving sorcerers; effete, cannibalistic underground civilizations; dinosaurs and demonic powers; and creatures from beyond the grave add up to equal parts fantasy, pulp, horror, and weirdness. The upshot of these comparisons being that the weird isn't confined to a narrow spectrum. Much like horror and fantasy, its remit is remarkably broad and overlapping. Certain stories from Lord Dunsany and MR James to Shirley Jackson, Jack Vance, or Stephen Graham Jones qualify.

I knew what I was in for when series editor Michael Kelly tapped me for the job of assembling this inaugural volume. Genre definitions are often nebulous, if not useless, and none moreso than the weird. Ask buyers for bookstore chains. Some of them will protest it doesn't even exist. That's all right—we know it exists, you and I. It's related to, yet palpably separate from, other genres. Neither fish nor fowl, the weird is either a subset of horror and fantasy literature, or it's the fathermother, or you're going to disagree entirely. As with any genre, the parameters of the weird are shaped and defined by the participants—editor and writer alike. In some respects, grappling with a serviceable definition is akin to the three blind men describing an elephant. Perhaps in this case, it's a diver in murky depths who spies the last meter of a trailing tentacle and innocently supposes he's apprehended a common specimen of octopi. The rest of the mighty Kraken, coiled within its lair, waiting. We catch mere glimpses of this beast called the weird and think we know it, can safely catalogue it.

Happily, there's a built in mechanism to deal with such difficulties. Among the more remarkable aspects of this year's best series, is the fact that it will evolve with each new volume and develop not unlike a sequence of snapshots. Every editor that rides herd on this series is going to brand it with his or her unique perspective. As I said at the top, I'm a horror guy, a connoisseur of the bleakly fantastic, the gothic, and the macabre. My choices reflect those predilections. Next year will feature a new guest editor with a wholly different slant on the subject. It will be, as they say, a completely different story.

That leads directly to another question I've received: What did I look for when selecting the stories of Volume One? My sense of a weird tale is that it contravenes reality in some essential manner; that it possesses at least a hint of the alien; and that it emanates disquiet or disorientation. If I may quote the answer from an interview I did with Weird Tales about what kind of story fulfills the weird criteria:

"When there's a sense of dislocation from mundane reality; the suspension      of the laws of physics, an inversion or subversion of order, a hint of the alien. Weird stories hit a different register than other genres. There's the experience of frisson, but it's a different thrill than the variety I receive from a good horror tale. Which is all to say, it's personal. I perceive the weird as a distinct literary tradition—one intimately related to fantasy and horror, and that relationship is fluid, maybe a little complicated."

Ultimately, I endeavored to choose a diverse table of contents. Diverse in voice, diverse in tone, diverse in theme, and diverse in the genres that are represented. Settling on finalists was painful. Peruse the honorable mentions—as may be evident, I could have assembled a second volume. In fact, the honorable mentions list by no means records all of the best material I read last year. The weird is alive and well.

A few more words before I go: Whittling the candidates down to a final table of contents was no easy task. I'm grateful for the efforts of the editors and publishers whom I consulted while compiling a massive reading list. Ellen Datlow and Gordon Van Gelder were extremely helpful in that regard. I'd also like to acknowledge the ongoing work of S.T. Joshi, and Ann and Jeff VanderMeer. This trio has worked diligently to bring the weird genre into the light and expand its audience. Hand in hand with the current horror renaissance occurring in the small press (and gods bless them too), through a series of excellent anthologies, essays, and lectures, they've helped create a climate where a book such as this might flourish. Thank you to the many readers who backed the original fundraiser that helped make volume one a possibility. Finally, my gratitude to Michael Kelly for his yeoman's labor in culling the K-2-sized slush pile that attended the open submission period. Mike has quietly and humbly become one of the finest editors currently working. It was a comfort to rely upon his skill and expertise throughout the process. He is the epitome of a professional and I can't imagine a wiser head to serve as series editor.

So it comes to this; the inaugural volume of the *Year's Best Weird Fiction* is at last a reality. Join us now. We are for the weird, else we wouldn't be here. Pull up a stone by the campfire of your youth and partake of a ghostly tale, or something far stranger.

—Laird Barron
May 17, 2014
Rifton, New York

# Simon Strantzas

## The Nineteenth Step

**Simon Strantzas** *is the author of four collections, including* Burnt Black Suns *from Hippocampus Press (2014). His writing has appeared in various "best of" annuals; has been translated into other languages; and has been nominated for the British Fantasy Award. He lives in Toronto, Canada, with his wife and an unyielding hunger for the flesh of the living.*

Broken shutters, boarded-over windows, a tree bent crooked and grey, leafless; the house was pressed between two other houses on the dismal November street. Mallory and Alex had already seen countless variations, each more unsuitable than the one before. This house appeared no better. But Mallory would go inside. Mallory *always* went inside whether her gut told her to or not. She held out hope that for once, she would be surprised.

And she *was* surprised. Surprised by the mess. Creaking floors covered in rancid stained carpeting, held down in places with nothing more than household staples. The walls in the rooms all were slate grey, the paint thick and filled with brushstrokes. Whatever it was meant to cover was going to stay hidden. The only pleasant surprise was the staircase to the second level. The surprise was that it was in one piece.

"It's a fixer-upper, for sure," the agent said, "which is why I brought you here. Alex is handy, and if you look past everything you can see that the house itself is in good shape. A bit of elbow grease and this place will double in value. See these floors? Underneath them, cherry hardwood." She stomped, then reached down and with the tips of her manicured fingers pulled back a corner of the grey wall-to-wall. The wood beneath was mottled but solid. "When they built these houses in the fifties, they installed hardwood floors as a standard. They just assumed people would cover them with carpet. Bare floors were for the poor. This carpet looks like it's original to the house, which means the floor has probably been protected since day one. Hire a team to do the sanding and varnishing and you'll have the sort of floor everyone pays through the nose to have nowadays. I'm telling you," she said, looking smugly at her surroundings, "if you're looking to flip a house, this is the one. A little work will get a big return. Get us *all* a big return, I mean." She winked, and Alex nodded. Mallory as usual acquiesced.

Flipping houses was the perfect solution for her and Alex's future. Mallory had been saving every penny she'd made for years, and Alex had spent a lifetime at his carpenter father's side, installing everything from shelves to roofs. They had no children, jobs without set hours, and were still young enough that they could do without much sleep. They both knew it wouldn't last forever, but only Alex was keen to buy right away.

"It's simple: we stop throwing money away on renting an apartment and buy a rundown house; we then live in the house while fixing it up; when it's fixed, we sell the house for a tidy profit." He did the math for her: if they worked hard for five years, flipping houses, by the time the two were thirty, they would have a big enough nest egg that they would never have to worry about their future again. This is what finally sold Mallory on the idea.

Alex noticed the problem with the staircase first, despite the number of times Mallory had travelled up and down it during the initial renovation, then during the final move, then during the rearranging and reorganizing. But why would it occur to her that anything might be wrong? She wasn't a carpenter, after all. She didn't know how these things were done. So when Alex said, in passing over the knock of his hammer against drywall nails, "Have you noticed the stairs?" she didn't know what to make of the question.

"What do you mean?"

"I mean, there isn't the right number of them. They're uneven."

"I have no idea what you're talking about."

"It's not up to Code. There should be an even number of stairs. But there's not. There are too many. Or not enough."

She must have betrayed her lack of comprehension, because he spoke slower, in that way she hated.

"These risers are seven inches tall, with a one inch tread. I've double-checked. This floor has ten-foot ceilings. Assuming two feet between floors, there should be exactly eighteen steps from this floor to the next. But there aren't."

"Is it really that big of a deal?"

"I don't know," he shrugged. "Probably not."

And they went on to talk about other things.

But Mallory didn't forget, and when breakfast was done and Alex was in the office, installing new shelving, Mallory paused at the foot of the stairs to the second floor and counted. There were eighteen, just as Alex had said there should be. So she counted them again to be sure. Even if she included the floors themselves and not the steps between, the number was even. She shook her head. What Alex was thinking? She put down the basket she'd been carrying and walked through the kitchen toward the office. There was quiet muttering, as though Alex were speaking to someone, but when she entered the room he was alone, tape measure against the wall. "Were you just on your cell phone?" He looked at her as though she were an alien. "No," he said, the word drawn out until it lingered between them. "Why?"

"Nevermind. Listen, I counted the stairs. There are eighteen of them."

"That's impossible."

"It's true. Come see for yourself."

He put down the tape measure and hurried out of the office, the shelves behind him instantly forgotten under the possibility of being proved wrong.

"See?" she said, narrow finger pointed as they stood before the staircase. "Eighteen."

She watched his head bob as he counted, then a perplexed look crept across his narrow face before his head bobbed once again. Without a word, he began to climb the stairs. Mallory watched him, amused at his need to prove himself, as though neither she nor his own eyes could be trusted. He'd always been that way, since the day they met. Sometimes, his inability to believe anyone else was infuriating, but often she simply found it charming.

"A-ha!" he said as he reached the top of the stairs. "I was right. Nineteen!"

"What?"

"Watch!" he said, and proceeded to descend quickly toward her. He led with his right foot, and counted the stairs off, one at a time. When he reached the last step, he landed on his right again, exclaiming "Nineteen!"

Her mind boggled. She pointed at the steps one at a time and counted. Then counted them again. No matter how she tried, there were only eighteen.

"I need to sit down."

Alex strutted back to the office, his reputation intact, while Mallory remained behind, seated on the living room sectional, her head a-buzz. It had to be a trick, she reasoned. Like an optical illusion, what she saw with her own eyes could not be trusted. There was something more to the stairwell, something she could not articulate. There wasn't any word for it, but it stayed with her the rest of the day, and kept her awake at night while Alex snored blissfully beside her. She flipped the covers back with irritation and put her feet in her slippers.

The staircase lay in half-darkness, shadowed by the odd arrangement of lights on the wall. In her tired state, she thought she saw the steps move ever so slightly, as though they had settled into place only as she'd turned the corner. She shuffled to the top of the staircase and looked down. The light stretched far enough to reveal the entirety of the staircase, and Mallory counted the steps again. There were eighteen. This did not make her feel any better. Alex's gentle snoring emanated from the bedroom down the hall. Mallory smiled. Then she turned back to the staircase and took her first step down.

She counted them off in her head as she descended, holding the bannister tight and watching her feet. Sixteen, seventeen, eighteen, nineteen—her foot landed safely on the first floor, and her concern carried with it. She looked back at the top of the stairs, dim light wavering as though about to flicker out. She shivered, her teeth chattering, and walked back up the stairs. When she reached the eighteenth, there was still one step between her and the second floor landing.

It made no sense. None at all. Something was wrong with the reality of the house, some bend in what she had until then believed was solid, and if something as simple as the number of stairs was wrong, then who knew what else could be? She went to take the final step, then stopped. Did the light grow dimmer, or was the staircase fading from reality, leaving her and Alex stranded on the second floor? Worry overcame her. What if she could no longer bring herself to put a foot down on the final stair in case there was nothing to bear her weight? What if she fell and fell and fell into a neverending nothingness?

# The Nineteenth Step

She carefully raised her foot and stepped over the nineteenth stair, stretching to reach the second-floor landing. As soon as she pulled herself to it, she dashed for the bedroom without turning around and leapt into the bed. She pressed her body as tight as she dared against Alex, blissfully ignorant and snoring, in hopes it would calm her uncontrollable shivering. As she tried to fall asleep, she wondered if it wasn't the fear of falling into nothing that terrified her most, but instead her desire to blindly leap.

In the wash of daybreak, Mallory was humiliated, and thankful there had been no one else present during the night to witness her foolishness. Lying in the soft sunlight, it all seemed so bizarre to her, and she wasn't absolutely certain it hadn't simply been some dream born of exhaustion. Of all things to be afraid of, after all: a stairwell? It was absurd. She was quite glad the day had returned, the morning sun clearing away the cobwebs of midnight hysteria. Alex remained sleeping beside her, and she rolled over onto her bent arm and watched his soft lips gently putter for a while.

Despite her waking confidence, she did her best to avoid the staircase afterward. Once descended, she refused to look back, to even acknowledge there were stairs present. Instead, she found work for herself amid splintering baseboards and chipped plaster. Resuming the renovations helped fade any lingering phantoms from the previous night—though much to Mallory's chagrin they did not dissipate completely. It only took Alex uttering a single phrase for the amorphous fear to rebloom.

"Hey, come look at this."

She wasn't sure she could move.

"What is it?"

Alex said nothing. Mallory shivered. She hoped he was in the room beyond the staircase, hoped he was any place other than on those wooden steps she'd taken such pains to avoid. But she knew hoping was no use. That would be exactly where he was.

"Are you there?" she said as she walked through the kitchen toward him, each step becoming progressively more difficult. She could not take her eyes from the other entrance, the corner around which she knew, if she turned, she would be face-to-face with her nightmare. She could feel her legs stiffening, each stride shortening, until she was barely moving at all. And then her legs decided to stop working completely, and she heard only her blood racing in her ears.

Then Alex materialized before her.

"You won't believe this. It's going to blow your mind!"

He grabbed her wrist too tightly and dragged her around that corner she had no desire breech.

Mallory did her best to avoid looking at the stairs, but Alex danced on them, calling for her attention and she knew he would not relent. He wanted an audience.

"I need you to tell me what happens."

"What do you mean?"

"Watch!"

Alex went back to the bottom of the stairs and started walking up them again, but slower. With each step, he called out its number.

"One!"

Mallory felt dread race down her spine. The narrow hallway, the wooden staircase, they began to take on a different aspect, shifting into a sort of hyper-reality. Like a nightmare. Each edge became crisper, every colour stronger—almost too crisp, almost too strong—and Mallory felt the oppressing weight of her terror mounting.

"Seven!"

"Alex, come back."

She did not want him to continue, did not want to even be in the same house as that horrible staircase. Why couldn't they leave, both of them, into the night? Simply drive away as far as possible? They could come back later for their things. Or maybe they could just flatten the house and burn it to ashes. Anything but stay as the were, her watching helplessly as he climbed the stairs to the unknown.

"Eleven!"

"Whatever it is, Alex, I don't care. Just come down." There was a sickening fear gnawing at her; a terrified scream raging to be born.

"Seventeen!"

"Alex, don't." Her throat was drier than it had ever been.

"Eighteen!"

"Alex, please come back!" she said, tears blurring her vision.

But Alex did not come back. Did not answer. Made no sound at all. Mallory wiped her eyes profusely, certain he would no longer be on the staircase when she could finally see again. But Alex was there, standing on the final step quietly, not moving, his back to her.

"Alex?" she said, her relief suddenly turning cold. "Alex? Are you okay?"

He remained perfectly still.

There were no thoughts in Mallory's shaking head. The walls

pulsed, throbbed like a beating heart. Mallory could not move, could not turn her head away. She could only stare at Alex, terrified he would never turn around. Terrified of what would happen if he did. Mallory stared and stared until—

"Nineteen."

Mallory couldn't speak. Alex slowly turned. His face was grey as ash, wrinkled as it had never been before. And his eyes, staring off into the distance, his eyes...

"Mallory, I—"

"What's wrong?"

"I—I can see..."

He paused one final time, and Mallory felt on the verge of losing everything.

"What is it, Alex? What do you see?"

And this is what he told her...

# Paul Tremblay

## Swim Wants to Know
## If It's as Bad as Swim Thinks

**Paul Tremblay** *is the author of the novels* The Little Sleep, No Sleep till Wonderland, Swallowing a Donkey's Eye, Floating Boy and the Girl Who Couldn't Fly *(as PT Jones with Stephen Graham Jones) and the forthcoming* A Head Full of Ghosts *(May 2015, William Morrow). His short fiction and essays have appeared in the Los Angeles Times and numerous Year's Best anthologies. He is also the author of the short story collection* In the Mean Time *and he co-edited (with John Langan) the anthology* Creatures: Thirty Years of Monster Stories. *He lives just outside of Boston, and when he's not writing about narcoleptic detectives, girls with two heads, or teens who float, he helps administrate the Shirley Jackson Awards. www.paultremblay.net*

W hat I remember from that day is the road. It went on for forever and went nowhere. The trees on the sides of the road were towers reaching up into the sky, keeping us boxed in, keeping us from choosing another direction. The trees had orange leaves when we started and green ones when it was over. The dotted lines in the middle of the road were white the whole time. I followed those, carefully, like our lives depended on them. I believed they did.

We made the TV news. We made a bunch of papers. I keep one of the clippings folded in my back pocket. The last line is underlined.

"The officer said the police don't know why the mother headed south."

᯿

# Swim Wants to Know If It's As Bad As Swim Thinks

I need a smoke break bad. My fingertips itch thinking about it. It's an early afternoon Monday shift and I'm working the twelve-items-or-less register, which sucks because it means I don't get a bagger to help me out. Not that today's baggers are worth a whole heck of a lot. I don't want Darlene working my line.

We've never met or anything, but Julie's youth soccer coach, I know who he is. Brian Jenkins, a townie like me, five years older but looks five years younger, a tall and skinny school-teacher type even if he only clerks for the town DPW, wearing those hipster glasses he doesn't need and khakis, never jeans. Always easy with the small talk with everyone in town but me. Brian isn't paying attention to what he's doing, lost in his own head like anyone else, and he gets in my line with his Gatorade, cereal, Nutter Butters, toothpaste, and basketful of other shit he can't live without. Has a bag of oranges, too. He'll cut them into wedges like those soccer coaches are supposed to. I'm not supposed to go to her games so I don't. From across the street I'll walk by the fields sometimes and try to pick out Julie, but it's hard when I don't even know what color tee shirt her team wears. When Brian sees it's me dragging that bag of oranges over the scanner, me wondering which orange Julie will eat, sees it's me asking if he has a Big Y rewards card, and I ask it smiling and snapping my gum, daring him to say something, anything, he can barely look me in the eye. Run out of things to say in my line, right coach?

I get recognized all the time, and my being seen without being seen is something I'm used to, but not used to, you know? I never signed up to be their bogeywoman. Yeah, I made a mistake but that doesn't mean they're better than me, that I'm supposed to be judged by them all the time. It isn't fair. Back when I could afford to see court-appointed Dr. Kelleher he'd tell me I'd need to break out the negative thoughts cycles I get stuck in. He was a quack who spent most of our sessions trying to look down my shirt, but I think he was right about breaking out of patterns. So when I start thinking like this I hum an old John Lennon tune to myself, the same one my mother used to walk around the house to, singing along. She'd drop me in front of the TV to do what she called her exercises. She'd put on her walkman headphones that just about covered up her whole head, the music would be so loud she couldn't hear me crying or yelling for her, that's what she told me anyway, sorry honey, Momma can't hear you right now, and she'd walk laps around the first floor of the house, she'd walk forever, bobbing her head and singing the same part of that Lennon tune over and over. So I find myself singing it now too. The song helps to ease me out of it, whatever it is, sometimes. Sometimes it doesn't.

I'm humming the song right now. The notes hurt my teeth and goddamit, I want my cigarette break. It'd take the edge off my fading buzz. I scratch my arms, both at once, so maybe it looks like I'm hugging myself to keep warm. It is cold in here but I'm not cold.

Monday normally isn't too busy but there's a nor'easter blowing so the stay-at-home moms in their SUVs and all the blue hairs are in, buzzing around the milk, juice, bread, cereal, cigarettes. Only three other lines open and they're all backed up so Tony the manager runs around, the sky is falling, and he runs his fingers through his nasty greasy comb-over, sending people to my line. Storm's not supposed to be bad, but everyone's talking to each other, gesturing wildly, checking their smart phones. I don't listen to them because I don't care what they have to say. I just keep humming my Lennon tune to myself and I keep scratching my arms, making red lines.

Darlene's fluttering around registers now, asking the other cashiers questions, eyes and mouth going wide and she puts a hand to her chest like a bad actor. She's checking her own smart phone. I don't know how she can see it or knows how to use it. Everyone but me has a smart phone. Like Dr. Kelleher, I can't fit a smart phone in my lifestyle anymore, financially speaking.

Tony sends Darlene down to me. Great. Not being mean or nothing, but she slows everything down. I end up having to bag almost everything for her anyway because she can't see out of one eye and her hands shake and she doesn't really have a gentle setting. Bagging isn't where she should be, and none of the shoppers, even the ones who pretend to be friendly to her, want her pawing their groceries, especially when her nose is running, which is all the time. Basically they don't want to deal with her at all. It's so obvious when you have Darlene and then no one goes in your line even when the other lines are backed up into the aisles, and it sucks because I have to talk to her, and she'll just ask me questions the whole time about boyfriends and having kids. I don't quite have it in me to tell her to leave me alone, to tell her to shut the fuck up with her kids questions. I guess she's the only one in town who doesn't know who I am.

The woman in the baggy grey sweatshirt and yoga pants stops her whispering with the woman behind her in my line now that I'm in earshot. I feel a stupid flash of guilt for no reason. I haven't even done anything to anyone here yet, you know, and I hate them and I hate myself for feeling that way, like yeah of course it's because of me and not a stupid little snow storm that everyone is freaking out in the Big Y. The woman says nothing to me, then takes over the bagging of her own stuff. She just about elbows Darlene out of the way, who for once doesn't seem all that crazy about bagging groceries.

I can't resist saying something now. "In a hurry? Leaving town?" I say the leaving town part almost breathlessly. Like it's the dirty secret everyone knows.

"Oh. Yes. No. I'm sorry. I'm so sorry," she says to Darlene but keeps on bagging her own groceries. Her hands shake. I know how that feels. I run the woman's credit card and have a go at memorizing the sixteen numbers without being obvious about it. You know, just for fun.

Darlene doesn't mind getting elbowed out of the way any. She's just staring at her phone, gasping and grunting like it hurts to look at. Humming my song isn't working. Seeing Julie's coach messed me up good.

Tony's still directing traffic into the lines, which is totally useless. We're all backed up and the customers are grumbling, looking around for more open lines. It's as good a time as any for me to yell back to Tony that I have to take a break.

He opens his mouth to argue, to say no, you can't now, but the look I give him shuts him down. He knows he can't say no to me. He shuffles through the crowd to behind my register, and takes my line. "Be quick," he says.

"Maybe." I grab my coat. It's thinner than an excuse.

Then he says something under his breath, something about not knowing what's going on here, not that I'm listening anymore.

Darlene with all her fidgeting, customers rushing around the aisles, cramming into the lines, just about sprinting out of the store, hits me all at once, and for a second it's like all the times I've blacked out then woken up with that feeling of oh shit, I wasn't me again, and the me who wasn't me did something, something wrong, but I don't know what. Like that one time in my newspaper clipping when just like the cops, I didn't know why the wasn't-me was going south with my daughter either.

I say to Darlene, "Can I see what you're watching, darling?" and I try to grab her phone. No go. Darlene has a death grip on the thing, and she taps my hand three times. Same OCD tap routine she goes through with the customers. Sometimes she'll tap the box of Cheerios before stuffing it into a bag, paper or plastic, or she'll tap the credit card if I leave it out next to the swipe pad instead of putting it back in the customer's hand.

She says, "It's a news video. Something terrible is happening. Something weird came out of the ocean," then she whispers, "Looks like giant monsters!"

"Well, I gotta see that, don't you think? Show me. Don't worry, I won't grab again. You hold the phone for me and I'll just watch."

I try and get close to Darlene but she's always flailing around like a wind chime in a storm. The video plays on the phone but she obsessively moves the little screen away from me and when I try to hold her still she clucks and starts in with tapping me again so I can't see much. What little I see looks like footage from one of the cable networks. A news ticker crawls along the bottom of the screen. Can't make out the words. I think I see what looks like giant waves crashing into shoreline homes, and then a dark shape, smudge, shadow, something above it all, and maybe it has arms that reach and grab, and Darlene squeals out, "Oh my god, there it is!" and starts pacing a tight circle around nothing.

"Hey, I don't think that's the real news, hon. It's fake. Pretend, yeah? I bet it's a trailer for a new movie. Isn't there a monster movie coming out soon, right? Next summer. There's always a big monster movie coming out in the summer."

"No. No no no. It's the news. It's happening. Everyone's talking about it. Aren't you talking about it too?"

Tony shouts over to me, "What are you doing?"

That's enough to chase me out. I wave bye-bye with my cigarette pack, the one with a little hit of yaba tucked inside. I say, "Don't wait up," loud enough for myself and I walk through the sliding doors and outside. I'm supposed to have four more hours on my shift. It'll be dark then. Who needs it. I'm still humming.

The snow is falling already, slushing up the parking lot. I dry swallow the yaba that I wrapped in a small strip of toilet paper, I imagine it crashing into my stomach like an asteroid, then I light up a cig. Breathe fire. I close my eyes because I want to, and when I open them I'm afraid I'll see Julie's coach waiting for me in the snowy lot. I'm afraid he'll tell me to stay away from the soccer fields. I'm afraid he and the whole town know that I'm not supposed get within two hundred yards of Julie's house when I do it all the time. I'm not afraid of Darlene's monsters. Not yet, anyway. I'm afraid of standing in front of the Big Y forever, but I'm afraid of leaving too. I'm afraid it'll be a snowy mess already at the bus stop. I'm afraid I didn't wear the right shoes. I'm afraid I don't know if Julie takes the bus home from school. I'm afraid of home. Mine and hers. They're different now. But her home used to be my home. Julie calls my mother Gran. Gran won't shop the Big Y anymore.

I'm still humming the song, through the tip of the cigarette now. Christ, you know it ain't easy.

You sing it, girl.

♒

After the Big Y, I don't go home. I take the bus to Tony's place instead. Dumbass gave me a key. I put on a pair of his boots that are way too big. I drink a beer out of his fridge and pretend to eat some of his food. I check his bedroom dresser drawers for cash. Find the fist-sized handgun he's waved in my face more than once and a wadded up thirty-six dollars, which isn't enough.

I'm not staying long. I have to go to the house again tonight. I have no choice. Living without choice is easier.

First I jump on Tony's computer and go online to the User Forum. It's a message board. It's anonymous and free. Both are good, because, you know, it's up to me to keep me safe, to keep me not dead. My handle is notreallyhere and yesterday I posted a question.

*Notreallyhere*

**eating meth**

swim wants to know if swallowing yaba messes up your stomach bad. swim or people swim know eats it occasionally, sometimes on an empty stomach, which probably isn't good, or swim knows it isn't good but wants to know if its really as bad as swim thinks. using toilet paper help? hurt?

I call myself 'swim,' which stands for *someone who isn't me*. I use swim even though it's against the forum rules to use it. Everyone else uses it too, so swim is kind of a joke. The first response is confusing.

*DocBrownstone*

**Re: eating meth**

SWIM has done this before and the toilet paper too. Little amounts dont do much and make you constipated. Huge amounts make you super sick... SWIM puked for hours and SWIM buddy had stomach pumped. So easy to OD this way too. Super harsh, esp. the stomach. You eat it, it eats you. So play it safe with meth. Dont eat it, dont stick it in your asshole. You wont like either result.

I don't know if DocBrownstone means little amounts of meth or little amounts of toilet paper make me constipated. I don't care about constipation. If it becomes a problem I can cut it with a laxative. I never eat food anyway. I only care about the stomach pain that bends me in half like a passed note. There are three other responses.

*brainpan*

**re: eating meth**

Better for you health-wise to take orally cause it keeps blood serum levels low and keeps neurotoxicity low too. SWIy wants it, oh yes. Pepper some of one's weight in their OJ or coffee in the AM and it's all GO GO GO all day. Did Swibf say its smoother?

*enhancion69*

**re: eating meth**

Swim heard eating meth almost gets same IV high. Swim eats and high is longer and stronger, even with smaller amount.

*snytheedical*

**re: eating meth**

hey all you little swimmies out of the water. did you see? looks like its not safe anymore.

I can't get past brainpan. He's always all over these message boards and he pisses me off because he's making me nervous and that makes my stomach hurt worse. I mean, there's no way he knows what he's talking about but he's trying to fake it, always faking it. Like he can walk around measuring blood serum and neurotoxicity like ingredients in a batch of cupcakes. I get a twinge of hunger somewhere underneath all the pain. Maybe I should eat something. Maybe thinking about eating cupcakes is all I have to do to make everything better. Then that hunger pang from Christmases past turns into a machete ripping through my guts, and I'm standing up screaming, "Fuck You!" at the computer screen, at brainpan. I stumble back and knock Tony's stupid computer chair over, so I stomp it with his boots, deader than it already is, and I push his keyboard, mouse, and all the stupid little shit he saves on his desktop to the floor and I rampage all over the stuff. I've never been thinner but I crush everything under my mighty mighty weight, and I'm still grinding it all under my heels when everything goes dark.

〰

I tell Julie that a transformer blew out and it's why there's no electricity anywhere in town, and it's why I came to get her too.

I tell Julie there's nothing to be afraid of.

I ask Julie if she remembers the Ewings and their tiny red house. It was even smaller than Gran's house, but kept nicer. It used to be in the spot where we are now. Their house postage stamped this big, hilly, wooded lot across the way from Gran's. Mr. Ewing died six years ago, maybe seven, and Mrs. Ewing was just shipped to a nursing home. Alzheimer's. Her kids sold the house and plots of land to a local contractor. He knocked the little red house down, ripped out just about all the trees, leveled off and terraced the lot, and is building this huge 2500 square feet colonial on the top of the hill. For months, I've been checking out the place, watching the progress. Makes me so sad for the Ewings. The contractor keeps the house key in the plastic molding that protects an outdoor outlet near the garage. I show Julie the bright blue key sleeve.

I tell Julie that when I was her age I used to run away from Gran's house all the time, but I'd only go as far as across our street, past the corner, onto Pinewood Road, and to the Ewings house. The Ewings had five kids but they were all grown and living on their own. I hardly ever saw them. After hiding from Gran and climbing trees in the Ewings' yard for a bit, Mrs. Ewing would let me in and I'd chase her cat Pins around. Such a small house, one floor with only three bedrooms, and the kids' beds still double-stacked up against the walls like planks. Pillows fluffed and sheets tightly made. It was like being in a giant dollhouse.

I tell Julie that Pins the cat loved when I chased her from bed to bed, up the walls and down. That black and white cat had a snaggletooth that stuck out beneath its upper lip. Pins let me touch the tooth, and it was sharp, but not like a pin, you know? I tell her that sometimes I pressed too hard on the tooth and we'd both cry out and then I'd say sorry and shush us both and say everything was fine.

I tell Julie I don't think Mr. Ewing trusted me much and blamed me for the missing loose change jar he kept on his bureau and wanted to send me home whenever he could but Mrs. Ewing was so nice and would just say, "Bill," all sing-song. That way she said Bill made my ears and cheeks go red because she was really saying something about me, or me and your Gran. I didn't understand what it was back then. Then Mrs. Ewing would make me PB and J sandwiches. She must've bought the apple jelly just for me since her kids were long gone.

I tell Julie we'll get some food later. Mrs. Ewing used to always say that I should smile more because I was so pretty, and she'd use that same sing-song Bill style though, which again, I knew but didn't really know that it meant something extra. I'm smart enough to not tell Julie that she should smile now. She's eight and too hip for that now, yeah?

I'm not sure if I'm making a whole lot of sense to Julie. I'm just so happy to be here with her. Here is the half-finished house. Walls and windows are in. Floors are still just plywood and there's sawdust and plaster everywhere. We're in a giant room he's building above a two-car garage. Twelve-foot high ceilings with enough angles to get lost in. Our shuffling feet and rustling blankets echo. It's like we're the last two people left in the world.

It's snowing hard outside. It's too dark and cold in here to do much besides huddle under the blankets, talk, watch, and listen. My arms itch and shake but not because of the cold. Julie is big enough to fit into me like I'm an old rocking chair. I hold her instead of scratching my arms. I hum the family song until I think she's asleep. But I can't sleep. Not anymore.

# Swim Wants to Know If It's As Bad As Swim Thinks

The wind kicks up and this skeleton house groans and rattles. There's a rumbling under the howling wind, and it vibrates through my chilled toes. I'm leaning with my back against the wall, arms and legs wrapped in bows around Julie. I tell Julie those aren't explosions or anything like that, and that sometimes you can get thunder in a nor'easter. I'm talking out of my ass, and it's so something a mom would say, right?

We get up off the floor. Julie is quicker than me. My bones are fossilized to their rusty joints and I need a smoke real bad again. Maybe I need more. There's no maybe about it.

Julie stands at a window, nose just about against the glass. Because we're higher up than the rest of the neighborhood, we can see Gran's house down the hill and across the way. It looks so small, made of dented cardboard and tape, and it disappears as Julie fogs up the window, putting a ghost on everything outside where it's all dark and white.

The rumbling is louder, and lower-sounding than thunder. By lower I mean closer to the ground, you know? It doesn't stop, fade, or become an echo, a memory. It turns our plywood floors into a drumhead. A power saw with its sharp angry teeth shakes and rattles on the contractor's makeshift worktable in the middle of the room. Then something bounces hard off the window behind us, and Julie screams and dives down into the blankets. I tell her to calm down, to stay there, that I'll be right back.

I glide through the darkened house. Been in here enough times that I've already memorized the layout. Practice, baby, practice. Julie's soccer coach approves of practice, yeah? Straight out of the great room for ten steps, past the dinning room, take that second left off the kitchen, no marble countertops yet but dumbass left some copper piping out, which I should probably take and sell, then a quick right, eleven stairs down into the basement, left then through a door into the two-car garage, left again and step out the side door, into the swirling wind that pick-pockets my breath.

Four, maybe five inches of snow on the ground, enough to cover the toes of Tony's boots. My feet are lost in the boots and can't keep themselves warm. Losers. My shaking hands fish for my cigarette pack. I only have one left, and *one* left. The world sighs, breathes, and it's so loud, like a whale breaching in my head. Trees crack and fall all over the neighborhood, London Bridge falling down around our new house on the hill. Sirens somewhere in the distance, in town, probably. More rumbling, more stuff crashing down, cratering into the ground, shaking everything. And that world-sighing stuff, it isn't just in my head, you know. That slow inhale and percussive exhale sound gets louder, and has company. Like more than one whale breaching. Beanstalk-high above Gran's house, almost lost in the dark, are thick plumes of white air, exploding along with the rhythmic deep breathing. Three, no four, separate clouds from walking smokestacks. Holy Christ, Darlene's video. They're here and they're walking and breathing somewhere above everything. A front section of Gran's roof is gone. Most of the roof is covered in white, but there's a section that's just a dark nothing space. Then those walking smokestacks move in and more of Gran's roof rips up and away, shingles flutter around Gran's yard like dying blackbirds, the ones that are always falling out of the sky dead somewhere down south, always south, and I think I know how that feels. The monsters are giant shadows with giant boulders attached to giant arms or giant legs, I don't know which, and they pile drive into the house smashing the chimney and walls, glass shattering, wood exploding, and always those white plumes of breath above it all, breathing slow, but loud, and constant, like they'll never stop.

Julie opens the window above me and starts screaming for Gran. I stick my head inside the garage, into more darkness, and I scream and yell at her, making sure I'm loud enough so I can't hear that goddamn breathing and the end of Gran's house, so I scream and I yell for her to shut up, to stop being a baby, why are you so stupid, they'll hear you.

Swim wants to know if it's as bad as swim thinks.

〰〰

The ground shakes worse than ever because they're all around us.

My stomach is dead and it hurts to talk, but I tell Julie to stop looking out the window. I tell her that they'll see her. I say it in my quiet, I'm-sorry voice.

I tell Julie that I'd been walking by Gran's house for a while now and I'd heard Gran yelling at her, calling her stupid and so bad, just like she used to yell at me, and it's why I'd always run away to the Ewings, remember the Ewings?, and they're not here anymore, you know, so that's why I went and got her out of the house tonight, got her away from Gran.

## Swim Wants to Know If It's As Bad As Swim Thinks

Julie hasn't said anything to me since we got here, but then from under the pile of blankets and the pile of bones that are my arms and legs, she asks me if I still have the gun.

I tell her my Mom became Gran to me the day they let her take you away from me.

And then I tell Julie about that first time, a little more than seven years ago, I went and got her when she was only eight months old. I was downtown by myself, and Joey, that prick, him and his bleeding gums and cigarette burns, he was so long gone it was like he was never even there, and I remember not being able to see Julie at all, right away, and worse, not being able to remember what she looked like or what her chubby little hands and feet felt like, how that must've been the worst pain in the world, right?, I mean what else could've mattered to me?, so when the pain wouldn't go away I went over to Mom's house, *Gran's* house, and I can't remember if I really remember because what I remember now is how they explained it all when I was in the court room, how the lawyers talked about me and what I did before me and Julie went south where everything was green. I remember them saying how I walked into my old house, calm as a summer's day (was how the lawyer said it, someone objected), me and a big knife, scooped up Julie out of the crib, though I don't know how it was I held her and a big knife at the same time, right? That doesn't make sense to me. I'd be more careful than that. So yeah, Mom wasn't my mom anymore but your Gran, which means she became someone else, and her stupid twelve-pack boyfriend whoever he was, the one with the junky red truck and a rusted plow blade hanging off the grill too low, the one with the easy greasy hands, the one who'd walk in on you if you were in the bathroom, he wasn't there, I was there, so was a knife, apparently, and this new Gran, she looked so angry, tough as a leather jacket, fists clenched, hair cut too short and tight like a helmet, and no wait, she looked like she wanted to give up, so old, thin, dry-boned, but she was screaming at me fine, like she was fine, just fine, like normal, or no, that's not right because then she was crying about how she couldn't take it, any of it, anymore, saying that she had cancer in her liver now, and go ahead she said, go ahead and do it she said, do it, and I ask Julie if she remembers Gran saying that and, and dammit I'm mixing up what happened when Julie was a baby with happened tonight. How do you keep everything that happened in order anyway? Doesn't seem like order matters much because it doesn't change what happened.

I tell Julie that swim didn't think this was going to happen.

We listen to sirens coming closer and we listen to breathing and stomping and everything outside. So loud, it's like we're in their bellies already.

I tell Julie there's nothing to be afraid of. I tell her that when it's morning everything will be all done. I tell her that all the houses around us and in the rest of the world will be gone, stomped and mashed flat, but we'll be okay. I tell her that we'll ride on the back of one the monsters. Its back plates and scales will be softer than they look. We'll feel the earth rumbling beneath us and we'll be above everything. I tell her it'll know where to go, where to take us, and it'll take us where it's safe, safe for swims. I tell her that I know she doesn't remember the first time but we'll ride it south again. The monster will follow the dotted white lines and instead of trees lining the roads there'll be all the rest of the monsters destroying everything else, watching us, leading the way south, not sure why south, swim south, but maybe it's as simple and stupid as that's where everything is green, because south isn't here, because south is as good or bad as any other place.

Outside there's flashing lights, sirens, pounding on the doors, walls, and roof. Dust and chunks of plastic rain down on our heads and we fall and roll into the middle of the room. Julie's yelling and crying and I brush away hair from her ear with one hand so I can whisper inside her head. Tony's gun is in my other hand.

I tell Julie, Shh, baby. Don't you worry about nothing. Your Mom's here.

# A.C. Wise

## Dr. Blood and the Ultra Fabulous Glitter Squadron

**A.C. Wise** *was born and raised in Montreal and currently lives in the Philadelphia area. Her fiction has appeared in* Clarkesworld, Apex, Lightspeed, *and the* Year's Best Horror Vol. 4, *among others. In addition to her fiction, she co-edits* Unlikely Story. *Visit the author at www.acwise.net*

Mars Needs Men!

But the Ultra Fabulous Glitter Squadron will have to do. At least one of them self-identifies as male. He tucks proudly, and fuck you very much if you don't like it.

By night, they work at clubs with names like Diamond Lil's, the Lil' Diamond, and Exclusively Lime Green. Every Thursday afternoon, they bowl. In-between, when they're not bowling, or dancing, or singing on stage, they kick ass harder than you've seen ass kicked before. And they do it all in silver lamé and high heels.

This is Bunny, their leader, born Phillip Howard Craft the Third. At the moment, she is up in the recruiter's face, waving a poster of Uncle Sam under the aforementioned tagline, a floating head against a backdrop of Martian red. Her nails are manicured perfection; each painted a different metallic shade, all the colors of the rainbow, and then some. Her hair is piled in a frosted bouffant so high it barely fit through the recruiter's door. Despite the anger written in every line of her body, she doesn't raise her voice.

"Your sign says you need volunteers. We're volunteering, and since I don't see your waiting room clogged with other candidates, dare I suggest: We're all you've got."

"I can't...I won't..." The recruiter turns bright red. He takes a deep breath, faces Bunny, and almost, but not quite, manages to look her in the eye.

"I can't just let a bunch of…"

Bunny's eyes, tinted violet today, shine cold steel. They stop the words in the recruiter's throat, hard enough that he looks like he might actually choke. Her tone matches her eyes.

"Think carefully, General. If the next word out of your mouth is anything but 'civilians' I will dismember you myself. You won't live long enough to worry about an invasion from Mars."

The General's jaw tightens. A vein in his forehead bulges.

"The Glitter Squadron's record speaks for itself, General." Bunny's voice is level. She places the poster on his desk.

"Cleaner than yours, I'll dare say. And," Bunny smirks, and points to the General's medals, "our bling is better."

Rage twists the General's features, but his shoulders slump all the same.

"Fine," he says. "The damned mission is yours. Add a little more red to the planet, if you want it so badly."

Bunny smiles, teeth gleaming diamond bright. "I promise you, General, the Ultra Fabulous Glitter Squadron is more than up to the task."

∿

They are loaded into the rocket by clean-cut scientists with white coats and strong values, men and women who believe glitter is for little girls' birthday cards as long as they're under six years old, and leather is for wallets and briefcases.

"Some people have no imagination," Starlight stage-whispers as they climb the gangplank. Starlight was born Walter Adams Kennett. Her mirror-ball inspired outfit forces the good, moral scientists to look away as light breaks against her and scatters throughout the room.

Starlight pauses at the airlock door, looking up at the floodlit rocket, all sleek length, studded with rounded windows, and tipped at the base in fins. "Well, maybe not *no* imagination." And she climbs aboard.

Bunny reads over a brief as they hurtle between the stars. "Imagine the outfit I could make from one of those," Starlight whispers, pointing to the stars pricking the vast dark.

"Hush." Esmerelda, born Christine Joanne Layton elbows her.

"Our target is Doctor Blood," Bunny says, rolling her eyes. She flips a page in the neatly-stapled file, scans, while the twelve other

# Dr. Blood and the Ultra Fabulous Glitter Squadron

bodies crammed into the rocket lean forward in anticipation.

"The least they could have done was give us champagne. We are off to save the world, after all. And this seating…"

No one answers Starlight this time.

For this mission, they've chosen strictly retro-future, which means skin-tight silver, boots that come nearer to the knee than their skirts, bubble-barreled ray-guns, frosted white lipstick and, of course, big hair. CeCe the Velvet Underground Drag King called in sick with the flu, so it's lamé all the way. Each member of the Squadron has added their own touch, as usual. Starlight's peek-a-boo cutout dress, which is really more skin than fabric, is studded with mirrors. Esmerelda wears a wide belt, studded with faux gems, green to match her name. Bunny is wearing her namesake animal's ears, peeking out from her enormous coif.

M is the only exception to all the brightness and dazzle. M wears leather, head-to-toe. Think Michelle Pfeiffer as Catwoman—erratic, angry stitches joining found leather so close to the body there's no chance for the flesh underneath to breathe. Only it isn't like that at all. There is a whip hanging from M's hip though, and plenty of other toys beside. Only eyes and lips show through M's mask, and their gender is indeterminate. No one knows M's birth name, and it will stay that way.

Bunny clears her throat. "Doctor Blood, born Richard Carnacki Utley, is a brilliant scientist. He was working on splicing human and animal DNA as a way to cure cancer, or building better rocket fuel using radioactive spiders and black holes. Blah, blah, blah, the usual. We've all seen the movies, right?"

Esmerelda giggles approval. Bunny goes on.

"He caught his wife cheating with his lab partner, or his brother, or his best friend. He tried to burn them to death, or blow them up, or turn them into evil monkey robots, and horribly disfigured himself in the process. So he did the only sensible thing, and shot himself into space where he built a gigantic impenetrable fortress on Mars. Now, he's threatening to invade earth, or shoot it to pieces with a space laser if the United Nations doesn't surrender all of earth's gold."

"Can they *do* that?" Esmerelda asks.

Starlight mutters, "No imagination at all," and shakes her head, sending bits of light whirling around the rocket.

"That's where we come in," Bunny says. "We take down Doctor

Blood, easy peasy lemon squeezy, and we're home in time for tea."

"Ooh, make mine with brandy!" Starlight says.

Bunny rolls her eyes again. "Look sharp, we're almost there."

※

Penny is the weapons expert. Born Penelope Jean Hartraub, she is the only member of the Glitter Squadron who has actually seen war. Her mini dress has a faint coppery sheen, befitting her name. She stands at the bottom of the gangplank, distributing extra ammo and back-up weapons as twelve pairs of chunky heels kick up the red dirt of Mars.

She keeps the best gun for herself, not just a laser pistol, but an honest to goodness Big Fucking Gun. It has rings that light up and it makes a woo-woo sound when it's fired and everything. Fashion-wise, it may be so last year, but it'll get the job done. As they leave the rocket behind, heading towards the ridiculously over-sized fortress, all done up in phallic towers and bubble domes, Penny takes the lead.

They encounter guards, dressed oh-so-predictably in uniforms purchased from the discount bin at Nazis-R-Us.

"Boring." Starlight buffs her nails to a high shine against a rare patch of fabric on her dress.

She delivers a high kick, catching the first guard in the throat with the bruising force of her extra-chunky, mirror-studded heel, not even bothering to draw her gun. Esmerelda uses her belt instead of the gun hanging from it, because it's more fun. She wraps it around the second guard's throat and neatly throttles him, before returning it to her waist.

The second wave of guards approaches with more caution. Penny singles out a man with a nasty grin, the one most likely to cause trouble. He reaches for her. She surprises him with her speed, and uses his momentum to bring him crashing down. He springs up.

"I won't make this easy on you, girly," he says, or something equally cliché.

Penny ignores him and goes in for a blow to the ribs. But it doesn't land. This time he's the one to surprise her with his speed. He catches her and spins her around, pinning her. She swears he tries to cop a feel, and his breath stinks of alcohol when he speaks close to her ear.

"You like that? You want a *real* man to show you how it's done?"

*No imagination*, she imagines Starlight saying, and smashes her head back against his, hoping it will break his nose. At very least it breaks his concentration. She slips free. The BFG is too good for this one.

He comes at her fast and hard, excitement clear in his eyes. She can see from their shine just what he thinks he'll do to her when he bests her, how he thinks he'll make her beg, and how he thinks she'll like it. She sweeps his legs out from under him; there's a satisfying crack as his head hits the floor. Even dazed, he grins up at her, blood between his teeth as she stands over him. She knows exactly what he's thinking: So, you like it rough, girly? Me, too. I like a girl who knows how to play.

Disgusting.

Fashion be damned. She pulls out a battered old 9mm pistol.

"Fetishize this, asshole." And she puts a single bullet in his brain.

〰

There are gorilla men—of course there are—all spliced DNA, dragging knuckles and swinging hairy arms. Bunny makes short work of them. There are radioactive zombies, slavering, pawing, glowing green and dropping chunks of unnamable rot in their wake.

Esmerelda handles them with grace and aplomb. There are even spiders, which sends Starlight into a fit of giggling, before she takes them out, singing Bowie at the top of her lungs. There are two female guards in the whole sprawling expanse of the base, both wearing bikinis, chests heaving before they've even thought to pick a fight.

"Oh, how progressive!" Starlight claps her hands in mock rapture. "I suppose there's a mud pit just behind that door?"

The girls in bikinis exchange glances; this is outside of their training.

"Look, honey. Honeys. Let me explain something to you. Super-villains pay crap. And there's no such thing as an Evil League of Evil healthcare plan."

One of the women takes a questioning step forward. Starlight holds up a hand.

"I won't make some grandiose speech about the fate of the world, or doing it for the children you'll probably never have, but I will say this – killing bad guys is a heck of a lot of fun. And we pay overtime."

And the forces of might and justice and looking damned fine in knee-high high heels swells to fifteen.

※

M is the one to find Doctor Blood, deep in his underground lair. He stands at a curved control panel, raised on a catwalk above an artificial canal, which more likely than not is filled with genetically enhanced Martian piranhas.

He screams profanities, his voice just as high-pitched with mania as you might imagine. He's wearing a lab coat, shredded and scorched, as though he has just this moment stepped out of the fire that destroyed his sanity and nearly ended his life. To his credit, the scars covering half his face are pink and shiny, stretched tight, weeping clear fluid tinged pale red when he screams. His finger hovers over a big red button, the kind that ends the world.

M approaches with measured steps. The profanities roll off the leather; the imprecation and threats don't penetrate between the thick, jagged stitches. Doctor Blood runs out of words and breath. He looks at M, wild-eyed, and meets only curiosity in the leather-framed stare. Oddly, he can't tell what color the eyes looking back at him are. They might be every color at once, or just one color that no one has though up a name for yet.

His voice turns harsh, broken, raw. The weeping sores are joined by real tears—salt in the wound.

"I'll make you pay. All of you. Nobody ever believed in me. I'll show them all. They'll love me now. Everyone will."

It comes out as one long barely distinguished string of words. M puts a hand on the sobbing scientist's shoulder. M understands pain, every kind there is. M understands when someone needs to be hurt, to be pushed to the very edge before they can come out on the other side of whatever darkness they've blundered into. And M knows when someone has had enough, too. When there's no pain in the world greater than simply living inside their own skin, and all the hurting in the world won't bring them anything.

Doctor Blood's words trail off, incoherent for the sobs. "Daddy never...I'm sorry mommy..."

"I know," M says softly. "Shh, I know."

And M does an unexpected thing, a thing M has never done before. M steps close and folds the doctor in leather clad arms, patting his back and letting him cry.

# Dr. Blood and the Ultra Fabulous Glitter Squadron

~~~
~~~

Sixteen bodies crowd the rocket ship hurtling back toward earth— just like Bunny promised, home in time for tea.

Starlight fogs the window with her breath, looking out at all that glittering black. Esmerelda discusses wardrobe options with the women in bikinis.

The others talk among themselves, comparing notes, telling stories of battles won, the tales growing with each new telling. Ruby and Sapphire, the twins who aren't twins and couldn't look more opposite if they tried, single-handedly took down an entire legion of Martian Lizardmen, to hear them tell the tale. Mistress Minerva knocked out a guard with her clever killer perfume spray and rescued a bevy of Martian Princes who couldn't wait to express their gratitude. Empress Zatar, who was born for this mission and didn't even get a single moment of screen time, fought off three Grons and a Torlac with nothing more than a hairpin.

And so the stories go.

Penny cleans her guns and her blades, humming softly to herself as she does, an old military tune.

Bunny uses an honest to goodness pen, and makes notes in a real paper journal.

Doctor Blood's head is bowed. His shoulders hitch every now and then.

M sits straight and silent, staring ahead with leather framed eyes, and holds Doctor Blood's hand.

All together, they tumble through the fabulous, glittering dark.

They are heading back home to claim their hero's welcome, even though every one of them knows this moment, right here, surrounded by so many glorious stars it hurts, is all the thanks they will ever get for saving the world. Again.

# Chen Qiufan

Translated by Ken Liu

## THE YEAR OF THE RAT

*Chen Qiufan (a.k.a. Stanley Chan) was born in Shantou, Guangdong Province. Chan is a science fiction writer, columnist, and online advertising strategist. Since 2004, he has published over thirty stories in venues such as* Science Fiction World, Esquire, Chutzpah!, *many of which are collected in* Thin Code *(2012). His debut novel,* The Waste Tide, *was published in January 2013 and was praised by Liu Cixin as "the pinnacle of near-future SF writing." The novel is currently being translated into English by Ken Liu.*

*Chan is the most widely translated young writer of science fiction in China, with his short works translated into English, Italian, Swedish and Polish and published in* Clarkesworld, Lightspeed, Interzone, *and* F&SF, *among other places. He has won Taiwan's Dragon Fantasy Award, China's Galaxy and Nebula Awards, and a Science Fiction & Fantasy Translation Award along with Ken Liu. He lives in Beijing and works for Baidu.*

**Ken Liu** *(http://kenliu.name) is an author and translator of speculative fiction, as well as a lawyer and programmer. A winner of the Nebula, Hugo, and World Fantasy Awards, he has been published in* The Magazine of Fantasy & Science Fiction, Asimov's, Analog, Clarkesworld, Lightspeed, *and* Strange Horizons, *among other places. He lives with his family near Boston, Massachusetts.*

*Ken's debut novel,* The Grace of Kings, *the first in a silkpunk epic fantasy series, will be published by Saga Press, Simon & Schuster's new genre fiction imprint, in April 2015. Saga will also publish a collection of his short stories.*

It's getting dark again. We've been in this hellhole for two days but we haven't even seen a single rat's hair.

My socks feel like greasy dishrags, so irritating that I want to punch someone. My stomach is cramping up from hunger, but I force my feet to keep moving. Wet leaves slap me in the face like open hands. It hurts.

I want to return the biology textbook in my backpack to Pea and tell him *this stupid book has 872 pages.* I also want to give him back his pair of glasses, even though it's not heavy, not heavy at all.

Pea is dead.

The Drill Instructor said that the insurance company would pay his parents something. He didn't say how much.

Pea's parents would want something to remember him by. So I had taken the glasses out of his pocket, and that goddamned book out of his waterproof backpack. Maybe this way his parents would remember how their son was a good student, unlike the rest of us.

Pea's real name was Meng Xian. But we all called him "Pea" because, one, he was short and skinny, like a pea sprout; and two, he was always joking that the friar who experimented with peas, Gregor "Meng-De-Er" Mendel, was his ancestor.

Here's what they said happened: When the platoon was marching across the top of the dam of the abandoned reservoir, Pea noticed a rare plant growing out of the cracks in the muddy concrete at the edge of the dam. He broke formation to collect it.

Maybe it was his bad eyesight, or maybe that heavy book threw him off balance. Anyway, the last thing everyone saw was Pea, looking really like a green pea, rolling, bouncing down the curved slope of the side of the dam for a hundred meters and more, until finally his body abruptly stopped, impaled on a sharp branch sticking out of the water.

The Drill Instructor directed us to retrieve his body and wrap it in a body bag. His lips moved for a bit, then stopped. I knew what he wanted to say—we'd all heard him say it often enough—but he restrained himself. Actually, I kind of wanted to hear him say it.

*You college kids are idiots. You don't even know how to stay alive.*
He's right.

Someone taps me on the shoulder. It's Black Cannon. He smiles at me apologetically. "Time to eat."

I'm surprised at how friendly Black Cannon is toward me. Maybe it's because when Pea died, Black Cannon was walking right by him. And now he feels sorry that he didn't grab Pea in time.

I sit next to the bonfire to dry my socks. The rice tastes like crap, mixed with the smell from wet socks baking by the fire.

Goddamn it. I'm actually crying.

〰

The first time I spoke to Pea was at the end of last year, at the university's mobilization meeting. A bright red banner hung across the front of the auditorium: "It's honorable to love the country and support the army; it's glorious to protect the people and kill rats." An endless stream of school administrators took turns at the podium to give speeches.

I sat next to Pea by coincidence. I was an undergraduate majoring in Chinese Literature; he was a graduate student in the Biology Department. We had nothing in common except neither of us could find jobs after graduation. Our files had to stay with the school while we hung around for another year, or maybe even longer.

In my case, I had deliberately failed my Classical Chinese exam so I could stay in school. I hated the thought of looking for a job, renting an apartment, getting to work at nine a.m. just so I could look forward to five p.m., dealing with office politics, etc., etc. School was much more agreeable: I got to download music and movies for free; the cafeteria was cheap (ten *yuan* guaranteed a full stomach); I slept until afternoon every day and then played some basketball. There were also pretty girls all around—of course, I could only look, not touch.

To be honest, given the job market right now and my lack of employable skills, staying in school was not really my "choice." But I wasn't going to admit that to my parents.

As for Pea, because of the trade war with the Western Alliance, he couldn't get a visa. A biology student who couldn't leave the country had no job prospects domestically, especially since he was clearly the sort who was better at reading books than hustling.

I had no interest in joining the Rodent-Control Force. As they continued the propaganda onstage, I muttered under my breath, "Why not send the army?"

But Pea turned to me and started to lecture: "Don't you know that the situation on the border is very tense right now? The army's role is to protect the country against hostile foreign nations, not to fight rats."

*Who talks like that?* I decided to troll him a bit. "Why not send the local peasants then?"

"Don't you know that grain supplies are tight right now? The work of the peasantry is to grow food, not to fight rats."

"Why not use rat poison? It's cheap and fast."

"These are not common rats, but Neorats™. Common poisons are useless."

"Then make genetic weapons, the kind that will kill all the rats after a few generations."

"Don't you know that genetic weapons are incredibly expensive? Their mission is to act as a strategic deterrent against hostile foreign nations, not to fight rats."

I sighed. This guy was like one of those telephone voice menus, with only a few phrases that he used all the time. Trolling him wasn't any fun.

"So you think the job of college graduates is to fight rats?" I said, smiling at him.

Pea seemed to choke and his face turned red. For a while, he couldn't say anything in response. Then he turned to clichés like "the country's fate rests on every man's shoulders." But finally, he did give a good reason: "Members of the Rodent-Control Force are given food and shelter, with guaranteed jobs to be assigned after discharge."

〰〰

The platoon has returned to the town to resupply.

In order to discourage desertion, all the students in the Rodent-Control Force are assigned to units operating far from their homes. We can't even understand each other's dialects, so everyone has to curl his tongue to speak Modern Standard Mandarin.

I mail Pea's book and glasses to his parents. I try to write a heartfelt letter to them, but the words refuse to come. In the end, I write only "I'm sorry for your loss."

But the postcard I write to Xiaoxia is filled with dense, tiny characters. I think about her long, long legs. This is probably my twenty-third letter to her already.

I find a store to recharge my phone and text my parents at home. When we're operating in the field, most of the time we get no signal.

The shop owner takes my one *yuan* and grins at me. The people of this town have probably never seen so many college graduates (though right now we're covered in dirt and not looking too sharp). A few old men and old women smile at us and give us thumbs-ups—but maybe only because they think we're pumping extra money into the town's economy. As I think about Pea, I want to give them my middle finger.

After the Drill Instructor takes care of Pea's funeral arrangements, he takes us to a cheap restaurant.

"We're still about twenty-four percent away from accomplishing our quota," he says.

No one answers him. Everyone is busy shoveling rice into his mouth as quickly as possible.

"Work hard and let's try to win the Golden Cat Award, okay?"

Still no one answers him. We all know that the award is linked to the bonus paid to the Drill Instructor.

The Drill Instructor slams the table and gets up. "You want to be a bunch of lazy bums all your life, is that it?"

I grab my rice bowl, thinking that he's going to flip the table.

But he doesn't. After a moment, he sits down and continues to eat.

Someone whispers, "Do you think our detector is broken?"

Now everyone starts talking. Most are in agreement with the sentiment. Someone offers a rumor that some platoon managed to use their detector to find deposits of rare earth metals and gas fields. They stopped hunting for rats and got into the mining business, solving the unemployment problem of the platoon in one stroke.

"That's ridiculous," the Drill Instructor says. "The detector follows the tracer elements in the blood of the rats. How can it find gas fields?" He pauses for a moment, then adds, "If we follow the flow of the water, I'm sure we'll find them."

〰

The first time I saw the Drill Instructor, I knew I wanted to hit him.

As we lined up for the first day of boot camp, he paced before us, his face dour, and asked, "Who can tell me why you're here?"

After a while, Pea hesitantly raised his hand.

"Yes?"

"To protect the motherland," Pea said. Everyone burst out in laughter. Only I knew that he was serious.

The Drill Instructor didn't change his expression. "You think you're funny? I'm going to award you ten pushups." Everyone laughed louder.

But that stopped soon enough. "For the rest of you, one hundred pushups!"

As we gasped and tried to complete the task, the Drill Instructor slowly paced among us, correcting our postures with his baton.

"You're here because you're all failures! You lived in the new dorms the taxpayers built, ate the rice the peasants grew, enjoyed every privilege the country could give you. Your parents spent their coffin money on your tuition. But in the end, you couldn't even find a job, couldn't even keep yourselves alive. You're only good for catching rats! Actually, you're even lower than rats. Rats can be exported for some foreign currency, but you? Why don't you look in the mirror at your ugly mugs? What are your real skills? Let me see: chatting up girls, playing computer games, cheating on tests. Keep on pushing! You don't get to eat unless you finish."

I gritted my teeth as I did each pushup. I thought, *if someone would just get a revolt started, I'm sure all of us together can whip him.*

Everyone thought the exact same thing, so nothing happened.

Later, when we were eating, I kept on hearing the sound of chopsticks knocking against bowls because our hands and arms were all trembling. One recruit, so sunburnt that his skin was like dark leather, couldn't hold his chopsticks steady and dropped a piece of meat on the ground.

The Drill Instructor saw. "Pick it up and eat it."

But the recruit was stubborn. He stared at the Drill Instructor and didn't move.

"Where do you think your food comes from? Let me explain something to you: the budget for your food is squeezed out of the defense budget. So every grain of rice and every piece of meat you eat comes from a real solider going hungry."

The recruit muttered, "Who cares?"

*Pa-la!* The Drill Instructor flipped over the table in front of me. Soup, vegetables, rice covered all of us.

"Then none of you gets to eat." The Drill Instructor walked away.

From then on that recruit became known as Black Cannon.

The next day, they sent in the "good cop," the district's main administrator. He began with a political lesson. Starting with a quote from *The Book of Songs* (10th century, b.c.) ("rat, oh rat, don't eat my millet"), he surveyed the three-thousand-year history of the dangers posed to the common people by rat infestations. Then, drawing on contemporary international macro-politico-economical developments, he analyzed the unique threat posed by the current infestation and the necessity of complete eradication. Finally, he offered us a vision of the hope and faith placed in us by the people: "It's honorable to love the country and support the army; it's glorious to protect the people and kill rats."

We ate well that day. After alluding to the incident from the day before, the administrator criticized the Drill Instructor. He noted that we college graduates were "the best of the best, the future leaders of our country," and that instruction must be "fair, civil, friendly" and emphasize "technique," not merely rely on "simplistic violence."

Finally, the administrator wanted to take some photos with all of us. We lined up in a single rank, goose-stepping. The administrator held up a rope that the tips of all of our feet had to touch, to show how orderly we could march.

≋

We follow the flow of the water. The Drill Instructor is right. We see signs of droppings and paw prints.

It's getting colder now. We're lucky that we're operating in the south. I can't even imagine making camp up north, where it's below freezing. The official news is relentlessly upbeat: the Rodent-Control Force units in several districts have already been honorably discharged and now have been assigned good jobs with a few state-owned enterprises. But among the lucky names in the newsletter I don't recognize anyone I know. No one else in the platoon does either.

The Drill Instructor holds up his right fist. *Stop.* Then he spreads out his five fingers. We spread out and reconnoiter.

"Prepare for battle."

All in a moment I'm struck by how ridiculous this is. If this kind of slaughter—like a cat playing with mice—can be called a "battle," then someone like me who has no ambition, who lives more cowardly than a lapdog, can be a "hero."

A gray-green shadow stumbles among the bushes. Neorats are genetically modified to walk upright, so they are slower than regular rats. We joke among ourselves that it's a good thing they didn't use Jerry—of *Tom & Jerry*—as the model.

But this Neorat is on all fours. The belly is swollen, which further limits its movement. Is the rat preg—ah, no. I see the dangling penis.

Now it's turning into a farce. A bunch of men with steel weapons stalk a pot-bellied rat. In complete silence, we slowly inch across the field. Suddenly the rat leaps forward and rolls down a hill and disappears.

We swear in unison and rush forward.

At the bottom of the hill is a hole in the ground. In the hole are thirty, forty rats with swollen bellies. Most are dead. The one that just jumped in is still breathing heavily, chest heaving.

"A plague?" The Drill Instructor asks. No one answers. I think of Pea. If he were here he would know.

*Chi.* A spear pierces the belly of the dying rat. It's from Black Cannon. He grins as he pulls the spear back, slicing the belly open like a ripe watermelon.

Everyone gasps. Inside this male rat's belly are more than a dozen rat fetuses: pink, curled up like a dish of shrimp cocktail around the intestines. A few men are having dry heaves. Black Cannon, still grinning, lifts his spear again.

"Stop." the Drill Instructor says. Black Cannon backs off, laughing and twirling his spear.

The Neorats were engineered to limit their reproductive capacity: for every one female rat born, there would be nine male rats. The idea had been to control the population size to keep up their market value.

But now, it looks like the measures are failing. The males before us died because their abdominal cavity could not support the fetuses. But how could they be pregnant in the first place? Clearly, their genes are trying to bypass their engineered boundaries.

I remember another possible explanation, something Xiaoxia told me long ago.

〜〜〜

Even though I'd had Li Xiaoxia's phone number in my handset for four years, I never called her. Every time I took it out, I lost the courage to push the "call" button.

That day, I was packing for boot camp when I suddenly heard Xiaoxia's faint voice, as though coming from far away. I thought I was hallucinating until I saw that I had butt-dialed her. I grabbed the phone in a panic.

"Hey," she said.

"Uh…"

"I hear that you're about to go kill some rats."

"Yeah. I can't find a job…"

"Why don't I take you out to dinner? I feel bad that we've been classmates for four years and I hardly know you. It'll be your farewell meal."

Rumor had it that luxury cars were always parked below her dorm, waiting to pick her up. Rumor had it that she went through men like a girl trying on dresses.

That night, as we sat across from each other, eating bowls of fried rice with beef, her face devoid of makeup, I finally understood. She really had a way of capturing a man's soul.

We wandered around the campus. As we passed the stray cats, the classrooms, the empty benches, suddenly I missed the school, and it was because of memories I wish I had made with her.

"My dad raised rats, and now you're going to kill rats," she said. "In the Year of the Rat you're going to fight rats. Now that's funny."

"Are you going to work with your father after graduation?" I asked.

She was dismissive of the suggestion. In her eyes, the business of raising rats was not all that different from working on a contract manufacturing assembly line or in a shirt factory. We still didn't control the key technologies. The embryos all had to be imported. After the farm workers raised them, they went through a stringent quality control process, and those that passed were exported, implanted with a set of programmed behaviors overseas, and then sold to the wealthy as luxury pets.

All that our country, the world's factory, had to offer was a lot of cheap labor in the least technology-intensive phase of the operation.

"I heard that the escaped rats had their genes messed with," Li Xiaoxia said.

She went on to explain that just like how some contract manufacturers had tried to produce *shanzhai* iPhones by reverse engineering and messing with the software, so some rat farm owners were trying to reverse engineer and mess with the genes in the rats. Their goal was to raise the ratio of females and the survival rate of babies. Otherwise their profit margin was too low.

"They say that this time the rats didn't escape," she continued, "but were released by the farm owners. It was their way of putting pressure on certain branches of the government to gain more handouts for their industry."

I didn't know what to say. I felt so ignorant.

"But that's just one set of rumors," she said. "Others say that the mass escape was engineered by the Western Alliance as a way to put pressure on our country in the trade negotiations. The truth is ever elusive."

I looked at the young woman before me: beautiful and smart. She was way beyond my league.

"Send me a postcard," she said. Her light laugh broke me out of my reverie.

"Eh?"

"To let me know you're safe. Don't underestimate the rats. I've seen them…"

She never finished her sentence.

~~~

From time to time, I feel many bright eyes're hidden in the dark, observing us, analyzing us, day or night. I think I'm going a little crazy.

By the bank of the river, we discover eighteen nests, low cylindrical structures about two meters in diameter. Several physics majors squat around one, discussing the mechanical structure of interweaving sticks. On top is a thick layer of leaves, as though the makers wanted to take advantage of the waxy surfaces of the leaves to keep water out.

"I've seen primitive tribal villages like this on the Discovery Channel," one of the men says. We all look at him oddly.

"It doesn't make sense," I say. I squat down, considering the trails of tiny paw prints that connect the nests to each other and the river, like an inscrutable picture. *Do the rats have agriculture? Do they need settlements? Why did they abandon them?*

Black Cannon laughs coldly. "You need to stop thinking they're people."

He's right. The rats are not people. They're not even real rats. They're just carefully designed products—actually, products that failed quality assurance.

I notice something strange about the paw prints. Most seem smaller than usual and only lead away from the nests. But in front of each nest there is one set that is bigger in stride length and deeper, with a long drag mark down the middle. The bigger trails only go *into* the nests, but don't come out.

"These are"—I try to keep my voice from shaking—"birthing rooms."

"Sir!" A man stumbles over. "You have to see this."

We follow him to a tree. Underneath there's a tower made from carefully stacked rocks. There's a sense of proportion and aesthetics in the pattern of their shapes and colors. From the tree, eighteen dead male rats hang, their bellies open like unzipped sacks.

A light layer of white sand is spread evenly around the tree. Countless tiny prints can be seen in the sand, surrounding the tree in ever-widening rings. I imagine the ceremonial procession and the mystical rituals. It must have been as wondrous as the scene in Tiananmen Square, when the flag is raised on National Day.

～～～

"Oh come on! This is the twenty-first century. Man has been to the Moon! Why are we using these pieces of scrap metal?" Pea, his head now shaven so that he looked even more like a pea, stood up and protested.

"That's right," I echoed. "Isn't the government always talking about modernizing defense? We should have some high-tech toys." Others in the barracks joined in.

"AT-TEN-TION!"

Complete silence.

"Hi-tech toys?" The Drill Instructor asked. "For the likes of you? You college kids don't even know how to hold a pair of chopsticks straight. If I give you a gun, the first thing you'll do is shoot your own nuts off! Now pack up. We're mustering in five minutes for a twenty-kilometer march."

We were issued the following kit: a collapsible short spear (the head can be disassembled into a dagger), an army knife with a serrated blade, a utility belt, a compass, waterproof matches, rations, and a canteen. The Drill Instructor had no faith we could handle anything more advanced.

As if to prove his point, at the end of the practice march, three of us were injured. One fell and sat on the blade of his knife and became the first to be discharged from our platoon. I don't think he did it on purpose—that would have required too much dexterity.

As we neared the end of training period, I saw anxiety in most eyes. Pea couldn't sleep, tossing and turning every night and making the bed squeak. By then I had gotten used to life without TV, without the Internet, without Seven-Eleven, but each time I thought about the idea of impaling a warm, flesh-and-blood body with a carbon fiber spear, my stomach churned.

There were exceptions, of course.

Whenever one of us passed the training room, we could see Black Cannon's sweaty figure practicing with his spear. He assigned himself extra drills, and constantly sharpened his knife with a grindstone. Someone who knew him from before told us that he was a quiet kid in school, the sort who got bullied by others. Now he seemed like a bloodthirsty butcher.

Six weeks later, we had our first battle, which lasted a total of six minutes and fourteen seconds.

The Drill Instructor had us surround a small copse. Then he gave the order to charge. Black Cannon went in first. Pea and I looked at each other, hesitated, and brought up the rear. By the time the two of us got to the scene, only a pool of blood and some broken limbs were left. They told me that Black Cannon alone was responsible for eight kills. He chose to keep one of the corpses.

At the meeting afterward, the Drill Instructor commended Black Cannon and criticized "a small number of lazy individuals."

Black Cannon skinned his trophy. But he didn't properly cure it, so the skin soon began to rot and smell and became full of maggots. Finally, his bunkmate burned it one day when he was out.

〜〜

Morale is low.

It's not clear what's worse: that the rats have figured out how to bypass the artificial limits on their breeding capacity, or that they have demonstrated signs of intelligence: construction of structures, hierarchical society, even religious worship.

My paranoia is getting worse. The woods are full of eyes and the grass is full of whispers.

It's night. I give up on trying to sleep and crawl out of the tent.

The early winter stars are so clear that I think I can see all the way to the end of the universe. The sound of a lone insect pierces the silence. My heart clenches with a nameless sorrow.

*Sha!* I turn around at the sound. A rat is standing erect on its hind legs about five meters away, like another soldier missing home.

I duck down for the knife in my boot sheath. The rat crouches down, too. Our eyes remain locked. The second my hand touches the knife, the rat turns and disappears into the woods. I grab the knife and follow.

Normally, I should be able to catch it in about thirty seconds. But tonight, I just can't seem to close the distance between us. From time to time, it even turns around to see if I'm keeping up. This infuriates me.

The air is full of a sweet, rotting smell. I take a break in a small clearing. I feel dizzy. The trees around me sway and twist, glistening oddly in the starlight.

Pea walks out of the woods. He's wearing his glasses, which ought to be thousands of kilometers away in his parents' possession. His body is whole, without that hole in the chest from that tree branch.

I turn around and see my parents. My dad is wearing his old suit

"Be careful that you don't drown along with him," he called out.

I tried to use my mirror neurons to understand what Black Cannon was thinking and feeling. I failed.

~~

The Drill Instructor stares at the map and the detector, looking thoughtful.

According to the detector, a large pack of rats is moving toward the edge of our district. At the rate we're marching, we should be able to catch them in twelve hours. If we can kill them all, we will have completed our quota. Yes, we'll be honorably discharged. We'll have jobs. We'll go home for New Year's.

But there's a problem. Regulations say that Rodent-Control Force units may not cross district borders for kills. The idea is to prevent units from overly aggressive competition, stealing kills from each other.

The Drill Instructor turns to Black Cannon. "You think we can contain the battle so that the whole operation is within our district?"

Black Cannon nods. "I guarantee it. If we end up crossing district lines, the rest of you can have all my tails."

We laugh.

"Fine. Let's get ready to leave at eighteen hundred hours."

I find a landline public phone at a convenience store. First I call my mom. When she hears that I might be coming home soon, she's so happy that she can't speak. I hang up after a few more sentences because I'm afraid she'll cry. Then I dial another number before I can stop myself.

Li Xiaoxia.

She has no idea who I am. Undaunted, I recount our entire history until she remembers.

She's now working at a foreign company's Chinese branch: nine to five, plenty of money. Next year she might go overseas to take some classes at company expense. She seems distracted.

"Have you gotten my postcards?"

"Yeah, sure." She hesitates. "Well, the first few. Then I moved."

"I'm about to be discharged," I say.

"Ah, good. Good. Stay in touch."

I refuse to give up. "Do you remember how when we parted, you told me to be careful of the rats? You said you had seen them. What did you see?"

A long and awkward silence. I hold my breath until I'm about to faint. "I don't remember," she says. "Nothing important."

I regret the money I wasted on that call.

Numbly, I stare at the scrolling ticker on the bottom of the static-filled TV screen in the convenience store: "The rodent-control effort is progressing well." "The Western Alliance has agreed to a new round of trade talks concerning the escalating tension with our country." "Employment opportunities for new college graduates are trending up."

Well, even though the rats have now bypassed the limits on their reproductive rates, our quota hasn't been adjusted in response. It makes no sense, but I don't care. It looks like we'll have jobs, and the export numbers will go up again. It doesn't seem like what we're doing here matters.

It's just like what Xiaoxia said: "They say that…" "Others say that…" It's just rumors and guesses. Who knows what really happens behind closed doors?

No single factor means anything. Everything has to be contextualized. There are too many hidden relationships, too many disguised opportunities for profit, too many competing concerns. This is the most complicated chess game in the world, the Great Game.

But all I can see is my broken heart.

♒

For the last few days, Pea had been going to the bathroom unusually frequently.

I followed him in secret. I saw him taking out a small metal can with holes punched in the lid. He carefully opened it a crack, threw some crackers inside, and murmured quietly into the can.

I jumped out and held out my hand.

"It was really cute," he said, "look at the eyes!" He tried to appeal to my mirror neurons.

"This is against regulations!"

"Just let me keep it for a few days," he begged. "I'll let it go." His eyes looked like the baby rat's, so bright.

Someone as nervous and careless as Pea was no good at keeping secrets. When the Drill Instructor and Black Cannon stood in front of me, I knew the game was up.

"You are sheltering prisoners of war!" Black Cannon said. I wanted to laugh, and Pea was already laughing.

"Stop," the Drill Instructor said. We stood at attention. "If you can give me a reasonable explanation, I'll deal with you reasonably."

I figured that I had nothing to lose, so I came up with an "explanation" on the fly. Black Cannon was so furious when he heard it I thought his nose was going to become permanently twisted.

Pea and I worked together the whole afternoon to dig a hole about two meters deep into the side of a hill. We lined it with a greased tarp. Pea didn't like my plan, but I told him it was the only way we could escape punishment.

"It's really smart," Pea said. "It can even imitate my gestures." He gave a demonstration. Indeed, the little rat was a regular mimic. I tried to get it to imitate me, but it refused.

"Great," I said. "Its IQ is approaching yours."

"I try to see it as just a well-engineered product," Pea said. "A bundle of modified DNA. But emotionally, I can't accept that."

We hid downwind from the hole. Pea held a string in his hand. The other end of the string was tied to the leg of the baby rat at the bottom of the hole. I had to keep on reminding Pea to pull the rope once in a while to make the rat cry out piteously. His hands shook. He hated doing it but I made him. Our futures were at stake here.

My whole idea was founded on guesses. Who knew how these artificial creatures felt about the bonds of kinship? Did adult rats have any childrearing instincts? How did their new reproductive arrangement—one female mating with multiple males, each of whom then became "pregnant"—affect things?

One male rat appeared. He sniffed the air near the hole, as if trying to identify the smell. Then he fell into the hole. I could hear the sound of its claws scratching against the greased tarp. I laughed. Now we had two rats as bait.

The adult male was much louder than the baby rat. If it really had a high IQ, then it should be issuing warnings to its companions.

I was wrong. A second male rat appeared. It came to the side of the trap, seemed to have a conversation with the rats in there, then fell in.

Then came the third, fourth, fifth…after the seventeenth rat fell in, I worried that the hole wasn't deep enough.

I gave the signal. In a second, men with spears surrounded the trap.

The rats were building a pyramid. The bottom layer consisted of seven rats leaning against the side of the trap. Five rats stood on their shoulders in the next layer. Then three. Two more rats were carrying the baby rat and climbing up.

"Wait!" Pea yelled. Carefully, he pulled the string and slowly separated the baby rat from the adult rats carrying it. The minute the baby rat dangled free of the adults, the adult rats screamed—and I heard sorrow in their voice. The pyramid fell apart as the spears plunged down, splattered blood beading against the plastic and rolling down slowly.

In order to rescue a child who was not directly related to them, the rats were willing to sacrifice themselves. Yet we exploited this to get them.

I shivered.

Pea pulled the baby rat back to him. Just as the baby was about to complete this nightmarish journey, a boot came out of nowhere and flattened it against the earth.

Black Cannon.

Pea jumped at him, fists swinging.

Black Cannon was caught off guard and blood flowed down the corner of his mouth. Then he laughed, grabbed Pea and lifted his skinny body over his head. He walked next to the trap, filled with blood and gore, and got ready to toss Pea in.

"I think the sissy wants to join his dirty friends."

"Put him down!" The Drill Instructor appeared and ended the madness.

Because I came up with the plan, I received my first commendation. Three times during his speech, the Drill Instructor mentioned "college education," but not once sarcastically. Even Black Cannon was impressed with me. He told me when no one was around that all the tails from this battle should be given to me. I accepted, and then gave the tails to Pea.

Of course I knew that nothing would make up for what I took away from Pea.

〰

Farm fields, trees, hills, ponds, roads…we pass like shadows in the night.

During a break, Black Cannon suggests to the Drill Instructor that we divide the platoon in half. He will choose the best fighters and dash ahead while the rest follow slowly. He looks around and then adds, meaningfully, "Otherwise, we might not be able to complete the mission."

"No," I say. The Drill Instructor and Black Cannon look at me. "The strength of an army comes from all its members working together. We advance together, we retreat together. None of us is extraneous and none of us is more important than any others."

I pause, locking my gaze with the furious Black Cannon. "Otherwise, we'll be no better than the rats."

"Good." The Drill Instructor puts out his cigarette. "We stay together. Let's go."

Black Cannon walks by me. He lowers his voice so that only I can hear. "I should have let you roll down the dam with the sissy."

I freeze.

As Black Cannon walks away, he turns and smirks at me. I've seen that curling of the lips before: when he warned me not to drown along with Pea, when he stomped on the baby rat and lifted Pea over his head, when he sliced open the bellies of the male rats.

Black Cannon was next to Pea that afternoon. They said that Pea left the path because he saw a rare plant. But without his glasses, Pea was practically blind.

I should never have believed their lies.

As I stare at Black Cannon's back, memory surfaces after memory. This is the most difficult journey I've ever been on.

"Prepare for battle," the Drill Instructor says, taking me out of my waking dream. We've been marching for ten hours.

For me, the only battle that matters in the world is between Black Cannon and me.

It's dawn again. The battlefield is a dense forest in a valley. The cliffs on both sides are steep and bare. The Drill Instructor's plan is simple: one squad will move ahead and cut off the rat pack's path through the valley. The other squads will follow and kill every rat they see. Game over.

I sneak through the trees to join Black Cannon's squad. I don't have a plan, except that I don't want him out of my sight. The forest is dense and visibility is poor. A faint, blue miasma permeates everywhere. Black Cannon sets the pace for a fast march, and we weave between the trees, among the fog, like ghosts.

He stops abruptly. We follow his finger and see several rats pacing a few meters away. He gestures for us to spread out and surround them. But by the time we get close, the rats have all disappeared. We turn around, and the rats are still just a few meters away.

This happens a few more times. All of us are frightened.

The miasma grows thicker, filled with a strange odor. My forehead is sweaty and the sweat stings my eyes. I grip my spear tightly, trying to keep up with the squad. But my legs are rubbery. My paranoia is back. *Things* are watching me in the grass. Whispers in the air.

I'm alone now. All around me is the thick fog. I spin around. Every direction seems full of danger. Desperation fills my head.

Suddenly, I hear a long, loud scream in one direction. I rush over but see nothing. I feel something large dash behind me. Another loud, long scream. Then I hear the sound of metal striking against metal, the sound of flesh being ripped apart, heavy breathing.

Then silence, absolute silence.

It's behind me. I can feel its hot gaze.

I spin around and it leaps at me through the fog. A Neorat as large as a human, its claws dripping with blood, is on me in a second. My spear pushes its arms against its chest and we wrestle each other to the ground. Its jaws, full of sharp teeth, snap shut right next to my ear, the stench from its mouth making it impossible for me to breathe. I want to kick it off me with my legs, but it has me completely pinned against the ground.

I watch, helplessly, as its bloody claws inch toward my chest. I growl with fury, but it sounds like a desperate, loud scream.

The cold claw rips through my uniform. I can feel it against my chest. Then a brief, searing moment of pain as it rips through my skin and muscles. The claw continues down, millimeter by millimeter, toward my heart.

I look up into its face. It's laughing. The mouth forms a cruel grin, one that I'm very familiar with.

*Bang*. The rat shudders. The claws stop. It turns its head around, confused, trying to find the source of the noise. I gather every ounce of strength in my body and shove its claws away, then I smash my spear against its skull.

A muffled thud. It falls against the ground.

I look up past him, and see a bigger, taller rat walking toward me. It's holding a gun in its hands.

I close my eyes.

〜〜〜

"You can all have a real drink tonight," the Drill Instructor said. He revealed a few cases of beer next to the campfire.

"What's the occasion?" Pea asked happily. He grabbed a chicken foot out of the big bowl and gnawed on it.

"I think it's somebody's birthday today."

Pea was still for a second. Then he smiled and kept on gnawing his chicken foot. In the firelight I thought I saw tears in his eyes.

The Drill Instructor was in a good mood. "Hey, Pea," he said, handing Pea another beer. "You're a Sagittarius. So you ought to be good at shooting. But why is your aim at rats so awful? You must be doing a lot of other kinds of shooting, am I right?"

We laughed until our stomachs cramped up. This was a side of the Drill Instructor we never knew.

The birthday boy ate his birthday noodles and made his wish. "What did you wish for?" The Drill Instructor asked.

"For all of us to be discharged as quickly as possible so that we can go home, get good jobs, and spend time with our parents."

Everyone went quiet, thinking that the Drill Instructor was going to get mad. But he clapped, laughed, and said, "Good. Your parents didn't waste their money on you."

Now everyone started talking at once. Some said they wanted to make a lot of money and buy a big house. Some said they wanted to sleep with a pretty girl from every continent. One said he wanted to be the President. "If you're going to be the President," another said, "then I'll have to be the Commander-in-Chief of the Milky Way."

I saw that the Drill Instructor's expression was a bit odd. "What do you wish for, Sir?"

We all got quiet. The Drill Instructor poked at the fire with a stick.

"My home village is poor. All of us born there are stupid, not much good at schooling, not like you. As a young man, I didn't want to work the fields or go to the cities and be a laborer. It seemed so futile. Then someone said, go join the army. At least you'll be protecting the country. If you do well, maybe you'll become a hero, then you can return home and bring honor to your ancestors. I'd always liked war movies, and thought it exciting to wear a uniform. So I signed up.

"Poor kids like me knew nothing except how to work hard. Every day, I trained the longest and practiced the most. If there was a dangerous task, I volunteered. If something dirty needed to be done, I did it. What did I do all that for? I just wanted an opportunity to be a hero on the battlefield. It was my only chance to do something with my life, you know? Even if I die it would be worth it."

The Drill Instructor paused, sighed. He kept on poking at the fire with his branch. The silence lasted for a long time. Then he looked up, and grinned.

"Why are you all quiet? I shouldn't have ruined the mood." He threw away his branch. "Sorry. I'll sing a song to apologize. It's an old song. When I first heard it, you weren't even born yet."

He was not a good singer, but he sang with his whole heart. The corners of his eyes were wet.

"...*Today all I have is my shell. Remember our glory days, when we embraced freedom in the storm? All life we believed we could change the future, but who ever accomplished it?...*"

As he sang, the flickering shadows from the fire made him seem even taller, like a bigger-than-life hero. Our applause echoed loudly in the empty wilderness.

"Let me tell you something," Pea said. He leaned over, sipping from a bottle. "Living is so...like a dream."

〰

The loud noise of the engine wakes me.

I open my eyes and see the Drill Instructor, his lips moving. But I can't hear a word over the noise.

I try to get up but a sharp pain in my chest makes me lie down again. Over my head is a curved, metallic ceiling. Then the whole world starts to vibrate and shake, and a sense of weight pushes me against the floor. I'm on a helicopter.

"Don't move," the Drill Instructor shouts, leaning close to my ear. "We're taking you to the hospital."

My memory is a mess of random scenes from that nightmarish battle. Then I remember the last thing I saw. "That gun...was that you?"

"Tranquilizer."

I think I'm beginning to understand. "So, what happened to Black Cannon?"

The Drill Instructor is silent for a while. "The injury to his head is pretty severe. He'll probably be a vegetable the rest of his life."

I remember that night, when I couldn't sleep. I remember Pea, my parents, and....

"What did you see?" I ask the Drill Instructor anxiously. "What did you see on the battlefield?"

"I don't know," he says. Then he looks at me. "It's probably best if you don't know either."

I think about this. If the rats are now capable of chemically manipulating our perceptions, generating illusions to cause us to kill each other, then the war is going to last a long, long time. I remember the screams and the sounds of flesh being torn apart by spears.

"Look!" The Drill Instructor supports me so that I can see through the helicopter cockpit window.

Rats, millions of rats are walking out of fields, forests, hills, villages. Yes, walking. They stand erect and stroll at a steady pace, as though members of the world's largest tour group. The scattered trickles of rats gather into streams, rivers, flowing seas. Their varicolored furs form into grand patterns. There's a sense of proportion and aesthetics.

The ocean of rats undulates over the withered, sere winter landscape and the identical, boring human buildings, like a new life force in the universe, gently flowing.

"We lost," I say.

"No, we won," the Drill Instructor says. "You'll see soon."

We land in a military hospital. Bouquets and a wheelchair welcome me, the hero. A pretty nurse pushes me inside. They triage me quickly and then give me a bath. It takes a long time before the water flows clear. Then it's time to feed me. I eat so quickly that I throw it all up again. The nurse gently pats my back, her gaze full of empathy.

The cafeteria TV is tuned to the news. "Our country has reached preliminary agreement with the Western Alliance concerning the trade dispute. All parties have described it as a win-win..."

On TV, they're showing the mass migration of rats that I saw earlier on the helicopter.

"After thirteen months of continuous, heroic struggle by the entire nation, we have finally achieved complete success in eradicating the rodent threat!"

The camera shifts to a scene by the ocean. A gigantic, multicolored carpet is moving slowly from the land into the ocean. As it touches the ocean, it breaks into millions of particles, dissolving in the water.

As the camera zooms in, the Neorats appear like soldiers in a killing frenzy. Crazed, each attacks everything and anything around itself. There's no more sides, no more organization, no more any hint of strategy or tactics. Every Neorat is fighting only for itself, tearing apart the bodies of its own kind, cruelly biting, chewing each other's heads. It's as if some genetic switch has been flipped by an invisible hand, and their confident climb toward civilization has been turned in a moment into the rawest, most primitive instinct. They collide against each other, strike each other, so that the whole carpet of bodies squirms, tumbles into a river of blood that runs into the sea.

"See, I told you," the Drill Instructor says.

But the victory has nothing to do with us. This had been planned from the start. Whoever had engineered the escape of the Neorats had also buried the instructions for getting rid of them when their purpose has been accomplished.

Li Xiaoxia was right. Pea was right. The Drill Instructor was also right. We are just like the rats, all of us only pawns, stones, worthless counters in the Great Game. All we can see are just the few squares of the board before us. All we can do is just follow the gridlines in accordance with the rules of the game: Cannon on eighth file to fifth file; Horse on second file to third file. As for the meaning behind these moves, and when the great hand that hangs over us will plunge down to pluck one of us off, nobody knows.

But when the two players in the game, the two sides, have concluded their business, all sacrifices become justified—whether it's the Neorats, or us. I think again of Black Cannon in the woods and shudder.

"Don't mention what you saw," the Drill Instructor says. I know he means the religion of the rats, Black Cannon's grin, Pea's death. These things aren't part of the official story. They're meant to be forgotten.

I ask the nurse, "Will the migrating rats pass this city?"

"In about half an hour. You should be able to see them from the park in front of the hospital."

I ask her to take me there. I want to say good-bye to my foes, who never existed.

# Sofia Samatar

## Olimpia's Ghost

**Sofia Samatar** *is the author of the novel* A Stranger in Olondria, *winner of the 2014 Crawford Award, as well as several short stories, essays, and poems. Her work has been nominated for multiple awards. She is a co-editor for* Interfictions: A Journal of Interstitial Arts, *and teaches literature and writing at California State University Channel Islands.*

My Dear S.,

Emil says you will not come to Freiberg this year; but Mother says you will. Who is right? We all know you hate Vienna with a passion; that is, Mother and Emil know it, and I know it through them, for Mother reads your letters aloud, and sometimes Emil, too, shares a few lines. Pray do not be angry! It is such a little thing, to hear of your successes, and it makes me very happy. And then, your sallies on your masters are so droll, and your remarks on Vienna—St. Stephen's steeple like a "great rolled-up umbrella"—Mother can hardly read for laughing.

I am sure you will not begrudge me this diversion, my dear S. On the days when there is no letter from you, life continues just as usual. The weather has been fine. There is fruit on the peach trees. In the long twilight, while Emil reads, I go up and down, up and down the stairs.

A few days ago I did have a new amusement: a marionette theater sprang up overnight in the square, like a white mushroom. I watched the marionettes for several hours, even though a light rain was falling, and the children screamed mercilessly. I suppose you would not have liked the noise, or the look of the dirty little boy who came around afterward, hat extended to gather our coins. As I left I saw him sharing a cigar behind the theater with the puppet-master, a rough, disreputable-looking fellow, undoubtedly his father. Oh, but the marionettes were so beautiful! The little Pierrot had a spangled coat, and two great tears shone under his eyes. He wore his heart on the outside, like any fool. As for Columbine, she carried a hand mirror that reflected her lavender hair.

I looked for them today, but they are gone.

I try not to be restless. Emil dislikes what he calls my "thumping." Tonight I will try to read. A volume by E.T.A. Hoffmann has been discovered in the library, and we think it must be yours, for it is certainly not ours. As I read, I will imagine that you are here again, seated in your chair by the window, teasing Mother as she chuckles over her knitting, and that you turn, with your hair lit up all reddish by the sunset through the window, and speak to me kindly.

Your
Gisela

My Dear S.,

I have had the most marvelous dream! And I believe I have you to thank for it—for it came directly out of the pages of Hoffmann.

I dreamt that I was entering the door of a very large eating-house, rather like a restaurant in the Prater. The door was of glass, with gilt lettering; I could not make out what it said, but I remember a large *O* with twisting vines. Inside everything shone: the glasses and tableware, the chandeliers, and the jewels and curled hair of the fine people at the tables. The walls were all covered with mirrors. I saw myself moving among the tables: I wore a mauve dress and, strangely enough, a powdered wig. I was not at all nervous, though the restaurant was very imposing. I went on walking, for I felt vaguely that I was supposed to be meeting someone. Then a young man caught my eye. He wore an old-fashioned frock coat and was talking earnestly to his companion, a lady in a powdered wig.

It was Hoffmann's Nathanael! I knew him at once: his thin face, very handsome if somewhat sickly; his black eyes; the trembling of his hands. He was precisely like the hero of that bewitching story, "The Sandman," which I had finished just before going to bed. And who do you suppose the lady was? Olimpia, of course! As I passed behind her chair, she made a wheezing mechanical sound, and then cried out "Ah! Ah!" It was she—Spalanzani's exquisite doll, so lovely and lifelike that Nathanael fell wildly in love with her. I knew I had stumbled into the part of the story that tells of their courtship. It is difficult to describe the elation I felt upon this discovery. To be in a story! All the

SOFIA SAMATAR |

chandeliers seemed to blaze more brightly, and I hurried around the table to look at Olimpia's face.

What do you think? She looked exactly like me!

Well, all but her eyes—these were quite fixed and strange, and glittered only when she nodded her head. This she did regularly, and then her eyes reflected the lights of the restaurant, creating an effect that was almost human. Poor Nathanael was smitten with her. I circled the table to look at him again, but just as he glanced at me, I woke up.

I suppose it should have been frightening—to see oneself as a doll. But it wasn't, not in the least! I woke up feeling rested and full of life. Indeed, I feel better than I have done for weeks. Both Mother and Emil commented on my color, and said I looked very well. "The summer has reached you at last," said Mother. You know she often calls me her "arctic chick"—a silly name, for I am not at all cold-natured. If I have been subdued lately, it is only because it makes me melancholy to think you will not come to see us.

Your
Gisela

S.:

So, you think I ought not to read Hoffmann? I am "too sensitive" for his art?

Then why could you not write to me yourself? Think how humiliating it was for me to be taken aside by Emil, like a child! He could hardly look at me; he knew himself it was wrong. "Don't be angry," he pleaded—as if I could help it! I felt myself growing hard and stony, absolutely petrifying with rage. When he left me, and I moved at last, raising my hand to smooth my hair, my own shadow startled me, shifting on the wall.

I have given the book to Emil. My dreams are my own.

I have been there again, you know. To the restaurant. I have walked between the smooth white tablecloths. No one seems to notice me there—except him. He sees me! Nathanael—he sees me. The first time he looked at me, he started like a hare. I was standing behind Olimpia, just at her shoulder, and Nathanael glanced at me and then down at his beloved and then up at me again, a potent horror dawning in his eyes. I realized then how disconcerting it must have been for him. Here was a second idol standing behind the first, and this one ever so much more alive than the seated one, more human, with vivid eyes aglow beneath the lights! He looked wildly at the mirrors, to find that I was also there. It was clear that no one else in the restaurant could see me. A waiter walked past me, brushing my arm. Nathanael paled; his hair went lank with sweat; I feared to see him faint.

I smiled at him, with the idea of calming his nerves. He flung his arm up before his face.

That made me hesitate. I watched him grope for his glass. He gulped the wine greedily. He was looking at Olimpia now, with a different kind of terror in his eyes. Of course, he believed her to be human. He was desperately in love, and would not wish to act like a madman in front of her. He straightened himself and smoothed his coat, and said something to her in a strange, shrill voice—a silly, drawing-room question about music.

Music: had she been studying it long?

It was—*comical.*

When he glanced at me again, I could not help baring my teeth. Just a little bit, to see what would happen. He shuddered and blanched more violently than before. It was as if he were a fish, and the hook had pierced his lip.

I winked at him. Very vulgar—but it was a dream! He danced at the end of the line, gasping for air. "Nathanael," I said. Great drops stood on his brow. "Nathanael!" I repeated. He babbled of Mozart, grapes and handkerchiefs while his clockwork darling answered "Ah! Ah!"

Such a ridiculous scene—I woke up laughing!

But I am not laughing now. Dear S., why could you not write to me directly? I would so love a letter from you, even a scolding one! If only you would reply, I would not ask to read E.T.A. Hoffmann or anyone else. And don't say "propriety"—you know I hate the sound of the word. We all hated it together when we were children, don't you remember? The Hochwald, and how you flung your hat into the weeds. You said hats were never worn in paradise. Can we not go there?

Your
Gisela


Dear S.—Dear Master,

Do you remember how we used to call you that? I suppose you think me too young to remember myself; but I recall every detail of your visits here, even the first year, when you wore a penknife on a chain, and the blackberries were so plentiful. I used to trail behind when you and Emil walked to the Hochwald. You talked of Cervantes and the noble Castilian tongue; you called each other "Don," and the two of you tied me to a tree by my apron strings and left me alone for half an hour. The sky grew dark, and the whole wood sighed. I twisted against my apron, trying to move my left arm, which was closest to the knot. The cloth pressed into my abdomen, the rugged bark scraped my forearm, and I closed my eyes as a cold wind shook the bracken. The first drop of rain struck my brow with such violence I thought it was an acorn. Then I heard voices calling me through the trees. "Gisela! Gisela!" You had lost me. I writhed harder against my taut apron, saying nothing, and then you crashed through a thicket and almost toppled into me. "Why didn't you answer? And what have you done?" you cried, having untied me to discover my arm rubbed bloody by the tree. "Why, Gisela?" Your eyes were dark with fear, your lips so close I could see the dim sheen on them, their texture of cranberry skins.

The family opinion that I am "strange" and "cold" dates from that visit. You knew better. Didn't you ask permission to bring my milk upstairs? I remember your face in the light of my little candle, the warmth of my heated blankets, the storm outside blowing as if it would knock the house down. You were too large for my room; you made it shrink. "You must tell me everything," you said, "everything, even if it makes you afraid. *Especially* if it makes you afraid." Such urgency in your voice. I was happy for the slight sting in my arm; without it, I might have thought I was dreaming.

Did you not say, dear Master, that the life of dreams is real?

I follow Nathanael through Hoffmann's streets. When he goes to the opera, I am there, in a great fur the color of horn. When he buys tobacco I am there, turning over some postcards. My favorite amusement is to run beside him when, in the evenings, he goes out to settle his nerves with a bit of air. He runs faster, and I run faster—my feet are so light, so light! I can hear him whimpering, and even praying in a low voice. His fear is so strong! I breathe it in, like the odor of aqua vitae. He is rather beautiful, his brown hair cut long, his face pale as a lamp with suffering. These days he has grown somewhat shabby: his coat is stained, and a faint beard blurs his cheeks. I wish he looked more like you.

G.

# Olimpia's Ghost

My Dear Master,

My dreams are so lovely, they really ought to be turned into something—perhaps an opera. Yes, why not? I should call it *Olimpia's Ghost*. Perhaps you and I could write it together: I would provide the dreams, and you the poetry. Let me know if you would like me to send you some notes. Like this: *Evening. A dark garret. NATHANAEL, a young man of gloomy aspect, paces between the window and the fire.* That was how I found him last night. When I entered, he crossed himself and sank to his knees, his upraised face capturing all the poor light in the room.

"Who are you? Who are you?" he whispered.

I said: "You know."

"No!" he said. "You are not she."

"But I am, Nathanael," I told him gently. "I am her soul."

He shook his head, recoiling toward the wall. "Never! I know my Olimpia's pure soul: it looks at me out of her tranquil eyes."

Well, I laughed at that. He covered his face. He cannot bear my laughter: Olimpia never laughs. "Come, show some spirit," I said, prodding him with my foot. He began to strike his head against the wall, and when he seized the poker, determined to do himself a mischief, I decided to leave the room.

Outside, the streets were lightly dusted with snow. Winter is coming early to the dream city, just as it is coming here. Walking beside the dream canal, I hummed a snatch of tune which, now that I come to think of it, might become an aria for *Olimpia's Ghost*. I think I should call it "The Hidden Life of Dolls." It will be sung by the Ghost herself, of course. The tune is similar to "Ach, du lieber Augustin." I am only really happy with two lines:

> *See! the midnight clock is shining brightly.*
> *It is the dolls' moon.*

Is it not rather fine? Perhaps it is not exactly poetry; but you will take care of that. I remember a golden day, so long it seemed nearly endless, and the strawberries in the meadow, and you told us a fortune-teller had predicted you would become a cabinet minister. Emil said it was possible; he might become one too, why not; you might both have distinguished careers, for being Jewish was hardly a handicap nowadays. You stared at him in amazement. "A cabinet minister! Is that what you envision for me? Boiled beef at dinner, and speech-writing afterward? Thank you very much!"

I understood you perfectly. I said: "Sigmund will be a poet."

You looked at me, grateful and sunburned, your shirt open at the neck. "There!" you said, triumphant. "Gisela knows me best, after all." And we both laughed at Emil, you and I together.

Then, of course, he blushed, and claimed he was only joking, and that he would be a painter. But he will do no such thing. He will inherit the dye-works.

What of you, dear Master?

This morning my eyes were crusted shut, as if I had slept for many days. The Sandman has been here!

G.

My Dear Master,

Last night I pursued him into a church. I wore a barometer at my waist like a reticule. Clumps of candles shone here and there in the huge dark sanctuary, tiny and far apart, like autumn crocuses in a plain of mud.

These lines, I notice, make me sound rather restless and unhappy. Be sure that I am nothing of the sort. My health is splendid: Mother has had to let out all of my dresses, and my hair has grown so thick I can scarcely grasp it in both hands. It is true that I go up and down the stairs more frequently than ever, but only because it is too wet to go out. I must tire myself somehow, and nobody likes my moving about so much, either in the house or in the dye-shop. And so: to the stairs. The old carpeting is almost all worn away, and the polished wood underneath gleams beautifully, rich as fat. I hurry down, for I get the most relief from climbing up again, toward the little hall window that frames a patch of sky.

I begin to be frightened for him. When I entered the church his shock and horror were so great that he collapsed in the aisle, foaming at the lips. The priest and the other good people there took him away to a back room, where I hovered anxiously until he regained consciousness. He looked very thin, very frail, like a glass angel. I slipped away before he noticed me. I could hear him weeping as I went out of the church. What if he should die? I am haunted by the awful conclusion to Hoffmann's tale.

Dear Master! I write because you said "tell me everything."

G.

# Olimpia's Ghost

And two years ago, the last time you came, you rushed past the house just as you were, all grimy from the journey, and you ran off into the meadow, and I ran after you, like a lunatic Mother said later, and we kicked through the grass, releasing a green, bruised odor, and you threw yourself into the arms of the cypress tree, the most somber tree in the meadow, certainly more funereal than the ones in Italian pictures, and perhaps there is something about our northern clime that makes them grow that way, almost black, absorbing all the light, not reflecting it at all, or perhaps it is only the paler light here, the paler sky against which they stand like sentries, and you seized a branch in your teeth and chewed it savagely, and I too pressed my face to the needles and bit, and you muttered *Freiberg Freiberg*, and I imagined that you were repeating my name.

My Dear Sigmund,

So, you persist in your silence. This is no more than I expected. Emil assures me that you will certainly not come now. Your zoology examination, it appears, is set for the end of the month. Well! I wish you success; though it is clear you need no encouragement from me.

You are resolved, he says, to become a man of science.

Perhaps you are thinking of my Nathanael, and wondering if he lives? Please do not distress yourself. Nathanael is quite well. Only last week I observed him consuming cakes on a balcony with his Olimpia. She, of course, ate nothing. It seems she is conscious of her figure. I peered at them from under my parasol, and walked on. I try not to let Nathanael see me these days. I imagine he and his darling will marry, and produce a line of human children with wooden hearts.

Sigmund, I know the secret.

Emil took me out this morning, at Mother's urging. The air was raw, the streets a rough mixture of frost and mud. To my amazement, the marionettes were again dancing in the square, before a paltry audience of mostly poor children. Pierrot's little face was so hard and sad, it brought the tears to my eyes. Columbine's hand mirror, I realized, is a lorgnette. She peered at me with an eye as gray as a clam. Her gaze quite went through me; but the magnification also revealed a great crack in her plaster forehead.

Thanks to the improved health I have enjoyed recently, I am very nimble and strong. I tore away from Emil and dashed behind the theater. The dirty little boy was sitting there, quite comfortable on an overturned pail, blowing vigorously on his gloveless hands. I could only see his father, the puppet-master, from the waist down: a pair of baggy trousers tucked into hobnailed boots. The boy stood, but I pushed past him and tugged the puppet-master's shirt. He lifted the spangled curtain and glared at me.

"What is it, miss?"

On the other side of the theater, the children had begun to roar their disapproval at the sudden collapse of the show. Emil rushed up behind me. The puppet-master, breathing white fog from his black beard, told us to be off, using a vulgar expression. "I know the secret," I told him. Emil had seized me now, and was pulling me away. He gave me a terrible lecture all the way home. I did not mind. Every time I raised my hand, as if sprinkling sugar, a host of swallows rose into the sky.

To climb. To climb.

This morning my eyes were crusted shut again. When I rubbed them, my fingers came away covered with brown flakes. Has the cold weather caused it somehow, or is it blood?

Now that I am avoiding Nathanael, I have had the chance to explore more of the dream city. I often find myself in black, narrow, odorous, humid streets: the streets where I used to chase him in merrier days. There is a certain alley that reminds me of the one behind the smithy in Freiberg, the one with a plaque commemorating the burning of witches. I always feel nervous in that dark dream street—yet at the same time I am drawn to the place. Last night, as I wandered there, a curious scraping echoed from the walls. A slow, uneven, tortured sound, the groan of an object moving with great difficulty over the slimy stones.

I paused. There was very little light—the buildings on either side shut out the moon—but the stones of the alley themselves possess a strange, greenish radiance. In that eldritch light, a figure came toward me, dragging itself painfully, a towering thing with an outline like a crag.

Closer, closer! I watched, frozen to the spot. For the first time in that place, I was terrified. The creature lurched toward me on heavy, jointless legs. I saw it was made of wood. And not just wood, but a wild patchwork of wood, painted pieces fixed haphazardly together. It was as if a crazed puppeteer had taken all the pieces left over from building his marionettes, and constructed one fabulous, horrible puppet, a creature taller than a man, its shoulders built up like buttresses, its sad face hanging down upon its chest. For it had a sad face, Sigmund, such a sad face! A face of flesh, very pale, the face of an invalid. Bloody tear-tracks descended from its eyes. I knew at once that it was the Sandman. It raised a clumsy arm and pointed toward the sky.

To climb. To climb.

The last time I saw you: Vienna, New Year's Eve. Your mother was distressed, as your father had not yet arrived. She kept running out to the landing to see if he had come. The parlor was hot from our dancing. I wore a white holiday dress and a black velvet ribbon. I had decided that there would be no more shyness on my part, no pretense. The flavor of bitter cypress was in my mouth. I had tucked a sprig of it inside the bosom of my dress, to bring you, there in the city, the delirious freshness of Freiberg. When we danced, I pressed close to you so that you would smell it. You pushed me back with a cold look. Later that night I heard you talking in the kitchen. "As for Gisela Fluss," you said, "once she was a decorous doll, and now she has become an indecorous flirt."

A doll, a flirt. But I shall become an artist. And you: you will be a man of science.

The Sandman jerked his arm, signaling to me. I realized that he was pointing to the single lighted window in the dismal tenement above the street. There, at a table, a man sat writing. His brown hair was tied in a pigtail. His coat was not clean. I thought, astonished, that this must be my Nathanael. Then he raised his head and looked out the window, eyes narrowed, pencil against his teeth, and I saw that he was an entirely different person. With his mobile face and pensive, furrowed brow, he looked more like the Sandman than Nathanael. He was, of course, the double of them both. Father, devil, puppeteer: he was Hoffmann. I glanced at the Sandman, who gestured eagerly at the drainpipe on the wall.

I am no fortune-teller, Sigmund. But I will make you a prediction. I predict that one day you will regret your choice. I predict that you will try to go back, to find your way to the dream city and the winding streets that might have made you a poet. You will search for Hoffmann, and you will not find him. It will not be your destiny to embrace him and kiss him on the mouth. Nor will it be your destiny to wind your apron string about his neck, and set free his collection of wooden birds.

The Sandman gestured to me, weeping blood.

I went to the wall and examined the drainpipe. Now I could no longer see Hoffmann in his room. The edge of the lighted window shone like frost.

I handed the Sandman my wig, grasped the pipe in both hands, and began to climb.

# Livia Llewellyn

## FURNACE

**Livia Llewellyn** *is a writer of dark fantasy, horror and erotica. A 2006 graduate of Clarion, her fiction has appeared in* ChiZine, Subterranean, Sybil's Garage, PseudoPod, Apex Magazine, Postscripts, Nightmare Magazine, *and numerous anthologies. Her first collection,* Engines of Desire: Tales of Love & Other Horrors, *was published in 2011 by Lethe Press.* Engines *received two Shirley Jackson Award nominations, for Best Collection, and Best Novelette (for "Omphalos"). "Furnace" has received a 2013 SJA nomination for Best Short Fiction. You can find her online at liviallewellyn.com.*

Everyone knew our town was dying, long before we truly saw it. There's a certain way a piece of fruit begins to wrinkle and soften, caves in on itself around the edges of a fast-appearing bruise, throwing off the sickly-sweet scent of decay and death that always attracts some creeping hungry thing. Some part of the town, an unused building sinking into its foundations, a forgotten alleyway erupting into a slow maelstrom of weeds and cracked stone, was succumbing, had festered, succumbed: and now threw off the warning spores of its demise. Everywhere in the town we went about the ins and outs of our daily lives and business, telling ourselves everything was normal, everything was fine. And every now and then a spore drifted into our lungs, riding in on a faint thread of that rotting fruiting scent, and though we did not pause in our daily routines, we stumbled a bit, we slowed. It was the last days of summer, I had just turned thirteen, and the leaves were beginning to turn, people were gathering the final crops of their fine little backyard gardens, culling the lingering remains of the season's foods and flowers, smoothing over the soil. My grandfather had placed a large red-rusted oil barrel off the side of the garage, and every evening he threw the gathering detritus of summer into the can, and set it on fire. Great plumes of black smoke rose into the warm air, feather-fine flakes of ash and hot red sparks. I stood on the gravel path, watching the bright red licks of fire crackle and leap from the barrel's jagged edges as my grandfather poked the burning sticks and leaves further down. An evening wind carried the dark smoke up into the canopy of branches overhead, tall evergreens swaying and whispering as they swept and sifted the ash further into the sky. We watched in silence. The air smelled gritty and smoky and dark, in that way the air only ever smells at the end of a dying summer, the smell of the sinking sun and dark approaching fall. The trees shifted, the branches changed direction, and the sickly-sweet scent caught in our throats, driving the smoke away.

—What is that? I asked.

—I don't know, my grandfather replied. He rubbed ash from his eyes, and stared out into a distance place neither of us could see. — Something's wrong.

〰

Summer officially ended, school began, and the town continued. It was easy for all of us to say that everything was fine. The dissonance in the air was the usual changing of the seasons, we told ourselves. Near the downtown area, on a small lonely street along the outskirts of the factories and warehouses that ringed the downtown district, that strange and troubling area where suburbia fizzled out to its bitter end and the so-called city proper began, a number of small businesses closed with no warning to their loyal long-time customers or to those who worked for them. I knew of this only because my mother drove down that particular street one early afternoon, having taken me out of school for a dentist appointment. My mother had frequented most of these stores in her childhood, and she loved driving down the street as an adult, pointing out to me all the various places she had been taken by my grandfather. A small confectioner's store that supplied those queer square mint-tinged wafers that were both creamy and crunchy, the pastel sweets popular at weddings and wakes. A stationers store, where my mother's family had bought boxes and boxes of thick cream paper and envelopes with the family crest, a horned griffin rampant over a field of night-blooming cereus, and where my grandfather bought business cards and memo pads with his name printed neatly in the middle, just above his title of supervisor for the town's electric and water company. A dilapidated movie theatre that showed films in languages no one had ever heard of, from countries no one could ever seem to recall having seen on our schools and library's aging maps and globes. A haberdashery where my father once had his soft brown wool felt fedoras and thick lambskin winter gloves blocked and stitched to his exact measurements and specifications. It had been taken over just that spring by the son of the former owner, an earnest and intense young man with perfect pale skin and unruly black hair, and unfortunately large black eyes. All three of those stores and more sat dark and fallow all along the block, faded red CLOSED and OUT OF BUSINESS signs swinging against padlocked doors, display windows choked with cobwebs and dust, the now familiar odor of sickly sweetness lingering in the air.

—Why do I keep smelling that, I said, pinching my nose shut.— What is it?

—It smells like camphor, my mother said.

—What's that?

—Like the moth balls in our closets, she said. —You know, what I use to keep your father's and grandmother's things from molding and rotting away. To preserve things.

—Preserve? Like jam?

—In a way. To protect things. So they'll never grow old, and always stay the same.

That afternoon as my mother steered the car along the narrow meridian dividing the street in two, the pale young man stood outside the haberdashery's doors, his long arms wrapped around a bolt of fabric as if he were carrying the body of a dead child. I started in shock to realize it was not a bolt of fabric, but a length of thick grey wool wrapped around the stiff body of a large bird with two beaks twisted into a hideous spiral and a spider-like cluster of lidless coal-colored eyes. My mother stopped the car, and we stepped onto the dry worn street sitting under a cool and cloudless sky crowned by telephone wires. No one else was here this time of the afternoon in this part of the town, a part of the town in the middle of everything yet nowhere in particular, where the buildings rose no more than two stories before flattening out in resignation and despair, where you could walk down the sidewalks for hours, see no strip mall or market or house that didn't look like the one behind it and before, hear only the soft crinkle of your shoes against cracked cement and the occasional miserable distant bark of a dog. In hindsight, we should have been more vigilant, more aware that these were the places of a town where septicemia and putrification creep in first, those lonely and familiar sections we slipped into and through every day without concern or care—not the seedy crumbling but flashy edges where decay was expected, and, from a certain element of our small society, even accepted and encouraged. These quiet streets of lonely backwater districts, these were the places we never gave a single thought about, because we thought they would be here forever, unchanging in the antiseptic amber of our fixed memories. These quiet streets of lonely backwater districts were always the first to go.

—Don't come any closer, said the pale young man to my mother as she stepped onto the sidewalk.

—What happened to all the stores? my mother asked. —When did everything close?

—Don't go near the windows, said the pale young man. —It's terrible, don't look. He stepped forward as if to block her, his already too large eyes widening further, the rims and lids as purple-red as the leaves on the trees, as if he had been weeping for hours, for centuries. My mother, a woman who, like her father, my grandfather, did not pay much heed to the general spoken and unspoken rules of a town, brushed past him, and I followed in her wake, already at thirteen very much a similar stubborn member of my family. My mother stepped up to one of the display windows, and I to the other, cupping my hands around my eyes to block out the sun as I pressed my face against the glass. —Don't look, the young man repeated, but he did nothing to stop us, only stood on the sidewalk cradling his many-eyed black-feathered bird wrapped in fabric, shivering in the afternoon sun. Inside the store, everything appeared covered in the light dust typical of such a place, but nothing appeared out of the ordinary. I had last been in the store five years ago, to help my mother pick out a fine linen handkerchief for my father for the holidays, before he had disappeared in the deep network of tunnels and passages owned by the town's electric and water company. I kept staring through the glass. Bowlers and fedoras slumping over the resigned foreheads of cracked mannequin heads, weary trays of uneven chevron-covered ties, unpolished cufflinks depressed into velvet folds of faded burgundy. My breath fogged the glass, and I wiped it away with a pass of my hands. Everything was quiet, peaceful, still.

—I don't see anything different, my mother said. —Everything looks the same as I remember. This is the way it should be.

—I know, the young man said. —It all looks the same on the outside. It always has. You have to look underneath.

—How can one look underneath? I asked.

—You just do. You just know.

I'm not certain how long we stood on the quiet sidewalk of the lonely street in that empty part of town, staring through fingerprint smeared windows into darkness. I now only remember how after a time had passed and as the afternoon sun hitched further down toward the town's jagged horizon, everything in the store seemed to recede, sink into an interminable black fuzz not unlike mold spreading across fruit. Soft sweet mold and mannequin heads, and no life at all in the displays and counters and fixtures and heavy folds of fabric, only the amber-tinged cool approaching dark. My eyes adjusted to the fading light, and everything in the haberdashery blurred and shifted into a single indistinct mass: for one wild terrible second I felt like I was staring into the only place left in the world, that there was only my face pressed to the glass front of a dead forgotten store endlessly out of the reach of my immovable limbs, and everything and everyone behind me, including myself, was forever gone.

—Nothing's changed except the sign, my mother said. —This is unacceptable. The stores must be reopened, so we can shop here, as we've always done. That's how it's supposed to be.

The young man replied, —Yes. And it will never end.

My mother looked at him, but did not reply.

I stepped back from the glass, and as I did, I caught a glimpse of the pale young man's face, reflected beneath the faded gold letters of the haberdashery that bore his father's name. I saw underneath him. I saw his wide unmoving mouth, his tiny painted teeth, his lidless lashless eyes, his cool matte porcelain skin. It was then I remembered I had crushed on him briefly, that last spring. I'd told my mother how handsome he looked, how comforting and familiar, and she'd laughed me into embarrassed silence, and so I'd driven it from my mind. The young man turned from us, and as he walked down the sidewalk back into suburbia, trailing oily iridescent feathers at his feet and the numbing sweet smell of camphor through the air, I caught a glimpse of his neck below his black, black hair, and the straight bloodless seam like a strange new road, slicing through every part of the town I'd ever known.

∿

My mother drove us home in silence, and we never spoke of the incident to each other again. I believe I was afraid to ask my mother what she meant when she said she saw nothing underneath, whether she meant she saw nothing out of the ordinary, or if she meant that she had perceived that same black nothingness the pale young man claimed he saw welling beneath the surface of the haberdashery, the nothingness that had spread throughout that entire row of stores. I was afraid to ask my mother what she meant when she saw nothing underneath, nothing changed, and said that was the way it should always be. I believe I knew then what I was afraid of, or rather there was a confirmation within me of what I had always known that I was afraid of; and my mother knew that I knew, and together in silence we drove home. We drove down the street several weeks later. All of the stores displayed their usual faded yet cheerful red and white OPEN signs, but my mother didn't slow the car, nor did she spin her usual tales of how her family had frequented the various shops over the years and what items she bought that were still somewhere in our house, carefully packed in cedar boxes lined with tissue paper and small white moth balls. I slid down in the car seat until my eyes were level with the plastic button lock on the door, and stared out the window at the haberdashery. Sitting on the sidewalk beside the dusty glass door, still holding the stiff deformed bird bundled in wool felt, I saw the pale young man that for one brief second in my past I had crushed on like the soles of my feet against soft gray gravel, standing, staring out into the street, the look on his face not unlike that of my grandfather when he stood over the can of burning leaves and ash. I had never told my mother what I thought I'd seen that strange afternoon in the face of the pale young man, or at the back of his neck. I didn't need to. My mother smiled, and stared ahead, and drove on.

Fall deepened and thickened and the air above and over our heads grew cold, but the gold and red leaves and the earth itself were still hot to the touch, as though the trees were drawing up and throwing off some unseen underground fire. I woke up early in the morning, having slept every night with the light at my desk never off and the small television always tuned to movies so old even my grandfather had never heard of them. I dressed for school to the snowy images of sleek, long-dead women and men, drifting through a world constructed solely of pixilated shades of black and grey. My grandfather seemed never to sleep, spending evenings after work in the kitchen, spreading maps and charts of the town's systems and infrastructures over the table, scribbling indecipherable equations and geometric shapes in blue ball point pen across the outlines of our streets and neighborhoods he'd traced onto wide sheets of translucent onionskin, the low light of the kitchen lamp falling over his thick white hair and worried face. I would tip-toe into the kitchen to make breakfast, expecting him to be fast asleep, slumped over the table, a pencil drifting out of his large hand. He was always awake, sitting straight in the chair, on his face the same indeterminable and unfathomable look as when we stood at the barrel while summer died all around us, watching the ash disappear into the thick grotto of whispering evergreens.

—What are you looking at? I asked, as I pulled up my chair and sat beside him. —What is happening? What do you see? I asked those questions every morning of him, never sure what I was really asking. Was I asking what he saw in the maps, or what he saw in the false autumn air? Every morning his answers were very different, and very much the same. Picking up a piece of onionskin paper covered in small diagrams and paragraphs thick with words, he would place it over the part of the town map to which it corresponded and point to a specific cluster of words or diagrams now floating over a specific building or street, I would ask the question, and he would speak.

—The B&I Circus Discount Emporium, along South Tacoma Way, where Mom used to buy my winter clothes?

—The woman found her children on the carousel, the one in the middle of the store. You remember it. Employees dressed as clowns, and a dying ape in a cage. She left the girl with the son, an older boy, while looking for a pair of boots that had a left and a right foot, and a pair of pants that had two legs instead of three. Popcorn crackling and calliope music filled the air of the low-ceilinged acre-wide room. Cash registers and conversations. No one could have heard the screams. Maybe there were none. They all left their children there. She returned, all the parents returned, to a circular wood platform wobbling unevenly. Circus animals taffy-warped, the bodies of their children spiraling in ropes of blood and bone around wooden saddles, wooden poles, wooden stars. Store mannequins, plastic boys and girls with bright-eyed smiles, inserted like obscene arrows into delicate flesh. Calliope music, warped and stretched, washing through the air with their howls. Across the store, across a forest of metal clothing racks and rotting sales signs under a flickering florescent sky, the woman saw a store clown, bloated and swaying around a cement pillar like a dying parade float, slowly tearing the ape apart like cotton candy and cramming the pieces into its peppermint striped mouth.

—The Safeway Supermarket, in the Highland Hills district, where you used to take me shopping when I stayed overnight with you and Granny?

—A young boy on a shopping trip with the mother of his best friend, was playing in the refrigerated food aisles. Opening the doors, letting the frost collect on the warming surface, then drawing pictures and writing his name on the glass, like you used to do. His friend and mother were gone only for a few moments, looking for ice cream in another aisle. When they returned to the aisle, the young boy had vanished. Everyone was gone. No traces—no half-filled shopping carts, no purses or wallets on the linoleum floor, no cash registers open in half-completed transactions. The woman saw the boy's words behind glass, the last letter elongated as if the hand writing it had slid down and away. She opened the door. Behind the milk bottle shelves and the thick strips of plastic curtaining, the movements of something quiet and colossal. A thick stench of sweet decay blossomed out into the aisle, hitting the woman so hard that she turned as if slapped, vomiting on herself as she ran from the store, ran from displays molding and blackening on the shelves, ran from open bins of vegetables exploding in clouds of insects and spores, ran from meat that slithered and whispered as it burst from its packaging, dissolving and reforming into something greater than the sum of its blood and gristle and bone, something that might have vaguely resembled a monstrous, profane, and profoundly damaged reconstruction of the missing young boy.

—Point Defiance Park, at the northernmost end of Old Town, where Mom and Dad took me to see the old fort, and the animals at the zoo? Mom got sick there one time. She said it was the hot dogs. We never went back.

—You were too young to understand. They took you along the road that winds through the old-growth forest, called Five Mile Drive, up to the abandoned logging camp. They took you to the small unpaved street of wood plank houses and shops, to the remnants of the railroad tracks where a single steam engine car sat for a century, its giant blackened pistons and wheels locked tight with rust and rain, the engine car your mother rested in while your father took you to the fort. Day and night, now, park rangers hear the thunder and roar of the engine, blasting and crushing and consuming its way through the woods, leaving behind two deep oily grooves of blistered burning earth that no normal plant or tree will grow in again. Other things are found in the self-made tracks, things the rangers have taken their axes to, then buried deeper in the ground. The desiccated remains of animals, lions and orcas, polar bears turned inside out, their bones splintered and shot through with iron splinters. Bubbling jellicular mounds of placenta, slick and hot with blood, the aborted machine-like creatures within them tearing feebly at the thick membrane with inverted limbs and jaws. The entire park has been shut down, but eventually, everything once alive within it will be eaten and rebirthed as something else. After that, who knows where it will go. There's nothing to keep it from leaving.

—Narrows View, in the University Place School District.

Our district. My fingers traced wild ink spirals over to my old elementary school, just a block away from our house. My mother used to walk me up to the corner every day, then watch as I made my way halfway down the block then across the two-lane road, walking carefully within the thick white lines of the crosswalk. I used to imagine that if I stepped out of the lines and onto the worn black surface of the road, I would sink into a river of soft blacktop and tar, be pulled under even as my classmates continued across the wide parking lot and onto the breezeway that connected each of the ten low buildings that made up the school. They would run and dash through bright orange painted metal doors, disappear down linoleum-lined hallways into warm and humid classrooms, shedding coats and fluttering into chairs like autumn leaves. Bells would ring out, harsh and long clanging that echoed over the rooftops and trees, and the heavy yellow buses would belch smoke and squeal out of the parking lot and down the road; and then silence. And I, slowly sinking in the road, my school just yards away, my hands outstretched as if I could grasp it. I couldn't. I never could. And my mother, standing at the crooked red stop sign at the top of our little street, hands at her side, the edges of her brown coat flapping in the cold morning air, watching expressionless as I screamed, then pleaded, then struggled, then gave up and stopped moving at all, just watched her watching me, watching the whole world around us grow dark and still, until we were both trapped in an endless moment in time, never to grow old, never to live, never to die. My hands, forever outstretched for her help. Her eyes, forever burrowing out hollows in mine.

I lifted my fingers from the map. The tips were so blue with ink, it looked like they were rotting away.

—They found a girl in the road, my grandfather began. His large hand covered mine, and placed it back down on the map. He looked so tired, so old. —The skeleton of a large girl, a colossal girl, a giantess. Rising up from the blacktop. Bones like deformed corkscrews, each bone fused from the skeletons of many smaller girls.

—Not different girls, I said, slipping my hand away. —The same girl, trapped in the same part of the road a hundred thousand times. Layers of the same girl, trapped over and over again from kindergarten to sixth grade. Seven years, ending only last spring.

—Yes. My grandfather rose from the table, and started to fold up the maps and diagrams before my mother came downstairs. He didn't have to ask me how I knew.

〜〜<br>〜〜

My grandfather abandoned his maps not long after that. It wasn't that he lost interest. So many incidents occurred, it became useless to record them all. All put together, the entire town became an incident, and the map drowned beneath the network of inky words and roads, until all that remained of white paper was the tiny dot we called home. I don't think either one of us could bear to fill in that small, lonely white circle. We knew it would happen. My grandfather placed everything in the trash can barrel at the side of the yard one day, and we watched it curl into grey ash and float away in the sweet hot air. And after a while, no one remembered what day it was, or what week, or whether the season was fall or winter or spring. It was all the same season, the same day. I woke up to the same ghostly, lifeless images on the television as the day before, dressed for a school day I wouldn't recall going to by evenings end, when I sat at my desk, looking through books and papers for homework I never found.

And then one afternoon, although which afternoon of which month of what year it was, I would never know, my grandfather didn't come home. He left early in the morning for his job at the electric and water company as he always had, his soft grey fedora over his white hair, a thermos of milky coffee tucked into his briefcase. He kissed me on the forehead and told me to be safe, then drove off in the large car he had bought years ago when he became supervisor. I got ready for school, but I can't say if I went or not. The day passed, like all the days, in a soft haze of warmth and numbing sweetness that festered into early evening; and then the sun was pushing long bands of shadow and sun through the windows, over the dinner table. My grandfather would never abandon me. He wasn't coming home, I realized, because he couldn't; and the shock and sorrow of it sent something cold and hard trickling through my veins, and for the first time in what seemed like forever, I felt I was awakening from a terrible, suffocating dream.

—Are we going to wait for Grandpa? I asked my mother.

My mother set the casserole dish on the table, and stared at me. In her face, traces of what I might become, in another time, in another town. Her eyes, bright and furnace dark. Unbearable and all-consuming; and in her pupils I saw the small reflection of myself sink into the road a million times. I knew her answer then, before she said it.

—No.

She poured me a glass of lukewarm milk, and sat down. We ate in silence. The shadows lengthened until there was no more sun, and in my mind, I saw my gentle grandfather filling in that one remaining dot of white on his map with ink as blue as his eyes. And then he, too, was gone.

The next morning was not the same as all the other mornings. In the sleepy-sweet air, I dressed for classes I knew I had never attended, and never would, for friends and teachers I had never met or seen. Silvery thin men and women danced and fought in the snow of a television set that had long ago lost its cord. Images that did not exist. Everything in the world around me, a perverted misremembering, a suffocating lie. I put my schoolbooks under my bed, then changed my mind and stuffed them into the backpack. I had wanted to go, I had wanted to learn. I wanted to grow up. I had wanted the pale young man with the red-rimmed, pool-black eyes.

In the kitchen, my mother folded the top of my paper bag lunch as I drank my lukewarm milk. She licked the palm of her hand and ran it across my hair as I stared at the empty surface of the table, where my grandfather's hands had drawn rivers of blue ink over the map of my life. Her breath was whisper-cloying, as though I had walked into a web. In the distance, a train sounded out, mournful and low and long. I stared up at the ceiling, watching small spores detach like faint candle sparks and float down through the thick amber air, wink out as they hit my face, my skin, the ground. Everyone had known that the town had been dying, long before I truly saw it. The ground trembled and buzzed beneath my feet. I thought of my grandfather and the pale young man, and my face grew porcelain-tight.

—I have to go to school, I whispered. Each word took a century to slip from my mouth, as slow as the dying spores.

—No, you don't. My mother clasped my hand in hers, hard, and I felt our bones shift and crackle, our skin cake and fuse together like velvet and mold.

—Let me go, I said.

—No, she said. —I don't have to.

—Yes, I said. —You do.

A century later or more, I pulled my hand from hers. Her fingers stretched like taffy, wriggled and dropped away. Centuries later, my other hand thrust my grandfather's pen at the pulsing hollow of her throat. Droplets hung in the air, ruby and indigo comets catching the light as they orbited our wounds. Outside, the sun fell and rose as many times as the stars in the sky, and in that epoch my mother curled back her cracking lips wider, wider until there was only teeth and the volcanic black of her open mouth. With each step back from her and away, she bloated and burst, exponential in rot, pushing away the flimsy walls of our home, her veined translucent flesh pulsing with all the unborn variants of my life pushing outward to be free. In the molasses air, I turned, a millennium spent directing my terror and trembling legs away and up to the end of our street. If I cried, time looped back and ate the tears before they fell from my eyes. Only the pounding of my heart, a beat for every revolution of the galaxy, only the echo of a footfall with every dying star, only my mother always behind me, exploding, grasping, expanding, only everywhere the low dark roar of thunder and never rain.

—*They found a girl in the road, my grandfather had begun, in another universe. —Bones like deformed corkscrews, each bone fused from the skeletons of many smaller girls.*

Down the street, past the crosswalk and the thick white lines, and after that each step was quicker, and the centuries burned away. I never looked back. I passed myself, stuck in the blacktop a hundred thousand times, the giantess made of a hundred thousand girls, each one falling apart and clattering to the ground. And I ran to the edges of my northern town and past it and slipped beyond into the world, as all the cold bright skeletons of who I could have been swarmed behind me, plunging into the quivering moist mountains of putrescent flesh that had birthed us all, sinking her into the road where she lost me, all of them dying within her desire like little miscarried dreams.

I never stopped running.

Neither did she.

∼∼∼

I've lived in this southernmost town for many lifetimes now, having lived in many other towns, each further south than the last. But all of the towns of this world have succumbed, as I knew they would, and there are no more towns beyond this one. There is nothing beyond this one, except the vast southern ocean, fields of ice, cold skies, colder stars. Here, winter is a diamond-hard fist, and summer an impossible dream. Or so it used to be, when I first made my way here, centuries or eons ago. I feel her now, again, in the air, in my bones. The days have begun to blend into each other as they did in all the other towns, the minutes and months and years, and a numbing sweet languor warms and slows us down until we no longer know or care. Everyone has known that the town is dying, long before we could see it. But only I know the reason why. My mother is coming for her little girl, once again burning the world away until there is only us and the memories of us together, until there is only her memories of how it used to be, how it should have been. And there are no more towns left to hide in, no more versions or dreams of me left to fight.

So I sit at the window of my apartment in that southernmost town, watching leaves turn red and gold that had only for the first time yesterday been green, watching the sun wax fat and throw off the late summer sparks I knew so well when I lived in the northern town, feeling the air grow camphor-bloated warm and sickly sweet. I sit at my window, turning the pages of school books I'll never learn from, watching the buildings do what I have never done. They age, morph, change. They bloat, fuzz over, and release soft spores from fat cankers sagging off their rotting faces, they malform and reform, they become more familiar with each calcifying day. The southernmost town is disappearing, and the northern town is rising, again. A steam engine howls in the distance as it gobbles up the miles, and so much more. The townspeople's movements weaken, slow, stop. They fade and drift away like vapor. The face of the pale young man appears in the windows, sliding from the flickering edges of my sight into full view as the weeks pass: and then the day will come when he will stand in the street below, as he has stood in all the other dusty streets of all the other towns, his large black eyes fixed on me as the twin-beaked raven in his grasp grotesquely struggles to call out my name, all the names of the monsters of my mother's memories. Behind and around him, behind and around me, the fully formed streets of my childhood soon will stand, birthed out of the ruins of the southernmost town like a still-born giantess, a puppet of calcified dreams and bone, pulled into unwanted existence by the strings of someone else's desire. This, this is my mother's endless suffocating desire, slowing time down around us, winding it back, back, until it becomes the amber-boned river in which I am always and only her little girl, eternal and alone.

I place the blue pen at the small pale circle of my throat.

I can stop time, too.

# Damien Angelica Walters

## Shall I Whisper to You of Moonlight, of Sorrow, of Pieces of Us?

**Damien Angelica Walters**' *work has appeared or is forthcoming in various magazines and anthologies, including* Nightmare, Strange Horizons, Lightspeed, Apex, Glitter & Mayhem, Shimmer, *and* The Best of Electric Velocipede. Sing Me Your Scars, and Other Stories, *a collection of her short fiction, will be released in Fall 2014 from Apex Publications.*

*She's also a freelance editor and a staff writer with BooklifeNow, the online companion to Jeff VanderMeer's Booklife: Strategies and Survival Tips for the 21st Century Writer. You can find her online at* http://damienangelicawalters.com.

Inside each grief is a lonely ghost of silence, and inside each silence are the words we didn't say.

≈

I find the first photograph face down on the mat outside the front door. In a rush to get to the office, I tuck it in the pocket of my trousers, thinking it a note from a neighbor. An invitation to dinner maybe.

I pull my car onto the highway, into a mess of brake lights and angry horns, and shake my head. Morning traffic is always the same. Not sure how anyone could expect otherwise.

When I reach for my cigarettes, I pull out the photo instead--you, with a lock of your hair curling over one cheek, the trace of a smile on your lips, and your eyes twin pools of dark, a touch of whimsy hidden in their depths. Beautiful. Perfect. A spray of roses peeks over your shoulder, the blooms a pale shade of ivory. Far in the distance, a faint

# Shall I Whisper to You of Moonlight, of Sorrow, of Pieces of Us?

strain of music, your favorite song, echoes away.

The surface of the photo is slick beneath my fingertips, and when I lift it to my nose I catch a hint of perfume. Sweet and delicate, but with an undertone of some exotic spice. I will never forget that smell.

I close my eyes tight against the tears. Yes, tears, even after all this time. I knew you'd find me. I've always known.

॥

*Please let me go. Please.*
    *Never.*

॥

In the middle of the night I wake to the smell of flowers. I move from room to room with a dry mouth and a heart racing madness, turn on all the lights, and check the windows and doors. Locked or unlocked, it doesn't matter. If you want to come back, they won't stop you. Nothing will. The photographs are proof of that. Still, the locks are a routine that makes me feel as if I'm doing something other than waiting.

I peer through the glass to the back yard where moonlight is dancing across the grass. The tree branches sway gently back and forth like a couple lost in the rhythm of a dance. I whisper your name, my voice breaking. Only house noise answers. I rake my fingers through my hair. I don't know if I can go through this again, but I also know I have no choice.

I never did.

॥

The next photo appears face up on the coffee table in the living room. Same smile, but with your hair pulled back in a ponytail. A thin chain of silver circles your neck; the fingertips of your right hand are barely touching the small medallion hanging below the hollow at the base of your throat. A trace of dark shadows the skin beneath your eyes.

*Baby*, those shadows say.

Yes, I still remember the sound of your voice.

I fumble a cigarette free from the pack; it takes three tries before

I can hold my lighter still enough to guide the flame where it needs to go.

When my job transferred me from one coast to another, I thought the distance would be too great for you. Even when I still lived in the old house, it had been over a year since you left the last photo. I'd thought you were gone.

I know it won't be any different this time, no matter how much I want otherwise. This hope is a strange thing, a wish wrapped in barbed wire. Or maybe delusion.

〰️

The smell of flowers again in the middle of the night. I stay in bed, the sheet fisted in my hands. Heart full of chaos; head full of images.

〰️

My coworker catches me at the end of the day when I'm slipping into my coat. "Hey, a bunch of us are going to happy hour. Want to come?"

"No, maybe next time."

He raises his eyebrows and shakes his head. "That's what you said the last time."

"Sorry, I already have plans."

"You said that, too."

I shrug one shoulder and step away before he can say anything else.

〰️

I sit with the television on mute, listening to the silence. A book sits unread on the sofa beside me; a glass of iced tea long gone warm rests on the table. Condensation beads around the base of the glass like tears.

The minutes tick by. The hours pass. I listen to nothing. I wait.

〰️

Another photograph. On the bottom step of the staircase this time. You, captured on a blue and white striped blanket, shielding your eyes

## Shall I Whisper to You of Moonlight, of Sorrow, of Pieces of Us?

from the sun. Even in the frozen bright, the shadows under your eyes are visible and your skin is too pale. Next to you on the blanket is a crumpled napkin, a plastic cup on its side, a bit of cellophane wrap holding a rainbow's arc on its surface, a few grains of sand. I hear the rush of a wave as it touches the shore then another as it recedes. The salt tang of the ocean hovers in the air, but only for an instant.

〰

I smell flowers in the night. Maybe it's my imagination, but the scent is growing stronger. A promise or recrimination?

〰

The landing at the top of the stairs. The next photo. Your face half in shadow, half in light. The almost-smile is still there in spite of the pallor of your skin, the hollows beneath your cheekbones, the scarf wrapped round your head. I hear the last breath of a laugh. Smell honeysuckle drifting on a cool breeze.

Always the same photographs in the same order. I don't know how, but the how doesn't matter. And I already know the why.

(*Please let me go.*

*Never.*)

It will be the last photo, just like the last time. I know it will, but I check the locks anyway. Everything is as it should be. It's too cold to leave the windows open or I would.

〰

A throat clears. I look up to see my boss standing in my office, a small frown on his face. "Are you okay?"

Yes," I say. "Why?"

"You look a little tired, that's all."

"Just a bout of insomnia," I say. The lie slips easily from my tongue.

"You have my sympathies. My wife's had that for years. Try a glass of wine before bed. That helps her."

"Will do."

He lingers for a few moments longer and for one quick instant, I think of telling him everything. I tried that once with your sister; she told me I should talk to a doctor, and then she stopped answering my calls.

〜

I unlock the windows, as always, but my hand remains on the lever. I am so tired of waiting. I'm wearing shadows under my eyes now and I have a knot in my chest that won't go away. Maybe I could learn to forget about you. To move on. Throw away the photographs, let time fade the memories. Lock the doors and the windows instead of unlocking them. Go out with my coworkers. And maybe you'll stop.

I flip the lock, sigh, and turn it back. No, I want you to come back. It's what I've always wanted. Maybe that small sliver of doubt is the reason you haven't yet.

〜

And then I find a photo in the hallway just outside the bedroom door. I sit with my back against the wall. I've never seen this photo before. You've never made it this close.

The smile is no longer a smile, but a grimace. The shadows beneath your eyes are now bruises of dark. I taste the bright sting of antiseptic. Hear the ticking of a clock winding down and down and down.

"Please, baby, please," I whisper, my voice hollow.

I take that tiny trace of doubt and shove it away. Hold the photo to my chest. This time will be different. I know it will.

〜

I toss and turn for hours, listening to the quiet. The distance between the hallway and the bed seems so small, yet miles, worlds, apart as well.

*Please, baby. Please.*

The last words you said to me.

〜

The next door neighbor is outside watering her plants when I get home. She waves. Smiles. I return the gesture, but not the expression.

# Shall I Whisper to You of Moonlight, of Sorrow, of Pieces of Us?

When she starts to head in my direction, I hightail it into the house. Rude, I know, but she caught me when I first moved here and kept me outside for an hour, her voice flitting from topic to topic like a bee out on a mission for nectar. She doesn't pick up on any of the signs that I want to be left alone, or maybe she does and just chooses to ignore them. The way she ignores the ring on my finger.

ᷔᷔᷔ

Another photo, left on the foot of our bed. It shows only clasped hands. Matching silver bands. Fingers entwined. One hand is hale and hearty; the other frail, the veins standing out like mounds in a field of fresh graves. I feel the paper skin beneath my palm. I hear a whisper of words, promising lies, promising everything. I taste a kiss laced with despair and loss.

I can't stop the tears. I can't stop my hands from shaking. But I run to the florist and buy three dozen red roses, long-stemmed with thorns, the way you like them. On the way back, I brave the mall and buy a fresh bottle of your favorite perfume.

ᷔᷔᷔ

But one day becomes two. One week turns three. No trace of flowers in the air. No new photos. I'm still alone with empty arms and a knot in my chest. I smoke cigarette after cigarette. Pace footprint divots in the carpet. Choke back tears as the hope leaks out, a little more with each passing day.

My boss was wrong about the wine. It doesn't help at all. Nothing does.

ᷔᷔᷔ

After two months, I slide the photographs into an envelope, tuck the flap over as best as I can, and pull a battered shoe box out from under the bed. Nine sets of photos. Ten envelopes, the last one sealed. The paper clearly reveals two small circular shapes. The saint on the medallion never offered assistance; the ring is only a circle of empty without your skin to bind it.

When I close my eyes, I recall every plane and curve of your face, before illness turned you pale and hollow, but I wonder, if not for the photographs, would I? Would time have turned my heart to scar instead of open wound?

I shove the box back under the bed, my mouth downturned. I should've known better. You've tried nine times in five years. All the want in the world can't bring you back.

〜

The next time my coworkers ask me to go to happy hour, I say yes. I say yes the second and third time, too. By the fifth time, I don't have to force a laugh at a joke or fake a smile when someone catches my eye. I feel a loosening in my chest. An ease in my breath.

I take the box of photographs and put them on the top shelf of my closet. I make sure all the doors and windows are locked before I go to bed. And, finally, I take off the silver ring. My eyes burn with tears, but I blink them away before they fall.

〜

"Please let me go," you whispered through cracked lips. "Please."

"Never," I said, arranging the scratchy hospital blanket around your shoulders.

Your bare scalp was hidden under a yellow scarf, but nothing could hide the matchstick legs, the grey tinge of your skin, or the pain in your eyes that morphine couldn't touch. No amount of perfume could mask the shroud of illness and breaking hearts.

I held your hand and told you for the thousandth time about that night, our first date, after I dropped you off. How I turned and saw you standing with your hair full of moonlight and your lips full of smile. How I knew I would spend the rest of my forever with you.

"Please, baby, please."

And then only silence. I sat with your hand in mine until your skin began to cool. I didn't cry until a nurse led me out of the room.

〜

I wake on a cool morning in early autumn to find the photograph on the mat outside the front door. The lock of hair, the little smile, the

## *Shall I Whisper to You of Moonlight, of Sorrow, of Pieces of Us?*

pale roses. I stand with my hands in my pockets for a long time, but eventually I carry the photo back into the house.

I'll leave the windows open every night, weather be damned. I'll put flowers out every day. Because you were so close the last time. So very close. That has to mean something.

I slip the ring back on my finger. It was a mistake to take it off in the first place. I won't make it again.

Please, baby, find your way back home to me. I'll wait for you no matter how long it takes. I promise I will. If you make it all the way this time, I'll say the goodbye I should've said in the hospital.

Maybe then I'll be able to let you go.

# John Langan

## Bor Urus

**John Langan** *is the author of two collections,* The Wide, Carnivorous Sky and Other Monstrous Geographies *and* Mr. Gaunt and Other Uneasy Encounters, *and a novel,* House of Windows. *With Paul Tremblay, he has co-edited* Creatures: Thirty Years of Monsters. *He lives in upstate New York with his wife, younger son, and a raft of animals.*

I love a big storm. I love the buildup to it: the meteorologists, flushed with their sudden importance, narrating the flow of the oranges and reds across the local maps; the supermarkets, crowded with people whose furrowed brows and pursed lips grant the soup cans and bottled water in their carts a promotion to provisions; the neighbors, diligently preparing their houses and yards for the high winds by rolling trash cans into the garage, securing the shutters as best they can. I love the storm itself: the house creaking as the wind moans against it; the rain rattling on the windows, reducing the yard to an impressionistic blur; the lightning burning the air white, the thunder shaking the walls. And I love the aftermath: the cautious step onto the front porch to survey the trees, their branches still saturated, bent; the walk around the house to pick up any items that were blown loose; the drive to town, to observe the storm's more general ruin.

It's the emotions that accompany each stage of the storm: I savor them. On one side, there's anticipation, a half-pleasurable dread at what's bearing down on us that makes the air hum, the way it does before any big event; on the other side, there's relief, which may also be tinged with dread at whatever damage awaits discovery, whatever crash must be sourced and reckoned with, but which is more an emptied-out feeling, as if, for a moment, we're as clear as the air the storm has just washed. In between dread and relief, though, is the most rarefied sensation, a terror at our utter powerlessness in the face of what's enveloped us, a panic at the trees whipping side to side deliriously, the power lines bouncing like jumpropes, the wineglasses ringing at each clap of thunder—which borders the ecstatic. When a storm is at its peak, and the world outside seems on the verge of tearing itself apart, a kind of radical openness comes briefly into view, as if, with each blanching of the view out the front window, something else, a more essential state of existence, draws that much closer to being unveiled.

At some point, I began to suspect that my figurative response to the violence of a severe storm might be pointing me in the direction of actual truth. I was a teenager, fifteen, sixteen, that point of maximum narcissism when it seems entirely reasonable to think that you are privy to special insight, able to intuit secret knowledge. However, unlike so many of the other notions that occupied my brain at that time, which steadily decamped as my teens drained into my twenties, this one dug in more firmly. It was buttressed by bits and pieces of magazine articles read in waiting rooms, by fragments of documentaries stumbled onto while late-night channel-surfing. The details were fairly incoherent, but the gist of the theory I assembled was, if there are other dimensions, parallel universes, alternate planes of existence—call them what you will—then mightn't the tremendous release of energy in a serious storm unsettle, destabilize things sufficiently for that other place to be glimpsed, even entered? Anyone with a modicum of scientific knowledge, let alone actual expertise, on whom I tried out this line of reasoning treated it with a species of amused tolerance, much the way they probably would have a declaration of belief in alien visitation. This lack of support did nothing to unseat my conviction; in fact, it was during my twenties that I first ventured out into the midst of a storm, to see what I could see.

Of course, this was nothing, which I blamed on the fact that I sat in my car the entire time, listening to the rain bang on the roof. It did not stop me from repeating the experiment with subsequent storms. Soon, I was starting the car, switching on the headlights, flipping on the wipers, and pulling out of the driveway in search of revelation.

For the next sixteen years, it eluded me. About the closest I came was during a storm that came over while I was driving back from a trip up into the Catskills with my then-fiancée. All afternoon, tall heaps of cloud had loomed over the mountains, dimming the sky, then moving east. When the air thickened, however, humidity pressing on us like a great, damp hand, a storm seemed in the offing, and we agreed it would be best if we beat it back to our apartment. Just the other side of Woodstock, a handful of fat drops of rain burst on the windshield, and then the world outside was swept away by a wall of water. Afraid to brake into a hydroplane, I downshifted as quickly as I could, stabbing the button for the hazards. Engine whining, the car slowed to a crawl, but even on fast, the wipers did little more than push the water screening the windshield back and forth. Lightning flashed, turning the rain into white neon, and the thunder that followed one-Mississippi two-Mississippi shook the car. I was already steering for the shoulder when the lightning repeated, the thunder answering one-Mississippi faster. Prin was telling me to pull over, the command a litany: "Pull over pull over pull over pull over pull over."

"I'm trying," I said, as lightning and thunder split the air together. Although I couldn't help my flinch, I wasn't worried as much about being electrocuted as I was about someone racing up behind and slamming into us. I knew the road wasn't that wide, the shoulder not that far away, but hours seemed to pass as the car eased to the right, lightning flaring like the flash of an overeager photographer, thunder overlapping, crashing into itself and forming an avalanche of sound that rumbled and roared over us. When I judged we had crossed onto the shoulder, I put the clutch in, shifted into neutral, and opened my door. I hadn't unbuckled my seatbelt, so I couldn't lean that far out of the car, and Prin didn't have to reach that far to grab my arm and haul me back inside. "Are you insane?" she screamed. "Close the door!"

I did.

"What were you thinking?" she continued, her eyes wide with terror. "There's a goddamn hurricane out there!"

"I was checking to make sure we were on the shoulder," I said, which was true: I was looking for the white strip that delineated the edge of the road. But once I'd pushed the door open and the immensity of the storm had rushed over me, I was swept by a feeling of such exaltation that the hand Prin had caught was stealing toward the release for my seatbelt. At her expression of utter fright, however, my exhilaration curdled to embarrassment. I took her hands and said, "It's okay."

"Asshole." She tugged her hands from mine.

"Yes, but I'm your asshole."

# Bor Urus

That brought a smile to her face, which disappeared as lightning stabbed the trees to our right, thunder cracking so loud it deafened us. Prin pressed herself into her seat as if it could conceal her, her hand groping for mine. Sheets of rain layered the windows; I switched the wipers off. "It can't last much longer," I said, speaking too-loudly because of the ringing in my ears. "These summer storms blow themselves out pretty quickly."

Prin didn't answer. I stared out the windshield, trying to distinguish the road through the water. For a moment, the rain lessened, and the world in front of us swam into view. Maybe fifty yards ahead, the road rose in a slight incline, more an extended bump than a hill. On the other side of that rise, something was crossing the road from left to right. It was an animal, easily as big as an elephant. For a moment, I thought it was an elephant, had visions of an accident involving a convoy of circus animals. But the silhouette was wrong: the back was longer, the dip to the hips less pronounced, the head shorter, blunter, crowned by a pair of heavy horns as wide as my car was long. With each step it took, the animal's head swung from one side to the other with a slowness that was almost casual, as if it were out for a stroll in a light mist, not a raging storm. My hand was back on the door handle, and then the rain picked up again, hiding the enormous profile behind a curtain of water. I opened my mouth; to say what, I didn't know. I was waiting for the rain to ebb once more, allow another glance at whatever that had been. When it did not, I turned to Prin and said, "Did you see that?"

"What?" she said. Her brown was level, her mouth straight, her cheeks pale. She was angry, I realized; she had witnessed what I had, and the experience had made her furious.

"I—"

"Do you think you can drive out of here?"

I wanted to ask if she was serious, remind her that this was a car, not a submarine, but what I said was, "Yeah."

Wipers whipping back and forth, defogger blowing, hazards blinking, I put the car into gear and turned toward the road. I was certain that I was going to drive into whatever had been crossing it. After five minutes passed with no collision, though, my hands began to relax their hold on the steering wheel, and once the dashboard clock had counted another five minutes, I knew that, even crawling forward as we were, we had passed beyond the place the great animal had been. I felt, not relieved so much as *full*, as if what I had seen were inside me, straining against the walls of my chest. I couldn't seem to draw enough breath. The sensation persisted all the long drive back to our apartment in Wiltwyck, where Prin led me directly to the bedroom, tugged down her shorts and mine, and pulled me onto the bed. We made quick, vigorous love, and once we were done, did so a second, and a third time.

When, aching, sore, we finally pulled apart from one another, we stood from the bed and stumbled into the kitchen and out the back door, onto the apartment's nominal back deck. Night had descended, bringing with it a fresh round of storms. Naked, we stood in the darkness, letting the rain pound down onto us. The pressure in my chest had eased, though it was not gone. It was more as if whatever was inside me had folded its legs and settled into sleep.

If I say that the babies—twins—who resulted from that afternoon occupied my attention for the next dozen years, there's enough truth to the words for them not to feel like too much of an evasion. What they are is incomplete. After all, there were a good four weeks between Prin's and my lovemaking and the baby-blue "+" appearing in the window of the home pregnancy test, during which time three more storms thundered through the area. I could have ventured out into any of them, could have tried to return to the spot outside Woodstock where my long-term intuition had seemed to flower into reality. For that matter, once Prin's pregnancy was confirmed, our hasty marriage accomplished, there were a handful of instances before the twins arrived when I could have resumed my investigation, as there were scattered throughout the years that followed. The most I did, however, was a cursory search of the web, which revealed that the place where Prin and I had seen whatever we'd seen was proximate to Dutchman's Creek, which had a vaguely sinister reputation; why, exactly, I couldn't discover. On a couple of occasions, I broached the topic of that day with Prin, but she met my question of what she thought we'd seen crossing the road with one of her own: "What? What is it you think we saw?" Strictly speaking, it wasn't a denial of our experience, but it was as if shutters dropped over her eyes, sealing off what might have been happening behind them. It stymied me into silence, which appeared to be the desired effect, since Prin did not continue the conversation.

It was as if the part of me that responded to storms so profoundly had become stuck, the memory of that huge form a gouge in the vinyl, stuttering my emotions. I would sit on the living room couch, Nina cradled in my right arm, Eddie in my left, as the rain washed the picture window, and the curiously hollow ring of water striking glass would absorb my attention, leaving it too saturated for any further response to the tumult outside. I would half-lie on Eddie's bed, my head and shoulders propped against his headboard, his face pressed into my chest, his arms wrapped around me with all his five year old's strength, as the air lit white and cracked, and I would stroke his hair, rub his back through his Spider-Man pajamas, telling him as I did that it was just the weather, keeping my voice calm, level, the steady rise and fall of my words, the slow circles my hand traced on his cotton top, smoothing away any emotions of my own that might have been threatening to bunch up. I would sit on the living room couch beside Nina as the CBS affiliate out of Albany interrupted our sitcom to discuss the severe weather rampaging across the area, and after leaving my seat to point out to her where Ulster County was on the regional map, I would explain why I didn't think we had to worry about a tornado striking us; although there was one that knocked down the wall of a school south of us, in Newburgh, some years ago— which led to us abandoning the TV to search online for accounts of that old catastrophe, channeling any impulses that had been stirred by the wind's shriek into research. The agitation, the exhilaration I had felt wasn't gone—it wasn't that far away, at all. It was...contained, dormant.

What raised it was my children; specifically, their decision to venture out into the woods behind our house on the brink of a storm. I saw the heavy clouds piling overhead; I had read the weather report, which put the entire region under a Severe Thunderstorm Watch; I could already hear the distant thunder, like big trucks bumping over a road. Nonetheless, when Eddie said that he and Nina were going outside to try his new two-way radios, I didn't object. "Don't go too far," I called after him, "it's supposed to rain," but my only answer was the screen door to the porch slapping its frame.

The thunder arrived first, a series of deep growls that rolled over the low hill behind the house. For long moments, the air was crowded with sound, and then it was full of rain, the lightning that flickered almost an afterthought. I sat on the living room couch, the book I had been reading lowered, and listened for the clump of my children's sneakers on the porch steps, their inevitable giggles at having run home through the downpour. Lightning flashed; the thunder's growl rose to a roar. I left my book open on the couch and hurried to the back door.

Rain hammered the porch. I opened the screen door, and the wind caught it and flung it wide. Leaning out into the storm, I cupped my hands around my mouth and called Nina and Eddie's names. There was no answer. I could picture the two of them crouched beside a tree, grinning like maniacs as they listened to me shouting, an image sufficiently annoying for me to consider leaving them to their sodden fate—an impulse that vanished a moment later, when a bolt of lightning speared the top of the back hill. Thunder boomed, shuddering the house; the rain redoubled. Before I fully knew what I was doing, I was down the porch stairs and running across the yard toward the woods, my bare feet kicking up sprays of cold water. By the time I reached the tree line, I was soaked, my hair and clothes plastered to me, my eyes full of rain. Bellowing my children's names, I plunged amongst the trees. Lightning whited the air; thunder shook the tree trunks. Every warning about what to do in a thunderstorm, especially the keeping-away-from-trees part, ran through my head. "Nina!" I shouted. "Eddie!" I dragged my forearm across my eyes, trying to wipe away water with water. Deep in my gut, dread coiled, while higher in my chest, a sensation of being absolutely overwhelmed threatened to force its way out of me in one long scream.

Strange as it sounds, only after Nina and Eddie had caught my arms and were guiding me toward the house did I realize that the tree I had been standing near had been struck by lightning. When the storm had burst, the twins had sought shelter in the garage, where they'd remained until they'd heard me calling for them. They'd emerged in time to watch me rush into the woods. After a brief deliberation, they'd set off after me. Fifty feet into the trees, they stopped, unable to tell which direction I'd gone. Nina was for splitting up and going left and right; Eddie favored staying together and moving forward. Their debate meant that they saw the lightning plunge into the trees somewhere in front of them out of the corners of their eyes. The attendant burst of thunder doubled them over, their hands clapped to their heads. Ears stunned, they stumbled to the spot where a moderately-sized tree had been detonated by the lightning bolt. Chunks of wood, some steaming, a few on fire, fanned out from the trunk's jagged remains. In the midst of the wreckage, the twins found me, standing with my eyes wide. Later, Eddie would tell me that he was afraid to touch me, because he was afraid that I might be electrified. No such worry disturbed his sister, who strode up to me, took my right arm, and turned me toward the house.

# Bor Urus

The worst effects of my experience—the almost-total blanching of my vision, the loss of my hearing—ebbed more quickly than I would have predicted. By the time Prin had returned from shopping and was driving me to the hospital, my vision had largely cleared, though colors still appeared washed-out, and while my hearing was little more than a high-pitched ringing, I was aware of my family's voices as disturbances in that noise. The E.R. doctor pronounced a cautious diagnosis that I was substantially unharmed, which my regular MD would second when I saw her the following day, and which she would amend to mild hearing loss when I checked in with her two weeks after that. I wasn't aware of any diminishment in my hearing as much as I was in my vision, specifically, my color vision, which remained less vibrant than it had been, as if I were viewing colors through a film. My ongoing complaints led to an appointment with my optometrist, who found nothing obviously wrong with my eyes and referred me to an ophthalmologist, a retinal specialist who spent a long time shining painfully bright lights into my dilated pupils, only to arrive at the same verdict. The specialist offered to send me on to a sub-specialist he knew up in Albany, but I demurred. By that time, I was starting to understand what had happened to me.

Two days before my appointment with the ophthalmologist, I dreamed I was back in the woods, searching for the twins in the midst of the storm. I stumbled into the small clearing where the twins had found me. Evergreens, interrupted by the occasional birch, stationed its border. I screamed my children's names, and as I did, a finger of lightning touched one of the trees across the clearing. For a dream-moment, the lightning hung in place, a blazing seam in the air, a brilliant snarl of glass through which I glimpsed a shape. It was a tree—but such a tree as I'd never seen. Leaves as green as an emerald, as one of those tropical snakes you see in nature documentaries, gathered into a globe atop a slender trunk whose bark shone like polished bronze. Simultaneously, this was a child's approximation of a tree, and the original tree, the Platonic ideal from which all others emanated. When the lightning was done plunging into the evergreen, the window it had burned into the air closed, a feeling of loss—of grief—as profound as what I'd felt at the death of my father made me suck in my breath as if I'd been kicked. Gasping, I struggled up to consciousness, to Prin asleep in the bed beside me.

For the next week, the image of that tree burned in my mind with such intensity that, had you placed a sample of my neurons under the microscope, you would have seen it lighting the center of each nucleus. Every time I closed my eyes, I saw those leaves thick with green, that corrugated bark. I didn't know if what I'd dreamed was an actual memory, retrieved from the trauma surrounding it, or a symbol, a way for my imagination to represent another, indescribable experience to me. I didn't care, because as the vision of that tree glowed in my brain, it illuminated the emotion that had accompanied the lightning strike, a terror that was exultation that was exaltation. It was the feeling that had stirred in me a dozen years before, more, while the wipers metronomed across the windshield, the rain jumped on the road ahead. It was the sensation of standing beside a fundamental openness, a Grand Canyon from whose space might emerge anything: an enormous beast, ambling over the blacktop, a tree glimpsed through a flash of lightning. As the huge shape that Prin and I had seen those years ago had seemed to take up residence inside me, tangling itself in this emotion and thus inhibiting it, so the sight of the tree roused the animal, set its nostrils flaring, its tail switching. Pulling my emotion along with it, the thing began to pace the confines of my chest, lowering its blunt head to test the thickness of the wall here, the padlock on the gate there.

Not at once, but over the course of weeks, months, the next couple of years, my actions, my behavior, shifted, became more impulsive, erratic. I noticed it first at work, where I was less-inclined to suffer the idiocy of either my co-workers or our customers. At home, the twins entering their teens provided both a prompt and an excuse for me to adopt a more authoritarian style of parenting. In my marriage, I became more vocal about my unhappiness with the long hours Prin put in at her job. And when a storm blew in, I was much more likely to grab the keys to the truck and announce to whoever was listening that I was going out. If one of the kids, or, more likely, if my wife asked why, I was ready with an excuse about us needing milk; although, on a couple of occasions, I declared that I felt like taking a ride, and since that provoked no further questions, it became my default response.

In nothing I did did I go too far, say words that could not be forgotten, commit acts that could not be forgiven. But in various ways, in all facets of my life, as time passed I drew ever-closer to a border to cross over which would bring disaster. At work, my responses to my district manager's suggestions for improving the store verged on outright mockery, while I had given a few dissatisfied customers such a run-around that one of them had been in tears. Within the house,

# Bor Urus

I became adept, not at criticizing the twins, but in remaining silent to the little they offered me, treating their adolescently-awkward gestures at communication with a bemused condescension. Within my marriage, I had stopped complaining to Prin; instead, through the miracle of social media, I had located the woman I had been involved with before Prin, and had started e-mailing, then calling her, late at night, when everyone else was asleep. Whenever lightning strobed the yard, thunder ground against the house, I reached for the keys. Sometimes, I would pull the truck into a lay-by and step out into the storm, let the rain needle me, the lightning arc overhead, the thunder shake me. No outsized animals emerged onto the road beside me, no lightning bolts opened views of other places, but I didn't care. Fear so pure it was joy made my blood sing in my ears, made my skin electric, made the animal confined in my chest toss its head and kick its hoofs.

When Prin realized the change in me—which is to say, when she sat down to the computer and saw one of the e-mails from my ex open on the screen—she attributed it to that cliché of our parents' generation, the mid-life crisis. This was during the first conversation we had over the phone, which had to wait a week after I came downstairs to the sight of her suitcase standing at the front door and the sting of her hand slapping my face. Had the twins not already left for their year abroad in Paris, no doubt they, too, would have been packed and waiting in the car. My cheek hot from her blow, all I could do was ask her what was wrong, what had happened. Of course, the instant my eyes fell on that black case, its rolling-handle extended, the explanation flashed through my brain: *She found out.* As she was stamping out the door, Prin's "Why don't you ask *Joyce?*" confirmed that she in fact had found out. A check of the computer showed my e-mail account open, the latest semi-flirtatious message from my ex on the screen. It had been forwarded, as had all the others from her, but I deleted them, anyway, then logged out of my e-mail, which I was certain I'd done the previous night—though it appeared I'd been mistaken.

That, or I'd been trying to force the moment to its crisis. I wasn't sure. The last few years, I'd largely abandoned the nuances of introspection in favor of the simplicity of action. Yet there had been something almost paradoxically private about my acts; rarely had I considered them in relation to anyone except myself. Mostly, I had luxuriated in the excess of emotion that had given rise to them and to which they, in turn, contributed. Now, left alone, my thoughts turned outward, to Prin, to the marriage which had canted suddenly to one side, its hull torn by the iceberg it had scraped against—the half-submerged danger I had been steering it toward. Back from the job at which I was subdued, distracted, I wandered the empty house, examining my behavior of the last several months—years—with the eye of an investigator attempting to reconstruct the precise sequence of events that had led to the jagged ice piecing the steel plates, the ocean's cold water pouring through the gap. I could identify a lengthy report's worth of instances, large and small, when Prin and I had been out of sync with one another, but I could not assemble those moments into a coherent and adequate narrative, one that explained not just my ongoing, secret communication with my ex, but my withdrawal from my children, my belligerence at work. There was only the great animal baying inside me, a torrent of emotion.

For the first time since I'd run out after the twins, however, that terrible awe was challenged by another feeling, by a fear more prosaic in its origins, but no less potent in its effects. Prin, Nina and Eddie, even my job: all had come to seem incidental to my life, barely-connected to its actual substance, to the fabulous tree burning in my memory. As if a lens had dropped in front of my eyes, I saw my wife, my children, my work, not as ornaments, but as the girders and beams giving my days what shape and order they had. To be the inhabitant of such a structure seemed the remarkable thing, the momentary tree and huge silhouette typical of a world that tended to formlessness and chaos. With my actions, I had steadily undermined the base of that construction, to the point that it was swaying perilously. How near to collapse my life was, I couldn't estimate with much accuracy, but it was certainly close enough for me to be overtaken by crushing sadness at the prospect of its fall. I was afraid, not of the sublime unknown, but for the domestic familiar, and the emotion transfixed me like a pin through an insect.

So absorbed was I by what appeared the imminent and inevitable end of my life as I had known it, that I barely registered the approach of Hurricane Eileen. Prior to Prin's discovery of my correspondence with my ex, I had watched the reports of the storm sweeping the northwest edge of the Caribbean, on path to make landfall somewhere between mid-Florida and north-Georgia, its course after that likely a coastal one, though the specifics would have to wait until the storm drew nearer. I heard the cashiers talking about the hurricane in the break room, directed customers to the bottled water, the propane tanks, the portable generators, agreed with my assistant manager's suggestion that we try to scare up some more portable jennies from the warehouse, but none of it registered as it would have only days before. I was absorbed by the fact that four days had passed since Prin's departure, and there was still no reply from her to any of the e-mails I'd sent, one a day. I wasn't sure if she'd headed to her parents, who were close but would require some measure of explanation, or to one of her friends', or to a motel. There'd been no word from the twins, either, which was probably due to late-adolescent obliviousness, but which I was afraid signified that Prin had contacted them, already.

Not until the end of my long conversation with Prin a week after she'd left, when she asked me if I were prepared for Eileen, did it dawn on me that this storm might be a cause for concern. A search online turned up articles about the mandatory evacuations of low-lying areas of New York City, the extra utility workers placed on standby, the state of emergency that had been declared for the area. Another click of the mouse brought me a satellite photo of the hurricane itself, a vast comma of thick, gray clouds whose margins reached from Virginia to Massachusetts. Rendered in the National Weather Service's color-coded pixels, Eileen was a wall of deep green sweeping around bands of yellow and orange, all of it arcing in front of the well-defined blank of the eye. Downgraded from a Category 2 to a Category 1 hurricane, the storm was still considered a serious threat to the City. Already, the first wave of showers was washing into the region, the winds were rising, the TV stations throughout the region had deployed whatever reporters had drawn the short straws to the locations that had been deemed suitably photogenic—the majority of which appeared to be located on or near the beach. Outside my window, the weather was quiet. I considered a run to Wal-Mart to pick up a few supplies, only to reject the idea as so much media-inspired hysteria. Likely, the storm would either skirt the City or miss it entirely, leaving me with a portable propane stove I could have bought for half the price using my employee discount at work. Anyway, I was preoccupied with my talk with Prin, the upshot of which was that, while far from happy, she accepted my assurance that my e-mail exchanges with my ex had not led to any other kinds of exchanges, and was willing to consider continuing our marriage. At least for the moment, our life together was not going to come crashing down; though how much repair would be required remained to be seen.

When I woke late the next morning, it was to wind moaning over the house, rain tapping on the bedroom windows. My prediction had been correct: the hurricane had missed the City. Instead, Eileen had swung inland, rolling over northern New Jersey and eastern Pennsylvania, losing strength as it went, until, by the time it reached the Hudson Valley, it had been demoted to a tropical storm. The difference, however, was academic, since even as a tropical storm, Eileen stirred the air into gusts that pushed against the house in long shrieks, drove the rain horizontally. Lightning stammered, an engine trying to catch, while thunder rumbled like the edges of continents scraping against each other. The cable was out, which was no surprise, but the power was on, which I wouldn't have expected. I found the transistor radio Prin had bought me last Christmas, slid out the antenna, and turned it on. Everything was already closed or closing. Whoever was responsible for such things had prohibited all non-essential travel. The storm had stalled overhead. Widespread power outages had been reported and more were anticipated; high wind advisories, flash-flood warnings, and tornado watches had been issued. Our house sat on a low ridge, paralleled by other ridges, so I wasn't worried about much except maybe one of the trees in the front yard falling into it—though none stood tall enough to threaten more than a prolonged inconvenience. Prin's parents' house, however—to which she had retreated—was separated from the Hudson by a modest lawn which terminated in a short slope to a narrow and rocky beach. On top of everything else, Eileen was supposed to draw the Hudson up beyond flood stage. I wasn't sure what the implications of this were for my in-laws' place, but it was a matter for concern. Our telephone was tied to our cable, though, as was our internet access, and since Prin had taken the emergency cell-phone with her, there was no way for me to contact her. I toyed with the idea of running out to the truck and navigating the deluge to Prin's parents', but couldn't decide how much peril my wife was actually in. With the slope of the lawn, her mom and dad's house was up maybe seven or eight feet from the river. Was that high enough? Not to mention, how would it look when I was pulled over for being on the road in the storm, as I probably would be?

There was nothing to do except to remain where I was and wait out the storm. On the kitchen table, there were stacks of paperwork I had been ignoring for a couple of weeks before Prin had left: sales figures, projections, and goals; a rundown of the coming season's new products, with suggestions on how best to promote them; three in-house applications for the assistant manager position that had recently opened, and another thirty-five applications for the single part-time job we'd advertised. It was the kind of work I daily found it more difficult to undertake, but which, given my need to fill the next several hours with some type of activity, was not without its use. I set up the coffee maker, switched it on, and dug a set of candles and a box of matches out of the junk drawer while the kitchen filled with the sharp odor of hot coffee. Then I settled down at the table and set to work.

Of course I wanted to be outside, letting the storm envelop me. Before I had processed the sounds to which I'd awakened, the beast in my chest had known them for what they were and been pawing the ground, pressing its thick shoulder against the wall surrounding it. Over the years, the tail ends of a few hurricanes had struck the area glancing blows on their way out to sea, but as far as I could remember, Eileen was the first storm of this magnitude to line us up in its sights like this. The house shifted and shuddered with the thunder; the bushes in the front yard cringed at the rain beating down on them; the woods behind the house creaked and cracked as the wind pushed them back and forth. The shrill, electric trill of the Emergency Broadcast System spilled from the transistor radio, and a woman's voice, sounding oddly muffled, announced that a tornado had been spotted on the other side of Wiltwyck, maybe ten miles away. As the voice went on warning about the dangers of a tornado and advising the best spots in a house for sheltering from one, the tips of my fingers, my toes, tingled, my cheeks flushed, and what felt like a space high in my skull opened. When I stood to take a break, I crossed to the kitchen windows and pressed one hand to each. Outside, Eileen was hurling itself against everything, was scouring the very air, wearing it thinner, bringing that other place, the home of the huge silhouette, the astonishing tree, nearer. It was close; I was aware of it at the edge of the space in my head, like something you know you have forgotten, a gap whose outlines you can almost picture. If I threw open the porch door and dashed out into the rain, into the woods, might I not find it? Might I not pass into it? I went so far as to unlock the back door and walk out onto the porch. A gust of wind made me stagger, while the rain drilled my arms, my neck, my head. Lightning filled the air in brilliant sheets; thunder shivered the porch under my feet. Terror as pure and pitiless as a bird of prey, as an eagle plucking a fish out of the water, gripped me. Here I was, on the verge. Already, my hair was soaked, my shirt and jeans drenched. How easy it would be to go the rest of the way into the storm, to let my fear carry me into it.

I couldn't say what returned me inside. One moment, I was leaning on the porch railing, squinting through the rain at the woods; the next, I had shut and locked the back door and was making my soggy way to the bathroom, where I pulled off my wet clothes and stepped into a hot shower. The terror that had seized me had not relaxed its hold; I could still sense the other place immanent in the air. The thing in my chest bellowed, ramming its head against its prison. But I stood letting the hot water chase the rain's chill from my skin, and when the water began to lose its heat, I turned it off, toweled dry, and went in search of fresh clothes. Once I'd dug another pair of jeans and long-sleeved t-shirt out of my dresser, I made myself an early lunch and ate it while I resumed my paperwork. At any time, I could have left the house for the storm. I didn't. It was as if—the very extremity of the emotion raging through me made it feel suddenly unreal. In comparison, the kitchen table at which I was seated, its top scuffed and scored from years of the twins' employing it as a workbench for school projects, felt solid, as much as the countertop behind me, which bore the scars of all the fruit, the vegetables, the loaves of bread I'd sliced through without using the cutting board. The refrigerator whose freezer tended to ice-up, so that it required defrosting at least twice a year; the electric oven that cooked too hot and that we'd been threatening to replace with a gas range for as long as we'd lived here; the coffee maker whose red CLEAN light blinked no matter how recently we'd cleaned it: none of these things, or any of the others filling the house, was as vivid as the tree I'd glimpsed through the lightning—but they seemed present in a manner I hadn't recognized before, and that was somehow sufficient to keep me working at the table.

By early afternoon, Eileen was starting to ebb. By mid-afternoon, the rain had diminished to a light shower. By late afternoon, the storm had slid to the north and east, Vermont and a corner of Massachusetts. I was congratulating myself for not having lost power when the lights went out. Exasperating, yes, but in a way that would I could tell would become funny when I related the event to friends—to Prin. Prin—without warning, I wanted nothing else than to see my wife, to gather her into my arms, to take her someplace, a hotel, a bed-and-breakfast, a motel on the edge of a highway, where we could be alone. I could not think of anything that was more important than this. I checked to be certain I hadn't left anything on that I shouldn't have—I hadn't, but she would ask, and I wanted to be able to say I'd looked—grabbed the keys to the truck, and locked the door behind me.

From the radio, I knew that 213, the route I usually took to my in-laws, was flooded. If I hadn't heard it on the news, I would have expected it: there was a stream that flowed right under the road about a mile towards Wiltwyck, and I imagined it would have submerged, if not carried away, the road there. What the news hadn't reported, and I hadn't anticipated, was that the road would be closed about a half-mile in the other direction, towards Huguenot, where the picturesque waterfall that descended from the hillside to the left had become a roaring Niagara. It had undermined the road it typically trickled below to the extent that the road's collapse was judged imminent, and the police had blocked it off already with sawhorses and barrels. I might have risked walking or running, across it, but the truck was far too heavy for any such adventuring. It appeared the only way to my in-laws would be to navigate the back roads that wound through the hills and mountains between here and the Hudson. While this wasn't something I did on a daily basis, I was reasonably sure I could manage it. When the twins had been infants, the one, guaranteed way to put them to sleep at the same time had been to strap them into their carseats and take them for a ride. As a result, I'd traveled the majority of roads between Huguenot and Wiltwyck, so, although Prin had the GPS in her car, I wasn't too concerned about being able to find my way. I turned the truck around and drove back to where one of the side roads intersected it at the bottom of a steep rise. I powered up the slope, and set off to join my wife.

As the crown flies, it was three and half, four miles from our front door to Prin's parents. Probably that distance doubled if you had to traverse it by car. And if the roads that vehicle was following had just been swept by a tropical storm, that seven or eight miles doubled, maybe tripled. The roads in here were narrow, with no shoulder, and bordered by more streams, swamps, and ponds than I'd realized, all of which had swollen and spilled their confines with the season's worth of rain that last fourteen hours had brought. Water lapped the edges of the road in some places; in others, it slid across in a glassy sheet; in still others, it covered the road in a new lake. After six, I lost count of the number of times I shifted into reverse for another three-point turn. One road was blocked by a massive tree that had fallen across it; another was fenced by power lines, one of whose poles had tilted toward the road; a third had mostly-disappeared under the hillside that had dissolved onto it. To either side, I saw houses damaged. Here was a raised ranch whose living room window had been staved in by the tree that had toppled through it. Here was a split-level built on a hill, its foundation laid bare by the rain. Here was a cape, an island in the center of a broad lake whose surface was ruffled by the wind.

When I drove across the black water, I thought I knew where I was. After almost reaching 9W, the major north-south route along the Hudson's western shore—which was not, as far as I could tell from the radio's updates, closed—a new stream galloping over the road had forced me to turn around. Feeling as if I were confined in a gigantic maze, I backtracked almost to my starting point for yet another try at the puzzle. It was not yet dark, but the sky was losing its light. On the right, a road t-junctioned the one I was driving. I'd noticed it on the way out, but had ignored it because I'd thought it joined another side road that emptied onto 213 this side of the flooding. Approaching it from this direction, however, I thought I remembered that this road in fact looped in the other direction, intersecting another side road that would bring me to 9W. It was worth a try, so I turned onto it.

Right away, I saw the water flowing across the road ahead, maybe a hundred yards distant. I knew enough to be aware of the danger of fording a flooded road, especially when the water covering it was moving; if I hadn't, there were warnings against doing so every ten minutes on the radio. Had I taken this road at the beginning of my journey, I would have reversed immediately. This far into it, however, with my options for reaching my wife dwindled almost to zero, I let the truck roll forward. The water didn't look that deep. Its blackness was no a trick of the light; nor was the water full of dirt. It was more as if it had been dyed black. The color didn't concern me: I assumed it must be due to some kind of microorganism that had been fomented by the rain. I eased the truck into it, unable to recall whether the road dipped here or not. The water eddied around the tires, rising up them as I continued. What was the minimum depth at which moving water could sweep your vehicle off the road? Was it different for a truck? I was approximately half-way across the stream, and the water seemed to have halted its climb at the bottom of my tires' hubcaps. I glanced to my left, where the water was spreading out in a broad pool over the small meadow there. If I were to be carried off the road, I was reasonably sure I'd be able to four-wheel my way out of it, and if not, I could abandon the truck and wade for it. It would be messy, and slow, and ultimately, costly, and it would mean having to return to the house, but it wasn't anything I couldn't handle.

And then I was on the other side of the water, pressing the gas pedal to make up for lost time. For the next mile or so, the road ran straight, its edges lipped by more black water pooling in the fields and forest alongside it. Where the remnant of a stone wall crossed the woods on either side, the road swung sharply to the right, before almost doubling-back to the left. I didn't remember this, but after all, it would have been fifteen, sixteen years since I'd last driven here, and anyway, that wasn't important. Standing amongst the trees on my right was the tree I'd glimpsed behind my house four years before.

Everything went far away, and it was as if I were seeing the tree at the end of long, dark tunnel. My head swam. Without thinking, I stepped on the brake, so that only the front right wheel left the road. The truck slowed to a crawl. Black spots dancing in front of my eyes, I brought the truck to a complete stop, shifted into park, and opened my door. The engine running, I stepped out of the truck. The ground here was slightly raised. I started to walk toward the tree. There was no water for me to trek through; though I wouldn't have cared—I doubt I would have noticed. All of my attention was focused on the tree, which I was certain was going to vanish any second, now.

It did not. My fingers brushed its bark, which was rough, fibrous, like that of the cedar in my front yard. It was warm, the way wood is at the end of a long day in the hot sun. Its surface shone with a dull, yellowed light, as if it was reflecting a brightness invisible to me. The faint odor of citrus, of oranges on the turn, hung around it. Overhead, leaves green as jade gathered in a heavy crown. I reached up my hand to one of them, only to snatch it back with a hiss. The edges of the leaves were serrated, and those teeth as sharp as fishhooks, a fact to which the beads of blood welling from my fingertips testified. Wincing, I shook my hand, and saw the other trees.

There were five of them, mixed in with the oaks and maples. Each was slightly different from its fellows, the trunk thicker here, the leaves higher there, but the bronze bark, the sea-green leaves, marked them as the same species. Almost before I was aware of it, I was half-running toward them, my uninjured hand held out to them. Their bark was full of the same heat as the first one I'd touched; I didn't need to touch their leaves to notice their sharpness. From tree to tree, I moved steadily deeper into the woods, farther away from the truck, whose engine sounded more distant than the hundred or so yards I'd walked. Beyond the last tree, there was a small clearing of reddish ground, across which, a grove of the trees stood. Somewhere deep within that grove, something was visible through the shining trunks. I was not afraid: at the sight of that first tree, my emotions had leapt over fear to wonder. As I took in each successive revelation, so did that wonder push toward joy. By the time I crossed the clearing, I was grinning.

Amongst the trees, the smell of citrus hung heavier. The air was warm, the post-storm chill chased from it by the heat radiating from the trees. The low rumble of the truck's engine had been occluded by another sound, a rushing like wind through the leaves, which was punctuated by an irregular boom. It seemed to be coming from the other side of the white objects in whose direction I was heading. There were several of them, standing straight and pale; they appeared to be another kind of tree, a grove within the grove. Their trunks were smooth, creamy; as with the trees surrounding them, these swept up to crowns I wasn't close enough to distinguish, but which appeared joined to one another. Only when I arrived at the edge of the space in which these white trees had been planted did I realize that they were not, in fact, trees, but columns. Perhaps a dozen, fifteen of them had been set in a wide ring, which had been roofed by the small dome they supported—which had partially collapsed on my side. The columns, the roof, seemed to be marble or a stone like it. The ground around the temple—that was immediately how I thought of it—was bare, only a couple of stray leaves marking it. That I could see, there was no writing, no marking, on the structure's exterior.

Tears streamed down my cheeks. The scent of oranges, the sound of rushing, surrounded me. My nerves hummed. Anything might happen here. Conscious of its damaged roof, I approached the temple cautiously. A heap of broken stone lay on the floor under the gap. Passing between a pair of columns, I saw that the rubble partially obscured the mosaic that took up the floor. Executed in the flat style of a Byzantine icon, the image showed the head and shoulders of a woman whose brown, ringletted hair spread down over the top of her peach robe. Most of her face was hidden by the fallen stone, which had also cracked and loosened dozens of the thumbnailed-sized tiles, but one wide, brown eye was visible. I knelt beside it, placing my palm on the iris. The tiles were cool, the seams among them imperceptible. I picked up one of the roof fragments. Though the size of a quarter, it was far heavier. I weighed it in my hand, listening to the rushing

# Bor Urus

noise, which sounded not so much louder as clearer, here, enough that I could identify it as the surf, throwing itself up the beach and receding, the occasional boom a collapsing wave. Between the columns opposite me, I could see out to where the ground lifted in a gradual swell. From the other side of it, the ocean sounded. I stood, fresh tears pouring from my eyes, and as I did, saw a shape moving over the rise.

It was an animal, crossing from right to left. It was enormous, its front shoulder a rounded mountain that dipped to a long back, which rose again at the hips. It paused, and swung its head in my direction, bringing a pair of widely-set horns into relief. It raised its snout, and with the whuff of a bellows inflating, inhaled. It did so a second time, and I realized it was sniffing the air. It dropped its head, and turned toward me. As it climbed the hill, I saw that it was a bull— but such a bull as might have stepped straight from an ancient myth. It wasn't only that it was far larger than any bull I had ever seen by a factor of two or three. Its skin shone the red-gold of the sun sliding toward the horizon; its horns were white as sea-foam. Its features were finely, even delicately formed, to the point that this animal could have served as the example of the species in all its varieties. Were it not for the great iron ring looped through its nostrils, I easily could have believed I was beholding a god who had elected to put on this form for his latest sojourn on earth. As it was, I was half-tempted to drop to my knees at the sight of it standing atop the rise, its presence there like the shout of a full orchestra. It threw its head back and bellowed, a deep, rolling roar that made the leaves on the trees shudder. I took a step backwards. The bull lowered its head, snorted, and pawed the ground. There was no need to wait for its charge; pivoting on my right foot, I sprinted out of the temple the way I'd come.

From this direction, the edge of the grove seemed to take much longer to reach. Already too close behind me, the bull was a wave of sound, rushing to overtake me. A glance over my shoulder showed it swerving from side to side as it sought gaps among the trees wide enough to allow its horns. Had its path to me been clear, the bull would have run me down in no time. As it was, I wasn't wild about my chances. My days of running high-school track were a quarter-century gone. If I could reach my truck, the odds would improve in my favor. But between the thunder of the bull's hooves on the ground, and the pounding of the blood in my ears, I had yet to hear the rumble of the engine—and that was assuming it hadn't stalled. The bull roared, and adrenaline fired my legs, carrying me out of the grove into the forest proper. To my left, my right, the scattering of the shining trees that had drawn me deeper into the woods flashed past. The ground here was slicker, slippery with storm-soaked leaves, treacherous with fallen branches, a couple of toppled trees. I hurdled a trunk thick with moss, slid under another whose collapse had been arrested by one of its companions. The first tree I had seen was ahead. Not too far beyond it, my truck appeared to be running. With a pair of titanic cracks, the bull struck and shattered the trees I had dodged over and under. I cleared the treeline. The truck was forty yards away, thirty-five. The bull's hooves pounded the earth. The truck was thirty yards away, twenty-five. The bull snorted like a steam engine. The truck was twenty yards away, fifteen. I could hear the engine's roll. The ground drummed under my feet; the bull was nearly on me. The truck was ten yards away, five. I could see the dome light on because I hadn't closed my door completely. The bull was burning behind me.

I cleared the hood, threw myself to the left, hauled open the driver's side door, and flung myself into the cab. Before I had pulled the door shut, the bull struck the right side of the flatbed with a shuddering boom. The truck swung hard to the left, the door snapping open and jerking me half out of the cab. Only a little of its momentum lost, the bull continued past, its hooves sparking on the road as it charged into the marsh on the other side, spraying water and mud as it went. Though slowed by the change in terrain, the bull did not stop, but wheeled to the left, commencing an arc that would return it to me in no time. Grateful to be on dry ground, I closed the door, shifted into reverse, and stepped on the gas. For a heart-stopping moment, the wheels spun, then they caught and the truck lurched backwards, flinging me forward with such force I smacked my head on the steering wheel. I stomped the brake in time to avoid plunging into the marsh, shifted into drive, and dragged the wheel to the left. The tires shrieked as the truck lurched around in the direction I'd come. I straightened the wheel and pressed the gas to the floor. To my right, the bull had adjusted its course and was on path to intercept me. Never the greatest when it came to quick starts, the truck gathered speed. The bull was churning up gouts of water and weeds as it went, dulling its hide with mud. I held the gas all the way down. The bull stumbled—my heart jumped—and caught itself. Just beyond where the bull was on course to hit me, the road turned sharply to the right, almost doubling-back on itself. If I took that curve too fast, the truck would flip, and I wouldn't have to worry about unearthly bulls. If I didn't keep the accelerator to the floor, though, the question of the curve would remain theoretical. The bull was practically galloping through the marsh. Even seated in the cab, I found it gigantic. The truck hurtled over the road. Fast enough—I was just about going fast enough. The bull's head, its great horns, loomed in the passenger's side window. An eye the size of a saucer regarded me with an emotion I couldn't identify.

For a second time, the bull hit the truck on the right side of the flatbed. There was a boom, the scream of tearing metal, the brass shout of the huge beast. The truck fishtailed left; braking, I overcompensated to the right and sent the rear end fishtailing that way. As the scene in the rearview mirror whipped back and forth, I glimpsed the bull plunging through the trees, shaking its head. It didn't appear to be turning as quickly as it had before, but I was too busy trying to bring my vehicle under control to do any more than note the difference. I succeeded in gaining command of the truck as the road bent into its acute angle, and while there was a second I felt the left-hand tires threatening to leave the asphalt, the truck remained upright. Fully expecting to witness the bull charging across the marsh after me, I looked to the right, to see it standing on the forest side of the road, watching me as I sped away. When I came to the black water still flowing across the road, I did not slow down.

Although I had no desire to return home, which seemed agonizingly close to where the bull had burst forth, I could not think of another route to Prin's parents, so home I drove. Once I'd parked the truck, I intended to sprint to the back of the house, where I'd use the basement door to let myself inside. I wasn't sure whether it would be better to shelter from the bull—which I was certain was making its way toward me—in the basement, or if I should choose the first floor, from which I could dash to the truck, if need be. However, when I stepped down from the cab, muscles tensing for the run to the house, something on the flatbed caught my eye. A quick survey showed the bull was not, as yet, near, so I hurried around the back of the truck. From just behind the passenger's door to the very end of the flatbed, the right side of my truck was crumpled and creased, the metal dented in half a dozen places, the liner cracked and pushed part of the way out. Between the rear wheel and the tailgate, a deep gouge ended in a jagged hole the width of my hand. Lodged inside that hole, jutting into the flatbed, was the object that had drawn my notice, a point of white horn a foot long, its tip undulled, its base rough from having been snapped off. Leaning over into the flatbed, I worked to free the horn. Except for a groove that had been cut into it by a metal shard, its surface was smooth, cool. It came loose without too much effort on my part, and was surprisingly light in my hand. Holding the piece of horn, I felt the panic that had spurred me home relax its grip—but I walked to the house quickly.

Inside, the house was dim, the power not yet returned. I lit one of the candles I'd left on the kitchen table, and used it to light my way upstairs to the second floor and the undersized room that served as my home office. There, I slid out the lower of my desk's drawers, in whose depths I stored those things I planned to find a more permanent home for, later. I placed the fragment of horn in there, along with the oddly-heavy piece of rock I'd picked up in the temple, and which at some point thereafter I'd dropped into the front pocket of my jeans. I closed the drawer, shut the office door behind me, and descended the stairs. I didn't enter that room again for weeks, didn't say anything about what was in my desk drawer or where it had come from to Prin or her parents, when they pulled into the driveway the next day, or to the twins, when they returned home for Christmas vacation. The damage to the truck, I blamed on an accident I claimed to have suffered while trying to reach Prin's parents' during the height of the hurricane. I had driven, I said, into a flooded section of road, only to find the water deeper and stronger than I'd anticipated. The truck had been swept off the road into a stand of trees, and it was only through some miracle that I had been able to engage the four-wheel-drive and escape. My story was helped by the large bruise that purpled my forehead where I'd smacked it on the steering wheel; though my father-in-law was visibly unsatisfied with my explanation. The insurance company wasn't any happier about my claim, which they first denied, then, when I proposed legal action, refused to cover fully, citing the role of my reckless behavior in causing the damage. I took what I could get, and the next year, traded in the truck for a small station wagon.

After arriving with her parents, Prin remained with me, as, over the next couple of weeks, she decided to remain in our marriage. I ceased contact with my ex, deleting the account from which I'd written to her. About ten days after the storm, I drove the road along which I'd sighted the shining tree; it ran straight and short, intersecting another after a few hundred yards. The twins returned from their study abroad

# Bor Urus

for their senior year of high school and plans to leave, again, for college. I did not leave my job; nor, when the next storm slid over us, did I do anything other than check that the windows were shut.

With each and every storm that followed, I have, when possible, done exactly the same thing: ensure that the windows are closed, and mount the stairs to the second floor and my office. There, I sit at my desk, which faces the window that looks over the backyard. I watch the rain bead the window, the wind toss the trees. I squint at the lightning's flare, listen to the thunder rattle the window. I try not to picture the face I saw on the temple floor, the single eye gazing up impassively. I try not to think about that other place, the grove in which I walked, the ocean whose waves I heard, lying on the other side of a veil as fine as spiderweb, as wide as the world. I try not to indulge the emotion that roils through me, that has continued to answer the summons of every storm. At some point, I will have retrieved the length of horn, the piece of stone, from the drawer and set them on the desk. My hands on either side of them, I gaze out the window, and remind myself how much I love my family.

*For Fiona*

# W.H. Pugmire

## A Quest of Dream

**Wilum Hopfrog Pugmire** *has been writing Lovecraftian weird fiction since the early 1970s. His identity with H. P. Lovecraft is now an obsessive lifestyle, and he is devoted to writing book after book in homage of HPL. That multitude of books includes* The Tangled Muse *(Centipede Press),* Uncommon Places *(Hippocampus Press),* Bohemians of Sequa Valley *(Arcane Wisdom Press) and* Some Unknown Gulf of Night *(Arcane Wisdom Press). His next book will be a collaborative collection with David Barker,* Spectres of Lovecraftian Horror *(Dark Renaissance Books 2015). WHP dreams in Seattle.*

I ascended the wide stone steps that led to Adam Webster's bookstore and stopped to smell the red frangipani. Moonlight beamed through the trees that surrounded the large house, and I paused so as to light an opium-tainted cigarette. I sucked, and then I sighed and lifted my eyes so as to watch Luna through the thin blue wreaths of smoke that curled fantastically. The tree that spread before me offered its fragrant flowers, and for a moment I fancied that these were blooms of blood I looked on. Ah, blood and moonlight, smoke and perfumed air. I was surrounded by enchantment. The moon was then veiled by clouds, and I passed through new-born darkness, up the wooden steps that took me to the large canopied porch. I sucked, and then extinguished my cigarette in a tall vase filled with sand and bits of bone. Adam stood before a hearth in the large bookshop that had been constructed by removing walls and turning separate rooms into one spacious chamber. Scented candles provided the sole source of light, the mellow illumination that felt so comfortable on my eyes. Sighing happily, I sank into an armchair and crossed one leg over the other.

"Simon's vanished," I informed him. "He was going to teach me the Ninth Diagram. I'm rather annoyed."

"He's in Prague," Adam informed me, his back to me as he fiddled with some tiny figurines that sat upon the hearth.

"Something's disturbed him. He was behaving so irrationally the last time we met. Rather disconcerting, to see the beast so thrown off balance." The fellow continued to ignore me. "So, what do you have for me?"

"Ah," he replied, pointing a finger upward as he walked to a bookshelf and removed a title bound in green cloth. "It's nothing special, but knowing your penchant for Wilde titles I thought you'd enjoy it." He moved to me and I took the book. *The Harlot's House and Other Poems* by Oscar Wilde, with "Interpretations" by the artist, John Vassos. I loved old editions of Wilde, and this 1929 title was in perfect shape. I opened to the title piece and read aloud:

> "Then, turning to my love, I said,
> 'The dead are dancing with the dead,
> The dust is whirling with the dust.'"

My recitation was followed by suggestive silence, and as I looked up I saw that the child of shadow was frowning at me. He said, "Wilde was called a corrupter of youth. This is something you share with him. You've been influencing Cyrus to dream. This must stop."

I made a rude noise with my lips. "Don't be a bore, Adam. Cyrus overflows with curiosity. He's hungry for new sensations. I taught him the art of concocting an absinthe cocktail the other day, and how happily intoxicated we were, nude and dancing beneath the autumnal moon. It was deliciously Greek. What have you against dreaming? You live in Sesqua Valley, where dreams are enhanced outlandishly. I have only to gaze for a length of time at the white mountain before falling into slumber to experience the most fantastic visions."

"It is dangerous for us to dream, Jonas. To dream in this valley is to open portals. Simon has explained this to you."

I squeezed my face so as to make an appalling expression. "The valley itself is a portal. It sucks one in, and twists one's psyche, and blasts one's brain. It gathers us, the valley does—we freaks of the world, and teaches us new ways in which to mutate. Ah, sweet intoxicating vale, poisonous and potent. We shut our eyes to your enchanted light, and in dream we follow your moonlit paths. As Wilde once said, so wisely, 'A dreamer is one who can only find his way by moonlight.' The moon over Sesqua is ripe for dreamers."

"Then dream on your own, Jonas. Do not coax my shadow-kindred to follow you. Cyrus is especially susceptible to mortal influence."

I rose out of the chair and winked at Adam's ugly face. "Thanks for the book, mate." Exiting the shop, I walked down the steps and onto the road that led to town. The moon had undressed herself of clouds, and her naked brilliance touched my eyes with wonder. Opening the book again, I whispered the title poem's opening lines:

> "We caught the tread of dancing feet,
> We loitered down the moonlit street,
> And stopped beneath the harlot's house."

I walked onto the planks of wood that are the sidewalk of Sesqua Town and stopped before one tall building so that I could listen to the noise that issued from its top floor. There were no blinds before the windows, no ghostly silhouettes; but there were moving shadows, and the tread of dancing feet. Silently, I passed the building's threshold and loiter up the flight of stairs that took me to the floor from which the curious din issued. Cautiously, I walked to where double doors parted and watched the unfathomable dancers as they moved as one within the silent room. I thought immediately of lines by Keats:

> "Heard melodies are sweet, but those unheard
> Are sweeter..."

I realized, as I peeped furtively into the room, that I had never before seen so many of the children of the valley gathered in one place; and my curiosity was so compelled that I failed to notice when someone moved behind me, until she pressed one hand upon my shoulder. By some strange instinct, the occupants of the room sensed intrusion and ceased their movement. A horde of silver eyes gazed at me. The female at my side linked her arm with mine and escorted me into the room.

"I can explain everything," I assured them. "You see, Adam just procured this delightful edition of Wilde's poetry, and I was contemplating its title poem as I passed by. And life, poor shoddy thing, imitated Art—for as in the poem the narrator passes and is perplexed by a room of inhuman dancers, so I became aware of your footfalls on this floor, and I was tempted to watch. I can resist everything except temptation, as you well know. I am human, all too human."

I turned to acknowledge the creature at my side and saw that she was not native of the valley. Marceline Dubois smiled at me, her eyes of altering shade set within the magnificent ebony face. I could smell the fragrance of her red tresses and for one moment disregarded all else. She turned to kiss the corner of my mouth and one breast brushed against my chest. I watched, as she moved away from me to the center of the room and raised her arms. Someone in the pack produced a flute and began to play a haunting melody, to which the sorceress moved. Other pipes were pressed to inhuman mouths, and the intoxicating noise drew me to the center of the floor, where I raised my arms and joined in the danse. The seductive music wrapped around me, and I knew that I wanted to be clothed in nothing else. Kicking off my shoes, I unzipped my trousers and let them fall to my ankles. Some kind creature helped me out of them and took my book as I began to unbutton my shirt provocatively, as though it were one of seven veils. I wished for a glass of scarlet wine to spill onto the floor, so that I could dance in its ruby pool.

The music ceased, and I wearied of my waltz. Laughing magically, Marceline helped me to retrieve my clothing, although I did not bother to don them. Nude, I allowed her to guide me from the room and down the bare steps, onto the moonlit road. I suppose I had suffered (happily) a kind of delirium and had no notion as to where I was being escorted until I saw the pale and mammoth monster. I opened my collection of Wilde's verse, but could not find "The Sphinx;" and so I racked my fevered brain and spoke one remembered line:

> "A beautiful and silent Sphinx has watched me through the shifting gloom."

Dropping everything except my trousers and book, I slipped into my pants and leaned my torso against the statue's moon-kissed stone. "Perhaps I'll go into the Hungry Place and dream of dead things."

"Whatever are you muttering about?" the black goddess asked me.

I blew air. "Oh, I've been reprimanded about dreaming; or, rather, about influencing Cyrus to dream fantastic things, to dwell in vision as I sing to him the language of arcane tomes. It's absurd, such caution and propriety. Adam lectured me after he gave me this book. 'Dreaming opens portals, Jonas.' Bah! He treats me as though I were a clueless clown."

"You are impulsive, and not wholly sane, Jonas Hobbs. Exactly the sort of fellow we like in Sesqua Town. But Adam is correct. One must use caution in evoking dreams. We dwell in close proximity to the dreamlands, a realm from which influences may leak."

"The *what*? Dreamlands? This is the first I've heard of it. Simon's never mentioned it."

The sorceress laughed. "He abhors the things utterly denied him. The dreamlands would never allow Simon access—he's too poisonous, too polluted from having memorized every known edition of *Al Azif*." She buzzed the title rather than articulating it as humans would.

"I think you're familiar with this place, this dreamlands. I think you've been there."

She bowed her head to acknowledge that I was correct. "It is where my Elder Brother dwells."

"Who's that?"

"The Strange Dark One."

She narrowed her eyes as I burst out laughing. "If you're trying to dissuade my interest, you're going about it ass-backwards. My brain itches with intrigue. How can I summon this realm?"

"One does not beckon the dreamlands. One enters into it. There is a place in the valley where Sesqua's woodland conjoins with the dreamland's forest. Oh dear, what dreadful curiosity shimmers in your mortal eyes. You've been tainted by the beast, and tingle for arcane manifestation." Ah, her sinister smile. I watched as she raised one sable hand to Luna and made a curious sign, a sign that I carefully observed and memorized. I listened, as a breeze began to blow, an element of which was caught within Marceline's magical hand. She tilted her head slightly and smiled at me in such a way that my blood prickled in its veins. Playfully, she moved her closed fist before my face, then took it away as I tried to kiss it. Finally, she blew into that hand and released the mingled air. I watched her fingers open, like petals of some obsidian bloom, and then I looked upward to watch the moon darken as it was covered with what I imagined was a spread of molten shadow.

"I thought you said the dreamlands can't be summoned."

"That is correct; but one may call the things that dwell within its precincts." The wind grew more vigorous, pushing the sweet scents of

# A Quest of Dream

Sesqua Valley into my face. Marceline's magnificent hair billowed in the tempestuous air. "Behold!" she exclaimed.

I raised my eyes and saw the fragmented patches of black cloud that wheeled in distant sky. No, they were not clouds; for clouds are not composed of rubbery texture that catches and reflects dim starlight. Clouds are not horned, nor do they spread membranous wings. I beheld the horde and guessed that they were perhaps fifty in number. I had seen their curious image before, on an antique piece of parchment that Simon had shown me in his round tower. When I asked him what the illustration represented, he tapped the image fondly and chuckled. "Night-gaunts," he answered.

## II.

I spent the next three days in Simon's cyclopean round tower, finding anything I could related to night-gaunts and the dreamlands; but I didn't know where to look, for his collection of arcane lore was vast and kept in a chaotic lack of order. Books, scrolls, bas-reliefs and maps were scattered everywhere. The circular walls and floor of the mammoth upper room were covered with cobwebs, dust and diagrams in chalk. Such a litter of lore, and yet I could not find the data that I sought. And then I had a hunch, and trotted down the winding steps of the ancient tower. Finding one of the queer stone circles that existed in the valley, I reclined therein and closed my eyes. I summoned the forest of the dreamlands as new sensation chilled my brain, and sang to valley air and sensed the things that pranced around me. When I partially lifted my eyelids I witnessed the blurry shapes of dark shaggy creatures of diminutive stature that danced around my circle of chiseled stones. Reaching outward, I touched the tiny paws that pulled me from the circle, and I knew that these wee creatures could lead me to the place where the valley's woodland met the land of dream. They did not do so; rather, they guided me out of the woods and onto a road that took me to town. Frustrated, I crept to the silent sphinx and violently knocked my head against its unyielding stone. I was about to repeat the action when I saw, through streams of blood and tears, movement in the Hungry Place, the neglected cemetery where outsiders to the valley are oft times interred.

The figure, book in hand, watched me as I entered the somber site, but did not cease his gambol until he noticed that beads of blood fell from my chin, to earth. Using the back of one hand, I wiped away the stream of blood that spilled from where my forehead flesh had torn. Reaching into a pocket, he produced a clean white handkerchief. "Use this. We do not want to titillate this earth with liquid gore. Hello, Jonas."

"Eldon, whatever are you doing here?"

How extraordinary, his laughter. "I've had *the most* delirious dream, of dancing on my tomb!" His voice was high-pitched; it quivered as it issued from his throat, emotional and mad. This was Eldon Prim, one of the valley's suicidal poets. That he was still among the living astonished us, for Sesqua Valley has an appetite for those so richly lunatic and plays with them, psychically, as cats play at tormenting mice. Eldon's supernatural scars ran deep. I saw that he was peering at me intensely, as if to read my mind. Again, his manic laughter. "But we are outsiders, Jonas—there'll be no *tombs* for us; there will be this hungry sod, and only that, unless we keep company with whatever crawls beneath it. This is where I'll be planted, this will be my grave. And so I dance upon it. Whee!"

I felt it then, the suggestion of a pulse beneath my foot, as if some stagnant heart had found resuscitation. Placid dizziness coaxed my knees to bend, and I knelt within the Hungry Place, before the dancing man. The earth on which I kowtowed was soft and enticing, and I pushed my hand into its depth. The mad poet fell beside me and set the book he held upon the ground. I saw that it was the thin hardcover collection of his poems that a friend in Boston had published in a very limited print run. The hand that had held the book grasped my wrist and pulled my hand from earth.

"No, Jonas, no. You're not the one who dreamed of dancing in the Hungry Place. It has not summoned thee. 'Tis not your paltry flesh for which it has an appetite. Nay, remove your mortal hide and let me plant mine own." He reached into his coat's deep pocket and pulled out a deadly ritual knife, the very sharp blade of which caught and reflected starlight. Looking up to the stars, Eldon raised one hand and made a little sign unto the sky; and then he rested his hand on the hard surface of his book and, using the dagger, liberated one finger from his hand. An undertone of hilarity issued from some deep place in his throat as he planted his severed digit into the cemetery sod. The valley pulsed more vigorously, and some snouted thing bayed beneath the peaks of Mount Selta. "Arthur Munroe is such a splendid sculptor, have him fashion me a tombstone. Farewell, Jonas Hobbs."

I stood and watched for just a little while, as the Hungry Place sifted its soil around the lunatic. He laughed, the sinking man, and sang, a noise that served as background music as I exited the place. I leaned against the moon-kissed sphinx until the distant noise silenced, and when I turned to look again into the Hungry Place I saw that it was void of occupant. But then a distant figure climbed onto a far section of the low stone wall that surrounded the cemetery and leapt into the graveyard. I turned away and leaned the back of my head against the smooth stone of the sculpted beast and let the moonlight play upon my eyes, and I wondered again at how singular the moon looked as it floated over Sesqua Valley, how its shadows formed faces that expanded, melted, and then blossomed again as other expressive things.

"Eldon's gone," a soft voice told me. I did not regard the young creature at my side. "I found his book in the Hungry Place. Guess I'll take it to the tower. You have it, don't you?"

I replied in quotation:

> "I hold it in, the hot and frantic breath.
> I won't exhale the words of lunacy.
> I won't pronounce your poison'd shibboleth
> And enter custom with insanity.
> Remember when you talked to me of pain
> And pierced a splinter into my soft eye?
> Remember how that splinter sliced my brain
> And planted dreams wherein the starlight died?
> Peace. Your language echoes on the wind.
> Silence all the shrieking in my brain.
> All your arcane lunacy rescind.
> I'll not mouth your fatal name again.
> I'll not move among your nightmare race.
> I'll find solace in some hungry place."

Cyrus nodded. "Weird. He wrote that before he came to the valley."

"It's not weird at all, young creature." I countered. "The valley seeks we who are demented, we who have been tainted by unholy alchemy. It lures us to its confines and sups upon our madness, thus nourishing its own."

"You're laughing at me, aren't you? You like to pose as so superior," the lad complained.

I shrugged. "For someone born of Sesqua's shadow, you're hopelessly innocent. Where is your edge of danger, Cyrus? One would mistake you for human."

"I'm not—human. Just because I'm not as diabolic as Simon and some others…"

I raised a hand to silence him. "No matter, I've been ordered to avoid you. Adam asserts that I'm corrupting your soul." Slyly, I smiled at him. "Do you shadow-spawn of this haunted valley *have* souls, I wonder? Or merely appetite?"

"You're talking a lot of nonsense tonight, Jonas. Leonidas must have slipped you some of his nasty narcotics. As for Adam, he's not my master, nor our concern. We'll continue with our studies. Good evening."

I smiled at the bravado in his voice and watched him walk away. Then I remembered Eldon's request, and so I sauntered up the road, to the large building that housed an artistic studio that was shared by members of the community. I did not care for the arrogant artist whom Eldon had named, but I knew his craftsmanship was exceptional, and so I entered the building and watched its few inhabitants at work. I was surprised to see that Arthur was working on a canvas rather than devoting his masculine hands to the sculptor's task; and as I gazed at his painting on its easel my curiosity was piqued, for the ebony beast that was gradually revealed in its dark surroundings seemed familiar. The artist ignored me as I stepped to him until I bent to stroke the piece of paper that had been thumb-tacked to the canvas. When Arthur spoke to me, his voice was low and haunting in its effect.

"They spill like patches of liquid shadow from their realm of fabulous darkness, and they esteem our adoration as our wonder-struck faces are reflected on their smooth blankness." I uncurled the piece of paper, which proved to be an image of a fantastic fiend. It was winged and faceless and incredibly lean; indeed, there was almost something sinister in its sinewy and compact form, and in its stance, which bespoke of incredible strength. Unpinning it from the canvas, I lifted the rectangular piece of paper to the overhead light and saw that it was indeed a photograph from life.

"Eldon has been swallowed by the Hungry Place. His last request was that you make a marker to his memory."

"Ah," the other fellow uttered, "do we know his birth date? No matter, we shall record the day of—well, one cannot quite call it extinction, from what we know of our fate beneath the Sesquan sod.

You were there?"

"Yes."

Arthur tilted his head and regarded me queerly. "I've heard about you, Hobbs. You like to dwell in the dangerous places. I'm told that you've actually ascended Mount Selta and swam in one of its sequestered pools."

"There's only one pool, inside a cavern of crimson rock. Yes, I found it curious, that a mountain with so white an exterior should have scarlet walls within. But you've journeyed yourself," I countered, holding up the snapshot. "You've found a way into the dreamlands."

He laughed. "No. The gaunts may be summoned if one knows the art. They love the light of our plump moon on their rubbery hide, and to feel the reflection of our faces on the surface beneath their horns." He noticed my expression and laughed again. "You're beguiled, Hobbs, and so you should be. The entire idea of a dreamland is hypnotic. How did such a realm come into existence? Is it formed of mortal dreaming, or is it the weave-work of some elder gods? Can we enter it as phantoms only, leaving behind our husks of flesh and bone? The night-gaunts are decidedly physical, and yet one senses that they are elementals of nightmare. So many scrumptious questions, so few boring answers."

I touched my free hand to the canvas on which the oblique silhouette of the depicted creature swam in gathered shadow. "Is this in preparation for a work in stone? I thought sculpting was your forte."

"No, this is just an idea I had. I'll give it to you once it's finished. You obviously have some kind of affinity with night-gaunts. You should see your face, Jonas—you're *caught*. Maybe they'll lure you to their ghoul-haunted woodland and let you cross over."

I didn't know how to answer him, for something in his words, and in the image on canvas, had indeed "caught" my imagination. He smiled at me as I opened my mouth to reply, and then he laughed out loud when the words caught in my throat. I had given the artist my message from the man who had been sifted through the cemetery loam, and my errand thus accomplished I made my escape. Night's wind had picked up considerably, and I raised my hands to push hair from my eyes; and I saw that I still held Arthur's photograph of his perplexing model, the silhouette of which looked different in the moonlight. Pushing the print into my pants pocket, I scanned the sky at the place where Marceline had conjured forth the horde of winged night-beasts, and then I followed the road away from Sesqua Town, toward a wooded area. Glancing over my shoulder, I saw the moon as an enormous disc just over the twin-peaked mountain.

I entered the silent woodland, escaping wind and starlight. The place seemed preternaturally hushed, and of a sudden some lines from a poem by Wilde oppressed my memory:

"To outer senses there is peace,
A dreamy peace on either hand
Deep silence in the shadowy land,
Deep silence where the shadows cease."

I wandered into deeper gloom, into a dreamy peacefulness. Although the place was dark, my vision had adjusted to my surroundings, and cool verdant shade soothed my eyes. As I marched along the path I could feel the photograph in my pocket as an entity near my inner thigh. My fancy dwelt on the fabulous creature, the night-gaunt of dreamland; and as I imagined it I held my arms aloft, as if perhaps I could sense the other realm with fingertips, for certainly its air would be of a different chemistry. I sought the essence of that incorporeal aether with my mind as my mouth hungered to gulp it, deeply.

I sensed another occupant of woodland, and looked about me until I saw the ghostly silhouette, the lissome outline, the phosphorescent eyes. Young Cyrus reached out to me with anxious hands, which I clutched. "It's insane to be out here alone at this hour. What the hell are you about?"

"I seek the dreamlands."

He shook his head ruefully. "Damn, you're crazy. Come on, let's return to town."

"No. Hang you, boy, I'm being called, compelled to find that other sphere. It summons me just as surely as Sesqua Valley once did."

"Jonas, you've been bewitched by magick, that is all. You've been staring too deeply into arcane lore, your eyes have drunk too deeply of sigils and schema. The beast of Sesqua Valley has corrupted you. I know too well that shimmer in your eyes, which is the sign of an intoxicated soul. I've witness it on Simon's lunatic eyes many times. Your quest is folly, my friend. You could never find the dreamlands."

I grabbed his coat by the shoulder and shook him. "How do you know? What's to hinder me?"

He leaned closer to me, and I could smell the fragrant valley on his inhuman hide. "You lack the required innocence," he stated simply, in his quiet voice.

"You've been there." I had a sudden hunch, and by his air of false nonchalance I knew that I had struck a note. "You've been to the dreamlands—you know the way. Admit it."

He shrugged and grinned. "I admit nothing. No, I've never been there, never set physical foot in that outrageous terrain."

I studied his bestial face. "But you've dreamed of it, and have been linked thereto."

"I've never dreamed, fool. It's not something we do, not easily. You think you can teach me with your fiendish ways to behave in a mortal way; but I am a child of Sesqua Valley, and we are not easily tainted by your insect race." I knew he wasn't being completely honest with me, and I did not blink as I stared accusingly. "Oh hell, follow me." Surprised, I watched him trot toward a second pathway and vanish from sight. I rushed after him, tripping over small shrubs and almost losing balance. Something tickled my sense of play, and I chuckled gleefully. Running through the woods reminded me of my childhood, when every summer was spent chasing through the mammoth woods of a lakeside park. I would sometime build small altars of twigs within those woods and dance around them; or oft times I would merely recline on supple and aromatic earth and daydream. Some pocket of my soul ached to stop and lay upon this earth—and dream. How dare the child of shadow say that I lacked innocence? At that moment I felt a purity of soul.

The woodland opened up as some gargantuan shape arose before me, and I watched Cyrus dig his fingers into the sharply sloping soil of a colossal mound that rose above the moon-drenched trees. Happily, I scampered up the slope in pursuit of my crony, not resting until I reached the mound's apex. Cyrus sat on the ground, and as I knelt beside him I looked behind me and saw that Mount Selta was far behind us. Distant hills surrounded us, as did the spreading woods.

"There," Cyrus whispered as he pointed to a far-off district; and there was an element in the tone of his voice that greatly affected me, an ache of longing, an aspect of sadness coupled with bewitchment. "Do you see the place where shadows cease, that region of verdant mist that captures moonbeams? Oh, it's so beautiful. How awesome it would be, to cross the barrier and stride its arcane turf!" He looked at me with impatience in his eyes. "Come on, use your arcane senses. Although we can never visit it, we can see it manifested."

I strained to see what he could perceive, but it was not to be. A sob of frustration caught inside my throat. Suddenly, the boy's hand combed through my hair, and then it wound through strands and tugged me to him. I felt his tender kiss upon my eyes. He leaned away from me as I looked again. I saw the eerie region. "The forests of dreamland," I sighed. Oh, the ache I knew within the pit of my being. I raised one hand as if it might somehow touch the other realm, and the sight of that hand held in the air reminded me of another hand, one that was beautifully black. Memory grew keen, queerly so, and I saw within its depths the movement of Marceline's hand, as she made weird gesticulations to the sky. I remembered *exactly* the formation of her fingers.

"What are you doing?"

I smiled but did not look at him, for my eyes were enchanted by remote movement. They rose, sleek and silent, from the outlying mist, dark patches of rubbery blackness that caught the sheen of moonlight on their immortal flesh. I stood to greet them as they sallied toward the mound, and I raised my hands to their horrendous beauty as they encircled me in the air. One member of the horde floated to me and hovered just above the ground on which I quaked. I thrilled at the movement in the air that issued from the noiseless flapping of its fantastic wings, at the rich smell of its ghastly inky flesh. As it hovered close before me rich moonlight fell upon its facelessness, and on that slate of jet I saw a vague reflection of my visage. I welcomed the clawed hands that reached for me, and shouted maniacal hilarity as I was fiendishly tickled. My lunatic laughter seemed to attract others of the flock, and soon I was being lifted off the mound, held by hands that tormented me with their touch. I did not look down as someone shouted my name, and soon I could sense nothing but the alchemy of aether that was kissed by the movement of membranous wings. Laughing, I sucked in the alchemical air, as I was taken to the other place and ushered into a realm of dream.

# Maria Dahvana Headley

## The Krakatoan

**Maria Dahvana Headley** *is the author of the dark fantasy/alt-history novel* Queen of Kings, *and the internationally bestselling memoir* The Year of Yes. *With Neil Gaiman, she is the New York Times-bestselling co-editor of the monster anthology* Unnatural Creatures, *benefitting 826DC. Her Nebula and Shirley Jackson award-nominated short fiction has recently appeared in* Lightspeed, Apex, Nightmare, The Journal of Unlikely Entomology, Subterranean Online, Glitter & Mayhem *and* Jurassic London's The Lowest Heaven *and* The Book of the Dead. *It's anthologized in the 2013 and 2014 editions of Rich Horton's* The Year's Best Fantasy & Science Fiction, *Paula Guran's 2013* The Year's Best Dark Fantasy & Horror. *Upcoming are* Magonia, *a young adult skyship novel, from HarperCollins, and* The End of the Sentence, *a novella co-written with* Kat Howard, *from Subterranean. She grew up in rural Idaho on a survivalist sled-dog ranch, spent part of her 20's as a pirate negotiator in the maritime industry, and now lives in Brooklyn in an apartment shared with a seven-foot-long stuffed crocodile. Twitter: @ MARIADAHVANA Web: www.mariadahvanaheadley.com*

The summer I was nine, my third mother took off, taking most of the house off with her. The night she left, I found my dad kneeling on the floor in front of the open refrigerator, and he looked at me for too long. He was supposed to be at work.

"What's wrong?" I finally asked, though I didn't want to know.

"No one's in charge of you," my dad told me. "No one's in charge of anything. Haven't you learned that yet?"

The cold fell out of the fridge like something solid, and I edged closer, hoping it'd land on me and cling. I was still vulnerable to the possibility that one of the mothers would work out.

"Alright then," my dad said. He left the ice cream out on the counter, along with the contents of his pocket: three charred sticks, one of them short, two of them long, and a list of dead stars, as in celestial, his specialty.

Then he went to work, driving in the dark up the spiral road to his job at the observatory. It was one of the great mysteries of the heavens that my father had been married three times. He only looked up, and he was awake all night. Each of my mothers had complained about this, and eventually I picked up some things about which direction you should be looking, and which hours you should be keeping if you wanted a woman to stay with you. I practiced eye contact. I practiced sleeping.

I ate the entire carton of Neapolitan, beginning with the chocolate. I visited the top of my father's closet, removed five Playboy Magazines, and read them. I considered my three mothers, and compared them favorably to the naked women. I turned on the TV, and then turned it off. She'd taken the rabbit ears from the top, and now all we got was static. She'd taken the doorknob too. It was made of purple glass. When you put your eyeball up to it and looked in, it was like you'd arrived on Mars. I'd gotten a black eye that way, when she opened it accidentally into my face. Getting out of the house now required kicking and a coathanger pushed through the hole where the knob had been, and by the time I arrived outside, it was seven AM.

My dad was sleeping at the observatory. There were bunks. The astronomers were like vampires, slinking around under the closed dome until the sun went down, at which point they swarmed out to look at their sky. My dad had once referred to the solar system as My Solar System. He seemed to consider himself the sun, but he was not, and if he didn't know that, I did.

We lived at the bottom of Mount Palomar, where the spiral road started. If you stayed on our road, you'd eventually make it to the observatory, a big white snowball of a building on the top of the mountain, and inside it, a gigantic telescope. The observatory, with its open and shut rotating roof, was like a convertible car and the astronomers were teenagers in love with black holes. Their sky made me miserable. I wanted humans. There weren't many of them on the mountain, and my options were limited. I rarely went up. I went down, if I was going anywhere, and that day I went to Mr. Loury's house.

Mr. Loury's wife had, two years earlier, gone into the Great White

# The Krakatoan

Yonder. That was what my second mother, the hippie one who'd thought that astronomy and astrology were the same thing, had said about it. I don't think she'd ever seen Jaws. I didn't know what a Yonder was, and so in my mind, Mr. Loury's young wife dove into the mouth of not just a great white shark, but a megalodon, every night for months. Then she got chewed up, and at the end she looked like canned spaghetti. My second mother hadn't had much patience for a year of me retching over ravioli. I was pretty sure that was why she'd left.

Mr. Loury, with his attempt at a handlebar mustache and his short-sleeved button downs, with his sadness, was a human fender bender. I couldn't stay away from his property. Normally I paced the perimeter, feeling his woe, but today, I had woe of my own and it entitled me to trespass.

He was sitting on his front steps drinking a beer when I arrived, and I sat down beside him, like this was something I did every day. My face was on-purpose sticky with ice cream, and it was beginning to acquire a furry stubble of dust. I was no longer nine years old, but a grown man in misery. My third mother was the one with whom I'd long been significantly and hopelessly in love.

"Hey, buddy," Mr. Loury said. Not kid. This was progress. "Want a beer?"

I took one. No one was in charge. It was known by men the world over. There was comfort in the shared understanding.

Mr. Loury was an astronomer like my dad, or he had been, until his firing due to an attempted sabotage of the telescope. I didn't know the details, and didn't care, beyond the thrilling fact of sirens making their way in slow frustration up the curve of the mountain. He'd been to jail. Again, this called to me. It seemed he never slept. I never slept either. I stayed up all night reading, and during the day, I patrolled the mountain, checking for aberrations. I felt like I'd know them when I saw them.

Together, we watched the goings on of the spiral road, first a rangy cat patrolling, and then Mrs. Yin, our local ancient peril, driving too fast downhill in her Cadillac. I didn't question the fact that it was seven in the morning and he was drinking already. It seemed reasonable. Some people drank coffee. Others drank beer. I was, I decided, a beer drinker. At last, Mr. Loury stood up, and looked at me for a moment, seemingly noticing for the first time that I was a kid. He waved his hand slightly. I thought he might be getting ready to send me home.

"My third mother moved to Alaska last night," I told him. "She's not coming back."

"My wife died," he told me. "That's like Alaska, but more."

I wanted to ask about the Great White Yonder, but I was worried he'd tell me too much, and so I didn't. I couldn't afford another summer of nightmares, the mouth of the shark opening and showing its chewed food like a cafeteria bully gone gigantic.

"Want to help me with a project?" Mr. Loury said. "A dollar an hour. Yardwork."

"If it's lawnmower," I said, negotiating. "I charge by the square foot." Lawnmowers weren't safe for me. My toes begged to be run over. There was a deathwish in me. One of my ears had been the recipient of eleven emergency room stitches. Hidden under the skin of my right knee, there was a jagged piece of gravel that seemed to have become permanent.

"Digging," Mr. Loury said. "Got a spare spade for you, you're interested."

*Spare spade.* I repeated the words in my head, a triumphant vision of myself at the bottom of a deep, dark hole in the dirt, looking up at a narrowed world.

Mr. Loury had already begun digging. He had a hole the size of a swimming pool, and a huge heap of dirt beside it. After an hour, the sun was high, and I yearned for the freezer, and the rocket-shaped popsicle I was pretty sure was left in there, amid the foil-wrapped unknowns.

"Why are we digging?" I asked Mr. Loury. I had a couple of ideas. One of them involved the burial of the Great White Yonder. I wondered if the stomach of the Great White Yonder still contained the body of Mr. Loury's wife.

Mr. Loury looked at me like I was very, very stupid.

"We're making a volcano," he said, jerking his head toward the heap of dirt, which I'd taken for beside the point.

I'd made a volcano once, in a science class, out of dirt, vinegar, red food coloring, and baking soda. It erupted in the car, and the screams of my third mother, caught in the lava flow, still echoed in my ears. She'd cried. I'd cried too, in mortification. I'd made it to woo her.

"I don't think real volcanoes are made the same way you make fake ones," I said.

"This is how they made Krakatoa," Mr. Loury said, with certainty. "This is how they made Pele."

I thought about this.

"This is how they made the volcanoes on Mars," Mr. Loury said, and went back to digging. "Don't believe me if you don't want to believe me, but you can look through the telescope and see for yourself."

Volcanoes made on Mars. Volcanoes made on earth. What if I could be one of the people who made volcanoes? What if this could be my career?

"*Who* made them?" I managed. I could hardly breathe.

"People like us," Mr. Loury said.

"On Mars? Martians?" I asked.

"Krakatoans, Martians, same thing," he said. "I knew it when I saw you. You're one of us."

I heard the distinctive sounds of my father's car coming down the spiral road. The brakes were failing, and so he kept an anchor in the passenger seat, attached to a rope, in case he lost control going downhill. I ignored the noise. No one was in charge, he'd said. If he wanted me home, he could scream.

I looked at Mr. Loury. He was offering me everything I'd ever wanted, and I was pretty sure he was about to laugh and take it back, the way adults always did.

"What are the volcanoes for?" I asked Mr. Loury, a last testing question. He eyeballed me. I swiped at my face with nervous, dusty fingers, but finally he nodded and surrendered everything.

"I wasn't sure you were ready for this, but you seem man enough to take it. They're observatories, but better. From inside a volcano, everyone knows you can look up. Almost no one knows that you can also look down."

It was not as though I hadn't been warned by my third mother about people who said things like this. It was not as though I cared. I was a goner. My dad, I imagined, would one day walk up the slope of this new volcano, and bend over to look down, startled to see me there inside it, my telescope aimed at the center of the earth. I'd be making charts of the things I saw there, the dark stars and explosions. There'd be worms the size of trains. I knew it, despairing with desire. There were mysteries on the earth, and wonders. Even my own bellybutton, and the possibility that through it I might reach blood and guts, had been known to obsess me. Volcanoes were portals too.

My dad shouted for me from our front door, but I didn't move. He increased volume and shifted to my full name. I didn't flinch.

Mr. Loury looked at me suspiciously.

"That you he's looking for?" Mr. Loury asked.

"Possibly," I said.

"I thought you were a boy," he said, and there was an edge to his voice now, a tightness. "You *said* you were a boy."

"I'm a Krakatoan," I said. Finally, with greed and great relief, I knew that I was one of something, part of a group. There was a destiny for me. My life wouldn't have to be this way forever.

"Your hair's too short for a girl," Mr. Loury said, still staring at me with an odd expression on his face.

"It got caught in a pair of scissors," I said, tersely. It hadn't been an accident. There'd been braids.

"Shit," Mr. Loury said.

"Shit," I replied, and threw another shovelful of dirt onto the volcano. I tromped it down with my bare feet, and spat on the new volcano section.

All the while, Mr. Loury shook his head, and muttered to himself.

"Volcano gods need sacrifices," he said, finally. "What are you going to do about that?"

"I have thirteen dollars in my piggy bank," I said. "You have beer."

"That won't work," he said, went inside his house, and slammed the door. "This one only wants boys. Don't you know anything about volcanoes? Don't you know anything about anything?"

His voice carried out into the yard, and it cracked at the end, with something I couldn't figure. I was repulsed by whatever it was. Crying was for babies.

I stared at his front door, kicked it once, and then went home to defrost something frozen. I asked my dad what Mr. Loury had done at the observatory to get himself fired.

"Said the sky was black and all the stars had gone out," my dad said. "Lost us a heap of funding, which is part of why we're where we're at now. Can't even afford a paintjob. You see how it's peeling."

"And so they took him to jail?" I was startled. My dad snorted.

"No. Rick Loury went to jail because he commandeered the telescope, and tried to crash it into the floor. He thinks there're stars inside the earth. He lost his wife, and then he lost his funding, and then he lost it."

Whatever *it* he'd lost, I wanted to find it and keep it for myself.

My dad was making another mark on the wall. There were three of them now, black X's in the places where his wedding photos had been. He didn't like the bare spots in the wallpaper.

# The Krakatoan

I didn't mind them. Sometimes I poked them with a pin, outlining perforations in each pattern. My first mother left right after I was born. She disappeared without warning, and the day after she left, the good part of the story, my dad discovered a new star. After my second mother walked out, my dad's team spotted an elusive comet.

"Did you find anything last night?" I asked my dad.

"Why would we?

"I don't know," I said. "I just thought you might."

Volcano gods needed sacrifices, Mr. Loury had said. I thought about Pele and her boys. I wondered if other volcanoes wanted other kinds of sacrifices. I wondered if observatories did.

I didn't know how telescopes worked. I didn't know what made up the center of the earth. I had muddled thoughts of lava. How would I know what the sky was made of, or that there was not another sky just beneath the surface of the ground? I thought it might be possible.

I knew that Palomar sometimes got angry. The shutters got stuck closed and the telescope couldn't see out. There'd been days of malfunction that week, things jammed in the works, and my dad had complained to my third mother about it. A grant had been lost because of observatory failure, and there were salary questions. They needed to find something new, something that would attract media. I'd heard a daylight argument.

"Did the roof open last night?" I asked my dad.

"Yep," he said, and went back to the X on the wall, going over it with his ballpoint. I thought about the picture that had been there until the day before, my third mother laughing, with her mouth full of cake. I wanted the photo back. I wanted her back. I wanted them all back.

I arranged the sticks on the counter into a triangle, the shortest one at the bottom, until my dad noticed what I was doing and took them away, breaking them on the way into the trash.

"Why'd she go to Alaska?" I asked him. "She never said anything about Alaska."

He didn't answer for a moment.

"She likes the cold," he finally said, and looked at me, his eyes wide and bloodshot behind his glasses. "Leave it alone."

I walked away from my dad, and up the stairs. I cranked open my bedroom window and looked up at the dark of the mountain.

I'd seen a television program about the explosion of Krakatoa, and in it, there was a fact that haunted me. Rafts made of hardened lava had floated up onto the coast of Africa, even a year later, passengered by skeletons. But maybe those people had been sacrificed to the volcano, and their bones thrown up into the air by the explosion. Maybe Krakatoa had exploded because it didn't like what it was being fed.

I wondered about my mothers. I wondered about Mr. Loury's wife. I wondered if there was a hole in the floor of the observatory, and if through it you might be able to see things beneath. I didn't want to wonder, but I wondered.

Later, I snuck out the window, and into the night. Did I even need to sneak? No one was in charge. No one saw me walking to Mr. Loury's house. I used my sneaker to open a hole in the top of Mr. Loury's volcano. After a minute, I used my hands. I was a Krakatoan. I stamped on Mr. Loury's volcano again, and then put my ear to the ground.

For a long time, I didn't hear anything.

But then, from far below me, I heard something stamping back, a pounding from the other side of the earth. Then a murmuring. I scratched harder with my hands, shoveling dirt away from the top of the volcano.

A light went on in Mr. Loury's kitchen, and his screen door opened.

"Hey!" he shouted, but I was gone, sprinting up Palomar, because whatever was in that volcano, I'd heard a sound, a ragged gasp of welcome as I moved the dirt away. And something else had happened too.

I had a piggy bank with thirteen dollars in it. I had three missing mothers. I dodged into the trees, and ran uphill, off the side of the road where he couldn't follow me. This was my territory. I knew how to run in the woods. He didn't even try, because he was a grown-up, and he had a car. I heard it start.

Trees leaning in, a no-stars, no-moon night and I thought maybe the sky had been swallowed by the observatory draining the stars into its mouth, sucking the darkness dry. There it was, in front of me, its glowing white snowcone looming against the horizon.

I scraped my hands on my jeans, once, twice, three times, until my palms stung, because from inside Mr. Loury's volcano, someone's fingers had reached up and touched mine.

I wasn't sure about breathing. I could hardly see. One of my knees was skinned. Maybe I was crying. I wanted my dad and I didn't. I wanted my mothers, even the one I never knew.

There was a set of headlights speeding up the spiral road and the observatory was full of astronomers without wives. Funerals sometimes. Car crashes and cancer. Other times the wives just went away and no one ever saw them again. This was the way the world worked, I'd imagined, but now I wondered if it really was.

My third mother, I thought and my brain got stuck on it. Katharine, called Kit, who sometimes called me Kit too, and sometimes called me Tool, for *toolkit*, as in a smaller, more equipped version of herself. But my real name was something else entirely. My dad called me Aulax, after a star. "The Furrow," that star name meant, and he'd stuck a Mary in as my middle name to make me more human.

The door was unlocked. I skidded in on my heels, and felt along the edge of the room. I knew my way around Palomar. The inside was like nothing, no sky on view, just the telescope stabbing through the sphere, but as I stood there, not hidden, uncertain, the shutters began to open to let the telescope look at the sky.

Mr. Loury's story was horrible all over my brain. *Look down*, he said in my head, *look underground*, and as I thought it, I felt those cold fingers again, touching my own, gripping my own, and I heard a car stop outside.

No one was visible inside the observatory. I wanted to look toward the center of the earth. I wanted to find my mothers. I didn't want to think about Alaska. I didn't want to think about Pele. I didn't want to think about who was underneath that dirt in Mr. Loury's backyard, nor about how far down the dirt went.

I ran to the telescope and slung myself up into its workings. The shutters were open and the sky was there, black. I held my breath and climbed.

Mr. Loury was in the building. I could feel him, making his way around the edge of the circle. The telescope was moving, and I was slipping.

"Kid," he called. "Hey, Buddy. Where're you at?"

I twisted my knees over the beam at the base of the telescope. I'd always wanted to climb the Hale. It was the biggest telescope in the world. Not in the dark.

"This isn't a place for little girls," he said, and his voice was closer than I'd thought he was. "They're going to look at the roots of the world tonight."

Where were the rest of the astronomers? Where was my dad, for that matter? He was supposed to be here. Nobody was in charge, I reminded myself.

I tied my shirtsleeves to the beam, because I felt the telescope moving. There was a sound, a squealing shudder, which I took for the roof shutters opening further, but when I arched my neck to try to look around the side of the telescope, I couldn't see anything.

I looked down. There was light below me, and the telescope rotated toward it, my fingers slipping on the metal as we tilted backward. I was not inside the telescope, could not see whatever it was they were seeing there in the cage, but whatever they were looking at, whatever it was they were trying to see, it was in the wrong direction.

"You aren't here," Mr. Loury said, from directly below me, and I could tell he was looking up at me, trying to reach me, but I couldn't do anything about it.

"I belong here. My dad works here, and you're trespassing. You got fired," I told him, clinging to the beam. I didn't care about quiet any more. I wanted someone to hear me, and yet, somehow, I didn't scream for help.

"I tried to tell you," Mr. Loury said. "The stars are gone and all of them are gone with them. They want boys, and that's all. She doesn't want me anymore."

The telescope completed its tilt, flipping me so that I faced down, and I saw what the open shutters looked into, what I was dangling over.

There was lava below us, a crater full of it, glowing orange and red, and in the lava there were women, stretching their fingers to touch the metal of the telescope, pressing their nails into it.

I saw the incandescent roots of the world, and the way the women were tangled in them, their mouths open, a deafening murmur like wind tearing trees. I saw Mr. Loury's wife, the Kodachrome version of her, her white skin and bright hair, her eyes big and black-rimmed with fake lashes. The sunglasses she always wore were missing. She was naked, her long arms savaged and blistered, her ribs skinny and her hipbones sticking out. *Come here*, she mouthed, and her lipstick was perfect. Other mothers were there too, and I knew them.

I'd been to their funerals and gone to school with their abandoned children. I'd seen the X's where they weren't. I saw all the dead women in the center of the earth, and then I saw them reach up toward where I dangled.

I saw my third mother, and she saw me.

# The Krakatoan

Somewhere I heard a door slam, a shout, and Mr. Loury, just for an instant, was silhouetted against all that light and fire.

Then, like the Krakatoans, the astronomer's wives were gone, and my mother was gone, and all that was left were black skeletons, ashes floating on rafts of darkness, lists of dead stars. I heard myself screaming.

The asbestos-tiled floor of the observatory appeared beneath my cheek, and my head appeared on top of my body, sharp pain and dull ache at once, and there was my dad, kneeling beside me, his eyes still bloodshot.

"Can you move?" he asked me. "Is anything broken?"

I could move. Nothing was broken. The roof rotated and where the sky had been dark, it was now all stars and Milky Way. I stood up, bruised, and tried to figure out where my feet were. My dad had me by the arm, and he was moving me out of there, faster than I wanted to move. I looked back at the telescope, and I could feel everything getting taken away from me, forever, and all at once.

My dad carried me to the car, fastened my seatbelt, and drove me down the spiral road, and to the hospital. He told the nurses I'd fallen from something high, and they looked into my eyes and agreed that I was looking out at the world through a concussion. They showed me my pupils in a handmirror, one big, one tiny, Martian moons in an eclipse, or the sun trying to shine through a sky full of ash.

I put my face into a crisp white shoulder and cried there, but when I lifted my head, I was done, and no one asked.

Mr. Loury's abandoned house and its volcano got paved over when they redid the spiral road in the late 70's.

My dad drowned in 1984, on a trip to the South Pacific, diving into an underwater cave and failing to equalize his pressure, but he was an old man by then and hadn't been in touch with me in a long time. There were no more mothers.

The astronomers at Palomar kept finding supernovae and charting galaxies, but the largest telescope in the world was surpassed in size in the early 90's. The last time I drove there, up the spiral road and to the tourist center, it was daylight, and the only person I saw was not an astronomer, but a painter pulleying himself around the walls, rolling white paint slowly over the dome.

When I tried to ask him a question, he shrugged and turned back to his job, pulling himself along the dome, hand over hand.

I stood there a while, watching him spackling the fine cracks all over the surface, the ones that stretched up from the gravel and all the way to the top of the dome itself. The observatory was getting old. I bent down, and put my ear to the ground, but there was nothing to hear. When I stood up, the painter was looking at me.

He reached into the pocket of his overalls, and tossed me a small white rock. Later that night, in my hotel room, I soaked it in alcohol. Underneath the paint, the rock was black and porous, but that was all.

# Anna Taborska

## The Girl in the Blue Coat

**Anna Taborska** *is a British filmmaker and horror writer. She has written and directed two short fiction films, two documentaries and award-winning TV drama* The Rain Has Stopped. *Anna also worked on seventeen other films, and was involved in the making of two major BBC television series:* Auschwitz: the Nazis and the Final Solution *and* World War Two behind Closed Doors—Stalin, the Nazis and the West. *Anna's short stories have appeared in a number of Year's Best anthologies, including* The Best Horror of the Year Vol. 4 *and* Best British Horror 2014. *Anna's short story* Bagpuss *was an Eric Hoffer Award Honoree, and the screenplay adaptation of her story* Little Pig *was a finalist in the Shriekfest Film Festival Screenplay Competition, 2009. Her debut short story collection,* For Those who Dream Monsters, *released by Mortbury Press in 2013, was nominated for a British Fantasy Award. You can view Anna's full résumé at http:// www.imdb.com/name/nm1245940, watch her films and book trailers at http://www.youtube.com/annataborska and learn more about her short stories and screenplays at http://annataborska.wix.com/horror*

So it's our last day together. You've been a good listener. And thanks to you I'll have a voice—albeit a posthumous one... I'm sorry—I've made you feel uncomfortable. But I believe that's what you wanted to cover today—my thoughts on my imminent demise. Well, we can do that, but first I want to tell you a story. I've never told it to anyone, but then again you're not really anyone—are you? Please don't be offended—you know I value your work, and one day you'll be a successful writer in your own right and under your own name. But today you're just the extension of a dying old man.

The painkillers they're giving me have stopped working; the pain is becoming unbearable, and soon I'll be on morphine. The doctors tell me I'll be hallucinating and delusional, and nobody will believe the ranting of a cancer-ridden old man... Is the Dictaphone working? Good... As you're my ghostwriter, the story I'll tell you is most appropriate because it's a ghost story—at least, I think it is... Do I believe in them? Perhaps once you hear the story, *you'll* be able to tell *me*. I don't know. It all happened long ago...

∿

I'd only been working at *The History Magazine* for four months, but they were pleased with my research skills, and I was the only person on the staff who spoke Polish. It was my second job since leaving university, and I'd already cut my teeth on an established, if somewhat trashy, London daily. So when the powers that be decided to revisit the Holocaust, the Senior Editor chose me to go to Poland.

I'd been to Poland before, of course. My mother's family hailed from the beautiful city of Krakow, and I'd been taken there fairly regularly as a boy to visit my aunt and cousins. But this time I was to travel to Międzyrzec—a small and unremarkable town, the name of which caused considerable hilarity among my colleagues, and which I myself could scarcely pronounce.

"You'll be going to My... Mee... here..." said my boss, thrusting a piece of paper at me with a touch of good-natured annoyance at the intricacies of Polish orthography. Foreign names and places were never his thing in any case. He seemed happiest in his leather chair behind his vast desk in the *Magazine* office, and I sometimes suspected that the furthest he'd been from Blighty was Majorca, where he'd holiday with his wife and children at every given opportunity. And nothing wrong with that; nothing wrong at all—I thought—as I drove my hire car through the grey and brown Polish countryside, trying hard not to pile into any of the horse-drawn carts that occasionally pulled out in front of me without warning from some misty dirt side track.

∿

I'd done my homework before driving the eighty miles east from Warsaw to Międzyrzec. Before the outbreak of World War II there had been about 12,000 Jews living in the town—almost three-quarters of the population. The town had synagogues, Jewish schools, Jewish shops, a Jewish theatre, two Jewish football teams, a Jewish brothel and a Jewish fire brigade. I wondered idly whether the Jewish fire brigade was sent to extinguish fires in Christian homes too, or just in Jewish ones. I figured it was the former, as by all accounts the Poles and Jews got on like a house on fire—excuse the pun—and most of the town's inhabitants worked happily side by side in a Jewish-owned factory, producing kosher pig hair brushes, which were sold as far afield as Germany. In fact, commerce in Międzyrzec flourished to the degree that the envious, poverty-stricken inhabitants of surrounding towns and villages referred to the place as 'Little America'... Does prosperity render a man better disposed towards his fellow man? I don't know. Certainly, during the course of my research, I read of various acts of generosity—big and small—which were extended to others regardless of background, so that, for example, when a film such as *The Dybbuk* came to town, the cinema owner would organise a free screening for all the citizens of Międzyrzec, and the queue stretched half way down the main street.

As with any positive status quo, the good times in Międzyrzec were not to last long. When war broke out in September 1939, the town was bombed, then taken by the Germans, before being handed over to the Russians, and finally falling into German hands once more. The horrors that followed were fairly typical for Nazi-occupied Poland. The Polish population was terrorised, while the Jews were harassed, attacked, rounded up and either murdered on the spot or sealed in a ghetto, from which they were eventually shipped off to death camps. Nothing new there, I thought, as by now I was becoming—not jaded by all the atrocities I'd read about, but something of a reluctant expert on Nazi war crimes and the pattern they followed in the towns and villages of German-occupied Poland. And yet something about the destruction of this surprisingly harmonious community—not just the murder of people, but the annihilation of a functional and thriving symbiotic organism formed from thousands of disparate souls— added to the customary level of distress that I'd somehow learned to live with since being assigned to the Second World War project.

Finally the countryside gave way to ramshackle housing, and the dark green and white road sign confirmed that I'd arrived at my destination. All I had to do now was find the town library, where I had a meeting with the librarian turned amateur historian—a pleasant fellow with a neatly trimmed brown beard, who furnished me with the details of several elderly local residents, including a lady who 'remembered the War'.

"She doesn't have a telephone," he told me as I thanked him and took the piece of paper with the names and addresses, "but she's almost certain to be at home. You can't miss the house. It's the last house but one on the left as you leave town, going east. It's one of the old wooden houses, and you'd be forgiven for thinking that you'd already left Międzyrzec, as those old houses are virtually out in the countryside."

I decided to start at the far end of town, with the old lady. Everything was as my bearded friend had said: the ugly apartment blocks and equally unattractive family houses (presumably built hastily after the war, to re-house those whose homes had been destroyed) gave way to what looked like small wooden farmhouses, with fields and meadows behind them stretching away into the distance.

I drove slowly in an effort to ascertain which house was the last but one on the left-hand side before leaving town. I was fairly sure it was a run-down wooden house with peeling green paint, set back from the road. I drove past just to check, but I'd been right—there was only one more house beyond the one I'd instinctively picked out. I turned the car around carefully and doubled back, pulling up on the grass verge by the side of the road. Chain-link fencing some six feet in height surrounded the property, and the only way in—from the roadside, at least—was through a gate, which was locked. There was a bell, but no intercom. I pressed the bell and waited. After a minute or so I pressed it again, not sure if it was even working.

After a couple more minutes, the front door of the house opened with a creaking worthy of an old horror movie, and an elderly grey-haired woman peered out apprehensively. I waved at her and after a moment's hesitation she waved back. Then she went back inside and shut the door behind her. I was taken aback and nearly rang the doorbell again, but then the woman reappeared, pulling a woollen shawl over her shoulders. I smiled at her reassuringly as she made her way slowly and painfully down the porch steps and across the front yard towards me.

"How can I help you?" she asked through the fencing.

"Hello, my name is Frank Johnson," I told her. "I work for *The History Magazine* in London, and I understand from Dr Lipinski that you remember the time when there was a ghetto..." I never got to finish my sentence. The old lady had been observing me with amicable curiosity, but now her face crumpled and she started sobbing uncontrollably, tears streaming down her face and gathering in her wrinkles. I was mortified and started to mumble a hasty apology, but the woman raised her hand in a conciliatory gesture.

"I'm sorry," she managed to say. "I'll take some medicine for my nerves. Please come back in an hour and I'll tell you all about the ghetto." I smiled at her as best I could and nodded my head vigorously. "The gate will be open," she added, trying unsuccessfully to stem the flow of tears with a shaky hand.

"I'll come back in an hour," I told her.

≋

There was really nothing constructive I could do in an hour, but I didn't want to make the old lady any more uncomfortable by sitting outside her house, so I drove back into the town centre, parked up and sat in my car. There was no decent pub to speak of and there was no point in getting a cup of tea, as I knew from my experience of Polish hospitality that I'd be having tea and cake at the old lady's house whether I wanted it or not.

I'd interviewed survivors of trauma before, and I'd had interviewees cry during interviews, but never before I'd even started. I'd always imagined Polish peasants to be a hardy breed, taking history's worst cruelties in their stride and not shedding much in the way of tears for themselves, let alone for the plight of an ethnic minority that shared neither their religion nor their cultural traditions. If nothing else, the old lady should provide some good first-hand material for *The History Magazine*—provided she was able to pull herself together and wasn't totally nuts.

After half an hour of sitting in the car, going through my notes and interview questions, I got bored and decided to drive back to the old lady's house and see if she'd talk to me a bit earlier than agreed. This time I knew exactly where I was going, so I was able to concentrate less on houses and house numbers, and more on the road itself. It struck me how deserted it was. Despite having only one lane in each direction, this was the main road heading east from Warsaw, all the way to Belarus; and yet my car seemed to be the only vehicle on it. Not even an old peasant on a hay cart in sight. Perhaps an accident somewhere further up had stopped the traffic, but that would explain the lack of cars in one direction, not both. Perhaps all the other drivers knew something I didn't... I chided myself for letting my imagination run away with me. But as I pulled up alongside the chain-link fence, I couldn't shake the feeling of unease.

The gate was open, as promised. I wondered if I should ring the doorbell anyway, to warn the old lady of my imminent arrival, but I didn't want to bring her all the way out in the cold again, so I slung my bag over my shoulder, locked the car and let myself in, closing the gate behind me. As I headed across the front yard to the rickety old house, a chill breeze stirred around me, whispering in the unmown grass and rustling the leaves of the sapling trees that had seeded themselves and sprouted unchecked on either side of the stone slab path. Although only a dozen or so metres separated me from the old lady's porch, I paused to zip up my parka. As I did so, the breeze grew stronger, making a high pitched sound as it weaved its way through the eaves of the house. Unexpectedly it died down, and the air around me was as still as the proverbial grave. Then a sudden gust of wind—this time blowing from the direction of the field behind the house. Urgent, angry almost, the wind brought with it something else: a sound—human, yet unearthly; a cry or moan—distant, but so heartfelt and full of despair that, despite the warmth of my down anorak, an icy shiver ran down my spine.

I made my way to the back of the house and looked out over the field that led away to a swampy patch of land, and ended in a stream or river of some sort—obscured by sedges and tall reeds. Beyond the line of water, a wasteland of grass, bushes and wild flowers stretched away to a railway track, and then further, to a dark tree line on the horizon. A mist was rising from the marshy land and, as I peered into the miasma, I thought I saw something: a flash of blue against the grey and brown. The wind blew in my direction again, and this time I was sure that the sound I heard was a young woman weeping.

"Hello!" I called out.

"Hello?" the voice came from behind me, making me jump. "Young man!"

I'd forgotten all about the old lady and my interview. She must have seen me out of a window, and was now holding open the back door, gesticulating for me to come inside. "You'll catch your death of cold!" she chastised gently. I noticed a slight frown crease the woman's already furrowed brow as I threw a last glance back over my shoulder before entering the house. Apart from that passing shadow on her face, my interviewee was a different person from the one I'd left sobbing her heart out almost an hour earlier. Calm and collected, she smiled at me in a warm and friendly manner. When she spoke, her voice was clear and steady.

# The Girl in the Blue Coat

In no time I found myself sitting in a worn armchair in a small parlour, nursing a glass of black tea in an elaborately engraved silver-coloured holder.

"I'm afraid I don't have much to offer you," said my hostess, holding out a plate with four different types of homemade cake. "You said you wanted to know about the War. I'll tell you everything I remember."

<center>~~~</center>

Her name was Bronislava. She was born in Międzyrzec and lived with her mother in an apartment block near the town centre. Her street was mixed Polish and Jewish. Not all of the Jews spoke Polish, but most of the Poles spoke at least some Yiddish, and it was normal for children from the two ethnic groups to play together in the street. Bronislava's father had died when she was little and, as her mother was out cleaning for some of the town's more affluent residents during the week, the little girl spent most of her time at the house of her best friends Esther and Mindla, so that her friends' mum was like a second mother to her. Bronislava and Esther were nine when war broke out; Mindla was a couple of years older. For a while not much changed, but slowly rationing and other increasing restrictions meant that hunger and fear crept into all their lives. Esther and Mindla's family was ordered to wear armbands with the Star of David, along with all the other Jewish residents, but at this point violence against the Jewish community was incidental rather than systematic.

Then one day, German soldiers with dogs and guns, and auxiliary Ukrainian militia, came marching into Bronislava's street. They swept through the houses, pulling out Jewish families, beating them and leading them away. Bronislava and Esther were playing with the other children. Mindla was out running an errand. When Esther's mother heard all the commotion, she came running out to the two girls, grabbed their hands and tried to pull them away from the shouting soldiers. The three of them were caught and shoved along behind the other Jews. Amid the blows and kicks that rained down on them from all sides, Esther's mother tried to shield the two girls as best she could. Then Bronislava's mother, who had been sewing at home that day, spotted her daughter out of the window across the road, and came running out, shouting that her child was Polish. Somehow she managed to fight her way to Bronislava, and yanked her away from

Esther and her mother. Bronislava screamed and grappled with her mother. She tried to go after her best friend, but her mother scooped her up and ran back to their building.

〰

The old woman spoke in a dry, dispassionate, almost robotic way, which I would have found a little disconcerting had I not known that she'd taken some kind of tranquiliser especially for the occasion. She spoke of street roundups, summary executions and coldblooded murder. When she told me about a hyped-up Ukrainian militiaman, in the service of the German military, ripping a baby apart with his bare hands, her voice wavered, and I realised that even with whatever drugs she'd taken, she was making a valiant effort to keep it together.

Some time after Bronislava's Jewish neighbours had been taken away, the German army took over the building in which she and her mother lived, and the remaining residents were evicted. Some of them moved in with extended family elsewhere; others were forcibly re-housed with other Poles.

"We were lucky," Bronislava told me. "My mother had cousins who lived on the outskirts of Międzyrzec—in this very house. Out here things were quieter. The Germans raided the farms to make sure that the peasants weren't hiding any livestock or reserves of grain over the allotted ration quota, but it was easier to grow some vegetables here and occasionally buy a few eggs from a neighbour who'd managed to hang on to a hen or two. My mother and I helped out in the house, and my mother still took on the odd cleaning or sewing job, so we got by somehow. We were hungry, but we weren't starving... Would you like some more tea?" I shook my head and she carried on.

"I quickly discovered that there was no love lost between our cousins and the family next door, and the reasons for this became clear soon enough. I know one shouldn't speak ill of the dead," Bronislava frowned, "but there is no other way to speak of those monsters. The farmer was a mean-spirited and violent drunk. His wife was a greedy, spiteful and malicious gossip, and their son, although slimmer in build than his bloated, overfed parents, was a vile combination of the two of them in both temper and habit. As soon as they laid eyes on my mother and me, they hated us with as much venom as they did the rest of our household.

"I asked my aunt how it was that the next door neighbours were fat and well dressed, while the rest of us were constantly patching up the tatters than hung off our emaciated bodies. And how was it that, when German soldiers carried out their 'inspections', they tore through all the houses—including ours—shouting, kicking things over and showering down blows on anyone who didn't get out of their way fast enough; and yet, when the same soldiers went next door, they joked and chatted with the owner, got drunk with him, and came out clutching food or a bottle of vodka, or sometimes a watch, a piece of jewellery.

"*We don't speak about it*, my aunt told me. *Just make sure you stay away from them.* Well, being told to stay away from something usually has the opposite effect on little girls, and—despite the horror of those times—I was no different. I spent all my spare time playing in the field at the back of the house and watching the neighbours' property. Then, one evening, my curiosity was rewarded.

"That day, a German patrol had swept through the street, looking for food and valuables. They were in a filthy mood, as nobody had anything left. They trashed our house and hit my uncle across the face when he was unable to give them anything of interest. Finally they went next door and left several hours later, singing and laughing. I figured they wouldn't be back again that evening, so I risked venturing outside.

"The sun had just gone down, but a strange light lingered. It was magic hour, and the field and marshland beyond it glimmered golden-blue. The peculiar light brought out all the blues and purples in the field, so that the cornflowers glowed like luminous azure eyes in the grass. I looked over the tumble-down bit of fence that separated my cousins' land from the neighbours', and my heart skipped a beat. Out in the neighbours' field, a brilliant swathe of bright blue shimmered in the shadows. At first I thought it was mist rising from the damp grass. But it was too solid to be mist and, when it moved, I realised that it was a human figure.

"As quietly as I could, I headed towards it. The figure was small and slim, and I finally worked out that it was a girl—a girl in a blue coat. And then it dawned on me that I'd seen that coat before. The girl turned suddenly, as though sensing my presence. She froze for a moment, then started to run back towards the neighbours' house.

"*Wait!* I clambered over a rotted piece of fence and gave chase. As the girl fled, the hood of her coat came down, and a flurry of matted black tresses flowed out behind her. Despite how thin she now was, I was almost sure. But how could it be? How could someone I'd grieved for every day for three years be alive and fleeing from me through a field that was rapidly turning a murky grey?

"The girl was evidently weak, but she had a head start, and I realised I wouldn't catch up with her before she reached the neighbours' house. Desperate, I took a risk and called out. *Mindla? Mindla, wait!* She heard me and stopped dead. She turned towards me slowly, her whole body shaking from the exertion of running barely fifty metres or so. She was emaciated—skeletal almost—no longer the chubby-cheeked twelve-year-old that I'd loved and looked up to, but a gaunt teenager with haunted, hollow eyes. Abruptly magic hour ended, and we were in darkness. We stood facing each other, trembling. Then a small gasp escaped Mindla's cracked lips and, as I rushed towards her, she slumped into my arms.

"From then on, Mindla and I met every night at the border of the two properties in which we were reluctant lodgers. I learned how Mindla had returned from the bakery on that day to find her mother and sister gone. The Polish family next door told her that it wasn't safe for her to stay in the street as the Germans could return at any moment to look for stragglers. She managed to get to the factory where her father worked, but all the Jewish workers had been taken away. So she hid in a series of attics and basements in Międzyrzec, moving on when each hiding-place became unsafe. Finally there was nowhere else to hide, so she left the town one night with a young Jewish woman and her fiancé. They'd tried to survive in the forest, hiding in a hollowed-out tree trunk by day and scavenging for food when it got dark, but when winter started to draw in, the cold and hunger became unbearable. They came across another group of Jews trying to survive in the open, who told them that a Polish peasant was taking in Jewish girls for payment. Mindla knew she wouldn't survive winter in the forest, so she decided to take a chance. She still had a couple of gold coins that her mother had sewn into the lining of her coat when enemy soldiers had first entered the town, so she followed the instructions given and made it to the peasant's house.

"*The man told me to give him everything I had*, Mindla explained. *In return he would hide me and feed me... But now he says there isn't enough food, so I only get a bowl of soup and a piece of bread a day. During the day I lie hidden behind straw on a kind of shelf above the animals, at the back of the house. That way the Germans don't see me when they come. Sometimes the soldiers stay for hours, drinking homemade vodka with the man and his son. I have to lie very still. I get cramps in my legs, and sometimes bugs crawl on me.*

"Mindla told me about two other Jewish girls who'd been hiding in the peasant's house when she arrived. They'd fled their home village of Rudniki when the roundups started, but the rest of their family had been taken away. One day the peasant and his son came for the sisters in the middle of the night, and Mindla never saw them again. When she asked what had happened to them, the peasant's wife told her to mind her own business, and the peasant said that a relative of theirs had come and taken them away. But Mindla must have had doubts as to the girls' plight because she kept returning to them in our conversations.

"I told Mindla that I would ask my mother if she could stay with us. *No,* said Mindla. *I won't put your lives in danger.* I related our conversation to my mother, and she said that Mindla was right; we didn't have the privileges that the next door neighbour had—unlike his house, ours got searched from top to bottom—and, in any case, there were no hiding-places in our house. So Mindla and I met outdoors, sometimes in the pouring rain. I lived for those meetings. I put aside what little food I could, as did my mother. We didn't tell my cousins what I was up to. The fewer who knew, the better. Sometimes my mother caught me sneaking out at night. She was very afraid for me, but she didn't stop me.

"One night Mindla was late to meet me. Finally she appeared, looking paler and more frightened than normal. She usually managed a wan smile and a few words when she saw me, but this time she was withdrawn and silent. It took me a while to get her to admit what had happened. The farmer had become tired of hiding her and feeding her. He said that he wanted payment. *I said that I'd already given him everything, and he said 'Not everything.'* Mindla cried as she told me that the man had tried to force himself on her. She was only saved because her screams brought out the man's wife, who called her 'an ungrateful little whore', and dragged her husband back to bed. I don't think I fully comprehended what Mindla was telling me—at twelve I was very naive about the ways of the world—but I knew that my beloved friend was in trouble and that I had to do something. *Let's run away together,* I told her. *Let's go right now—tonight.* Mindla looked at me with love and sadness. I've never seen such sadness in anybody's eyes. *We can't run away,* she told me. *There's nowhere to run.*

"That night I had a terrible nightmare. Mindla was standing by the marsh at the bottom of the field. She was only in her underwear. She reached out to me and at first I thought that she had that same sadness in her eyes, but as I drew closer, I saw that her eyes were gone." Bronislava paused. I had been engrossed in her recollection, and the sudden silence startled me. I looked at her, but she avoided my gaze. She turned away and pretended to blow her nose, but I could see that she was wiping her eyes.

"The next night Mindla didn't come," she finally said, then fell silent once more. I waited in vain for her speak. After what seemed like a long time, but was probably only half a minute, I finally asked her what had happened.

"I waited for hours," she said. It was raining and very cold. Eventually my mother came out and found me by the fence, soaking wet. I contracted pneumonia and nearly died." Another pause.

"What happened to Mindla?"

"She was never seen again."

"Well, what do you think happened to her?"

"I don't *think*. I *know* what happened. They killed her. The farmer and that son of his. As soon as I saw my Mindla's blue coat stretched over the grotesque body of that woman, I knew that they'd killed her."

"You saw the farmer's wife wearing Mindla's coat?"

"Yes. When I was well enough to get out of bed, I looked out of the window and saw her parading around shamelessly in it. It had always been too big for Mindla. I remember, she'd seen that coat in a shop and fallen in love with it. That was just before war broke out. She persuaded her mother that she'd 'grow into it' and eventually her mother gave in and bought it for her. But Mindla never grew into it. Instead of filling out like other girls her age, she'd been starved and the coat always hung off her. But it was too small for that awful woman— she couldn't even do the buttons up, and yet she strutted around in it as though Mindla had never existed. God knows why she wanted it—it was tattered and badly worn, but it was a pretty colour, and the woman was greedy.

"I flew out of the house before my aunt could stop me, and I confronted her. I asked what she'd done to Mindla. The woman shouted at me to mind my own business. Her husband came storming out of the house and told me that if I didn't shut up, he'd make sure that something very bad happened to me.

"The next thing I knew, German soldiers came storming into my cousins' house. They beat up my uncle and tore up the floorboards in the kitchen. The next door neighbour had told them that we'd hidden grain under the floor. They didn't find anything, and the farmer got a clout round the earhole for making them waste their time, but he'd made his point.

"I didn't confront him again until the war was over. The communist authorities weren't interested in the wild accusations of an adolescent girl—or her mother. In any case, the farmer was a man of influence. He had grown wealthy on the suffering of the unfortunate souls he had exploited and, although the other residents on the street viewed him with distaste and went out of their way to avoid him, he didn't care. He now drank with the NKVD, and, when the Soviets left Poland to the Polish communists, he drank with the chief of police. It was made very clear to me that if I continued with my accusations, things would end very badly for my mother. By the time the communists were overthrown, the farmer and his family were dead. The man and his wife died of natural causes, but not until they had buried their only son. It's said that he was drunk and—for some inexplicable reason—wandered out onto the tracks beyond the field at the back of his parents' house, where he was hit by a train." The old lady paused, and I thought that she'd finished her story. I tried to think of something appropriate to say, but after a moment's hesitation, during which she seemed to be sizing me up, she carried on.

"Sometimes I dream about her," she said. "Sometimes, especially in autumn and in early spring, when the mist rises from the marshy ground, I see her walking along the ditch at the far end of the field. Mostly I just hear her crying..." The woman broke off, tired and sad. I could tell I wasn't going to get much more out of her. She fixed her rheumy eyes on me, and seemed to wait for my full attention. I placed my glass of tea carefully on the table and returned her gaze. Something in her tone changed; became more urgent, almost pleading. "I've waited fifty years to tell her story to someone who would listen," she finally said. "To someone who could tell her story to the world and... right the wrong."

I lowered my eyes and finished my honey cake, weighing up whether or not to tell my down-to-earth editor the story of the girl in the blue coat. As I sipped the last of my tea, I already knew that the 'ghost story' wouldn't make it into my research notes... I know what you're thinking, but, in any case, it wouldn't have made a difference; my boss dropped the Międzyrzec story. It wasn't that he was unhappy with my report—quite the contrary; I'd managed to find two credible eye witnesses of the so-called 'ghetto liquidations', during which the Jews who had been rounded up or enticed out of hiding with promises of immunity were robbed, beaten and murdered, or herded onto trucks and driven to the local train station for transportation to the gas chambers of Treblinka and Majdanek... No, my research had been thorough, as ever, but the ghetto liquidation story was abandoned in favour of the Chelmno death camp; aerial photography had uncovered a hitherto unknown mass grave in the nearby forest, and my boss was keen for *The History Magazine* to be the first publication outside Poland to cover the find.

And so I forgot all about Międzyrzec, and the old lady, and the girl in the blue coat. Until fifteen years later—when I was working as a war correspondent for Reuters in war-torn Iraq. I'd been stationed with the US regiment I told you about for over a month. We'd been lucky: the territory that came under our patrols was fairly quiet, and the worst thing about the posting was the heat and the desert wind. No matter how carefully you covered up, you could always taste sand in your mouth, and the grit would irritate your nose and make your eyes run—despite the shades we all wore virtually around the clock.

Then one night I saw her—the dead girl from Międzyrzec. She stood in the mist at the bottom of the old woman's field, looking at me with eyes of death and sorrow. The cold blue-grey of that Polish landscape couldn't have been further from the blistering yellow of the desert into which I awoke, and yet no amount of burning desert dust could dispel the horror I felt. That day the convoy I was travelling with drove into a trap—a double whammy, if you like—of a landmine and a car-bomb driven by a suicide bomber, who died on the spot, along with five of the soldiers who'd become my friends over the past few weeks. Nobody escaped without injury; some of us lost limbs, one young man from Idaho lost an eye, another boy lost part of his jaw. I was lucky; I escaped with shrapnel in my knee and cuts to my back and arms. But it shook my confidence in my indestructibility—for a while, at least.

With all the blood and guts and horror of the aftermath of the attack, I forgot about the girl in the blue coat once more. But she came back. Whenever I became complacent, whenever things were going a bit too well, or when I simply forgot about my own mortality, she came back. Don't get me wrong, people weren't blown up around me every time I dreamt about her, but each time reminded me of the unpredictability and cruelty of the world we live in; of death which will one day come for all of us, and of the fact that she's still waiting—waiting out there in the cold, the damp and the dark for her story to be told... And I've been dreaming a lot lately.

I see I've rendered you speechless. Well, I'm sorry. Like the old lady in Międzyrzec, I've waited many years to tell that story. I realise it doesn't quite fit with the image of the tough old reporter that we've created together, but you must promise to allow me to tell it to the world as I've told it to you today. You know it now. And, believe me, if either of us is to have any peace in this world or the next, then it must be told. Promise me.

≈

"His words, not mine," the ghost writer looked his publisher straight in the eye. "So you see, we have to keep it in. It's what he wanted." It was a plea more than a statement.

"Nonsense!" the publisher scoffed. The writer's sentimentality and inexperience were starting to annoy him. Perhaps it had been a mistake to give the Johnson gig to someone so young. "Don't you see? A supernatural yarn about a dead girl goes against everything else you've written. It's out of character, it's completely inconsistent with the rest of the book; it will alienate our readers and ruin Johnson's reputation."

"You don't understand..." the writer implored.

"But I do understand. I understand that including a drugged up old man's fantasies in what is to be his legacy to the world wouldn't just be *unfair* to Frank; it would be a total violation of the trust he placed in all of us to tell his story." The publisher studied the writer closely. The young man's face had blanched and he was starting to sweat. "Look," the older man's voice softened a little, "Frank Johnson was hard as nails. Not a fanciful bone in his body. If he'd been in his right mind the last time you saw him, he'd never have said what he said. He was a tough, unshakeable war correspondent who did a dangerous and responsible job, and did it well—you know that better than anyone. Now his reputation is in our hands. And there's no way this publishing house is going to destroy his legacy for the sake of some crazy story that he told you in his last days, high on morphine."

The writer had lowered his gaze to his hands, which were clasping and unclasping in his lap like the death throes of a beached fish. When he raised his eyes again, the publisher was shocked to see in them a look of desperation and—perhaps—fear. When he finally spoke, his voice shook, and for a moment the publisher had the worrying notion that the writer was going to burst into tears.

"You don't understand," the young man practically begged. "I've... seen her."

"What?... Who?"

"The girl." The publisher stared at the writer uncomprehendingly. "The girl in the blue coat."

"What do you mean? Where?" The publisher wasn't sure what disturbed him more: the writer's evident breakdown or the fact that he now found himself alone in a room with a madman.

"In my dreams... Nightmares." The writer looked down at his now motionless hands. "She walks along the ditch at the bottom of a field. It's cold. It's lonely. When the wind blows in my direction, I can hear her crying. And then she looks at me... I see her every night... Her eyes are like death. Full of betrayal and sorrow that can never be healed. Grief not just for her own short, painful existence, but for all those whose bones or ashes lie in unmarked graves. I can't stand her eyes. The desolation in them gets inside you. It makes you wish you were dead. Makes you wish you'd never been born..." The publisher was too stunned to react and, after a moment's pause, the writer carried on. "I don't know how Frank Johnson lived with it... He was a... strong... man." The writer raised his eyes once more, but did not meet his boss's incredulous gaze. His attention was focused on the window at the far end of the office, behind his listener's back, where something—a gust from the air-conditioning unit perhaps—caused the reinforced textile strips of the cream-coloured blind to stir and rattle softly against the glass pane. He added quietly, "I'm not... that... strong..."

# Joseph S. Pulver Sr.

## (HE) DREAMS OF LOVECRAFTIAN HORROR…

**Joseph S. Pulver, Sr.**, *is the author of the novels,* The Orphan Palace *and* Nightmare's Disciple, *and he has written many short stories that have appeared in magazines and anthologies, including* Weird Fiction Review, Lovecraft eZine, *Ellen Datlow's* Best Horror of the Year, *S. T. Joshi's* Black Wings (I and III), Book of Cthulhu, The Children of Old Leech. *His short story collections,* Blood Will Have Its Season, SIN & ashes, *and* Portraits of Ruin, *were published by Hippocampus Press. He edited* A Season in Carcosa *and* The Grimscribe's Puppets. *He is at work on two new collections of weird fiction,* A House of Hollow Wounds, *and* The Protocols of Ugliness, *both edited by Jeffrey Thomas. He is currently editing* Cassilda's Song, The Leaves of a Necronomicon, *and* Unlanguage of Unknowing: Examination No. 1 COMMON QUESTIONS *for 2015 release.*

*You can find him on the internet at: http: https://sites.google.com/ site/thisyellowmadness*

*{for my dear brother, a certain Mr. Hopfrog, Esq.}*

( T hen) *(by the light of an East Coast moon…)*
after the beans.
after coffee.
after the day's vigorous adventure in sunlight, the walk, enjoying the blue. a pen in silver hands, prizing. dreaming—'**wholly overruled by the newer and more bewildering urge.**'—from (and laced with) mathematics, and physics, and hints… '**Subterranean region beneath placid New England village, inhabited by (living or extinct) creatures of prehistoric antiquity and strangeness**'. . . '**Lonely bleak**

islands off N.E. coast. Horrors they harbour—outpost of cosmic influences'…'A very ancient colossus in a very ancient desert. Face gone—no man hath seen it'…words, aware—of history and science, and ancient fruits (and the embrace of Eternity)… 'There was the immemorial figure of the deputy or messenger of hidden and terrible powers – the "Black Man" of the witch cult'… astonished words. of cellars and cobwebs, of the inquiries of a madman. the hunger of the engine in the fountain burns in the nest. winter. telling farther. shaking with the moments when the clock faces the stars. the race to the gate. leaping with fast dreams. today. yesterday. a cold year (wrapped in beauty and loneliness) that disappears in a stream of years. words. dreams. words. words, lost and found…and melted.

dreaming (dusk) (shadows) (dark corners)… revising.

in the tomb. dreaming. and other tales of terror. . .

*(now) (by the light of a West Coast moon…)*

after coffee.

after Thai food.

after singing along with the new Streisand cd—*twice*. the hungry hands (of the poet) at the keyboard. mining (commitment). deeper and deeper to emerge with landmarks. words. each dreaming of the master…each in sorrow and ecstasy, formed by heart. words. no make-up today. {ashton}ished WORDS—rising, leaping (soon to be thrust into the hands of The Editor), fast as midnight explored. fingers in the unwound mists of a woodland asylum, eyes in the master's *Commonplace Book*. more words—'He kissed the instrument, then held it to the moon, that globe of dead refraction'…, more phrases—'Autumn is my favorite time of year; it heralds absolutely the death of torturous summer'. . .'She placed her hands together in a semblance of prayer'…more (legions of deliberateness, each raindrop-tongue pulsing) grow (in Sesqua Valley) (and other haunts). words, stitching blight on the doorways of abandoned streets. blue-veined words, caging the empty-handed prayers of the garden. carved words that must weight in. *sign and sentence, lamps in the witch-house*! (tearswept) words. choirs of words, gut and reflexes that won't hide, or stop…the stain of dark blossoms covering the page. words, plucked (from the master's territories) by the velocity of his nets, and piled high on his altar of

Lovecraftian dreams . . .

face pressed to words, roots (of death and decay and dark black earth) and raven stars. briars—burdens, shaking with burdens. the movement (every knot and gesture lit) of association and choice.

> words.
> flares.
> bells.
> bells. and smoke fermenting. bells. thrust into technique,
> banging on the strictures the stars possess.
> bells.
> bells. the luminous baptism—cooking genesis in the
> decomposition of apocalypse.
> words.
> wild. decadent.
> falling. shedding restraint. dancing…
> dancing—
> FASTER.

words. nouns and periods, and the commas (that map caves, and understand night infused with crossings), all—the recipe of every leaf, all—loaded with dread. italics diagnosing the rent of blood and butcher's bill. gang & timber! south, all the way to "There!" with claws in the game. wordshed—strata-phrase, uncork the tears. wordshed—lifting dauntless verbs. *words!* that light the doom felt last night in Sesqua, to prowl the warrens of Kingsport with kisses of corruption. witness words from hands that reek of smoke. a swirl of thorns hunting marrow… words. gathered. the mirrors and thunder of unshuttered words (glowing and trembling)(each a drum and blade and portal), at the threshold with their avid flint harvesting observations of moor and orbit and afflicted memory. words (explorations and ecstasies… built for whomever listens)…and tangled, uncommon yesterdays (wrapped in beauty… and loneliness) (like those of the master) that cannot disappear in the stream of years.

> dreaming (dusk) (shadows) (dark corners)… revising…
> in the tomb of the master. dreaming. and other tales of terror.

*{Jon Hassell "Last Night the Moon Came"}*

# Jeffrey Thomas

## In Limbo

**Jeffrey Thomas** *is the creator of the acclaimed milieu Punktown. Books in the Punktown universe include the short story collections* Punktown, Voices From Punktown, Punktown: Shades of Gray *(with his brother, Scott Thomas), and* Ghosts of Punktown. *Novels in that setting are* Deadstock, Blue War, Monstrocity, Health Agent, Everybody Scream! *and* Red Cells. *Thomas's other short story collections include* Worship the Night, Thirteen Specimens, Nocturnal Emissions, Doomsdays, Terror Incognita, Unholy Dimensions, AAAEEEIII!!!, Honey is Sweeter Than Blood, *and* Encounters With Enoch Coffin *(with W. H. Pugmire). His other novels are* Letters from Hades, The Fall of Hades, Beautiful Hell, Boneland, Beyond the Door, Thought Forms, Subject 11, Lost in Darkness, The Sea of Flesh and Ash *(with his brother, Scott Thomas),* Blood Society, *and* A Nightmare on Elm Street: The Dream Dealers. *Thomas lives in Massachusetts.*

Anderson awakened to a quiet hissing. As he lay in the dark, his mind scrabbled to make sense of the sound. Steam? Had he left a tea kettle on, to make instant coffee? No, lately he only used his coffee machine. Water running in another apartment, as one of his thinly-partitioned neighbors took a shower? He decided it must be his TV. It was his sole source of companionship these days and he had left it running in the living room, thinking only to lie down in his bedroom for a late afternoon nap.

That was one of the benefits of being unemployed: being able to sleep whenever the inclination occurred. One of the *only* benefits of being unemployed. Three hundred dollars a week hardly seemed a benefit, when it took three weeks for him to accrue enough to pay the rent for this one bedroom basement-level apartment. The last time he'd been laid off, he had been getting five hundred dollars a week, but he had exhausted that claim. Fortunately, a week after the money ran out he'd finally found himself a job via a temp agency, at a biotech company. For all of three months, that is, before he'd been laid off again, and his new unemployment claim was based on that brief tease of employment.

He wondered what it said about his his career choices, his life, or his country that he had been laid off from almost every job he had ever held over the past three and a half decades, since he'd started working at nineteen. He was in his fifties now, and where once he had dreamed he'd be enjoying his last decades in a mellow glow of comfort, here he was having to start anew...and start anew again.

So that muted sizzling sound; was that television static, then? And if so, did that mean his provider had finally moved from threats to actually cutting off his TV service? If that were the case, then he was probably without telephone or Internet service, as well, since all three were part of a bundle deal. Assuming this scenario were correct, he could call the company from his cell phone to restore service, exhausting what he had in the bank, but he'd been saving that for the rent due next week.

Feeling more fatalistic than alarmed, tiredly irritated rather than outraged (one became accustomed to life's subtractions), Anderson swung his legs out of bed and sat on its edge for a moment, waiting for his mind's fog to clear a little. It wasn't just sleep obfuscating his mind. He'd been drinking earlier and earlier each night, and today had begun in the afternoon with his lunch of microwaved lasagna (hard as plastic outside, a cool mush at its center). Three small glasses of cheap, 80 proof rum. Maybe the static he was hearing, he idly thought, was in his own head.

He felt further displaced by the darkness that had fallen since he'd laid down. The sun hadn't fully set then. He looked at his clock radio, saw that it was eight-thirty at night. He'd slept almost three hours.

At last he stood, and padded barefoot across the carpet toward the subdued light from his kitchen, which was separated from his tiny living room by only a low half partition, providing an unconvincing illusion of two rooms. He wore his usual uniform of t-shirt and sweatpants, hadn't even bothered to shower today. Hadn't shaved in a week.

The static sound grew louder, and as he turned into his living room his suspicions were confirmed. A pale gray glow radiated from his dated model TV, its screen showing only a field of sparkling, gritty static. His television looked like a box filled with millions of frenzied, angry little flies.

"Bastards," Anderson muttered, next turning to check his telephone. He didn't expect a dial tone when he lifted the handset to his ear, and sure enough there was none, but instead he heard soft, fizzing static. This wasn't the first time his phone had been cut off, so this static instead of dead air seemed irregular to him. Well, in any case he still had his cell phone, and he had no plan for it that might be canceled; he just added minutes via cards purchased at the supermarket.

After locating his latest unpaid service bill he tapped out his provider's number on the cell phone's keys, but when he sent the call and lifted the little device to his ear, instead of the automated menu he expected would greet him he was simply met with more static. Just as on his home phone.

Murmuring a less articulate curse than before, Anderson studied the phone's tiny screen, saw that he still had seventy minutes of air time. He punched in the number again. Listened again. Static.

"What the fuck?" he hissed, his first thought one of conspiracy. Somehow, they had cut off even his cell phone! But how was that possible? No, that was illogical. He decided to try another number. His parents were both deceased, but he had a sister in New London, Connecticut...

Static.

Okay, he considered, maybe because it wasn't a local call. Randomly, he tried his favorite pizza restaurant, just a short walk from his apartment, because it was an easy number to remember (and if they answered, well, a pizza delivery was always a good thing). But even though he knew the pizza place remained open until ten at night, not only was there no answer, but there was nothing at all except that now familiar sound of millions of trapped flies.

"Doesn't make sense," Anderson complained, shoving the phone across the kitchen table in disgust.

He turned toward his computer, its screen black in sleep mode. His only remaining window on the world, at least in the technological sense. He moved to it, impatiently roused his monitor to brightness.

His desktop image was a photo of himself with his wife taken at Acadia National Park in Maine. They had asked another vacationing couple to take the picture for them. They were standing in front of Jordan Pond, at its far end the softly rounded twin peaks nicknamed the Bubbles. He almost winced when the photo materialized, and wondered why he tormented himself with it.

Tammy had been diagnosed with breast cancer at twenty-seven. Anderson had held her hand through it all: the double mastectomy, the hysterectomy, chemotherapy, radiation. But the cancer, even more determined than Tammy in her struggle, had insinuated itself into the lymph nodes along her trachea and she had died just a year after this photograph was taken—at the young age of thirty-two. Twenty years ago. She'd been gone longer, now, than they'd been married.

Anderson had never remarried, and they had never had children.

When he thought of the jobs that had come and gone, particularly when he'd been drinking, he reflected on the impermanence of anything he had ever produced. His first long-term job, five years working in a boot company—how many of those boots were likely to still exist now? Various positions in a printing company over a span of fifteen years, churning out business cards and stationery, all of that ephemeral paper probably reduced to dust and reabsorbed into the stuff of the universe. Other jobs, some lasting years but others mere months. And never had he helped create anything truly lasting. A bridge, a museum, let alone a painting to hang in a museum, something to outlive him. No, he didn't even have a child to allow him the notion of a borrowed immortality.

But even museums crumbled, he consoled himself. Every painting would degrade and return to a state of disorganized matter, too, eventually. Before that happened, their artists would be forgotten by all but dust-sniffing scholars.

It was natural. It was the way of things. Anderson was not a religious man. He didn't believe he would rejoin Tammy one day, except in the sense that they would both be part of the eternal stew of atoms, ever in flux, ever in the process of construction and destruction.

He had no idea what he was trying to say to himself, with all this muddle. He thought: I'm in a state of *self*-destruction. He smiled at that, sadly, and looked away from his perpetually young wife's face to click on the icon for his web browser.

A window opened, filled the screen. It was entirely white, as Anderson's home page waited to load. It was taking a bit too long.

And then, the flat screen of the LCD monitor was filled with static. Furthermore, he had left his volume turned to 75 the last time he'd used the computer, probably after listening to a poor copy of an old music video on YouTube. So the sound of the static was a roar, and he was startled, fumbled with his mouse to lower the volume to

0. He Xed the window, banishing the static. Back to the placid photo, his wife's gentle smile.

He opened the browser again. Waited again. Static again.

He typed in different web addresses. Google. YouTube. Hotmail. Every time: only static.

"Static on a fucking *computer?*" he exclaimed out loud. He'd never seen it...never heard of such a thing. His fatalistic numbness had turned to rage at last. He ranted, "All right...what the *hell's* going on?"

The droning noise of TV snow exasperated him, and he whirled at the machine vengefully and shut it off altogether.

Yet the whispery background noise continued. More subdued, but it was still there. At first he thought he might not have turned his computer volume down all the way, but then Anderson realized the truth. The sound was coming from outside his apartment.

There were two small windows in the living room, on level with the ground outside, decorative hedges partially obscuring their view. Two small windows in the bedroom, too, all four looking out on the driveway that led to the apartment building's parking lot, around back. On the other side of the driveway was a Knights of Columbus hall, which on every Wednesday night held a bingo game—its yellow windows filled with white-haired heads—and on most Friday nights, rented for parties, boomed annoyingly with either Indian or Brazilian music.

He went to one of the twin living room windows now and pulled the cord to raise the blinds. Then, he took hold of the bottom of the window frame and pushed it upwards, after which he put his face close to the screen, expecting to smell the crisp cool air of an October night.

The air had no smell, but with the window raised the hissing had grown louder, almost as loud as the roar of static had been through his computer speakers. Yet even gazing out into the night, he couldn't tell what was causing the sound, because it was utterly black out there. Normally, however much those hedges might obstruct his view, he'd be seeing streetlights along this tree-lined side street, the floating windows of neighboring houses, even a faint ambient glow rising from the town all around him.

"Power failure," he said to himself, his voice sounding too close, as if the screen trapped it. Yes, it had to be a power failure. It hadn't reached as far as his apartment building, thank God, but had still affected his TV, phone, computer. His services hadn't been shut off, necessarily, after all—thank God. So what had caused the failure? Considering the interference with his devices, he wondered if it had been a solar flare, but then dismissed that as farfetched. Probably something as prosaic as a car hitting a pole. Or while he slept, had there been an unseasonal lightning storm, bringing down a power line? He hadn't listened to the news today. Being laid off, he lived in a kind of insulated world, sometimes not venturing outside for days at a time, sometimes close to a week. The weather had almost become an irrelevancy. The outside world, full of busy workers and married couples, an abstraction.

Since his eyes couldn't penetrate the darkness—it was so inky he couldn't even make out the hedges, so close to his screen—he focused on listening to the hissing sound instead. What *was* that? Static from all the TVs in the other thirty-plus apartments in this cheap little building with its faux brick facade? No, he thought, it must be the stirring of a strong breeze, wind blowing the leaves of trees. Sure, a windstorm could have brought down a power line. During Hurricane Irene, last year, he'd lost power for a day and a half.

Or maybe the hissing was rain. The sibilant noise also sounded like a crackling fire. Or the blown sands of a desert storm. Any or all of the four elements.

Voices behind him caused Anderson to whirl around. Gooseflesh spread down his arms; he had mistakenly believed the voices were coming from his computer speakers, but they were in Spanish, and passing through the hallway on the other side of his flimsy, dung-brown kitchen door.

He crept to the door quietly, not wanting to give himself away as he pressed an eye to the tiny peephole lens.

There had apparently been a string of people chattering past, maybe a family, headed in the direction of the building's front door. (There was another entrance at the other end of the corridor, opening onto the parking lot.) Anderson caught a fleeting, distorted glimpse of a young girl—late teens or early twenties—he saw from time-to-time, though he didn't know which apartment she lived in or even on which of the building's three floors. He always noticed her, however, because she had a pretty face and a very short, curvy body with a protuberant bottom, typically outlined by tight black jeans. He took her to be Mexican, or from somewhere in Central America, like most of the tenants in this building. When he'd first moved here, going on three years ago, he'd been wary of these tenants, particularly the men, but none of them had ever seemed threatening or impolite, even behind his back. Quite the opposite: even the most thuggish-looking teenage boys were quick to hold the door for him if he were carrying groceries, and he had occasionally chatted with a couple of the older women, who seemed to enjoy testing him on what he remembered of his high school Spanish lessons, once he'd admitted to them that he had studied their language for two years.

He held no illusions about inspiring this young woman—any young woman, any woman of *any* age—to fall in love with him, at this stage in his life, but that didn't mean his libido had expired. He felt like the proverbial young man trapped inside an aging man's body. At nineteen, working in that boot company, he had been befriended by an Armenian man in his forties. That man, nicknamed Johnny, has once confessed to Anderson that the years had flashed by like a comet. He was still *young* inside, he protested...as if a cruel trick had been played on him. Anderson had never forgotten those words. Now he was living them.

He figured those people who had passed his door were going to check out what was happening...were going to look out the front door. He was tempted to unlock and open his door, step out into the corridor and join them, but a shyness prevented him. He withdrew from the peephole. Anyway, in case the apparent power outage did spread to their building, he should make preparations.

Anderson drew a kitchen chair over to his refrigerator, stood on the chair to reach a set of cabinets above the fridge, dug out two large candles, a lighter, a flashlight. His "apocalypse stash," he had joked to himself when he'd put these meager supplies aside after the Hurricane Irene experience.

Next he went to his bathroom and started filling his tub with water, in case he did lose power and needed to scoop water into his toilet in order to flush it.

A little excitement didn't really hurt, did it? He almost welcomed this event, whatever its cause. Anything to break up life's monotony.

〰
〰

Anderson was frying two steaks for himself—wanting to use up whatever he had in his fridge before a power loss descended, rather than have to throw food away later—when peripherally he thought he saw a face surface through the shifting pool of interference framed in his computer monitor. He snapped his attention in that direction.

He had shut off his TV, but not his computer, though its volume had remained muted. After some more attempts to go online, he had left a window open. A feed of restless nothingness. As he stared directly at the monitor now, he saw nothing changed. For all its crackling and popping activity, it was as inactive as a gravestone slate blown up to the highest magnification, its molecules electrified yet bound.

Just his imagination, he decided, superimposing structure on chaos. Meaning on the meaningless.

And then he heard a woman scream.

It was out in the hallway. It had made Anderson jump. This time he rushed to his kitchen door and flung it open before he could consider that he might be exposing himself to some danger...or at the very least, to a problem that had nothing to do with him. But the wild, panicky crying that followed the initial cry drew him into the hallway and toward its source: the vestibule of the apartment building's front entrance.

On either side of him, the hallway's walls were plastered with broad trowel strokes, giving them the look of being covered in dirty cake frosting. A number of brown doors interrupted the hall throughout its length. They tended to seal certain odors in the spaces between them. One section might smell enticingly of hamburger cooking for some Mexican dish or other. Another section might smell of incense. This one stank of trapped cigarette smoke, even though smoking was supposed to be against the rules for tenants. At least it beat the chemical fumes that wafted down from the apartment upstairs sometimes. Another tenant had confided to Anderson he believed the young couple up there had a meth lab going.

Anderson pushed through the door before the short set of steps that took one up to ground level and the front vestibule. This was like a little airlock, a cramped telephone-booth space between two glass doors. Within it, on either side, were the apartments' tiny mailboxes. And standing in this tight space, her hands pressed to the glass of the outermost door like suction cups, was one of the female tenants who had tested Anderson on his Spanish. She was still sobbing, staring out into the night.

"Hey," he asked her, "are you okay?"

The short, stocky woman whipped around to face him. Her eyes were ballooned with frenzy, and she started babbling in Spanish, pointing through the glass. "*Mi marido desaparecido!*"

"Slow down," Anderson told her, "I don't understand you...uh, *no lo entiendo.*"

The woman took hold of Anderson's forearm, still pointing behind her at the outer glass door. "My friends...my friends from Apartment 18, upstairs, they went outside to see what was going on. They told my husband they were going to go look..."

"Yes?" Anderson prompted her. Had that been the family he had heard passing his door? That attractive young girl amongst them?

After drawing in a shuddery gulp of air, the woman continued, "They didn't come back...we checked. We knocked and knocked on their door. They left it unlocked, so we went in and no one was there. So my husband, Enrique, Enrique said let's go outside and see if they're out there." The woman glanced over her shoulder at the door. Her bright but transparent reflection was superimposed over the darkness. "When I saw it was so black out there, I told Enrique don't go. It didn't look right...I was afraid..."

Anderson looked through her reflection. So he wasn't the only one who had thought it just looked too dark out there. Unnaturally dark. Even, perhaps, for a power loss.

"Enrique opened the door." Her sobbing was growing breathless, her words harder to get out. Her fingers crushed Anderson's arm. "I told him don't step outside...*I told him!* But...but..."

"But what? What happened?"

She looked up into Anderson's eyes beseechingly. "He stepped into the black and he was gone! In one second...just gone! I couldn't see him! I couldn't...I couldn't hear him! Only that *sound.*"

"Look," Anderson told her soothingly, "there's been a power outage. It's just really dark out there." Somehow he didn't sound convincing even to himself. What they were both feeling...about the unnaturalness of the darkness...it was an instinctual, intuitive reaction.

"No...*no!*" she insisted, hysterical. "It's like the black just *swallowed* him!"

Then, something beyond the woman caught Anderson's attention, and he said more to himself than to her: "Hey."

The woman turned to follow his gaze. When she saw that thin black wisps, like inky tendrils of smoke, were flowing around the edges of the door, she shrieked.

Was it smoke? Was there a fire nearby, and the smoke was so thick out there it obscured all vision? But why then wouldn't they be smelling it? And somehow these wisps—though pitch black—suggested to Anderson a grainy, gritty, and restless quality...as if the snaking tendrils were composed of millions of tiny seething particles. Like the swarming flecks of static on his computer screen.

The lights went out in the hallway.

The woman's wailing was ear-piercing. She clawed at Anderson irrationally, and he ducked his face away from her. Still, her nails raked his neck. And then she seemed to fall at his feet. Anderson reached down for her, and for a second his fingers brushed against her back, but then she didn't seem to be there anymore.

Her screams were abruptly cut off. The hallway became silent... except for the muffled hiss beyond the glass door.

Anderson spun away, blundered in the direction of his apartment, so unseeing that his eyes might have been burnt out of his skull. His left hand felt ahead of him along the wall, with its rough plastered texture. He struck one of the hallway's interspersed doors, shoved it away from him, and now felt at the wall on the left-hand side. Desperately, clawing like the woman had clawed at him. He resisted looking over his shoulder. It would be pointless. His right hand finally closed on a doorknob. What if he had the wrong apartment, and the door was locked? But it turned in his hand, he slipped inside, slammed the door shut and locked it.

The smoke had got around the edges of the glass door...the gap under his door was much wider. Still, with no other plan, Anderson felt his way across his lightless kitchen to where he always draped a bath towel over that little half partition between rooms, to dry his hands on when he worked at the sink. Groping wildly, he found the towel, turned back in the direction of the door (he hoped) and got down on hands and knees. He felt for the door, found it, pressed the towel against that empty wedge at its bottom. The act offered scant relief, but again, at the moment it was better than nothing.

He got back to his feet, next felt for the counter. His heart's hammering seemed to cause his every movement to misfire. Finally, though, he located the candles and lighter he had set down there a short time earlier. He thumbed the lighter's grooved wheel, got a flame, and lit the wick of first one fat candle in its jar, and then a second.

Now holding one of these candles before him—as if its ghostly flame and meager fluttering light were enough to ward off the unknowable immensity of the universe—he stepped a little closer to the door, staring at the towel he had pushed up against its bottom edge.

He expected to see tendrils curling and coiling into the room around this paltry barrier, a blacker black than the room's darkness, but as yet there were none.

Anderson remembered the window he had left open. Would its flimsy metal screen be enough to hold back the blackness, or would it now be filtering its way through the mesh? He turned quickly and, still holding the candle before him, hurried to the far side of the living room. To think he had put his face close to the screen, only a brief while ago! Now he was reluctant even to reach out and close the window, lest a thick black tentacle formed of coalesced darkness tore through the screen and wrapped around his wrist. But he got the window closed, and turned the lever to lock it. He then locked the window beside it, moved into his bedroom to lock those two windows as well.

He stepped backwards from the windows, into the middle of his bedroom floor, and stood there with his candle.

He realized he was holding his breath, as if afraid to draw the darkness into his lungs.

He realized he was waiting.

〰〰

When he returned to the kitchen, to check on the door again—still no insinuating tendrils—he glanced at the counter beside the sink and saw his flashlight lying there beside his lighter. Stupid: in his panic he had forgotten the most important of the supplies he had stashed after last year's hurricane and outage. He set down the candle and picked up the flashlight instead.

After sweeping a beam of light across the bottom of the kitchen door he switched off the flashlight to conserve its batteries. Then, by candlelight, he rummaged in the cabinets under his kitchen sink until he found what he was looking for: a silver-gray roll of duct tape.

He got down on the floor beside the bottom of his apartment's door, moved the towel aside, and before any fingers of blackness could come creeping under the door drew a long strip of tape across the gap. He fortified that with several more strips. Then, he sealed the length of the door on both sides, and finally the thin space across the top.

Every residence by law was required to have two means of egress in case of fire, preferably a back way out. His own second way out—typical of all the building's apartments—was simply another door opening into the same hallway. In his case, this door was right around the other side of the kitchen wall, near his bathroom. So he went to this door and outlined it in duct tape as well.

What about the four little windows? He considered this, told himself the windows were fairly new and had never been drafty, seemed pretty airtight.

But moments later he was sealing the edges of the windows with duct tape, too.

He used up what he'd had left of tape on the roll, but at least it wasn't until he'd covered the edges of all four windows. Then he remembered he had another roll in the cabinet under his bathroom sink, because his shower head had been leaking and he'd once done a bandage job on it.

Duct tape against the universe. Sure, it made sense to a human and an American, he thought, trying to humor himself. Not that he succeeded much in that attempt. His humor was as pathetic a protection as the tape itself.

Whatever this phenomenon...this *force*...was, it would have him when it was ready. When the stain had spread further. Stain? There he was thinking like an arrogant human again. This blackness was purity, wasn't it? He and his kind were the stain. A stain to be cleansed... eradicated.

The thought that the blackness might be sentient terrified him. But even more terrifying, perhaps, was the thought that it held no intelligence. That it was mindless...indifferent. That it had no intent, no mission. That it just *was*.

Creeping stealthily from room to room (all two of them), Anderson listened for sounds of humanity around him. Often on the other side of the wall from his sink, he'd hear the neighbor's shower running and running. God, did they take long showers. But now, nothing. Above him in the kitchen/living room, he'd frequently hear children running up and down the creaky floor. Sometimes, when he lay in bed, directly overheard he'd listen to the rhythmic squeaking of bed springs. People making love (maybe that young couple who were rumored to be running a meth lab). The sound would torment him with memories of his young wife. Torment him with the fact that he hadn't been to bed with another person, even casually, in almost a decade.

But there were no sounds from the apartment above, either. He was tempted to fetch a broom, pound the tip of its handle against his ceiling to see if he could establish communication. And then what? Communicate in Morse code? He didn't know it. And what if by making a loud sound he attracted the blackness to him? Maybe it didn't realize he was still in here. Maybe he had slipped past its notice altogether, where the others had been less lucky.

Maybe he should blow out his candles, lest the blackness peek in through the thin slits in the Venetian blinds over his windows. Maybe if he sat here in the dark, overlooked, until...

...until what? Help came? The National Guard? The cavalry? The *day*?

He greatly suspected that day would never dawn again. Once more, it was an intuition. He felt it in his gut.

He found himself standing unmoving in the center of the kitchen floor, tensed up as if he might bolt into a run at any second. Run where? Into a wall?

Slowly he became aware of dumb physical sensations. For one, his throat was dry. He was thirsty. He had milk in the fridge and he told himself he should start drinking it before it went bad. But at the same time, even the thought of putting anything into his knotted stomach at this point made him want to vomit. Besides, when the milk had run out, when the food had run out, and all he had left was tap water, then what? Slowly starve? So why even bother at all?

He was going to die. Or maybe not so much die, he thought, as cease to be...as if there were a difference. Curiously, he was not falling to his knees weeping, pounding the walls with his fists, yelling at the top of his lungs. Despite his fear, running through every nerve like an electrical current, despite the nausea, he was oddly calm. Was it brave acceptance? More likely it was the soul having been clubbed down so thoroughly that all it could do was blink and...wait. But this clubbing hadn't only occurred tonight. He felt it had been going on for decades now. Since Tammy's death, but even before that, really. Maybe from the day of his birth, that beating, that hammering, had begun. Maybe that was why new souls came into this world screaming.

He had made the mistake, and not just once, of watching videos on the Internet of beheadings by Middle Eastern terrorists and by Mexican drug cartels. Morbid curiosity, he supposed, some kind of masochistic fascination. Masochistic, because these videos had horrified and depressed him. And they had frustrated him, too, because not once did he see one of these victims really fight back, spit or curse at his executioners, kick at them or struggle much. But now he understood what they had been feeling. That clubbed sensation. Dazed, waiting for the *coup de grace*. Breaking the neck off the bottle was only an afterthought. The soul had already been voided.

Another dumb sensation niggled at him. He realized he had to urinate.

"Stupid cow," he chuckled, speaking to his own body. He realized a tear dribbled down one cheek. He wiped it away on the back of his hand, and turned toward his bathroom. He took one of the candles with him, along with the flashlight, figuring he'd leave that candle burning in the bathroom when he was done. The other candle he left on the kitchen counter.

As he started around the corner of the kitchen wall, into the tiny hallway that ended at his fire escape door, the kitchen went dark behind him.

The candle had been snuffed out, just in the time it had taken him to turn his back on it. Had the wick drowned in the liquefied wax cupped in the top of the candle? Or had the candle ceased to exist?

These questions fired through his brain in the merest fraction of a second. He didn't look back. His only instinct was to thumb his flashlight on and dive into the bathroom. Inside, he hastily set down the remaining candle on the sink, then slammed the door shut behind him. He turned the lock in the knob.

Then, however much he had been philosophically ruminating on his fatalism, he still squatted down and searched under the sink until he uncovered the other roll of duct tape.

He commenced sealing off the bathroom door. Well, why not? These pitiful impulses toward survival were just more dumb physical urges, like wanting to drink and to pee. Let the poor cow go through its motions. He pitied it, as if he were an entity apart from it.

With the four sides of the door patched over, he set the tape aside and stood there facing it. Was this the last little cube of humanity, this room? The final cell for the last human soul? A toilet. How ignoble, he thought. How fitting.

While he was waiting he might as well empty his bladder, so he did. He didn't flush the bowl, though; didn't want to make undue sound. Candlelight reflected on the water standing in his tub. It was like the surface of some pond at night. Mellow. Calming. He sat down on the closed lid of his toilet. He stared at the water. He thought of Jordan Pond.

His candle flickered for one instant, as if a breeze he couldn't feel were passing across it, and then the flame was extinguished.

He wanted to jump to his feet, but he didn't think his legs would support him. Though he held no religious beliefs, Anderson whispered, "Oh God."

He thumbed the switch of the flashlight. It was as if the batteries had died. There was no beam.

The blackness was absolute. Was this what it felt like, then, to be swallowed as that woman's husband, Enrique, had been? And yet he still drew air into his lungs. He was still conscious of his body. Was this how he was to spend eternity? Not tortured by demons, but locked alone in a little room? Not the acute agonies of Hell, but a subtler kind of suffering? The suffering of being apart…disconnected? Now that the end had come for his kind—for whatever reason, if there needed to be a reason for an ant hill to be trampled—would every soul be caged in its own tiny cell, isolated from every other soul? Though in a way, hadn't it always been that way? Each of them caged in the cells of their bodies?

Then Anderson became aware that he could see the door in front of him. Dimly, but he could just make it out in the murk. The silvery duct tape even seemed to be reflecting a soft radiance. He could see his hands, gripping his knees as he sat there on the toilet lid.

Anderson stood up, turned and faced the source of the strengthening glow.

He was face-to-face with a screen of silent, seething static. Gray and white and black pixels, dancing like agitated subatomic particles. But this was not his TV screen, nor even his computer screen. This field of shimmering static was the mirror over his bathroom sink.

Anderson gazed into the mirror. It being a mirror, he waited for his own reflected face to form from those electrified motes. Was his the face he had glimpsed peripherally on his computer monitor? Did the end entail looking into your own soul?

And a face did begin to materialize, vaguely, from the churning interference. It didn't come into sharp focus, and it was not in the colors or textures of physical life, and yet he recognized its outline, the shape of its features.

He recognized it as Tammy's face.

A tear coursed down his cheek again, but Anderson was smiling as he stretched out his arm.

Smiling as he reached through the glass.

# Richard Gavin

## A Cavern of Redbrick

**Richard Gavin** *writes numinous fiction in the tradition of Algernon Blackwood and Arthur Machen. To date he has published four short-story collections, including* The Darkly Splendid Realm *(Dark Regions Press, 2009) and* At Fear's Altar *(Hippocampus Press, 2012). He has also authored esoteric works and essays that explore the philosophical underpinnings of Horror. A resident of Ontario, Canada, Richard welcomes readers at richardgavin.net*

See now as the boy sees. Bear witness to a summerworld, a place sparkling with clear light and redolent with the fragrance of new-mown grass and where the air itself hosts all the warmth and weightlessness of bathwater.

It is the first morning in this summerworld and, knowing that autumn is but a pinpoint in the future, Michael stands on the porch of his grandparents' country home and allows the elation to erupt inside him. He then mounts his bicycle and rides headlong into the season.

The town whisks past him in a verdant smear. But Michael holds his destination firmly in his mind's eye.

The gravel pit on the edge of town has long been his private sanctuary. He has escaped to that secret grey place more times than he can possibly remember. It is his own summer retreat, one of the many highlights of spending the summer with his grandparents in the little village of Cherring Point.

Visiting the pits is technically trespassing; his grandfather, who is charged by the government to occasionally man and maintain the place, has often told him to keep away from the place. Thus Michael keeps his mild transgressions to himself. Clearly he isn't the only one to sneak into the secluded area. He isn't the one who has cut the hole into the chain-link fence that distinguishes the property line, though he *does* always make sure to re-cover this portal with the brush that camouflages it.

Michael consoles himself with the logic that he really never disruptes anything in the pits. On his bike he would race over the mounds, which he likes to imagine as being the burial sites of behemoths. He loves watching his tires summon dirty fumes of gravel dust. Often that instant when his bike soars past the tipping point at the mounds' summit, Michael feels as though he is flying.

It is his private ritual of summer elation; harmless and pure.

Except that today, on his inaugural visit of the season, Michael discovers that his ritual ground is no longer private...

His initial reaction to seeing the girl beyond the fence is shock, a feeling that gives way to an almost dizzying sense of disbelief.

At the far end of the lot is a large redbrick storage shed, its door of corrugated metal shut firm and secured with a shiny silver padlock. Michael has often fantasized about all manner of treasure being stored within those walls.

Standing on the shed's roof is a girl whom Michael guesses to be no older than he is. She is dressed in a t-shirt only slightly whiter than her teeth. Her straw-coloured hair hangs to the middle of her back. Her bare feet are uncannily balanced at the very summit of the shed's pitched roof, yet she does not teeter or wave her arms to maintain this daring balance. She is as stationary as a totem.

Michael can feel her eyes upon him.

He veers his bike away and rides the paths above the gravel yard for a while, cutting sloppy figure-eights in the dirt while wrestling with whether or not he should retreat. What exactly is she trying to prove standing on the shed that way? What if she tries to speak to him, to suss out his reasons for coming here? What if this place is in fact *her* special place? Perhaps *he* has been the real outlander all this time.

Michael veers his bike cautiously back to the hidden gap in the fence, hoping, foolishly, that the girl will flee. He crouches low on his bike and glides to where the brush is thickest.

"*What's your name?*"

The sound of her voice chills Michael. He wonders how she has spied him. Does her position on the roof make her all-seeing?

Like a surrendering soldier, Michael rides out from behind the greenery, clears the entrance to the pits and eases his bike toward the shed.

"How did you get up there?" he asks.

"*Do you live near here?*"

Michael frowns. "No. My grandparents do."

*"You're not supposed to be in here, you know."*

"Neither are *you!*" Michael spits. He feels a strange and sudden rage overcoming him. Somehow his childish anxiety over seeing an interloper in his sanctuary pales beneath a fiery anger, something near to hatred. It erupts with such sharpness that Michael actually feels himself flinch, as though he's been shocked by some hidden power line. Why should the girl anger him so? He wonders what it is about the nature of her innocuous questions that makes him despise her.

He pedals closer and is opening his mouth to say something, just what Michael isn't sure, when a searing glint on the girl's body forces him to screw up his face. Shielding his eyes with one hand, Michael gives the girl a long and scrutinizing glare.

And then he truly sees her...

Sees the flour-pale and bruise-blue pallor of her skin, sees the nuggets of crystallized water that form in her hair, in the folds of her oversized T-shirt, on her rigid ill-coloured limbs. Her eyes are almost solid white, but instinctively Michael knows that blindness is not the cause.

When she again asks Michael what his name is, her voice rises from somewhere in the gravel pits and not from her rigid face, for the girl's jaw remains locked. For a beat Michael wonders if she is frozen solid.

To answer this thought, the girl suddenly raises her ice-scabbed arms as if to claim him.

Michael's actions are so frantic they must appear as one vast and hectic gesture: the shriek, the rearing around of his bike, the aching, desperate scaling of the gravel mound, the piercing push through the tear in the fence, the breathless race across the fields.

Michael rides. And rides.

The distance Michael places between himself and the gravel yard brings little relief. Not even the sight of his grandparents' home calms him. He rushes up their driveway, allows his bike to drop, then runs directly to the tiny guestroom that serves as his bedroom every summer vacation.

Burying his face in his pillow, Michael listens to the sound of approaching footsteps.

"Mikey, you all right?"

His grandmother's musical voice is a balm to him. Michael lifts his head, but when he sees the reddish stains that mar his grandmother's fingers and the apron she's wearing he winces.

"What is it, son?"

He points a bent finger and his grandmother laughs.

"It's strawberries, silly. I'm making jam. I saw you come tearing up the road like the devil himself was at your heels."

Michael wipes his mouth. "Grandma, do you believe in ghosts?"

Her brow lifts behind her spectacles. "Ghosts? No, I can't say that I do, Mikey. Why?"

His account of the experience reaches all the way to the tip of Michael's tongue, but at the last instant he bites it back. He shakes his head, stays silent.

His grandmother frowns. "Too much time in the sun, dear. Why don't you lie down for a while? I'll wake you for lunch."

Michael nods. His grandmother's suggestion sounds very good indeed. He reclines his head back onto the pillows and shuts out the world.

He doesn't realize he's dozed off until he feels his grandmother nudging him. Perspiration has dried on his hair and skin, which makes him feel clammy. He shivers and then groggily makes his way to the kitchen to join his grandparents for sandwiches.

"What happened, sleepyhead?" his grandfather teases. "You didn't tire yourself out on the first day, did you?"

His grandfather receives a sardonic swat from his grandmother, which makes Michael laugh.

"He probably just rode too long in the heat," she says.

"Oh? Where'd you ride to?"

"Just...around." Michael bites into his sandwich, hoping that this line of questioning will end.

"Mikey asked me a little earlier if I believed in ghosts." His grandmother sets a tumbler of milk down in front of Michael as she settles into her chair.

"Ghosts? What brought that on?"

Michael shrugs. "Nothing. I was just wondering."

He cannot be sure, but Michael feels that his grandfather's glare on him has hardened.

〰〰

Michael remains indoors, the only place he feels relatively secure, for the rest of the day. He helps his grandmother jar up the last of her jams and wash up afterwards. He watches cartoons while she prepares supper. His grandfather is outdoors, labouring on one of the seemingly endless projects which occupies so much of his time. He is a veritable stranger in the house. Last summer Michael had tried to assist him with the various chores, but he got the feeling that his grandfather found him more of a burden than an aid. So this year he takes his mother's advice and just stays out of his grandfather's way.

Though he's never been mean, his grandfather does give off an air that Michael finds far less pleasant than that of his grandmother. She is always cheerful, brimming with old family stories or ideas of various things that he could help her with. Grandma's chores never feel like work.

After supper Michael's mother phones to see how his first day went. He is oddly grateful for the deep homesickness that hearing her voice summons; it means that he doesn't have to think about what he'd seen that morning. His mother says she'll be up to visit on the weekend.

The late morning nap and mounting anxieties make sleep almost impossible for Michael. He lies in his bed, which suddenly feels uncomfortably foreign, and wrestles with the implications of what he has seen, what he has *experienced*, for the encounter was far more than visual. Standing in the presence of that girl, whatever she had been, made the world feel different. Just recollecting the event made Michael feel dizzy.

Maybe his grandmother is right, maybe he has been riding too hard under the hot sun. After a time Michael understands that the only way he can put the incident behind him is to return to the pits, to test what he'd seen or thought he had seen. His teacher last year told him the first rule when learning about science and nature is that you must repeat the experiment. If you want to know the truth about something you have to do the same thing more than once. If the results are the same, then what you've found is something real.

Tomorrow he will go back. He will find the truth.

〽

The girl is nowhere to be found. Michael rides out after breakfast, despite his grandmother advising him against it. He promises her he will ride slowly and in the shade, and that he'll be home to help her with lunch.

Michael is so elated by the absence of the ugly vision that he plunges through the rip in the chain-link and begins to scale and shoot down the gravel mounds at a manic pace. Dust mushrooms up in his wake. Michael feels unfettered from everything.

The sound of an approaching vehicle startles him to such a degree that he almost loses his balance.

Glancing up to where the country lane meets the gate of the gravel pit, Michael spies his grandfather's pickup truck. He performs a quick shoulder check, panicked by the distance that stretches between him and the hole in the fence.

His grandfather steps out of the cab. Realizing that he has no time to escape, Michael hunches low and pedals behind the farthest gravel mound. There he dismounts, crouches, and is punished by the thundering heartbeat in his ears.

The gate is unlocked, de-chained. The pickup truck comes crawling down along the narrow path, parking before the shed. Michael doesn't hear the engine shut off and he wonders if his grandfather is just waiting for him to come out from behind the mound so he can run him down.

But then the engine is silent and is soon followed by the rumbling sound which signifies the corrugated metal door being opened. Has the ghost-girl flung the door open from the inside? Perhaps she has attacked his grandfather. Michael swallows. With utmost caution he creeps to the edge of the mound and peers.

It is dark inside the shed, so dark that it looks boundless; a deep cavern of redbrick. Michael can just discern the faintest suggestions of objects: power tools, equipment of various shapes, overfilled shelves of metal. The only item that stands out is the white box. It glows against the gloom and puts Michael in mind of Dracula's coffin. But the sight of its orange power light glowing like a match flame confirms to Michael that it is nothing more than a freezer.

The shed's corrugated door is drawn down. His grandfather must have chores to attend to in the shed. It likely won't take him long to locate whatever tools he needs. Michael steals the opportunity to rush back to the tear and escape.

He races out to the bridge above West Creek. There he settles into a shady spot, dangles his legs over the bridge's edge and studies catfish squirming along the current. Near noon, Michael mounts his bike and rides back to his grandparents' home.

The pickup truck is parked in the driveway. He takes a deep

breath, praying that his grandfather hasn't seen him making his escape.

"I'm home, grandma," he calls from the foyer.

Entering the kitchen, Michael is startled by the sight of his grandfather fidgeting at the counter.

"She went into town to run some errands," he says. "Sit down, your lunch is ready."

Michael does as he is told. His grandfather plunks down a bowl of stewed tomatoes before him, along with a glass of milk. He nests himself at the far end of the table and chews in silence.

His stomach knots. Michael chokes down the slippery fruit in his bowl.

"I suppose I should have had you wash your hands before we sat down," his grandfather remarks. "You're pretty filthy. You've got dust all over your clothes and hands."

Michael freezes. His grandfather's gaze remains fixed on the food in his dish, which he spoons up and eats in a measured rhythm.

When his bowl is empty, his grandfather sets down his spoon and lifts his eyes to Michael's. "I have a confession to make," he begins. "You know yesterday when your grandmother brought up the topic of ghosts? Well, can you keep a secret, just between us?"

Michael nods.

"You swear it?"

"I swear."

"Cross your heart?"

Michael does so.

"All right then. I wasn't being honest when I said I didn't believe in them. The fact is I do. I saw a ghost once myself."

"You did?"

"Yes. Well, it was something *like* a ghost. I think what I saw was actually a jinn."

"A jinn?"

"A jinn is a spirit, Michael. Legend says they are created by fire. They can take all kinds of forms; animals, people. But they're very dangerous."

"What did the jinn that you saw look like?" Michael asks breathlessly.

"It was in the form of a young girl."

Michael feels his palms growing damp. "Where did you see her?"

"In the woods, not too far from here. I think she was planning to burn the forest down. That's what the jinn do; they bring fire."

"And did she?"

His grandfather shakes his head.

"So what happened?"

His grandfather tents his hands before him. "They say the only way to combat the element of fire is with ice..."

And with that, a silent tension coils between child and elder, winding tighter like a spring. Michael is confused, curious, and scared. He doesn't know what to do or say.

"Young boys get curious, and when they get curious they sometimes discover things that give them the wrong impression of what the world is like. There are always two sides to things, Michael," his grandfather advises. "There is the appearance of things and then there is what lies beneath. I want you to remember that, boy. Don't base your opinions of the world on how it appears. Always try to remember what lies beneath. Sometimes the things that appear to be the most innocent are the most dangerous, and vice versa. It was a long time before I knew this, so I want you to learn it while you're young. You understand?"

Michael nods even though he does not at all understand.

The sound of his grandmother turning into the driveway brings Michael a relief that borders on gleeful. He runs to her. His grandfather rises and dutifully clears the table.

～～～

The remainder of the day moves at a crawl as Michael searches for a way to probe his grandfather further about the jinn. Is this what he has seen? No, what he's seen looks more like a spirit born of ice. Either way, the woods that surrounded the old gravel pits are obviously haunted, and that means they are dangerous. By bedtime that night Michael has resolved to never again visit the gravel pits. He will find other ways to amuse himself.

He has almost managed to convince himself that everything is right with the world when the girl appears again, this time inside his grandparents' house.

It is the dead of night and Michael is returning to his bed after relieving himself. She stands in the hallway, her flesh phosphorescent in the darkness. The nuggets of ice sparkle in her hair like a constellation of fallen stars.

Michael is bolted in place. His jaw falls open as if weighted. He looks at her but somehow isn't truly seeing her. In the back of his mind Michael wonders if what he is experiencing is what lies beneath the surface of the girl and not merely her appearance.

The girl neither speaks nor moves. She stands like a coldly morbid statue, with one arm jutting toward the wall of the corridor.

Michael's gaze hesitantly runs along the length of the girl's extended arm, and her pointing finger. Is she indicating the unused phone jack on the wall? Michael turns back to face her but before him there now stretches only darkness.

He lingers in the vacated hallway for eons before finally crouching down to investigate the phone jack. It is set into the moulding, which Michael's grandmother always keeps clean and waxed. Michael clasps the jack's white plastic covering and tugs at it. It pops loose.

Within it Michael discovers a pair of keys. One of them is larger than the other and has the words 'Tuff Lock' engraved on its head. The smaller key is unmarked.

A creak of wood somewhere inside the house acts as a warning to Michael. He hurriedly recovers the jack and slips back to his room where he lies in thought until the sun at last burns away the shadows.

〰

Only after he hears his grandfather fire up his old pickup and drive off—Is he going back to his secret redbrick vault at the gravel pits?— does Michael leave his room.

His grandmother is sitting on the living room sofa. She seems smaller somehow, almost deflated.

"Morning," Michael says, testing her mood.

"Good morning, dear," she replies. Her tone is distant, a swirl of unfocused words.

"Where's grandpa?"

She stands. "He had some chores to do. Are you hungry?" She advances to the kitchen without waiting for Michael's response.

"You all right, grandma?"

She forces a chortle. "I'm fine, Mikey, just fine. Your grandpa just seemed a little out of sorts this morning and I guess I'm a bit worried about him, that's all."

Michael feels his face flush. "What's the matter with him?"

"He didn't sleep well." She seems to be attempting to drown out her own voice by clattering pans and beating eggs in a chrome bowl. "Your grandpa has bad dreams sometimes, and when he does he wakes up very cranky and fidgety."

"Oh."

When they sit down to eat Michael wrestles to find what he hopes is a clever method of interrogation. He needs so badly to know...

"Does grandpa ever talk about what his bad dreams are about?"

"No."

"Do you ever have bad dreams?"

"Almost never, dear. I think the last time was a couple years ago when there was some bad business here in the village."

"What happened?"

"A girl went missing." She speaks the words more into her coffee cup than to Michael, but even muffled they stun him.

"Missing?"

His grandmother nods. "She was one of the summer people, came up here with her family. I'd see her walking to and from the beach almost every day by herself. Then one day she went down to swim but never came back. Must have drowned, poor thing. They dragged the lake but she was never found. A terrible event. Felt so bad for her mother and father. That's why your grandfather and I never let you go to the beach unsupervised."

"Do you remember what she looked like?"

She shrugs. "Thirteen-years-old or so. Blonde hair, I recall that much."

Michael excuses himself from the table. His jimmying open of the phone jack is masked by the noises of his grandmother washing the breakfast dishes.

"Think I'll go for a ride," he tells her.

"Be careful, dear. Have fun."

⁂

Throughout his race to the gravel pits Michael senses that the village is somehow made out of eyes. He passes no one, but is terrified by the prospect of encountering his grandfather at the pits.

The area is equally abandoned. The cavern of redbrick sits snugly locked, illuminated by a hot dappling of sunlight. He enters the breach in the fence and fishes out the pair of keys from his pocket.

He marries the one labelled Tuff Lock with the padlock that bears the same engraving. The lock gives easily. The clunking noise startles a murder of crows from their nest. Michael cries out at their sudden cawing, wing-flapping reprimand. He quickly looks about, terrified of being caught.

The gravel mounds are as ancient hills, silent and patient and indifferent to all human activity. Michael removes the padlock and struggles to raise the corrugated door. It rattles up its track, revealing the musty, cluttered darkness.

Like an ember, the orange light of the freezer gleams from the back of the shed.

Michael feels about for a light switch but finds none. With great care he makes his way to the light. He is like a solider crossing a minefield. Every motorized tool, every stack of bagged soil, is a danger.

He reaches the freezer. Its surface is gritty with dust. He sees the metal clamp that holds its lid shut. It is secured with another padlock. Before he's fully realized what he is doing, Michael inserts the smaller key and frees the open padlock from its loop. He can hear the freezer buzzing and he wonders if he is truly ready to see what it contains.

'You've gone this far,' he tells himself. He pulls the lid up from the frame.

Frost funnels upward, riding on the gust of manufactured arctic air. Like ghosts, the cold smoke flies and vanishes.

A bundled canvas tarp reposes within the freezer's bunk. Its folds are peppered with ice, its drab earthy brownness in sharp contrast to the white banks of frost that have accumulated on the old freezer's walls. The tarp is secured with butcher's twine, which Michael cannot break, so instead he wriggles one of the canvas flaps until his aching fingers can do no more.

But what he has done is enough. Through the small part in the bundle the whitish, lidless eye stares back at him, like a waxing moon orbiting in the microcosmic blackness of the canvas shroud.

Michael whimpers. All manner of emotion assails him at once, rendering him wordless.

A shadow steps in front of the open shed door. Michael spins around, allowing the freezer lid to slam down. His grandfather has caught him. Michael sees his future as one encased in stifling ice.

But the figure in the doorway is too slight to be his grandfather.

Michael then sees the ghost-eyes staring at him from the dim face. A face that is brightened by rows of teeth as the girl grins. She bolts off into the woods.

"Wait!" Michael cries. He stumbles across the littered shed, but by the time he reaches the gravel pits she has gone.

*What do I do?* Michael keeps thinking as he locks both freezer and shed. He needs help.

His confusion blurs the ride back to his grandmother.

It also makes him doubt what he sees once the house comes into view.

His grandfather's pickup is once more in the driveway. Beyond it the entire house is engulfed in flames.

Neighbours are rushing about the property, seemingly helpless. Michael speeds up to the lawn, jumps off his bike and attempts to run through the front door.

A man stops him. "No, son! We've called the fire department. Stay back, stay back!"

Ushered to the edge of his grandparents' property, Michael can see the window of their bedroom. The lace curtain is being eaten by fire, allowing him a heat-weepy view of the figures that are lying on the twin beds inside. He sees his grandmother, who appears to be bound to her bed with ropes. Next to her, Michael's grandfather lies unbound, a willing sacrifice. The large can of gasoline stands on the floor between them. The pane shatters from the heat.

Michael feels his gaze being tugged to the trees at the end of the yard, where some kind of animal is skittering up the limbs with ease.

In the distance, sirens are wailing their lament.

# Scott Nicolay

## Eyes Exchange Bank

*Over half a century back a child was born amidst the toxic waste dumps and devil haunted swamps of New Jersey ... 26 years later that child packed all he could fit in a '72 Dodge Challenger and lit out for the high desert of northwest New Mexico and the Navajo Nation, where if the dogs bark at night it is only the skinwalkers ... along the way he had three children and held jobs including dishwasher, restaurant and hotel cook, factory worker, camera salesman, DJ, security guard, teacher, and sheepherder ... as a teacher he and his students cofounded the New Mexico Youth Poetry Slam and the National Youth Poetry Slam ... as a caver and archaeologist he studied and explored the caves and lava tubes of Belize, Easter Island, and the U.S. Southwest ... several years ago he tailed Jack Spicer's Martian to the uncertain boundary between our reality and the cobbly worlds ... now he spends his nights there peering through a grimy window and reports what he sees. Fedogan & Bremer published* Ana Kai Tangata, *his first book of weird horror tales in 2014.*

"*On prend un peu de recul. On abandonne la douleur un instant—on s'éloigne. IL N'Y AVAIT QU'à FERMER LES YEUX—*"
—Maurice Roche, *Compact*

Ray Bevacqua hated what winter did to central Jersey, but he was barely over the bridge from Lambertville before he decided he hated it even worse in eastern Pennsylvania. The everywhere dull grayness, the dirt and soot fouling the plow-curled mounds of snow along the roads, all that was the same. But west of the

Delaware, rows of low and lumpy hills ate the daylight, and last week's snow had not even begun to melt.

Route 202 was a tunnel through a shadowed world whose brightest color was brown. Woods that in spring or summer would offer green relief from the drab and dreary towns were gnawed to bleak orchards of black bone. Ray's mood already sucked, and the PA landscape only aggravated it.

Even without the miserable scenery, Ray experienced increasingly mixed feelings about this trip. Spending the weekend with Danny and Colleen, having to sit through their lovey-dovey bullshit...this was not looking like the best way to heal his own mangled emotions. Worse, the last time he saw them was the day he and Lisa drove down to help them move into that same dingy little apartment in Lansdale. The high point of their trip was almost getting caught mauling each other in Danny's bathroom when they thought everyone else was downstairs, and that meant he would be reminded of Lisa every time he took a leak, standing there with his dick in his hand...

Lansdale. It looked even more dismal than the other sorry-ass towns he'd driven through to get there. More boarded up shops, more abandoned vehicles, everything grayer, deader. A total shithole. But this was where the last of his three best friends had packed off to with his just out of high school girlfriend.

It was always the four of them: Danny, Luke, Lisa, and Ray. Danny and Ray grew up in the same central Jersey burb, friends since junior high. They met Luke and Lisa freshman year at Rutgers. Lisa that first week of Freshman Comp, when she leaned across the aisle to him while their untenured junior prof scrawled a line from "Sailing to Byzantium" on the board, and said, "I must tell you, this man knows absolutely fuck-all about William Butler Yeats." And, oh, there it was: that accent...Dublin and Manchester blended so smoothly as to give the lie to the shattered marriage that produced her.

Two months later they met Luke at a party in Frelinghuysen, the tower dorm on the Raritan River where he lived on the special floor reserved for students in the Fine Arts Honors program. It was Lisa who got the invite, but she and Ray and Danny were already inseparable by then and she brought them along. Luke, Mr. Perfect Hair and Tortoise-Shell Frames, cornered Ray to ask who his friend was, the blonde, and they struck up a conversation about *symbolisme* in art and literature, Odilon Redon and Rimbaud. And then they were four. Ray always considered himself the pivot that brought them together, made them a group, the Nick Fury of their Avengers. Had he thought they'd be a team forever? Wrong again. Truth was, the whole thing began falling apart months before the class of '90 walked.

First Danny found this young bimbo from Temple over Christmas Break, just a frosh, and they saw less and less of him until June when he finally packed off to Colleen's hometown in PA. That meant back to working in a garage, same as high school. Brand new BA in Communications and he's replacing fan belts. The rest of them didn't even need to look at each other to share their disgust. But Ray hadn't complained: his roommate's departure left room for Lisa to move in. First girl he actually lived with after dating all those others, the one he wanted all along.

Next Luke got a plum design job in the city and an apartment in the Village. Which left Ray the last one still at RU, in grad school and switched from English to Comp Lit, dissecting Poe and struggling through Maurice Roche with a measly three semesters of undergrad French. *Tel quel*...if he could just tell what the hell...

But he still had Lisa. They finally started up as a couple third quarter senior year. None of them had discussed that this was a big part of the reason Luke left, but Ray was sure they all knew it. Well, maybe not Danny, but Danny was busy with his own thing. And Ray kept asking himself why he hadn't asked her out way back freshman year, back when he wasn't buried in grad work and she didn't have a full-time job. Back when his dad was still around. He remembered how she hit it off with the old man when he discovered they both smoked Benson & Hedges Multifilters. "Why don't you strike up with this one?" he asked one night in front of them all, and who squirmed worse: Ray or Luke?

Problem now was Ray *didn't* have Lisa anymore, had lost her long blonde hair, her freckled cleavage, her Dublin accent that wasn't all Dublin and only came all the way out when she was drunk. He still had no clue how he blew it, but he had and she was gone. No more Friday night road trips to Princeton for ice cream, no more plying her with Zinfandel for pre-coital readings of *Finnegans Wake*.

A year earlier, three best friends would've closed ranks to carry him through a breakup. But dating Lisa meant losing Luke, and Lisa's own departure left him without his closest confidante, the one person who stuck by him through three years of breakups. Of course Danny, his original roommate and oldest friend, had already done his own up-and-run.

But now, surprise, surprise, it was Danny to the rescue, calling out of the blue as if he already knew the situation: "Come on out to our place for the weekend! We'll hang, have some brewskis, watch some movies, take your mind off things! It'll be just like old times." And there was the vague suggestion that Colleen had an available friend or sister. Or was it a cousin? Probably some steel-town girl with an ass like a Budweiser Clydesdale. Which, yeah... He would. No question. Even sober. He'd gone without for more than a month.

When Ray was a kid, Pennsylvania was a special destination. His dad drove the family out to the Poconos several times each summer. They'd cross the border at the Delaware Water Gap, and Dad always told him to look for the Indian chief's face on Mt. Tammany. Ray would press his own face against the glass and twist his neck at odd angles, desperate to puzzle any kind of image at all out of that blocky granite ridge while his father cruised by without slowing. It was years before he realized the face was a *profile*. By then it was a disappointment all round. He was past the age where a face in a rock formation held any magic, and his dad had long since given up on him anyway, in more ways than that. Not like there was anyone better than the old man at missing what was staring him in the face: 10 year old Ray's mom jetting off to Cali with her boss, or the way a three-pack-a-day habit was going to put him in the ground eight days before exam week Ray's sophomore year at RU. Least his friends were there for him then.

The night's black mist soaked through everything by the time Ray entered Lansdale proper but the streetlights were late coming on... city fathers probably skimping on electricity. The Interstate T'ed out, forcing him to navigate a broken grid of backstreets to reach Main. Rills of dirty snow lined them all, covering the walks on the side streets and rising up the walls of buildings.

Last time he came through here he hadn't noticed just how many storefronts were empty. But Lisa rode with him that time, so he wasn't paying much attention to his surroundings. He was more interested in copping a feel, while she kept shoving his hand away and telling him to keep his eyes on the road. Now he had nothing to feel, nothing to watch except the progression of empty shops, windows soaped or boarded, some even broken. The recession hit Lansdale hard as a Mike Tyson uppercut.

Though it wasn't much after 5:00 p.m., the streets were all but empty. He passed a handful of gray, shambling figures, heads hunched against the bitter wind, and in some of the more sheltered entrances, vaguely human bundles of rags, but these scattered souls comprised the visible extent of Lansdale's citizenry.

Here and there where a building flaunted an expanse of wall, rising one or two stories above its neighbors or turning full broadside at a corner, painted advertisements for vanished businesses still clung to the bricks like giant splotches of lichen: Nehi, Something-Something Hardware, "Hickiry" Broom and Cigar Box Factory. Lansdale was a ghost town haunted by its own lost prosperity.

Ray cruised rapidly down Main until a light caught him close to what he took for the center of town. He could've run it, there was no other traffic and no cops—at least none he could see. But it would suck ass to get pulled over in this shit berg, so he stopped.

Drumming his impatience against the steering wheel, Ray flicked his eyes left to right. No traffic crossed in front of him, none waited. His gaze caught on a broad building of pale brick to the left. It was vacant like so many others, "FOR RENT" sign taped askew to the inside of its door, but a pale lemony glow from inside highlighted the forlorn arc of gilt uncials that spanned the wide front window. A pair of the scrubby, leafless trees that ran up either side of Main, relics of early '80s optimism, blocked parts of the text, but for a moment Ray was sure he read: "EYES EXCHANGE BANK." Which, no fucking way: that was Roche, not reality. Great. His goddamn thesis was affecting his vision now.

He moved his head forward, back, angling for a clearer view of the floating letters, even pulled up a couple feet, but only made it worse. Now he couldn't be sure of a single word, couldn't be sure he'd ever been sure.

But he could see that the light in the building came from a single bare bulb on a sagging wire. It revealed an interior empty except for a crooked stepladder and newspapers spread across the visible portion of the floor. And the shadows. They registered all at once: elongated inky streaks unfurling over the dim, scattered sheets of newsprint. He was positive they weren't there initially—their appearance was as sudden as if some person or persons unseen hurled broad streamers of black velvet from the near end of the empty lobby. But Ray saw no one. The light was poor, but enough to be almost certain the building's interior was vacant. And still the shadows moved, angling over each other and lengthening until they stretched up the back wall to the ceiling. Probably vagrants who wanted out of the cold and found an open door, but kept hidden from his sight by some trick of architecture and optics. He oughtta report them. But to whom? He had no idea where to find the local police station. Not that he could picture himself strolling into a Pennsy cop shop to report invisible bums in an empty bank.

The patterns of their movements reminded Ray of searchlights over a dark cityscape, except these were beams of moving, searching darkness. He watched them, forgetting the traffic light, until all at once they poured out from the front window, over the dirty sidewalk and straight toward his car.

His forehead struck the wheel before bouncing back against the headrest. Outside a dark tree trunk not much thicker than his arm rose above a visible crease in the car's crumpled hood, faintly backlit by the glow from his headlamps. He was on the sidewalk, the better part of a block west of the bank. On the left side of Main. He'd traveled over two hundred feet, crossed the center line, popped the curb, hit a tree. He recalled none of it. The burnt-syrup smell of hot antifreeze stung his nostrils and he knew the radiator was probably leaking.

Had he zoned out, fallen asleep at the wheel? No one had stopped to check him out. No cops, no cars, no pedestrians. Adrenalin took hold and he got wild, restarted the engine and threw the car in reverse, bouncing back over the curb with a loud scrape from the undercarriage. He hoped it wasn't the oil pan or the tranny. The Slant-6 Duster that served him all through Reagan's second term and now into Bush's first wasn't making it much farther without help. Danny and Colleen's place was close. His friend would fix the radiator and whatever else was screwed up—he had the skills, he had the technology. This visit might be serendipitous after all. Danny would make it all better. And that was *all* Ray wanted now: someone to make it better.

Continuing down otherwise empty Main, he looked left and right into storefronts, compelled to search for more of the long shadows. Several times he thought he glimpsed the interplay of dark streaks within other buildings that proclaimed themselves empty, down alleys, even once in a recessed doorway. He wondered if the whole town was infested with the mobile strips of darkness and he'd only now become attuned to their presence. Were they a trick of the light? But there hardly was any light now. Still they showed, dark on dark. Ray shook his head to clear his vision and fixed his gaze straight ahead. He didn't need this. Whatever caused the shadows, they were not his problem, not something he wanted to see. He had other issues to deal with. Plenty. He kept his eyes on the road and soon emerged from the moribund downtown into the side streets that led to Danny and Colleen's crummy apartment.

Ray was in full panic mode by the time he steered off Main. His heart pounded and it was all he could do not to pin the accelerator. He glanced at the scribbled sheet from his notebook on the passenger seat, then snatched it up and pressed it to the wheel with his right hand. He'd forgotten the way since that day he helped Danny and Colleen move, so he needed to ask for new directions over the phone. But when he came up on their apartment complex a few minutes later, he immediately recognized the plain brick U, a blocky three-story magnet drawing him back to his last significant human contact. He pulled in beside Danny's restored '72 Challenger, braking at the last second so as not to slam the lot's grimy border of plowed snow. Snow got like rock when it was hard and crusted. The front of his vehicle was already fucked, and the snow would sure as shit mash it worse. No telling how much more his radiator could take before it was a complete write-off. No need to compound his problems.

He got out and inspected the damage in the scant light of a single flood high up the side of the building. It was enough to see the deep vertical crease that traversed the grill. Viscous coolant dripped steadily to the pavement. No question the damage breached the radiator. At least the headlights were intact. But what about him? He never blacked out before. Not sober anyway. True, the anxiety attacks came more often since Lisa split—but he never lost consciousness during those.

He cursed and muttered a line of verse: "my wife my car my color and myself." The final entry in Charles Olson's *Maximus Poems*, an accounting of everything the poet had lost by then, dying in his hospital bed, jaundiced with liver failure, car repoed, wife dead...

This wasn't like that though. Lisa was gone, but not dead. And Danny would fix his car. He still had his health, of course. He hustled to the entrance and up the stairwell, gripping the rail with one hand and probing lightly at the bruise on his forehead with the other.

Seven rings before Danny answered the door, and when he did, the wave of musty reeking air that rushed out drove Ray back a step. Rank mildew, mixed with something worse. Colleen must not be much into cleaning. Not surprising. He hadn't pegged her for the type.

Not much of a cook, either. Even in the dim light, Ray could see Danny had lost weight. Slouching and shirtless, skin gone gray and sheened with sweat, short greasy curls glued to his forehead, the man looked like deep-fried shit.

After a blank, awkward moment, Danny stepped aside for Ray to enter. "Oh hey man, come on in. Have a seat. Lemme get you a cold one." Random sputtering candles provided the only light, but it was enough for Ray to see the junk piled everywhere. The place was a goddamn mess. He squeezed into the only clear space on the sofa. Loose stacks of women's clothes took up the rest. Heaps and boxes and mounds of clothes and other personal effects sprawled across the floor. The apartment looked about the same as it had when Luke, Lisa, and Ray had first helped Danny and Colleen move in—except for the trash. Had they even unpacked?

Danny returned from the kitchen, an open Bud in each hand. Ray held his to his nose, half-expecting the taste to be as off as the stifling smell in the room, but all he smelled was hops, and the beer was cold and crisp. He relaxed a little. Danny shoved another pile of folded clothes off the easy chair so he could sit.

"So where's Colleen? Work?"

"Ah. Yeah. Well, basically man, Colleen ain't here no more. She split. So we're kind of in the same boat, you know, you and me."

"She dumped you?"

"Just up and left, man. That's why I'm glad you're here. You and me can help each other through this."

"What the hell? When did all this happen?"

"Oh, 'bout a month ago."

"A month ago? You made out like she was still here when you asked me to come down. Why didn't you tell me?"

"Yeah, well I was kinda thinkin' you might not wanna come if you knew. On the other hand, you never liked her much anyway, so I figured you wouldn't mind once you got here."

"So I guess you won't be hooking me up with her cousin or sister or whatever? What was that all about?"

"Sorry, bro. I just really needed some company, you know? But hey man, if you want chicks, we can go to Pizza Uno. We'll find some chicks there, guaranteed."

Ray stared across the room at his friend. Danny looked ill and definitely needed a bath. It bothered Ray to see the man this way: Danny who had always been so fastidious, who even when he was working as a mechanic kept a special brush handy for scrubbing the black grease and dirty engine oil from under his nails. No way he was gonna be picking up any chicks tonight. None with eyes or a nose anyway. And Ray wasn't going to get any action hanging with him. He really shoulda stayed home. Now his car was fucked and he was looking at doubling down on his loneliness. Or worse.

On the plus side, he at least had someone to drink with, and that was what he and Danny had always done best together. So after finishing their Buds in the parking lot as Danny inspected the damage to Ray's car, they climbed in the old Challenger and headed to the local mall. It was a relief for Ray just to get out of that reeking apartment.

"How the hell does this dump support a mall anyway? From what I saw downtown, the whole place is pretty dead."

"Well, people 'round here say it was the mall killed the downtown. Then again, the mall ain't exactly hopping neither. Hey, at least it ain't Scranton. Remember Schmitty?"

Schmitty was a grizzled old laryngectomy in Middlebrook, Ray and Danny's hometown, a local character who walked the neighborhood and periodically wandered into the service station where Danny worked and Ray joined him most evenings to hang out and drink. No matter what the topic, the old man inevitably began reminiscing about his formative years in Scranton, and when he did, he always came to his tag line: "When I was your age, you could get a blowjob for a quarter in Scranton."

Neither Ray nor Danny had ever felt the need to test the assertion for themselves, but this and several of Schmitty's other buzzing pronouncements had entered the long catalog of their personal in-jokes.

"Well, I'll tell you," Ray replied, "Right now I might go for a 25 cent BJ."

"Pizza Uno, that's the place, I'm tellin' you man."

"We'll see man. We'll see."

The drive took less than 10 minutes, but they each managed to kill two more beers along the way. The Montgomery County Mall occupied a low rise west of town in an otherwise isolated area. Leafless second growth forest surrounded the hill, the mall, and its broad but almost empty parking lot.

As Danny wove up the serpentine access road, movement to the right caught Ray's attention. A high tier of business signs rose from the crusted snow on a single whitewashed pole, and the second sign from the bottom was gliding smoothly to the left: "eyelab." Six thick sans-serif letters, all lower case, black on a yellow background. This gimmick seemed an extravagant expense for any business in such a depressed area. As Ray watched, the sign reached its apogee halfway out and began sliding back. It passed the halfway mark on the right and continued on until it floated unsuspended in the night. "Whoa, fuck man...do you see that?" he asked Danny, but at the same moment, he realized the eyelab sign stood on a separate pole behind the others, that the illusion of its motion was the result of its position behind a gap in the first tier of signs and their car's progress up the mall's rising, curving entrance drive. Probably also the three beers he sucked down so fast. Still, it was trippy—what were the odds against everything being positioned like that? And the confluence of "eyelab" with "EYES EXCHANGE BANK"...of both with Maurice Roche, Poe, and the central focus of his thesis...he did not like that at all. Synchronicity could go fuck itself for all he cared right now.

Danny parked near the glass doors of JCPenney's, which appeared to be this mall's sole anchor. "Pizza Uno's down the other end. There's no parking there. Probably 'cause it's the only restaurant and they want people to walk through the whole place to get there."

Ray followed his friend inside. They traversed the department store in less than a minute and entered the mall proper. Ray kept his attention on the central corridor and avoided looking closely at the stores to either side. He did not want to see any more shadows, not here where he had no vehicle to provide even the illusion of a barrier. What he saw instead was too dreary for reassurance: dry fountains, dusty plastic replicas of tropical plants, abandoned kiosks that should have been selling smoked almonds or blown glass art, shit like that.

They encountered only a handful of shoppers, most headed for the Penney's exit. The conversation had never really gotten going in the car, and neither of them said a word until they were well into the mall. After several false starts, clearing their throats and grunting, it was Danny who at last managed a legit opener. He asked Ray about his MA thesis, if he still had the same topic. Not that Danny remembered it. The best he could manage was, "That thing about Poe." Even that much surprised Ray.

So Ray ran with it. Anything to fill the awkward silence. "Yeah, that's it. Working title is *A Long Shadow: Poe's Legacy in France*. I'm focusing on the way Poe controlled his readers' perceptions to create optical illusions in print. And how the French picked up on that, starting with Baudelaire and Mallarmé. For Poe, think of "The Sphinx" or "The Man of the Crowd."

Danny nodded as if he understood. Ray knew he had no fucking clue.

"Or take this scene in *Pym* for example, Poe's only novel, where the narrator and his friends are trapped on the hull of a wrecked ship. They're desperate: no water, no food. Finally they see another ship headed right towards them. There's a guy on the bow smiling and nodding and waving at them...only when it gets closer, they see the guy is dead and tangled in the ropes, and a big-ass seagull is pecking out his brains, which was why he was moving. That's classic Poe horror: what's worse than being trapped in your own skull because your own eyes betrayed you?"

Danny nodded again. As if.

Ray turned to his friend: "Aren't you hot man? I'm burning up in here." The mall interior was warm, humid, stuffy. Ray could even swear he caught a whiff of the same musty stink that had all but overwhelmed him at Danny's apartment, but maybe it was just coming off Danny. He hadn't smelled it in the car though.

Danny shook his head, but then he hadn't worn a coat. Just a faded Styx concert jersey with holes in the armpits he pulled on before they left: "Grand Illusion Tour." Ray shrugged off his own coat, a bulky suede Polo number, tucked it under his left arm, muttered: "Damn, man," shook his head, and continued his thesis filibuster:

"Mallarmé is really the key. The guy even built an altar to Poe and prayed at it. Fast forward from him to Maurice Roche in '66, a major Mallarmé disciple, and he picks up on Mallarmé's idea of creating optical illusions with the text itself. Well, maybe not illusions, but *distortions*. Like he makes a skull out of letters, calls it 'Mnenopolis,' the city of memories. But he mainly uses this trick called anamorphosis: you get to this part in *Compact* where there's all these long stretched out lines on the page, but if you tilt the book way over on its edge, the lines are letters that spell 'EYES EXCHANGE BANK'—in English, which is weird 'cause the book is in French. And my French ain't that great, so I'm having trouble working through the rest of it."

"Anal-what-a-sis?" asked Danny. "Sounds like some kinda porn."

"Ana*morph*osis, dude. It's an old trick in painting. Luke taught me about it. The most famous example is this painting *The Ambassadors* by Hans Holbein, where there's a long gray diagonal blur floating near the floor in front of these two dudes dressed all fancy, like kings on playing cards. But if you get close and look at the blur from just the right angle, it's a skull."

For a moment, Ray imagined Danny and himself as shabbier versions of the figures in Holbein's painting. Danny already seemed like an ambassador from some foreign land. His best friend since junior high, and Ray hardly recognized him. Living out here in Pennsy had changed him, made him strange.

"A floating skull? What's that all about?"

"It's a *memento mori*. It's there to say 'Remember you will die.' Folks were big on that sort of thing back then."

They arrived at the Pizza Uno entrance. Here at least they found signs of life: colored light gleamed out and WMMR played loudly from inside. But when they approached the hostess, a lifeless and dispirited brunette, she told them the wait for a table was 20 minutes.

Ray challenged her immediately: "What the hell? We can see a buttload of empty tables right from here. How can you have a 20 minute wait?"

"Because we've only got one server on tonight," she droned. "Unnerstand? So do you wanna make a reservation or not?"

Danny gripped Ray's arm, pulled him away from potential confrontation. "C'mon man, let's check out the rest of the mall for awhile and come back." Then to the hostess: "It's cool, we're cool. Reservation for two, Bevacqua." He spelled it out, and Ray knew right then who was going to pay for this meal.

Danny's hand felt too warm and damp on Ray's forearm. His gut reaction was to shake it off. But he didn't dare offend the mechanic he relied on to help him escape from Lansdale, so he was relieved when his friend let go.

A final section of the mall angled away to the west past Pizza Uno, and they took off down this way. Ray checked his watch and marked 6:18 p.m. Plus 20 minutes = 6:38.

He saw right away it would be hard to kill 20 minutes in this wing. There weren't many stores, and even fewer of those were open. A jeweler, a shoe store, a leather goods emporium...nearly all the rest were vacant, their facades sealed with panels of raw plywood. It was worse than downtown. They soon entered a zone where every storefront was empty. Most looked as though they never opened. Plywood covered some, others were sealed with nothing more than thick hanging sheets of translucent plastic. Construction here had progressed no further than the steel framing. They advanced regardless.

Altogether, they passed only five open stores in the entire wing, and all those near the east end, close to Pizza Uno. No plastic plants here, just empty fixtures. There were long patches where the tile was out or had never been laid and the bare concrete was exposed. Sheets of water-stained plywood covered the floor in other places: subterranean ducts and pipes still under construction. Ray crossed one panel and it echoed hollow and bowed beneath him. He avoided the others after that. This wasn't a mall. It was an abandoned construction site, a skeleton. And an obstacle course. Before long they confronted the end of the corridor: a blank wall of unpainted cinderblock.

Ray turned to Danny. "Dude, what's with this place? It's totally decrepit."

"Yeah, well you know: the economy, man. That fucker Bush... everything went downhill after Reagan."

They began their retreat from the dead end, but as they passed the first derelict kiosk, Ray noticed his shoelaces were loose. Again. Both sides. He'd been partial to Sperry Top-Siders since sophomore year, ever since Luke turned him on to them. Luke was from North Jersey, Englewood: not rich but upper middle class. Ray had tried to emulate his friend's effortless preppy style, looking to recreate his own image and cut the stink of the burbs, projecting himself into the academic future he envisioned: Top-Siders, Bass Weejuns with pennies inserted, argyle, chinos, Bean Boots, buttondown shirts from Land's End. But his current pair of boat shoes just wouldn't stay tied.

Ray stepped over to the kiosk, set his coat lightly on the blank, dusty counter, and bent to grasp the squared leather laces. He had tied only one side when a noise came from inside the kiosk, a kind of exhalation or sigh. He froze, laces drooping through his fingers. What the hell? He listened for a 10-count. Nothing. He let out his breath and was beginning the other side when something thumped the panel in front of him so hard it bulged out in his face.

He shot to his feet and staggered backward, footsteps echoing off another plywood sheet. Where was Danny? Ray looked wildly for his friend before spotting him about 50 feet back down the corridor, still walking. Ray scrambled over to him, making frequent backward glances at the kiosk. As soon as he was close enough, he stage-whispered, pointing back toward the now-silent structure: "Dude, did you hear that?"

"Hear what?"

"There's something in there. Someone."

"Probably a rat."

"This was no rat. Whatever it was, it was way bigger than a rat!"

"Some homeless dude then, looking for a place to sleep. You woke him up."

Ray shuddered. He knew the stats: a million millionaires under Ronnie Raygun—and a million people on the streets, many of them mental patients released when Reagan shut down the state mental hospitals. He'd done some work with the campus solidarity group "RU With the Homeless," even volunteered in a soup kitchen in Morningside Heights during a visit to a high school girlfriend who'd gone on to Columbia. But this was not the kind of controlled circumstances under which he interacted with the homeless before. "C'mon, let's get out of here," he said to Danny, who shrugged but turned and continued toward the finished section of the mall as Ray hustled to catch up.

He forgot to check his watch when they returned to Pizza Uno, but the hostess sat them regardless of the time. "Bevacqua, party of two. Follow me." Her voice remained empty of intonation. She led them to a gloomy corner booth, lingered for their drink order: two Coronas.

At first they just stared at each other across the table as they waited for their beers. Ray was still shaken from his experience at the kiosk, and he had no idea what else to say to this pallid drone that replaced his oldest friend.

The blank-faced hostess returned with a brace of Coronas and lingered to take their order. It appeared *she* was the one server on duty. Danny immediately ordered a chicken and artichoke heart pizza without consulting either Ray or the menu, "And two more Coronas." The girl shuffled back to the kitchen.

And then Danny showed a spark of his old self: "Dude, what if she brings an artichoke and chicken *heart* pizza? Remember Bill Cosby when we were kids, the chicken heart? 'Pum-pum. Pum-pum.' Just like the heart under the floorboards. That's Poe, isn't it? You should put that in your thing."

Ray mustered a grunt of feigned enthusiasm. Like he really needed thesis advice from a fucking mechanic. But his thoughts turned anyway to the familiar tale of the sinister eye and the heart buried beneath floorboards, how Poe controlled the reader's perceptions through his unreliable narrator. How could he have missed that one?

He *would* have to work it into his thesis somehow. Not that he'd tell Danny, who would probably expect credit for something Ray would have picked up on soon anyway.

The waitress/hostess returned with their drinks. Danny raised the dewy bottle before him and said:

"Remember you will die, huh? Well, we ain't dyin' tonight, bro. To the single life!"

Ray reciprocated, mechanically. He would rather die himself than take any more academic advice from Danny, even if it was good, so he stabbed at another topic. "So, Dude, what's the deal with Colleen? I thought you two were mated for life."

"Yeah, well, she got really bitchy after I lost my job. Not like *she's* got any income you know—just sponged off her family before I came along, and after that, she started hangin' with them more even though she was spongin' off me. They're a mess, just the mom and the two sisters sittin' around bitchin' about men this, men that. It's a regular estrogen fest, Y-chromosomes beware. But she probably would've come back this last time except for that whole thing with her cat."

"What whole thing with her cat?"

"Kitten really. Dude, it was totally justified. She brought this thing home and it was always whinin' and gettin' in my shit. And she left it for me to take care of when she got pissed about my job and ran back to her mom's, like I could really give a shit about some stupid furball. It kept buggin' me when I was tryin' to watch TV, climbin' up on the Barcalounger and meowin', lookin' at me all sad. Finally I picked it up by the fuckin' neck and squeezed it, and it felt good, so I kept squeezin' till it didn't move. So then she comes back the next day, and she's all, "Where's my cat?" and I told her the fuckin' thing was dead, and she got all pissed, started screamin' at me like it was a real pet, a dog or a turtle or somethin', said she was movin' back to her mom's for good. I was too wasted to argue, and that was that. So what about Lisa, *your* perfect woman? How did that go south?"

The shift in topic caught Ray unprepared—he wasn't ready to answer, not after the cat thing. He bought time by mouthing his beer, then stammered out a response. "Man, I, uh, don't really know. I think she got pissed over my lifestyle, working on my thesis all the time. She just wasn't ready to be with a serious academic. One day she came home and just started crying. I tried asking her what was wrong, but she locked herself in the bathroom for a whole hour. When she came out, she told me we needed time apart. Just like that. No explanation.

Then she packed up her shit and split. That was it. Haven't heard from her since. She hasn't been back to her job, either. I don't know where she went."

Which wasn't really true. He was pretty sure she was shacked up with Luke in the City. Luke who conveniently wasn't answering his calls either. But Ray wasn't about to let the conversation stray in that direction. Instead he rose, mumbled, "Man, I gotta take a leak," and made his unsteady way to the restroom. At least it was true.

When he returned, Danny took a deep pull from his beer, looked across the table at Ray, and said, "She came here for awhile. Right after Colleen left."

"Who came here?"

"Lisa."

Ray gaped. "You're fuckin' shittin' me, right?"

Danny shook his head, "No man, seriously. She was here. Her and Luke. She needed someone to talk to, so we all got together."

"Did she talk about me? What'd she say?"

"It wasn't all about you. She kept saying, 'I know it's me, but...' Her but's were mostly about how she felt jealous of the attention you were givin' Poe and all these frogs you're into—but she knew your thesis was important—but you were losing touch with reality—but you were ignoring her, etcetera, etcetera..."

"She never said any of this to me."

"What she told us was she didn't feel like she could talk to you about it. Said she tried but you didn't listen."

"Man, that's bullshit. I always listened to her."

But had he? How many times had he blown her off for the work, for another session with Roche and his copy of the *Robert et Collins Dictionnaire Français-Anglais*? "So how long did she stay? And what was going on with her and Luke?"

"I know what you're thinkin' man, but that wasn't it. She just needed friends, and we were here for her, like always. That's all."

"Bullshit. I know Luke's been after her for a long time."

"Yeah, maybe, but not this time.

"Whaddaya mean: 'not this time'?"

"Nothin' man, give it a rest. She ain't fuckin' Luke. I guarantee that."

Their pizza arrived. Gray Danny regarded him across the table. "You still havin' those anxiety attacks, man? 'Cause you look a little pale right now."

Deep breath. He'd mentioned the attacks to Danny over the phone. "Yeah, but this isn't one. They're just something I've been getting on and off since my dad died. They don't last long. Nothing to sweat over." Yet he already felt a cold, greasy sweat leaking over his body from every pore.

"You oughtta get seen to man, that shit can't be good. But not now, huh? For now, dig in. A full stomach's just what you need."

With trembling hands Ray nodded and tore loose a slice of the lumpy, pus-colored pizza. The waitress returned with a fresh round of Coronas, and Ray took a deep pull from his to wash that first pasty mouthful down.

They ate and drank for several minutes without further conversation. The bland waitress brought more Coronas even before their last round was empty. Danny must have told her to "Keep 'em comin', honey," while Ray was in the can. That was okay with Ray. All he wanted was to get tanked. But then, Danny had convinced him to come here for more than beer...

"So Dan-man, where's all the chicks you said would be here? 'Cause I'm not seeing 'em..." Fewer than a dozen other customers were visible. None were unescorted women. The bar was empty.

"I dunno man...must be an off night. Most nights this place is crawlin' with chicks."

"So...are we just cursed or something? I mean, c'mon, seriously, this is pathetic."

"What about the waitress? She should be gettin' off soon, and she looks kinda game..."

"You're kiddin' right? Game? She looks half dead to me..."

She returned even as Ray spoke, however, and he examined her again. Lank, dark hair fell evenly around her face from both sides, maintaining the almost parallel lines of her figure. Almost sexless. But she did have tits, suppressed and taut within the white men's dress shirt she wore. A plastic rectangle engraved with her name rode askew above her left breast. Rochelle. He imagined her coming to life in a threeway: Danny, her, him. He never had a threeway. Maybe that's what he needed to cheer himself up.

Danny faced her, a sagging pizza slice held aloft in his left hand. There was something wrong with his eyes, but Ray couldn't place it. Too sunken, too glassy, the pupils too wide...

"So my buddy here was wantin' to know where you're from," Danny said to Rochelle.

She turned her head slowly, right, left, looked at them each in turn, then replied, sans inflection, sans expression:

"Scranton."

Ray sputtered into his fist and glanced at Danny. Their history was filled with hundreds of moments like this, secret in-jokes mutually acknowledged and achieving fruition at some third party's expense. Ray could not hold back. He expected Danny to bust out too, but his friend just stared, his glassy gaze the same—as Rochelle's.

"Can I get you anything else?" she asked, her voice even colder, if that was possible. Danny said no, they were okay, and she walked off toward the kitchen.

"Dude, I was looking at you, trying to tell you not to laugh. But you blew it." Danny shook his head. His timing and rhythm the same as Rochelle's...and the same as the motions of the "eyelab" sign outside. Except Danny's head didn't float off into the night. Ray watched to be sure of that.

"Sorry man. I couldn't help it."

"Well, we ain't nailin' her now. I don't know what's wrong with this place tonight. There's usually lots of chicks."

"I find that hard to believe, myself. This is some pathetic town you've found yourself in if this joint is the best you can do for a singles bar."

"Don't knock it, man. I tell you, livin' here has changed my whole outlook on life. All that study, study, study, work, work, work—it doesn't really matter. None of it matters. I got a different way of seein' things now."

Ray was lost with this line of reasoning, but he didn't much care. At this point, his only plan was to get drunk and ask Danny to fix his car in the morning so he could get the hell out of Lansdale, before dark, if possible. He'd pretty well accomplished the first part already.

They both drank on in silence as beads of suspicious moisture oozed from the cooling cheese on the half-eaten pizza. By the time Rochelle brought the check, Ray was pretty much shitfaced. He paid it, just as he had expected he'd have to. Even flipped her a fiver for a tip, he didn't know why. The booze, no doubt.

Danny and Ray were the final customers to exit Pizza Uno, and they had to duck under the burnished aluminum rolling grille already pulled down to within a few feet of the floor. The corridor outside was dim, all the stores were closed and only a single row of fluorescent panels high above provided illumination. Ray thought again of the derelict bank he had seen downtown just before his blackout and the accident, the lone bulb on a wire that lit it.

At first neither spoke as they made their unsteady way toward the exit. Then Ray tried to focus and said, "Dude, I can't believe you didn't tell me Lisa was down here. To be honest, I feel kind of betrayed." He kept his eyes on the floor, not Danny, struggling to keep his steps within a single row of tiles.

He felt Danny turn to him. "You feel betrayed? You know what dude? You always act like Lisa was such an angel, and she wasn't. You wanna know the truth? Luke didn't bang her this time, but he already banged her like way back sophomore year. And so did I. A buncha times. Once we had a threesome, some night when you were too busy writin' one of your damn English papers and we all went to the Roxy without you. It didn't mean nothin', you know. We were pretty wasted, anyway. But she made us promise not to tell you because she knew you had this crush on her. Fact is, by then she was already gettin' tired of waitin' for you to ask her out. But that's not the way it went this last time. She just hung out, told us her troubles and stuff, that's all."

Ray opened his mouth to reply, but his tongue had gone numb. The space between them stretched as long as a football field, as if Ray were staring at Danny through the wrong end of a telescope. He didn't want to believe his friend, but he knew his words were true. He knew it in his guts, he knew it from a dozen tiny suspicions that clicked into place all at once, memories he'd shunted aside. But that was all he was going to learn from his guts, because it was happening again: an elevator shaft opened in his torso and everything inside collapsed down a vast abyss. He thought helplessly of Pound's line: "But Sordello, and my Sordello?" All at once there were two Lisa's, and both were lost to him. Now he clung to a ledge in a deep, dark pit as her image receded. The inexorable pattern had begun once more, and all he could do was ride it out. In rapid succession his mind played host to a slideshow featuring his father, his MIA mom, his scant remaining handful of distant aunts, uncles, cousins...Lisa. He grasped for each as they faded in turn. None could hold him. He shrank, diminished, dwindled to a pinpoint, a dust speck no Horton could hear in a universe of immense galaxies isolated by stifling, incomprehensible spans of emptiness. There was nothing to hang onto, no one to hold him back from the pull of oblivion. The void sucked him in, crushed him to nothingness. All he was, all his memories, vanished, gone forever. He shuddered and gasped an inchoate syllable with what seemed the last breath in his lungless chest.

And then, as quickly as it had taken him, the spell began to fade. He found himself gripping the edge of a thick concrete planter with both hands. A plastic tree trunk rose from it, almost as thick as the one he struck on Main. They were just outside of Penney's. He staggered toward Danny and threw both hands out to shove him. "You fucker!"

Danny sidestepped with surprising ease, considering how sick he looked. Ray swung a roundhouse punch at him, but Danny caught Ray's right with his left, ducked under, and slammed him in the stomach. Ray collapsed to his knees and puked a sour stew of pizza chunks and Corona.

Danny stood above him. "Fuck you man. I try to open your eyes, show you how it really is, and you take a swing at me. You wanna live in a fantasy world, that's your own problem. You'll see when the snow melts. Everyone will see. But I'm finished with you here." And he strutted off into Penney's.

Ray fought for breath and spewed his guts out a few more times before he could struggle to his feet. Puke spattered the backs of his hands, and he wiped them on his pants, though those weren't much better. He checked all round, but saw no one watching him, no customers, no security. He made for Penney's and the mall exit.

It wasn't until he was outside that he felt the sting of the winter wind and realized he'd left his coat behind. Where? In Pizza Uno? No, on that kiosk. Shit. Only a handful of cars remained in the lot, and Danny's was not among them. Triple-shit. Ray hadn't anticipated returning to the rear of the mall, but wherever he was going tonight, he was walking, and there was no way he was doing that without his coat. Not to mention his car keys were in the pocket, for what they were worth.

The mall was empty now. The grille was all the way down outside Pizza Uno and the lights were off. He expected to have to feel his way through the section beyond in total darkness, but a lone panel of fluorescents lit the aperture to the west wing. Others glowed at uneven intervals further down the corridor, hanging exposed from bare steel beams.

Ray picked his way down the aisle from one oasis of light to the next. He had not gone far before flashes of maybe-movement began to register in his peripheral vision: more of the long shadows. They never approached him head on—instead they pulsed over and over at the corners of his sight, independent of the angles of the overhead lights and showing no conformity to objects on the floor. He tried to focus on his feet, ignoring the dark streaks that crisscrossed each other and rose up the walls, the hollow echoes from the plywood panels he trampled, the way the plastic sheeting over empty storefronts rippled without any breeze. Just keeping his feet together and moving forward dizzied him, and his stomach still threatened.

His worst fear was that when he arrived at the kiosk, his coat would be gone, but he saw it from a good distance off, resting almost right beneath the final flickering light panel. At last—his ordeal was almost at an end. Just grab the coat and strike a fast pace back to the exit. Maybe Danny would be waiting for him after all. Of course he would be: he wouldn't leave Ray stranded. The coat was here, and Danny would be outside, parked at the curb with the heater running. It was all gonna be OK.

Ray was only a few yards from the kiosk when the buzzing of the fluorescents overhead cycled to the level of an angry hornet swarm, and the panel shut off altogether with a loud pop. He held his breath, straining his ears, but heard only the rippling of plastic. Yet it was not completely dark. To his right, a rectangular panel glowed softly from behind the plastic curtain that spanned an empty steel frame. Black on yellow, six letters: "eyelab." It was the twin of the one on the pole outside, only this one didn't move. It hung in place, pressed against the milky membrane as if straining to be born.

The overhead lights clicked back on. At once, Ray recognized the streaks of shadow everywhere, clearer than before. He turned to stare at one on his left, and this time, instead of shifting, it rolled up—rolled up and *rose*—contracted toward him, no longer a shadow, but a hunched figure wrapped in foul, uncertain rags. Shadows on either side underwent the same transformation, at least a dozen, and began to shuffle toward him. He gasped in drunken shock, but he was so close to his coat now. He could get it and get out before the gray figures reached him. They were slow, and Danny would be waiting outside.

Ray stumbled up to the kiosk and stretched his arm toward the coat, not wanting to approach any closer than necessary. In his mind's eye he saw with absolute clarity the gaunt, discolored limb that would whip across the counter and clutch his wrist, filthy jagged nails piercing his skin, but it never came, and with one lightning motion, he jerked his own hand toward his coat and gripped it by the collar. The instant his fingers closed on the fabric, he took half a dozen quick steps backward, never taking his eyes off the kiosk, and thus fell directly into the uncovered pit behind him. He hadn't heard the plywood cover move.

One sharpened spike of rusted rebar drove straight through his right kidney, and Ray would have screamed if another hadn't pierced the back of his neck and pinned his tongue flat in his mouth. Before the light clicked off again, he caught one brief glimpse of the gray, eyeless faces leaning over him. Then they climbed down in the darkness and slid the plywood back in place.

# Anne-Sylvie Salzman

## Fox into Lady

**Anne-Sylvie Salzman** *is a French writer and the co-editor of the* magazine Le visage vert. *As a translator, her many authors include Mary Shelley, Kris Saknussemm, Lord Dunsany, Fritz Leiber, Arthur Machen, Arthur Conan Doyle, Wilkie Collins, Sax Rohmer, Iain M. Banks, Jim Shepard, L. Frank Baum, Herman Melville, Henry Darger, and Willa Cather. Prior publications in French include two novels—* Au bord d'un lent fleuve noir *(Joëlle Losfeld, 1997) and* Sommeil *(José Corti, 2000) — as well as a short story collection,* Lamont *(Le Visage vert, 2009). It is available in English in the collection* Darkscapes *(Tartarus Press, 2013). A second collection of stories,* Vivre sauvage dans les villes *(also available in* Darkscapes) *was recently published by* Le Visage vert. *Her novel* Dernières nouvelles d'Œsthrénie *is forthcoming from Dystopia Workshop this fall.*

Keiko is lying in the grass of the narrow garden, her head against the cement wall, her mind a blank, when she is seized again in the pit of her stomach, in the place where, she imagines, her ovaries are located, or perhaps her Fallopian tubes, she doesn't know which, by incomprehensible pangs of pain. They come and go, and have been twisting in this part of her body, soft and defenseless, since the small hours of the morning. Feeling her abdomen with both hands Keiko detects a growth the size of an apricot which rolls beneath her fingers and which appears half an hour later (she has fallen asleep again and reawakened) palpably larger.

She goes back into the house. The passage from light to shade makes her heart falter. Everything is green within and the interior of the house seems to her tapestried in a huge net. She thrusts her finger into the net, chokes with disgust, then pulls herself together. These specks moving before her eyes, these trembling limbs, they are nothing. Once in the bathroom she has already recovered her spirits—low as they are at this end of a summer in which the wind has never ceased, or the bad news. She is leaning on the rim of the bathtub when another sharp pain catches her. She sits on the floor panting. An iron tube is passing through her pelvis, from the labia to the uterus. A sudden spurt from this scorching passage of hot black blood, clots that the tormented girl could almost squeeze in her fingers to break them open; then in the thickness of the discharge there is formed something with a head and limbs. "Lick it, lick it," says an instinct which Keiko in her terror cannot hear; "it is the fruit of your belly."

Keiko washes it clean in the hand-basin. It is a little animal with brown fur, the size of a mole, and its eyes are not yet open. Pensively she washes the private parts between her legs while the little creature mews in the basin. What is she to do? What to make of this blood-smeared apparition? Keiko opens the bath taps, fills the tub to the brim with water that is rather tepid than hot, and lies down in it. At the end of an hour of lassitude she finds the misshaped birth still alive at the bottom of the basin, and trying to escape from it by means of paws with transparent claws. Before her sister can return—the two girls are sharing the house, which had been the home of their dead parents—Keiko has time to find in the downstairs lumber-room a box in which to shut the animal away; her idea is to let it die of hunger. Then she waits for her sister, sitting in the drawing room with the television switched off, and sees in her mind's eye the animal's tiny mouth, its eyes protruding beneath lids still gummed together, its soft ears. The sun enters through the top of the window and falls slanting on the floorboards. When it reaches the foot of the wall her sister returns and wakes Keiko who has fallen asleep, her back to the television, and has dreamed fitful disturbing dreams of landscapes with towering rocks that scraped the low-flying hunting aeroplanes.

Night comes. Keiko goes down to see if the creature is dead. It is not. Lying in a corner of the box it trembles when Keiko touches it, yet appears to have grown bigger. Returning to her bedroom Keiko feels fear. The newfound gaze of the beast, limpid and black, sticks to her heels, and climbs back up her leg to the damp nest from which it emerged.

Her sister is asleep, her right hand over her breast. Very softly she snores; from time to times her lips sketch a mimic sucking. Keiko looks at her as she sleeps. Terror so grips her muscles that she is without power to move. For a moment she imagines that she is no more than a skin stretched over a huge, formless, palpitating amoeba. The skin bursts; Keiko returns to protozoan disorder. Neither in the next few days nor in those that follow does Keiko tell her sister of this creature so unexpectedly come into the world. The box is hidden in a cupboard off the hall which her sister, Keiko thinks, will never open. Nor does she speak to anyone else of this unnatural birth. The desire is not lacking—but the words?

The first day, having left the house without so much as visiting her beast in its infancy ('If only it would die!') Keiko is gripped at midday by a nameless panic. Her sister will have found the animal, she will have taken it to the vet, the apparition will have been registered officially. "But this little monster," says Keiko grasping her hair in both hands, "this blood-sucking witchling wants our skin."

Her sister has done no such thing. Returning at lunchtime in a state of collapse Keiko takes her beast from its box. It has gained strength. Its fur, softer now, is growing out light red. It has no teeth as yet; nor, so far as Keiko can tell, has it any inclination to cry.

Keiko returns to the garden. The sky is uncertain. The creature, probably, is puling and twisting in the darkness of the cupboard, far from the woman who gave it birth. Keiko likewise is restless. She would like to go to bed, to sleep—no, she goes out again to work. In the street she stops, a dart planted under her heart. What is the beast doing in the dark? What is in its mind? How is it nourishing itself? Has it perhaps crept back unobserved to its nest, and is it devouring Keiko from within?

♒

The second night of her strange calamity Keiko falls asleep numb with fear. Her sister is away in Yokohama till the end of the week. In the hall close to the cupboard where the creature is living out its agony there hangs a smell of sweat turning to gangrene. But Keiko, terrified of finding the creature more vigorous, provided now with claws and teeth, will not open the door. She cooks spaghetti, sits up late watching television, allows a dark languor to turn her bowels to water; then goes out, vacillating, into the garden, breathes the air, puts off the moment of going to bed. The moment comes all the same. And

Keiko wakes up in the middle of the night, a weight on her chest, in her mouth a taste of tainted food. By the light of her bedside lamp she sees on the skin of her ankles and calves the marks, hardly darker than the surface of her skin, of the greedy lips of the creature now launched at last upon the world.

She gets out of bed, rigid from head to foot. The animal is not in her bedroom. It has escaped out of the cupboard, that is all, that is as much strength as it has acquired. Keiko searches for it all through the house, cupboards, attic, under the furniture, and in the little garden. The beast has returned, Keiko prays, suddenly furious, to its foul beginnings. Through the hour that follows, seated in the chair she often leaves leaning against the wall of the house, she listens to the thunder of the motorway and the stray sounds of the neighbourhood. Two or three houses away a raucous discussion breaks out between students; somewhere else they are trying to start a car; a small dog yaps. Keiko recalls how her elder brother (he has been in the north for two years) went out into the garden to sleep under just a blanket. "It was a starry sky," thinks Keiko, "a night that no one could fear." Vain memories; the fear returns even though the sky is clear and the garden small and without hiding-places. Keiko sees passing shadows denser than they should be. Going back into the drawing room she seats herself before her mother's shrine and addresses to her a useless prayer. What can she, dead as she is, do against this beast that is now on the loose? Keiko looks at its scratches on her legs; no, the beast is not in the land of the dead.

Perhaps it has been run over by a car, or perhaps, this is her secret hope, it has drowned in the sewers. Her sister is back from Yokohama. The marks fade away. Keiko spends a night at the Hotel Vukuran in a red bedroom with her lover, who is a divorcé living in Kamakura. But although he strokes the underside of her breasts and works upon her tenderly, Keiko bites her lips and weeps tears of misery when his back is turned. The passage of the beast has seared what for the time being she calls her inner parts. From the window of the room nothing can be seen except one of the walls surrounding the commercial centre, and to the right of it, the end of a neon sign which Keiko deciphers and reconstructs as "Tobacco Baruder". "The beast knows, it smells the fire," thinks Keiko, squeezing her legs, "it knows where to find me." The question keeps recurring: has the creature come back to rest in the girl's womb? Is it not consuming her in an evil feast, inch by inch?

# Fox Into Lady

"I have hurt you," whispers the man, seeing Keiko arched up, with her veins standing out. "It's not that at all", Keiko would have liked to say, shrugging her shoulders and breathing slowly to calm the frantic beating of her heart. She stays silent. The man, not without uneasiness, takes her in his arms again. She suffers less this second time. The man, as is their usual custom, goes off to take the early train, leaving her asleep. At about seven o'clock, before going to work, she spends a long time washing her pubis and the lips of her vagina. She strives with the aid of a mirror to see what has been scorched. Nothing. Then the creature, whether it has ventured to creep back into Keiko or is leading a half-wild existence in the marginal areas about the town, falls slowly into oblivion.

$$\approx$$

Comes November. Keiko returns home one evening by Meguro, along the river which laps coldly against its enclosing walls. She looks at the movement of the water under the trees. Her fear returns, she could not say why. The river flows unbroken. She halts on the bridge, and her eyes sweep round in search of what can have awakened a fresh alarm. She enters the supermarket at the station to buy octopus and instant noodles; then takes the metro with her anxiety unabated, though it is still broad daylight. Her sister being again in Yokohama the house is empty and dark. Keiko switches on a light in every room and mortise-locks the door, something she ordinarily does not think to do. For the last four months she has been carrying a child of which the man from Kamakura is the father. She learnt this only this morning; he does not yet know. In point of fact she asks herself with an increasing melancholy if she has to tell him. Not that she is afraid he will cease to love her; rather, she thinks as she enters the garden, it is of the child that she is afraid. What will it be? At the bottom of the garden, which is bordered by three gloomy cedars, the darkness, into which she stares unthinkingly, causes her to tremble. She is now swimming in a sea of anguish which tosses and batters her. The darkness of the night is streaked with threatening lights. Waiting in shadow, more and more distinct, is a creature with the form of a fox—a vixen, rather, for its limbs are slender and its muzzle delicate. And this animal, the moist smell of which comes now to Keiko's nostrils, growls and whimpers, and in the middle of its inarticulate cry pronounces with horrible distinctness the word "Mother". Keiko puts out her hand towards the beast, motions angrily to drive it away. The word is repeated. She bolts into the house, slides shut the glass door and slams down the catch. The beast approaches. Keiko can see only the depths of its eyes shining with a yellow-orange light on the other side of the glass. She draws the curtain and sits with her face towards the animal she can no longer see. It scratches at the door and whines; then 'Mother' in a voice that is thick and inhuman.

Seated in the middle of the room Keiko hears the slightest sounds of the vixen. Her thumb and index finger at her throat count the beats of her heart, the pace of which subsides as the beast grows calmer and withdraws. But that is not for long. It returns to rub against the fastening of the window, against the walls and shrubs; it barks. She ought to leave the house, but an insurmountable weariness has seized Keiko. She gets as far as the front door, which gives onto a small flagged courtyard; but at the moment when her fingers touch the door handle she knows that the beast is waiting for her, plaintive and ubiquitous.

She puts her hands flat on the door. "What do you want?" she asks. "Mother," comes back the voice. "Never," replies Keiko, choking with horror and fury.

At the door into the garden on the other side of the house there are the same sounds, the same exchanges. "The night is multiplying the monsters around my house. I'll wait for morning; then they'll have disappeared."

She goes upstairs to bed, her knees like cotton. She recalls for the first time without the veil of self-deception the day the beast was born. It is not so late. She calls her lover (he is on a business trip to Tomakomai) to talk to him about that child that is on its way; but there is no reply and she puts down the receiver without leaving a message—her broken voice, she is afraid, will betray her. She lies on the bed fully dressed, she unbuttons her shirt, she places both hands on her belly and her fingers discover again this object which more resembles something invertebrate than an embryo, an amorphous mass with languid movements floating in her bowels. She falls asleep in the familiar hollow of that jellyfish to which the darkness gives gigantic proportions; she returns to consciousness aching. The beast to which she gave birth in the past summer, now large and pale, is stationed at her threshold. It comes forward. Keiko backs off and falls to her knees, lips compressed. The beast has become the size of a wolf. Its hair is long, its limbs are powerful. It circles round Keiko and nudges her with its paws and muzzle, but without biting or scratching. Twice it forces its huge groin between its mother's thighs, which it could have opened wide with a single snap of its teeth. As it does this it pants and grunts with pleasure. Keiko tries to rise to her feet. The giant vixen reseats her with a heavy blow of its back leg.

Presently the body of the girl is in the stomach of the beast, and her spirit flutters briefly between the separated pieces. The vixen leaves the house and stalks through the streets under the cover of the night. Sounds travel through its fur, skin and intestines, which the scattered parts of Keiko would still be able to hear: sounds of car-engines, of asphalt brushed by wheels, of human voices, but also of the puissant heart-beats of the animal, the creaking of its bones as it trots in the ditch beside the road. Then fallen leaves, the smell of decaying undergrowth, earth scraped by the monster. What had been Keiko succeeds at last in dissolving itself in the recesses of the gigantic beast, which, wearied by its running is now gone to rest in a hole in the forest. Winter is on its way. It will sleep and, alone of its species, bring forth young at the return of the spring.

—*Translated from the French by William Charlton*

# Kristi DeMeester

## Like Feather, Like Bone

*Kristi DeMeester lives, loves, and writes dark, weird fiction in Atlanta, Georgia. Her work has appeared or is forthcoming in Jamais Vu, Shock Totem, Shimmer, and others. Growing up both Southern and Pentecostal, she has witnessed traveling preachers cast out demons. These demons still haunt her writing. Find her at www.oneperfectword. blogspot.com.*

The little girl is under my porch eating a bird. Her hair is matted. She did not bother to push it back before she began, and blood has clotted against the white strands. I try to ignore her, but she is crunching its bones, and the sound is like the ground cracking open.

I creep under the porch, squat near her, but not too near. She still has her milk teeth, and they are sharp, a tiny row of pointed knives. Small feathers cling to her heart-shaped face.

"You shouldn't do that, sweetheart. It isn't good for you," I say.

"I want wings. Wings the color of the sky," she says and slurps at the bird's eyes.

"What's your name, darlin'?"

"Momma said I don't have one. But your name is Caitlin."

"How do you know my name?" I say, but the little girl shakes her head.

"It's a secret," she says and licks her hands, her small pink tongue darting in and out of the spaces between her fingers where the blood has dripped.

I feel I should take her inside; put her in a hot bath, wrap her in the thickest, fluffiest towel I can find, but it's her mouth that keeps me from taking her in my arms and carrying her into the house. She gobbles down a slimy string of meat, and I look away.

"Where's your Momma?"

"Under the water, under the water," she says, and her voice lilts up and down as if reciting a nursery rhyme. My skin blossoms into goose flesh despite the warmth of the late September afternoon.

"She went under the water. Like your Jacob. The sky doesn't go in the water. I want to be like the sky."

I haven't said his name in six months. Not since Colin left.

I pretended to listen as he spoke. "I'm sick of your fucking judgment, Caitlin. Like losing him didn't tear me open. Like you're the only one allowed to mourn. My boy. My baby boy in the goddamn ground, and I kept thinking that it wasn't right for him to be down there in the dark. He would be scared. Cold. It isn't right. I can't do it, Caitlin. I can't. " he had said. But I was happy when he left. He didn't know what it had been like to find Jacob, his eyes glassy, unfocused, his skin blue, his mouth filled with water.

"Jacob," I say and my mouth is full with the sound of his name. The little girl cocks her head, watches me, her eyes glinting in the shadows.

"Do you want wings, too?"

I think of the heaviness of Jacob's body when I pulled him from the water, my fingers scrabbling through his hair, dipping inside his mouth as if I could pull the water out of him.

I kneel beside the girl and watch her pluck the feathers from the bird. She gathers them in her hand one by one, and she laughs. It is like music, and I am so tired. I lie down in the dirt. It is cold and damp like the fistful of earth I placed on top of Jacob's small coffin.

The little girl hums, her voice high and quavering, and arranges the feathers around me. Her fingers are streaked with blood, but I do not care, and she places the feathers in my hair, tests their color against my eyes until she is satisfied. She pats my cheek, and her hands are sticky.

"There. Now you're like a bird, too," she says and resumes her song. Her voice is delicate, fragile, a thing I could take in my hands and crush. So much like Jacob's cold hands, tissue paper skin stretched across bone. So easily breakable.

Something flutters at my feet. A small sparrow hops toward us, its beak opening and closing.

"You're calling them," I say, and she snatches the bird, watches it wriggle against her grip before snapping its neck. The sound seems to echo against the slats of the porch, fills up the space. I think of screaming, but if I start I'll never stop.

She grins, her mouth all teeth and gore, and holds out her hand. The bird is still. I want to take it from her, breathe life back into it, but I remember Jacob, my mouth working to push air into his still lungs.

"Look," she says and turns, lifts her shirt to expose bare shoulders. "You see? It's working."

Dotted against smooth flesh are small bumps, dark specks against pale skin. Tiny feathers beginning to sprout.

Something sharp gnaws at my stomach. I am hungry. So, so hungry, and the girl turns back to me, places the sparrow near my mouth.

"Don't you want wings?" she says, and her voice is Jacob's voice. There is a roaring in my gut, an aching screaming to be filled, and I take the bird in my hand, bring it against my lips. It is so small. I do not think it will be enough.

"I can get more," she says. Behind her, small wings the color of the night sky unfold, flutter for just a moment before settling.

I bare my teeth, press them against warm flesh, tear at the soft feathers. It burns as I swallow. The little girl sits with me, sings her song into the growing night. Beneath my skin, my bones shift, and the dead make room for something new.

# Jeffrey Ford

## A Terror

**Jeffrey Ford** *is the author of the novels,* Vanitas, The Physiognomy, Memoranda, The Beyond, The Portrait of Mrs. Charbuque, The Girl in the Glass, The Cosmology of the Wider World, *and* The Shadow Year. *His story collections are* The Fantasy Writer's Assistant, The Empire of Ice Cream, The Drowned Life, *and* Crackpot Palace. *He lives in Ohio.*

Emily woke suddenly in the middle of the night, sitting straight and gasping as if finally breaching the surface of Puffer's Pond. The last thing she could remember was the shrill cry of the 6:00 a.m. whistle from the factory down Main Street in The Crossing. Then a sudden shuddering explosion behind her eyes; a shower of sparks.

She pulled back the counterpane and moved to the edge of the bed. There, she rested; her bare feet on the cold floor, letting the night's hush, like between the heaves of storm, settle her. Only when a fly buzzed against the windowpane did she remember everything.

Her health had been bad, her spirit low. She'd felt so weak for days on end that she could barely make it out into the garden to cull wilted blossoms. Her pen, which usually glided over a page, sowing words to correspondents or conjuring a poem, had become a weight nearly too burdensome to bear. At her father's insistence, the doctor had come the previous week and demanded to examine her. She'd reluctantly allowed it, in her way. He stood in the upstairs hallway, peering through the partially open door of her room as she shuffled past the entrance, back and forth, three times, fully clothed. He'd called out to her, "Emily, how can I diagnose anything other than a case of mumps in this manner?" but she was loathe to see him, to have him or any other stranger to the Homestead near her.

All that had somehow passed, though, and she no longer felt a slave to gravity. Gone was the perpetual headache like the beating of a drum, gone the labored rasping for breath. That frantic confusion of thought that had plagued her seemed only a fading nightmare, as if now, at the start of autumn, there'd been a spring cleaning in her mind. Before standing, she took stock to make sure she wasn't deluding herself, but no, she felt calm and rested. She stood and stretched, noticing a dim reflection of her loose white nightgown in the window glass, a floating specter that made her smile.

Moonlight sifted in through the two windows and showed her the way to her writing table. There, she lit the taper in the pewter candlestick and took it up to lead her through the darkened house. She wanted to let them know that she'd recovered from her spell. Turning right, down the hallway, she stopped first at Lavinia's room. A tapping at the door brought no response. She rapped louder, but still couldn't raise Vinnie from sleep. Quietly, she opened the door and crossed the dark expanse. Bringing the candlestick down in order to light her sister's form, she was surprised to find the bed still made, empty. She left that room and hurried further down the hall to her parents'. Her mother had been in the poorest health, and Emily was reluctant to wake her, but concern for Vinnie overcame her caution and she knocked heavily three times. Silence followed.

The raised lantern revealed her parents' bed to also be empty, still made from the day. She hurried back up the hall to the top of the stairs and called out for her father. The glow of the candle only reached halfway down the steps. Beyond was a quiet darkness from which no answer came. She felt the nettle sting of fear in her blood and called again, this time for Carlo, her dog. At any other time the Newfoundland would have been right by her side. Slowly, she backed away and returned to her room. She set down the candlestick on her writing table and stepped toward the bed. After a quick look over each shoulder, and a moment of just listening, she pulled the nightgown off and tossed it on her pillow. She was paler than the garment she discarded, glowing within the glow of the candlelight. From the closet, she removed her white cotton day dress from its hanger and slipped it on with nothing beneath. She found her walking boots in the shadow at the end of the bed and guided her bare feet into them while standing. Not bothering to tie the laces, she picked up the candlestick and left the room.

The untied boots made a racket on the steps—better, she thought, than having to utter a warning to whatever revelation lurked in the dark. She discovered that the clock on the mantel in the downstairs parlor had stopped at 2:15. Stillness reigned in every room, from her father's library to the kitchen. She fled to the conservatory, to her gardens, for comfort. As soon as she crossed the threshold from the house into the growing room, the aroma of the soil soothed her. An Aeolian harp in the one open window made music, and she turned to the plants, desperate for a moment's distraction.

It seemed to her like it had been weeks since the last time she'd inspected the exotics. September had definitely come and was drawing the summer out of blossoms. The peonies, gardenias, jasmine drooped dejectedly, their closed petals half-wilted. The summer gentian were long shriveled, and she knew she must pick them before they fell in order to make the purple tea she'd dreamed of. Resting the candle in a patch of thyme, she leaned over pots of oregano to reach the plants and pinch the desiccated flowers from their stems. Only when she had a handful did she recall that her family had vanished in the night. She shook her head, muttering recriminations at herself, put the petals in the pocket of her dress, and blew out the candle. Her eyes had adjusted to the moonlit night.

Before leaving through the door at the end of the conservatory, she grabbed from a peg the tippet of tulle she often wrapped around her shoulders when walking or working in the outdoor gardens. It was a flimsy wrap, and did little to warm her against the wind that shook the trees in the orchard. She thought of it more as a familiar arm around her shoulders. She kept to the path and called out in a whisper for her father and then Vinnie.

Upon reaching the heart of the gardens, she rested upon the log bench her brother, Austin, had built when just a boy. She resolved to go next door to The Evergreens, Austin's house, and get help. She had a choice to either reach it by traversing a lonely thicket or going round to the street. For the first time ever, she chose the street.

She hadn't been in front of the Homestead in over a year, and the thought of being seen drained her will. She found it ever preferable to be in her room, sitting at her writing table, watching, through the wavy window glass, the traffic of Main Street. For long stretches in the afternoon, before she'd put pen to paper again, she'd watch her neighbors come and go. Her imagination gave her their names and their secrets, but she felt in her bones that only at a distance could she know them.

It was different when the children came into the yard and stood beneath her window. They could smell that she'd been baking. When the cookies cooled, she'd slip them in a crude envelope she made from butcher wrap and then attach a parachute of green tissue paper her mother had been saving and forbade anyone to use. There'd be three or four children on the lawn, looking up at the white form behind the glass, a mere smudge of a phantom. Opening the window, she'd say nothing, but launch the cookies, the green paper cupping the air. The parcel would float gracefully down into their grasping hands. They'd hear her breathy laughter, the window would slam shut, and they'd scurry in fear.

She opened the wrought iron gate of the fence that ran between the property and the sidewalk, cringing with the squeal of its hinges. Looking around, she waited for someone or something to come at her out of the dark. She left the gate open so as not to make it cry again and headed right, toward The Evergreens. The wind pushed against her and dry leaves scraped the street. She shifted the tippet on her shoulders but it could do no better. It was only early September, yet she smelled a hint of snow and felt winter in her brain. A line from a poem she'd written surfaced, and she spoke it under her breath: "Great streets of silence led away . . . ."

She'd taken no more than fifty steps, head down, anticipating the comfort she'd find in the presence of Austin and the arms of his wife, Susan, when from the street behind her rose the sound of horses' hooves, the clickety-whir of carriage wheels. The noise slowed and then stopped her; zero at the bone. She dared not turn to look, and hoped the late-night travelers would pass her without notice. From the corner of her left eye she saw the contrivance pull just ahead of her and halt. It was an elegant black brougham with a driver's seat, a cab, and two white horses dappled with dark spots like a leopard's markings.

Emily turned and lifted her head but couldn't make out the driver beyond his silhouette. He was dressed in a heavy coat, collar up, a wide-brimmed hat, and gloves. He turned and lit the two lanterns that were attached to the front of the cab and then resumed his slumped posture. The door swung open and a male voice called out of the dark compartment, "Miss Emily Dickinson?" She blushed as she always did when confronted by a stranger. A man stepped out of the brougham. She took two steps back.

In that instant, she hoped and then thought for certain it was Sam Bowles, editor of *The Springfield Republican* and her clandestine correspondent. His stream of letters had dried up since his wife had discovered that he and Emily referred to her as "the hedgehog." Emily missed him so dearly since his departure for the sanitorium to treat his nervous condition. It would be like him to surprise her with his return in this way. But just as quickly she saw the features weren't Bowles', and her joy curdled.

It was a gentleman, finely dressed in a black tailcoat and trousers, a spotless white shirt. There was a lovely white rose in his lapel. He wore leather gloves and carried a walking stick. The last she dared to take in was his face, which was adorned by a thin mustache but otherwise smoothly shaven. His eyes were dark yet glimmered with the light of the lanterns. His smile was, considering her anxiety, enormously appealing. He took a gold watch from his vest pocket and held it on its chain up close to his eyes. "We're running late," he muttered, as if to himself, but loud enough for her to hear. This fact didn't seem to distress him in the least. In fact, he smiled more broadly.

Her manners obliterated, she called out louder than she'd intended, "Who are you?"

The gentleman stepped up out of the street and onto the sidewalk. "I'm nobody, who are you?" he said and laughed. "You know me," he added.

He wore some subtle cologne that reminded her exactly of the scent of the garden at the height of summer. The chill left her immediately and her breathing eased. "What do you want?" she asked, now more relaxed but still with a fading memory that she'd meant to be defensive.

"I'm here to bring you where you need to go," he said. "I know you're busy so I've taken it upon myself to come for you."

"I'm only going up the street to my brother's house."

"Oh, no, Miss Dickinson, you'll be going much farther than that."

"Please. I'm in a hurry. An emergency."

He took the glove off his left hand and held it in his right. She was incredulous at the effrontery when he reached down and lightly clasped her fingers. At his touch a blast of cold, like a January wind, ran through her body, lodging in her mind and causing a sudden confusion. He had no right to touch her. She meant to protest, to pull her hand away, but every time forgot what she'd intended and then remembered and forgot again.

"If I might call you Emily?" he said in a soothing voice.

"How civil," she thought while still searching within herself for the panic she expected. The cold that had invaded her slowly diffused into a sense of utter calm more comforting than an afternoon with Susan and the new baby. He gave a half-bow and led her toward the brougham as if her fears about him had never existed. She stepped off the curb convinced that a journey was precisely what was needed.

Emily woke to the movement of the carriage. The shades were up and the sunlight shone through the window to her left. She pushed against the hard bench to straighten her posture and yawned.

"You'll want to see this," said the gentleman, sitting opposite her.

He smiled cordially and her spine stiffened, a scream rendered numb fell to the bottom of her throat. He pointed out the sunlit window and his gaze insisted she look. The view was dizzying as the rig sped madly through town. She thought they were caught up in a twister, but then she was able to identify a section of street, and the whizzing scenery slowed to a crawl, as if it and not the carriage were moving. The sidewalks were empty in the late afternoon light, and the aroma of the oyster bar downstairs in the Gunn Hotel pervaded the cab. The very next thing she noticed was the spire of the First Congregational Church, and that was all wrong, for it should have been in the opposite direction.

They went a few more yards down the road and, impossibly, were passing the grounds of Amherst Academy. Whereas the church and hotel were steeped in the summer heat, the three-story school was surrounded by trees whose leaves had gone golden. There were children sitting on the steps of the building and some playing Ring A Rosie in the field out front. Emily remembered that the school had closed just that year, as a new public school had been built. She wondered what had brought the old place back to life. As the carriage rolled by, the children turned in the ring and she glimpsed the laughing face of her second cousin, Sophia.

She gasped and closed her eyes, averting her gaze from the window. "It can't be," she said.

"What's that?" asked her traveling companion.

"My cousin, Sophia. She died of typhus when we were children."

"You don't understand yet, do you?"

"You're taking me to my family, I thought."

"In a sense," he said.

"But then what is all this, this journey through the town all crossways and confusing?"

"You're taking the tour, Emily. Everybody gets the tour."

"The tour of what?" she begged, her voice raised.

"Why, your life, of course. A little summing up before nestling down into your alabaster chamber."

"How do you come to use my private words?"

"I can see you're beginning to see now," he said.

She turned quickly and caught a glimpse of Mount Holyoke Academy, miles away from Amherst, in the early evening, and right after it Amherst Town Hall, with its giant clock lit by morning light.

She looked back at him and asked, "What happened?"

"It comes to all, my dear. You were weak and had one of your seizures and . . . well . . . I have my job to do."

"But Vinnie and Mother and Father?"

"Oh, they're all as well as when you last saw them. It'll be a while more before they get the tour."

"I want to say goodbye to them." Tears formed in her eyes.

He shrugged and opened his gloved hands as if to indicate there was nothing that could be done.

"Where are we going?"

The gentleman banged on the ceiling of the cab with his cane, and the horses instantly set into a gallop. "Toward eternity," he said.

She fell back into the corner of the bench, her face turned toward the window. It was night, no stars visible. Only the bumping of the carriage and the sound of the horses' hooves gave any indication they were moving. They traveled on for what seemed hours and hours, and then she blinked and it was as if they'd arrived in a moment. In the carriage lantern's glow, she could see they'd halted in front of the Amherst Town Tomb, a stone structure built into the earth with a grassy hill of a roof and its cornice in the ground, like a sinking house.

"You are Death," said Emily.

Her fellow traveler sat in shadow. "Call me Quill." He leaned forward so that she could see his face and nodded. "Go ahead. I know you have questions."

Emily knew there was no point in trying to escape or cry out. Although she was terrified, her curiosity was intact. "Which direction am I heading once I'm interred?"

"That's the thing," said Quill, lighting a thin cigar. He swung open the carriage door to blow the smoke out. "I've got nothing to do with that. I don't know what happens after. That will always remain a mystery to me. My specialty is the moment *of*, so to speak, an entire life squeezed down into a flyspeck on the windowpane of the universe. I wish I could tell you more."

"I've done bold things in my life, as quiet as it might have seemed."

"You don't have to convince me, Emily," he said. "I know everything you've done and thought. You've nothing to be ashamed of. Even the falling sickness you tried to hide. It was nothing more than some twisted little knot in your brain work. You and Julius Caesar, my dear. Two emperors, one of men and one of words."

"My secret afternoons?" she whispered.

He shook his head. "I just deliver the spent to their rest."

"But why am I being put into the Town Tomb? It's only for the bodies of those who die in winter when the ground is too hard to dig a grave."

The gentleman clasped the cigar between his teeth and then removed his left glove with his right hand. He snapped his fingers. "There, look now," he said as he pulled the glove back on his hand.

She peered out the carriage window at a snowy scene, the wind howling, drifts having instantaneously formed around the entrance to the tomb.

Quill took a drag on his cigar and tossed it out the door of the cab. As he spoke his words traveled on curling smoke.

*The brain is just the weight of God,*
*For, lift them, pound for pound,*
*And they will differ, if they do,*
*As syllable from sound.*

"You see what I mean?" he asked. "It's metaphorical."

"What is?" she said.

"Everything. The world," he told her. "Come now, let's get to it." He reached his gloved hand out.

She appreciated his gentleness, his friendly manner, but still she pressed her back against the seat and didn't reach to meet his touch. "I'm only thirty-one. A dozen unfinished poems right now await me in my dresser drawer." Her breathing grew frantic.

"Unlike you, Emily, I never tell it slantwise."

"Is there nothing?"

He sat silently for a moment, and then reached out, grabbed the carriage door by the handle, and swung it shut. The sound of it latching brought a change to the scene outside the window. They were no longer in front of the tomb. It was early autumn again, twilight, and the carriage was moving along Russell Street, west, through Hadley, harvest fields to either side.

"Are you much for deals, Miss Dickinson?" asked Quill.

"Deals?" she asked.

"Yes, it so happens I'm in need of a poet. If you'll help me, I'll erase this evening and not bother you again until, uh . . ." He paused and reached into his jacket pocket for a small notebook. Flipping the pages, he finally landed on one and stopped. Running his finger down a list of names, he said, "You'll have another quarter century. It's the best I can do."

"You're saying I can go home?"

"Yes, when we're finished with my errand. It's somewhat dangerous and there's a chance you still might wind up in the tomb if things go awry, but this is the only way."

Emily remembered from her reading of fairy tales the dangers of deals with Death, but she was flattered that he knew her as a poet. "What do I have to do?"

"I want you to help me kill a child," he said.

She shook her head vehemently.

"Hear me out, Miss Dickinson, hear me out," said Quill, and tapped his stick twice on the carriage floor.

"Speak," she said.

"First, keep in mind what I told you about the world being made of metaphor. I know you're an adherent of reality, a devotee of science. 'Microscopes are prudent in an emergency,' you write. Yes, sound advice, but there are those moments of—shall I call it magic? Sorcery? The supernatural, let us say . . . ."

"You mean something like a coach carrying Death, pulling up to take you hither and yon?"

"Well put," he said. "Now, this is where things stand—there's a child, a boy, who has for all intents and purposes died, succumbed to scarlet fever. But his mother has cast a spell upon him to keep him living."

"Can this be real?" she asked.

"It's real. I'm speaking of the power of words. Your father, a devout preacher, would be disappointed in you, not to mention what Reverend Wadsworth might think. In Genesis, God spoke the world and all that's in it. He said, 'Let there be light,' and there was."

"Sophistry," she said. "But go on."

"The fact that I'm prevented from taking the child has caused all manner of problems. In fact, I'd not have had to come for you so early if it wasn't for this one boy—you, and a dozen more whose times were not nigh. I've got to compensate for the aberration. It's not right."

"Why a poet?"

"The spell has to be undone. I'm not sure how, but word magic, I'm guessing, can best be subdued with words. You know, I almost decided to snatch Walt Whitman instead."

Emily winced. "The man's pen has dysentery."

"For me, there's a method to his madness," said Quill. "Like you, he writes about my work quite a bit. He writes that the grass is 'the beautiful uncut hair of graves.' Now that's the spirit. He writes, 'And to die is different from what any one supposed, and *luckier*.' You can see why I appreciate the gentleman."

"Please, allow Mr. Whitman the honor."

"For this task, though, I need a surgeon not a dervish."

She turned again to look out the window and noticed the road was lined with trees. "Where are we?"

"Just beyond Holyoke, heading toward the Horse Caves. The woman in question, the Widow Cremint, has a fine old home there in a clearing just a few hundred yards off the road. It's recently come to my attention that she's been advertising for domestic help in town. We will apply for the positions—a governess for the child and a laborer. No one else will dare to apply. They've all heard rumors and know what she is. I spread those rumors myself in the guise of a traveling preacher. She'll have to take us on."

"You're sure?"

"Nothing's a certainty, but I've been doing this for millions of years."

"Oh, my," said Emily, and brought her open palm to her mouth. "I just remembered one time when a very old woman came to the door of my father's house inquiring where she might find lodging in Amherst. This was when I still answered the door. I gave her directions that would eventually lead her to the cemetery, and told myself, this way she wouldn't have to move more than once in a year." She shook her head. "How I laughed at that mischief. I was laughing at myself."

She looked up for his reaction and noticed some commotion on his shadowed side of the compartment. There was a sound like the flapping of wings, and then something flew toward her. She closed her eyes and brought her arms up.

"Gather yourself," said Quill.

Emily lowered her arms and opened her eyes to morning sunlight. She blinked and then focused on a set of steps before her. When her gaze widened, she took in what she could see of a large, sprawling house that seemed to surpass the Homestead in size but not in upkeep. White paint was peeling, porch railing supports were missing, and one of the front windows had a meandering crack traversing its pane.

The suddenness of day forced her to adjust her balance, and she took a step back and then one forward. Quill, somehow she knew it was Quill, although he was no longer the gentleman of the brougham, stood next to her in front of the door. He was older, tired-looking, with a puffy, wrinkled face and white hair. His drab jacket and trousers were on the verge of tattered. She looked down and saw that she was now wearing a dark blue day dress, but thankfully her walking boots were her own.

"I wear white," she said.

"Not for this," he said, and stepped forward to rap on the door. "All that white you wear; I have a theory that it's symbolic of the blank page."

"Think again, Mr. Quill," she said.

"I hope you don't mind, I've supplied you with undergarments. White, by the way."

"I'll treat them like a blank page," she said, and noticed now that he was carrying a large sack over his shoulder.

The door opened and a tall young woman stood before them. Quill stepped forward and said, "Good day, Mrs. Cremint. I heard in town that you were looking for a laborer and a woman to watch your child. Allow me to introduce myself: I'm John Gullen and this is my daughter, Dagmar."

Emily wondered if the witch would know there was treachery behind Quill's smile. She averted her gaze, but not before noticing the woman's voluminous hair and the inordinate length of her neck. When Emily looked down, she realized that she was wearing the very same blue day dress that Mrs. Cremint wore.

"You, there," said the woman. Emily looked up. "Do you have any experience with children? Have you cared for them before?" Her tone was demanding, and the poet was too nervous to answer. She merely nodded.

"We have a letter of recommendation from our last employer,

Jessup Halstone, Albany, New York. A very wealthy and well-respected gentleman," said Quill. He handed Mrs. Cremint a piece of paper, folded in half. The woman took it and read through it quickly. She handed it back to Quill.

"You can see the place needs work," she said, her voice softening. "I'll take you on. But I want the young lady here—Dagmar, is it?—to know that my child is very frail. He has a serious condition that the doctors cannot diagnose. I should say, those from outside might think his demeanor something strange. If she thinks she can bring herself to treat him as she would any other child, she can have the position."

"I understand," said Emily.

Mrs. Cremint stepped beyond the doorway, approached Quill, leaned forward, and sniffed. She paused for a long spell as if contemplating his aroma while the breeze, laced with pine, played in the surrounding oaks and a chime sounded in the corner of the porch. Then it was Emily's turn, and the woman drew closer than the poet could tolerate. A lump formed in her throat but she dared not swallow. She feared that at any second, she'd tremble and give herself away. A few more moments of deep thought and the lady said, "Come in. I'll show you to your rooms."

She led them down a hallway, Quill directly behind Mrs. Cremint and Emily following. The hall they traversed was lined with the most magnificent paneling, a butterscotch wood with a thousand dark knots visible. There were daguerreotypes lining the walls; sienna portraits of an older gentleman with prodigious mutton chops and dressed in a military uniform. "The pictures are of my late husband, General Cremint," the woman called back. "You may call me Sabille."

"Sabille, very good," said Quill, and the party turned left into a large parlor. The furniture was plush and the books and figurines were arranged neatly on the shelves, but all was cast with an indefinable dinginess, as if the very atmosphere and light had been corrupted. Emily wondered if nature itself might be in revolt against a child denied his death.

After Sabille had shown them to their separate rooms, and she'd briefly haggled with Quill over the terms of employment, she came to Emily and said, "Come and meet Arthur." Her tone was far more pleasant than before, almost conspiratorial. She led Emily back toward the front of the house and then mounted the steps leading to the second floor. "As you can see, there's a lot that needs to be done here. I just haven't had the strength to do everything since my husband died, and also watch the child. The accounts alone—my husband was a well-to-do gentleman—have been neglected, and I need to give them attention before I lose money. Your father will be a godsend in reviving the house."

At the end of the upstairs hallway, there was a door that Sabille waited at as Emily caught up to her. The woman reached out and gently touched the poet's shoulder to draw her near. She whispered, "The boy is very frail, very frail. He likes to hear stories and to play with his wooden soldiers. You'll see that his vitality diminishes with the day. By late afternoon, you'll not recognize him as the child of the morning." She opened the door.

The room was circular, no doubt a turret Emily had not caught a glimpse of in front of the house. There were five windows evenly spaced along the circumference. There was a small bed, a bookcase, a dresser, and a play table with a child's chair, all resting upon a large braided rug. In the miniature chair, there was a boy with his back to Emily. The first things that drew her eye were the intermittent clumps and strands of brown hair on the otherwise bald head. The sight of it depleted her.

He wore a red flannel shirt and a pair of overalls; moccasins on his feet. There must have been a hundred wooden soldiers, each the size of a thumb, arranged on the table as if on a parade ground, readied for inspection. The boy held one in each hand and mumbled to himself. Sabille cleared her throat and spoke. "Arthur, I want you to meet someone."

The boy turned at the sound of his mother's voice, and Emily desperately tried to stifle her astonishment, knowing her life depended on it. Still, an expression of awe escaped her lips, and she instantly recovered by turning the sound into the boy's name. "Arthur, I'm Emily and I've come to keep you company."

His complexion was tinged green and there were scabs and oozing scrapes across his cheeks and forehead. The whites of his eyes were yellowed and the pupils faded to white. Behind his crusted lips, his teeth were brown pegs. He looked to his mother and grunted. Cautiously, he left his chair and stepped across the room to hug Sabille's legs.

Emily lowered herself on her haunches to the child's height. The boy smelled like a muddy streambed, and there was something shiny dribbling from the side of his mouth. "I'm Emily," she said again. She reached out to take the child's scabbed hand, but at the last second he drew it quickly away. His sudden movement frightened her and she reared backward, nearly falling over. As she stood, he opened his horrid mouth at her. A second later, she realized he was laughing.

"A joke?"

Arthur nodded.

"Well," said Sabille, "I see you've got an understanding. I'll leave you two to get acquainted." The boy went back to his chair and soldiers. When the door closed, Emily took a seat on the bed and watched as if she was watching a neighbor through wavy glass on Main Street. The child seemed some kind of little beast sprung up from the forest floor. She worked to reconcile this with the fact that she could detect a child's spirit within the rotting husk. As horrid a figure as the boy cut, something about him reminded her of Austin and Susan's Ned, just born in June. *And I'm to kill him with words*, she thought.

Arthur mumbled continuously, the two soldiers in hand, facing his troops, for over an hour. She waited for something to happen, for war to break out or for the wooden men to suggest an adventure, but the game, in which he seemed entirely invested, was all talk. She listened to make out his words and heard nothing but low barks and burbling mumbles, occasionally a heave, like a fatalist's sigh.

"Arthur," she called to him. "What's happening to the soldiers?"

The boy stared at her over his shoulder. Emily waved to him. Then he turned, put the two soldiers in their empty places in the parade ground revue, and walked to the bookcase. He took a book down. She was horrified at his approach. She knew he would want her to take him in her lap and read him a story. No sooner had that realization dawned than she noticed his flesh had gone from a pale green to a light morbid blue. A clump of his hair fell out as he came across the room, a thin lock tumbled off his shoulder.

He held the book out and grunted. She took the volume from him and then, holding her breath so as not to smell him, she reached out to take him into her lap. His flesh was the slick consistency of rotting mushrooms. When she began to read, she had to eventually breathe, and his aroma conjured in her mind an image of her holding a boy-sized toad. When Arthur made noise and pointed to the book's illustrations, she heard it as croaking.

Only a chapter into the story of Saint George and the Dragon, the boy fell asleep in her arms. His stillness won over her revulsion, and she grew accustomed to his weight and scent. She thought of a spring day a few years earlier when last she'd gone out walking. Carlo was at her side. Just beyond town, the meadow was full of black-eyed Susans. The day was warm and the sun bright. Across the meadow she and the dog moved in among the birch trees and continued on for a mile or more. As she approached a pond, leaves floating upon its surface, she felt a sharp pain in her breast, and woke to Arthur trying to bite her through her day dress.

She cried out and quickly set him on the floor. He showed her his big mouth full of brown shards and she smacked his face. The boy crumpled down onto the rug. She called out his name in a whisper, so as not to let his mother hear. He sprang up onto all fours, gave her another smile, and crawled in circles around the table and chair. To her horror, she noticed her hand print in pale green against the darker blue of his flesh. For the rest of the afternoon, he kept his distance from her and growled if she made any overture of contact.

Luckily, by dinner her handprint had vanished into the overall violet of his face. His flesh seemed to have come unstrung, sagging down in ripples around his neck and making cuffs at his wrists. His breathing had grown labored, and he cried out occasionally as if in pain. He sat, at the head of the dining room table, strapped into a high chair that was much too small for him. Sabille sat to his right and Emily to his left. For the sixth time his mother lifted a spoon of gruel into his mouth, forcing it far down his throat. The child gagged the portion into his stomach and a moment later Emily lifted the half-full bowl she held in order to catch his vomit. The process was repeated with each spoonful. "It's the only way," Sabille repeated as if saying a prayer. Emily was desperate to scream, "The dead don't eat," but held her peace.

At the other end of the table was Quill in the guise of the old laborer, John Gullen. He watched the bizarre feeding, seemingly unable to touch his stew. At one point, Emily looked at him and caught his eye. In her mind she heard his young gentlemen's voice say, "I've seen few things grimmer than this."

"I'm nauseous," Emily told him in her thoughts.

"At bedtime tonight, try to be near enough to them to hear the spell. If I have to spend another day here chopping wood, *I'll* expire."

The last spoonful had been loaded and returned, and Sabille said, "Dagmar, if you'll clean him and bring him upstairs in a minute, I'll prepare his bed."

"Yes, ma'am," said Emily.

Quill stood when the Widow Cremint left the table. Emily set to washing up Arthur, who was slick with gruel and vomit. She gagged more than once in the process. The entire time she worked on him, the boy mumbled at a furious pace, and every now and then released a weak howl of pain. When she was finished cleaning him, he pulled his thumbnail off. It came away from its bed easy as breathing. He dropped it into her open palm, and she put it in her pocket. She hugged him to her and thought she felt him kiss the spot he'd earlier bitten.

Sabille stripped the day's clothes from Arthur's sagging, violet body, and then she and Emily fitted him into the felt bag he slept in. His head stuck out of the end of the sack, and a drawstring was tied snugly around his neck. Carrying him to the bed, Sabille called him "my little caterpillar." When she set his head upon the pillow, strands of hair fell free. Emily waved and wished the boy a sweet night's sleep. She stepped back but didn't leave the room.

"You may go now," said Sabille.

"Yes, ma'am," said Emily, and exited but made sure to only close the door partway. She hid just outside in the darkened upstairs hallway and waited. Through the sliver of an opening, she watched as the mother knelt next to the bed, cooing and shushing the child who rocked frantically from side to side. After a time Arthur finally lay still. She watched Sabille lean over, her mouth near the child's ear.

Emily turned her own ear to the opening. Sabille's whisper was so very low, but each of the words of the spell registered in the poet's mind with utter clarity, like the tap of a pin against a crystal goblet. There were three stanzas and she thought she knew them. She pulled away from the door and leaned back against the wall. "I've got it," she thought, hoping he would hear her.

His voice sounded behind her eyes. "Good. Now *run*," he yelled, and the words echoed through even her most distant memories. "Run to the road."

She slipped away from the open door and crept down the stairs, easing her boots down on each step so as not to be discovered. When she reached the door, her fear banished caution. She flung it open and trounced across the porch, knowing now she'd be heard. Emily hadn't run since she was a girl, but her walking in the woods with Carlo allowed her to keep a steady pace. She dashed along the winding, tree-lined path that led to the road. Only ten yards into her flight, she heard the ungodly baying of some creature. She ran faster, but before long heard the thing galloping behind her.

She pictured a muscular, sleek animal with six legs. When she turned to steal a look, she saw it in the moonlight. It was no beast, but the gentleman in the daguerreotypes, General Cremint. He was naked and wielding a saber. Both the sounds of galloping and baying issued from his open mouth. His eyes were missing, just two black holes. When he noticed Emily glance at him, Sabille's voice came forth, "*Spy,*" she screamed. "*Spy.*"

The old man gained on her, and she could feel the breeze of his flashing sword at the back of her neck. Up ahead she saw the end of the path and the silhouette of the brougham, waiting. Just then the carriage's lanterns blossomed with light. She was tiring, her legs cramping, and she heard Quill calling from the open door, "Lap the miles, Miss Dickinson. Lick the valleys up." She pushed harder but felt the sword tip slice through her hair. The brougham was only feet away.

As she reached for Quill's outstretched hands, Emily saw the driver stand in his box, his arm moving in a sudden arc. She heard the crack of his whip. General Cremint whimpered and fell behind. Quill grabbed her then beneath the arms and lifted her into the brougham. The horses sprang forth, the door of the carriage slammed closed, and they were off. Emily looked quickly to catch one more view of her assailant, the general, sitting in the road, crying, turning slowly to smoke. She moved to the bench across from Quill. Leaning back, catching her breath, she said, "I've forgotten the spell."

"Don't worry," said Quill, again a young gentleman, the rose still fresh in his lapel. "Once you heard it, *I* was able to hear it, and I've got it. Part of the spell was that every night when she used it on the boy I'd never be able to hear it. Once *you* heard it, though, I could hear it in your thoughts. Sabille is already weak. Evidence of that is the illusion of her dead husband she set on you. She must be going mad."

"An illusion?"

"A deadly illusion, but still conjured from nothing."

"It's inevitable she'll lose the child?" Emily asked.

"Exactly. And now you must get to work on the counterspell." The brougham came to a halt. She looked out the window to see that they'd returned to the Town Tomb. Again it was snowing and the drifts around the entrance to the sunken house were ever higher.

"Why are we here again? I've done what you asked."

"I certainly didn't recruit you for your running prowess," he said. "You're a poet, and now begins your work. Come see," he said. "I've brought your writing table from home." He'd removed his glove again. His fingers snapped.

She stood in freezing, damp darkness. She heard the wind howling as if at a distance, and then heard the scratch and spark of Quill lighting a match. The flame illuminated his face. He smiled at her, his breath a cloud of steam, and tossed the lit match over his shoulder. A moment later there was a hushed explosion, a sudden burst of flame, and the place came into view. At first she thought she was in a cave, but a moment later realized it was the Town Tomb.

Quill stood warming himself before a fireplace dug into the rock wall. She saw her writing table and chair. "See here," he said, and pointed to a swinging iron bar that could put a cauldron of water over the flame. "I've acquired your gold and white tea set. You can make tea. What type are you partial to? I'm guessing marble."

She glared at him. "Something strong, and I'll need a bottle of spirits."

"Spirits?"

"Whiskey," she said. "I'll need paper and a copy of the spell."

"There you are," he said, and pointed to her writing table, now complete with pen and inkwell and a stack of fresh paper. He turned and pointed again, and a few feet left of the fireplace there stood a wooden bar, a decanter of whiskey, and glasses. "If you need ice, you can go outside," he said. "It will always be winter while you're here."

"What exactly am I to do?"

"Create a counterspell to Sabille's spell."

"How is one to begin on something like this?"

"That's the challenge," said Quill.

"How long do I have?"

"Eternity, or until you succeed."

"Then I go back."

"For twenty-five years," he said.

"It's blackmail," she said.

"Laws don't apply here, Miss Dickinson. Death is no democracy." He walked toward the door of the tomb. "Might as well get started," he said.

"How will I know if I'm even close?"

"That'll be up to you." The huge door of the tomb slid open. As Quill went out, winter came in, snow flying and a wicked chill. With a distinct click, the door closed, and the wind and world were again distant. Emily took her seat at the writing table. She lit the taper in the candlestick for extra light and adjusted the tulle across her shoulders, a meager attempt at protection against the darkness of the tomb. She felt its blind depths like a breathing presence behind her. Lifting the page on which Quill had copied the spell, she noted his clear and elegant handwriting. The paper smelled of saffron.

She read the words of the spell, but nothing registered. It didn't seem to be what she'd heard. Leaning over the scented page, as if to communicate with it as much as read it, she recited its stanzas in a whisper.

*Stir, stir, stir*
*And stay*
*No leave to go away*
*Burn, burn, burn*
*And rise*
*The sun will be your open eyes*
*Stir, stir, stir*
*And stay*
*All of time to love and play.*

After an hour of contemplation, Emily decided that the spell was useless to her. The magic of the words sprang from the traditions of a culture she knew nothing about. She surmised that her first solution, attempting to rearrange the words of the spell into a poem in order to counteract it, would have no effect. Dogmatic belief in anything was foreign to her. She crumpled the sheet of stanzas, got up, and threw it in the fire. The moment the flames licked the balled sheet black, she felt lighter, like a boat cutting loose its anchor and drifting. She made tea and put whiskey in it.

Sitting, sipping her brew, she noticed that she again wore her own white cotton day dress. She was clear that what she would do was simply write a poem, whatever came to her, and hope that somehow it would have some bearing on the spell. Presentiment, something she'd written about before—"The Notice to the startled Grass that darkness is about to pass"—was to be the order of the long night. She set a sheet of paper in front of her, moistened her pen in the inkwell and then sat there, staring, listening to the blizzard outside, searching for words in its distant shriek. An hour passed, maybe a day or year.

Later, she was brought to by the sound of a groan emanating from the dark back of the tomb where the winter's harvest lay frozen. When the enormous stillness had swallowed the noise, Emily was unsure if she'd really heard it or only heard it in her thoughts. She turned in her chair and looked into the shadows. "Hello?" she called. While she waited for a response, she realized that as long as she'd been in the tomb, she'd not been hungry, she'd not slept, and had no call for a chamber pot. No answer came back from the dark.

She put the tulle around her shoulders and opened the door of the tomb. She was surprised by how easily the enormous weight of it slid back. In a moment the blizzard was upon her. She took two steps out into a drift that reached to her thighs and looked up into the snow-filled night. It wasn't long before the fierce wind forced her to retreat. Once back inside, the tomb door closed, she swung the water cauldron out over the perpetual fire. Tea and whiskey were her only pleasures. She'd noticed that, when she wasn't looking, the decanter refilled itself.

Waiting for the water to come to a boil, she rubbed her hands together in front of the fire, and once they'd warmed she shoved them into her dress pockets. When first she felt the dried gentian petals, she thought them just some scrap of paper she'd jotted a line on at some point. But when she touched the child's nail, she remembered. The water boiled, and she made the tea she'd dreamed about, lacing the brew with a generous shot of whiskey to offset the taste of the boy's nail that twirled atop its plum-colored depths.

In the dream the gentian tea, tasting like the sweetest dirt, had made her mind race, and now too, beneath the ground, her mind raced. Phrases flew, their letters visible, from every grotto of her mind. She stood at the center of the storm, scythe in hand, cutting through the dross. Eventually she lifted the pen and drew ink. The first line came strong to the paper, and there was a pause—a moment, a day, a year—before she hesitantly began on the second line. Slowly, the poem grew. Midway she sat back and wondered which came first, the words or the visions. Her thoughts circled, and then she leaned forward and resumed her work. When she finished, she read the poem aloud.

> *The night woke in me—And I rose*
> *blindly wandering in a Snow*
> *To the Sunken house—*
> *its Cornice—in the ground.*
> *Parlor of shadows—in the ground*
> *The distant Wind—a lonely Sound*
> *Winter's orphans and Me*
> *Undoing knots with Gentian tea.*

# A Terror

The instant the last word was spoken, she rejected it; too obvious to undo a spell of life. She crumpled the sheet and tossed it into the fire. A belief in complexity and complication crept into her thoughts and with that the years fell like an avalanche. She drank tea, and stared at the blank sheet, went outside, and listened for groans in the dark back of the tomb. A million times, a place to begin arrived, and she would think of Arthur trapped in his high chair at dinner, and the line would vanish, too insubstantial to survive.

Later, she was brought to her senses by the sound of something shuffling in the dark behind her. She spun in her chair, her heart pounding. It sounded like weary footsteps. Realizing the sound was approaching, she stood and backed against the writing table. Out of the gloom and into the glow of the fireplace, a wasted figure staggered, an old woman, dressed in black, wearing a black muslin cap atop her white hair. Her face was wrinkled and powdered with dust, and there were patches of ice on her brow and sunken cheeks. She clutched a Bible in her crooked hands.

"Hello," said Emily, surprised as she did so. Even before the old woman stopped and looked up, the poet knew it was the same woman who'd come that time to the house for directions to a place she might stay.

"Excuse me, miss, could you tell me where I might seek lodging in town?" Her voice was low and rumbled in echoes through the tomb. Emily noticed part of the woman's nose had rotted away and that there was something alive in her glassy left eye by the way it bulged and jiggled.

"Go that way, into the dark," said the poet and pointed.

"Thank you for your kindness, dear." The woman turned and shuffled into the shadows.

Emily stood numb from the encounter. "Is the gentian tea still steering my mind?" she whispered.

"No," came the old woman's reply from the back of the tomb. "It's the rising tide of years."

Some piece of eternity later, she sat with pen poised above paper, her arm aching for how long it had been in that position. She barely recognized anymore the crackle of the fire, the distant wind. The pen's tip finally touched the blank sheet, and she heard a new sound that distracted her from her words. The nib made a fat black blotch, and she drew her hand back. "What was that noise?" she said. In her loneliness she now spoke all her thoughts. Finally it came again, something outside. "A person shouting?" No, it was the barking of a dog. She leaped up from the chair and rushed to the door of the tomb. Opening it, she stepped out into the blizzard.

Sitting a few feet off, up to his chest in snow, was Carlo, her Newfoundland, a bear of a dog. He barked again and bounded the drifts to reach her. She was overwhelmed and blinked her eyes to be certain he was there. But then she felt his furry head beneath her hand and he licked her palm. It came to her as if in a dream that she was freezing and she stepped back into the tomb. The dog followed. After closing out the winter, she sat in her writing chair, leaning forward, hugging Carlo to her. "You're good," she repeated, stroking his head. When she finally let go, the dog backed away and sat staring for a long while. His sudden bark frightened her.

"What?" she asked.

The dog barked three more times and then came to her and took the sleeve of her dress. Carlo tugged at her, long his sign for her to follow. It came to her, with his fourth tug and tenth bark, that he was there to take her back. "You know the way," she said to him. The dog barked. She turned to face the writing table and lifted her pen. She quickly scribbled on the blotched sheet, "Gone Home. Mercy." Dropping the pen, she stood and wrapped the tippet around her shoulders. The dog came to her side and she took hold of him by the collar. "Home," she said, and Carlo led her into the dark back of the tomb.

They walked forever and before long he led her by way of a narrow tunnel back into the world. When the moonlight bathed her, she felt the undergarments Quill had given her vanish like a breeze. The dog led her down a tall hill to the end of Main Street. Walking the rest of the way to the Homestead they encountered no one. Quietly, in the kitchen, she gave Carlo a cookie and kissed him between his eyes. After taking off her boots, she tiptoed up the stairs to her room. She removed the white dress and hung it in the closet. She swam into her nightgown and got back into bed.

As her eyes began to close, she felt a hand upon her shoulder. In her panic, she tried to scream but another hand covered her mouth. "Shhh, shhh," she heard in her ear, and feeling cold breath on the back of her neck knew it was Quill. "Lie still," he said. "Let's not wake your parents."

"Leave me alone," she said. She lay back on the pillow without getting a look at his face.

# A Terror

"I intend to," he said. "I merely wanted to tell you that the piece you left in the tomb worked the trick. Three simple words were the key to the spell's lock; a mad but marvelous thing. Arthur is resting peacefully, so to speak."

"So I owe you nothing."

"I'd like to ask you a question, if I may."

"What?"

"All these poems you've written and hidden—so many poems. Why?"

While she thought, morning broke and the birds sang in the garden. "Because I could not stop," she said, and he was gone.

# Michael Blumlein

## SUCCESS

**Michael Blumlein** *is the author of* The Movement of Mountains, X,Y, The Healer, *and* The Roberts, *as well as the award-winning story collection* The Brains of Rats. *He has been nominated twice for the World Fantasy Award and twice for the Bram Stoker Award. His second story collection,* What the Doctor Ordered, *has recently been released. In addition to writing, Dr. Blumlein is a practicing physician. You can find out more about him at michaelblumlein.com and at facebook.com/ blumleinonline*

Dr. Jim lost his job at the University at the unripe age of thirty-six. As brilliant as he was (and this was one brilliant man), his eccentricity had mushroomed during his tenure, and in the end this made him a liability. In his early years at the U, he had published extensively, dozens of papers, all of them notable and a few truly groundbreaking. Then, abruptly, he stopped. Not for lack of results or new ideas (or, for that matter, requests from eminent journals for a submission—any submission—he might deign to send their way), but because, in his words, he had better things to do with his time.

"Better? Meaning what, exactly?" the chairman of his department had asked.

"Meaning I can't be bothered with publishing papers. Meaning the answer is bigger. Meaning I have an idea how it all fits together. All of it. Molecule, cell, person. There's a Unifying Theory of Life, and I get a glimpse of it sometimes, and I feel it sometimes, too, in my body, a tingling, a premonition, but I can't feel it, or see it, for long. Holding on to it is like balancing a pin on my forehead. I need practice. I need time. I can't be interrupted. Grant applications are an interruption. Bench work is an interruption. Thinking up one new experiment after another gets in the way. I'm not interested in data collection anymore. I need to do research of a different kind."

These were not the words of a man who valued his professional career, and certainly not of a man who lived to please his employers. Still, the University indulged him. His work was too respected and important not to. But after several years of escalating complaints from colleagues and students—he was rude; he was unprofessional; he was unapproachable; he was monstrous; he was grandiose—they cut him loose.

Over the next year, reports trickled in of continued erratic and unpredictable behavior (spending sprees, email rants, public and professional diatribes), and at length he was admitted to a psychiatric hospital. All such admissions require a diagnosis, and his, provisionally, was Mania, of the sub-type Accelerando, of the sub-sub-type Non Fugax. Mania Accelerando Non Fugax, known commonly as Flaming Man Disease. By this point he had been flaming for quite some time and had burned many bridges: he'd spent all his money, lost his home, his professional standing, his friends, and, finally, his wife.

There was some disagreement among the psychiatrists as to his diagnosis. There were features that didn't fit the classic definition of FMD, one being that he had no history of mental illness. Another: there was no family history of it, either. Most troublesome of all (and most problematic, diagnosis-wise), he didn't respond to medication. And FMD did, reliably. If not one drug, then another. And if not a single drug, then a combination of drugs: two, three, sometimes four of the bad boys, what they liked to call a cocktail.

But two, three, four had no effect on Dr. Jim. No matter what he took or was forced to take, he remained the man who first was wheeled down the corridor: wild-eyed, wacky, savage at times, brilliant at other times, hyperactive, insomniac, volatile, and unreachable, as detached from his caregivers as a hinge torn free of its door.

A meeting was held regarding what to do next. When a treatment that is known to succeed one-hundred percent of the time does not, there are basically two choices, as his panel of clinicians well knew:

1. Question the diagnosis.

2. Question the treatment.

In the best of all worlds, the questioning should proceed in that order, but time was short, the budget was tight, and there were other meetings to attend and other patients to cure. And while diagnosing a tricky illness was always satisfying, discovering a new treatment, for those impatient to get on with things, was an order of magnitude more satisfying: it was the difference between building a rocket and flying a rocket, between Sherlock and Santa.

A combination of electric, magnetic, and sonic shock, both extra-corporeal (at a distance) and intra-corporeal (by means of a cranial stimulator, linked wirelessly with esophageal and anal emitters), delivered in asynchronous "swan-neck" pulses over a period of hours, was settled on. (The idea, basically, was to shock the bejesus out of him and hope for the best.) The night before he was to enter the pantheon of brave and nameless medical pioneers (in this case, as the first to receive a treatment that would later, god help us, become the standard of care), he was shaved, showered, and dutifully prepared.

At nine o'clock he was seen nervously pacing his room. He looked agitated. His eyes were as wild as ever and he appeared to have no idea who or where he was.

At ten o'clock he was seen lying on his bed.

At eleven o'clock he was still lying on his bed, but this time his eyes, thank god, were closed.

At midnight the room was empty. It was as if he'd vanished into thin air.

The alarm was raised. Patients were roused from sleep. Every inch of the hospital was searched. Eventually, the police were called in, but they had no better luck than the hospital staff in finding him. A day went by, then another. His disappearance fueled rumors among the patients of alien abduction, interdimensional travel, suicide, homicide, and your basic institutional foul play. A meeting was scheduled to squelch these rumors, but the night before, the third night of his disappearance, an orderly and a nurse slipped into his now vacant room for a quick one.

It was dark, and they didn't see the shape stretched out on the bed. Didn't know there *was* a shape, much less a human one, until the nurse, straddling the orderly's hips, arching back and uttering a crescendoing series of deep-throated moans as he acrobatically and prestidigitationally multitasked her voluptuous external and internal parts, felt the touch of flesh on her shoulder blade. She let out a yelp.

# Success

The orderly, fully aroused, delivered his package, then eased her down to the floor. Hurriedly, they reassembled themselves, then flicked on the light. Lying on the bed, freshly shaved and in a natty new set of threads, was Dr. Jim. His eyes were closed, as though to spare them the embarrassment of having been seen. Neither of them believed he was asleep.

The nurse smoothed her blouse, cleared her throat and said his name. His eyelids fluttered open and he turned his head. He looked surprised to see them, or at least he acted surprised, along the lines of "what a nice surprise," as though theirs was an unexpected but welcome visit. Pointedly, he didn't act crazy.

He sat up in bed, and he and the nurse had a conversation. It was lively, amicable, comprehensible, and sane. In short, nothing like previous conversations he had had. What it wasn't was informative. Dr. Jim offered no explanation for where he'd gone or what had happened. When asked, first by the nurse and later, repeatedly, by a procession of psychiatrists, he professed ignorance. But clearly something had happened.

He was changed in nearly every way, from his appearance, which was no longer slovenly, to his manner, which was no longer like a relationship gone bad. His voice was calm and composed. His speech was clear, his reasoning logical and precise. He looked his interlocutors in the eye when he spoke. His facial expressions were appropriate accompaniments to what he said. He smiled when a smile was called for, knit his brows when a difficult question was asked. His behavior, which, at best, had been bizarre, and at worst, menacing and provocative, could have been lifted from Emily Post.

He was, in short, an exemplary patient. A civilized, approachable, exemplary man and a credit to his—the human—race.

They observed him for a week, tested him, retested him, then let him go. With no job, no house, and no wife, he pretty much had to start from scratch.

※

Fast-forward five years. Dr. Jim has a new wife. He has a new house, a modest two-story post-and-beamer with a basement and a fenced-in backyard. His dream of finding and elucidating the Unifying Theory of Life on Earth is very much alive, as is his faith that the answer lies in the biological sphere, and further, in the molecular biological sphere, to wit, the gene, the epigene, and the perigene, the so-called holy trinity of creation and life. There are, of course, other spheres, non-biological ones, along with non-biological answers, and these, he assumes, will make themselves known when the time is right.

For now his hands are full. There's the house to take care of. There are his daily visits to the basement. There's his wife, Carol, a stellar woman of unparalleled beauty and intelligence. And of course there's the dream, which occupies center stage.

For the past four years, Dr. Jim has been working feverishly to put his dream into words, to make it concrete, comprehensible, and readable, so that others can know it, too. He no longer uses a lab of his own, has no need of a lab—his mind is a lab, and it pullulates with thought experiments. In addition, he culls through the work of others. He has learned the rudiments of half a dozen languages, reads extensively, and keeps in touch with researchers around the globe. His name can still open doors (though with roughly equal frequency it closes them); to avoid awkwardness or misunderstanding he mostly uses a pseudonym: Dr. Jean Marckine, a play on the great Jean-Baptiste Lamarck, unjustly disdained and discredited in his own time and for many years thereafter, and presently in the process of being rehabilitated. And soon, if Dr. Jean Marckine has anything to say about it, to be raised to the pedestal upon which he belongs.

Dr. Jim is writing a book. Already it's more than five hundred pages long. The first three hundred pages describe, in the briefest possible terms, the gene, a hopeless but necessary task. The next two hundred concern the epigene, and he is far from done. The complex of histone, protein, and DNA, the shifting chimera of amino and nucleic acids, forming and breaking covalent and ionic bonds like on-again, off-again lovers, deserves a book of its own. For if the gene is the key, the code of life, the epigene is the hand that turns the key, the force behind the code. The epigene cradles the gene, it gives structure and organization and flexibility to the genome. Elucidating it has been his life's work, up to now.

Of late the going has been slow. Some days he sees clearly and writes up a storm; other days his vision is clouded, cataracted, and he produces little of worth. The epigene will not give up its secrets lightly, and the closer he gets, the more it seems to resist his efforts. Now and then he feels as if he's in a dogfight, much as he feels when he goes downstairs. But it will yield to him: in time it will yield completely. Of this he has no doubt.

# Success

The perigene, he hopes, will also yield, though the when and the how are less certain. The task confronting him is so much greater and will therefore require commensurately greater, deeper, and more profound levels of imagination and thought. For as the epigene is to the gene, so the perigene is to the epigene: more complex by far, cryptic, Delphic, cosmic, grand, and elusive. It will be the final section of the book and its crowning achievement, the centerpiece of the Unifying Theory of Life.

He can't wait to get started on it and at the same time is almost afraid to begin, a paradox common to all great endeavors and forays into the unknown, and the perigene most certainly is this. Its existence, far from being the subject of a healthy debate, is on nobody's radar, nobody's tongue. It's a mystery of the most mysterious sort—one that is never mentioned, never acknowledged, never discussed. One might say it's his own conceit and creation.

To which he would respond: not a creation but a prediction, along the lines of gravity, relativity, and the Higgs boson. The perigene is a fact of life and law of nature, merely waiting for the proper experiment to be observed firsthand.

But that's in the future. His present task is to do justice to the epigene, which is taking all his considerable mental muscle and then some. In periods, like now, when the going is slow, frustratingly so at times, calculated, or so it feels, to bleed a man of his confidence, he gives thanks for the two pillars of his life, without whom he would almost certainly crumble:

First and foremost, his wife Carol, an impeccable woman of energy, stability, self-discipline, and mental prowess. She heard him lecture once when she was in graduate school, was duly impressed, ran into him years later as a post-doc, and from there things evolved. Like him, she values the life of the mind, but she's not apt to go overboard and lose her mind—to impulse, say, or whim, or folly. She's as balanced as a judge, as organized and orderly as a statistician. She's driven, but not to distraction, has a clear vision of her future and feet that are planted firmly on the ground.

Second and also foremost, the creature downstairs, who is nameless. He gives himself no name, and Dr. Jim is not about to give him one either. Providing him a name would be like bestowing on him a quality he lacks, legitimizing and at the same time compromising him, robbing him in a sense, like offering a man a suit of clothes in exchange for the man himself.

≋

*From Dr. Jim's Diary:*

*Wednesday, October 14th. Wake up, roll out of bed, throw on some clothes, go downstairs. He's waiting for me, as usual.*
*We fight.*
*I win.*
*Hunker down with Chapter Seventeen (Epigenetic Control of Transcription). Progress slow, then sudden. Inch inch inch along, then leap ahead.*
*Very much like evolution.*
*Which had a middling good day.*

*Thursday, October 15th. Wake up, stagger out of bed, take a leak, stop in the kitchen for a mini-bowl of Mini-Wheats, then down to the frigid basement. There's a twisted hairline crack developing in the concrete floor. Resembles a helix, smashed and flattened like a bug on a windshield. The bars of the cage are icy cold.*
*He looks sleepy. I'm unimpressed. He has a million looks.*
*We fight.*
*I win.*
*Get stuck on the idea of the histone as a spool of thread. Perseverate. Get nowhere. Rescued by Carol, who takes me to lunch.*

*Tuesday, October 20th. Get downstairs later than usual on account of last night, when Carol came to bed after I was half-asleep and made it known by lying absolutely and unnaturally still and quiet that she was not about to fall asleep anytime soon but was determined not to make me pay the price for that, bless her heart, although if I, of my own free will, chose to wake up in order to find out what was bothering her, not that I need to know everything, or that she even wants me to, but it's a relief to talk and have someone listen, or even pretend to listen as long as it's convincing (and why that is I don't think anybody knows for sure... question: does talking upregulate genes, leading to more talking, and is this Lamarckian, i.e., inheritable? Will future generations of upregulated talkers increase their affinity for oxygen so they don't turn blue in the face, or talk themselves to death? Will listeners similarly upregulate their listening genes? Crazy people often talk—and listen—to no one, and no* one wants to be like that, but I digress), then that would be a mark in my favor. It's the little sacrifices that keep the marriage ship on course.

So we talked, and after that we made love. Carol was a hellcat, which talk can do to a woman. She tore off my clothes, then pushed me down, sat on my chest, and raked my sides with her nails. While she was doing that, she bent over and poured her tongue into my mouth, soft and sweet as honey, then hardened it and rammed it at my throat, like I was ramming her. She bit my neck, then moved south and had a go at my nipples. I wasn't complaining through any of this, except when she got carried away and took the poor little nubs between her canines. I yelped then and she stopped, no blood drawn.

Woke in the morning with the sun on my face. Still wiped out from the previous night, but do what I have to. He's standing on the other side of the cage when I stumble down, big and tall and hairy, puffed out in the chest like a bag of Cheetos. He smiles that toothy smile of his, looking smug, and sensing an advantage, takes a step forward. The punk. Trying to get me to make a false move. That, and pull me down to his level. That low-ass level of his. Daring me to dirty my hands.

Thing is, I got no problem with that level. I like that level. He of all people should know.

We fight. Boom boom. It's over in an instant.

I'm buzzing with energy when I get upstairs, but for some reason it doesn't translate into progress on the book. This is becoming more and more of a daily occurrence, and I can't begin to describe how frustrating it is. It's not like the epigene isn't known. It's been studied and characterized in a fair amount of detail, and while it's true that I'm breaking new ground, it shouldn't be this hard. The damn thing should be there for me, but I keep hitting a wall, and I know it's a wall of my own making. Can't see over it and can't quite punch through it. As if something besides the epigene is at work, raising and thickening the wall, making it impervious to me. This, I'm convinced, can only be one thing: the perigene, its commander-in-chief.

So elusive. So potent. Taunting, humbling, and, so far, defeating me.

Carol's in the kitchen when I come downstairs from a wasted morning in my study.

"How's it going?" she asks.

I grunt my displeasure.

She motions toward the basement. "How about down there?"

I shouldn't have to tell her that conversation's off-limits.

There's an awkward moment, then she hands me a king-size box. "I *bought you something yesterday."*

*Inside is a brand-new shirt with a matching tie and a crisp new pair of pants. The woman is devious.*

*"A little pick-me-up," she says. "That's all."*

*"Dress for success" is one of her mottos. Meaning, do something for yourself, and your self will thank you. She's very Lamarckian that way.*

*"You might want to shave, too."*

*It's been a few days. I see where she's going with this.*

*"Don't worry," I tell her.*

*"I'll wait," she says.*

*I end up doing the whole works—shave, shower, shampoo, new duds. Half an hour later I return to showcase the updated product.*

*"How do the pants fit?" she asks.*

*"Perfectly."*

*"You look good."*

*"I feel good."*

*She nods, as though this were obvious. "I'm going to be gone for a couple of days. There's a conference I need to attend. It's a last-minute thing."*

*"I'll miss you."*

*"I'll call."*

*She's standing by the window that overlooks our weedy and neglected yard. Usually she keeps the curtains drawn because she hates how it looks. She hates clutter and chaos of all sorts, whether natural or man-made. You'd think we'd get out there and do something about it, but neither of us has had time.*

*Today, for whatever reason, the curtains are open. I find myself staring.*

*"See something?" she asks.*

*"I don't know. I had a thought."*

*"Which was?"*

*"The weeds. Look at how they grow—higher and higher, as though reaching for something."*

*"The sun."*

*"In their case, yes. But something else could reach for something else."*

*"Such as what?"*

*"I'm not sure."*

*"You going to cut them down?"*

*"The weeds? I might."*

# Success

"Do you know how happy that would make me?"

"Put something else in their place."

"Anything would be better."

"Not just anything."

She gives me a look. Her eyes like diamonds. Her short blond hair (which is how she wears it, having no use for the long and messy curls nature gave her) rimming her perfect face like a nimbus.

"You had a glimpse of something," she says. "What?"

I shrug.

"C'mon. You did. What was it?"

"It's gone."

She comes up and punches me on the arm. "It's not gone, bozo."

She tightens the knot on my tie, straightens my collar and smoothes my shirt. Making me neat and tidy, folding me—like the stuff she brought in the box—into the right shape, bringing order to chaos, bringing me, that is, into her own special universe, accepting no less. In response, I throw back my shoulders and straighten my neck, as if rising to her expectations, and in a flash it comes to me, like a bolt from above: the epigene is a marriage. It's the union of two separate and complementary entities, two lovers—gene and protein—in an ever-changing dance. And if all goes as it should, an ever-changing harmony. It's a piece of work that's never finished, like a building under continual construction and remodeling. One small alteration—to the histone, say, the protein scaffold—and the entire complex changes. If one were to build the epigene, represent it visually, in space, it would be a structure of constant self-adjustment and shifting shape, with a default of perfect balance. It would be mobile and highly internally interactive. A thing of perfect logic and supreme beauty.

A ballroom of coupling and uncoupling molecules.

A church, wedding form and function. A reflection, however pale, and a conduit, however hidden at this point, to the Highest Power, The Unifying Principle of Life.

This is the epigene, and I can demonstrate it.

And the perigene? The Highest Power itself?

That comes next.

All this occurs to me in the blink of an eye. Carol, my delivering angel, smiles a knowing smile, takes me by the shoulders, turns me around and gives me a gentle shove in the back.

"Go get 'em, champ."

It's a huge relief to use his body instead of his head. He spends a good week clearing out the yard. Gets rid of junk, pulls weeds, digs up roots, cuts down shrubs and the one small, disease-ridden tree. When he's done, there's a clearing about half the size of the house's footprint.

For the next stage, he's jotted down some notes and drawn up a preliminary design. The idea is that the structure will be a bridge to the book. When completed, it will loosen his tongue, unblocking whatever it is that has him at such a standstill, and the rest of the epigene section will write itself. That's the plan, and why the hell not? Man had hands long before books, and he used them quite nicely to express himself. Caves were painted long before the Dead Sea Scrolls were inscribed. Pots were thrown. Figurines were sculpted. Cairns and henges were built to communicate complex ideas, only much later transcribed with ink and pen. All of which merely goes to show what every monkey knows: the spatial brain underlies the speaking brain, just as the roots and trunk of a tree prefigure its crown. Dreams and wordless visions traffic between the two, and Dr. Jim intends to take advantage of this by writing his dream and his vision in space.

He's no Michelangelo. But what he lacks in expertise, he makes up for in panache. He uses bought, found, and scavenged materials— from copper pipes to plastic tubes, from lengths of wood to auto parts (axels, shafts, and rods), from moving gears to strips of sheet metal, from circuit boards to computer screens—basically anything he can lay his hands on. These he attaches and assembles in whatever way seems most suitable and appropriate: by bolt, nail, glue, duct tape (naturally), wire, rivet, weld. A fat extension cord snakes from the house to power the electronics as well as the small motors that move the various ball joints, winches, chains and gears. The years he spent in his uncle's machine shop, daydreaming and slaving away, are finally rewarded. In a month, his creation stands five feet tall and ten feet wide. It moves with a ceaseless, jerky, rickety-rackety energy, somehow managing not to tip over. It resembles a spastic, multi-limbed robot that can't make up its mind what to do with itself. That, or a primitive, possibly alien, probe. It also resembles what it is: a junkyard raised by its bootstraps. To Dr. Jim, however, who knows that the epigene is comprised of molecules at least as odd-looking and diverse, it's just the beginning of his life-sized model of reality.

He works nonstop, from dawn to dusk, breaking only when Carol happens to come out. He loves her visits, which never fail to take him by surprise, so absorbed is he in his project. He loves her fearless eye and supple intelligence. He loves how she keeps her distance, allowing him his freedom, and at the same time finds ways to encourage him. He loves her face and her body, and how, on occasion, usually at his instigation, that face and that body attach themselves to him.

She, in turn, loves to see him being productive again. She loves to watch him from the kitchen window, half-hidden, before she leaves for work. His boundless energy. His brain. His hair, which is lengthening, and the way he tosses his head to get it out of his face. His shirt (she makes sure he wears a clean one every day) stained with sweat. His facility with tools. His creative bursts. It's as though, through this new, sideways endeavor, this temporary substitution of one form of expression for another, he's been unchained.

Like Hercules, she thinks proudly.

Like Samson.

Like that animal...what's its name? The one with three heads. The dog, straining at its leash. Cerberus.

But no. That would not be her Dr. Jim. Dr. Jim has freed himself of his leash.

Cerberus would be someone else.

〰〰

*Carol's Diary:*

Carol's diary is blank.

Carol, née Schneeman, now James, took her degree in anthropology, with a minor in biology, and parlayed these into a doctorate in one of late-century academia's favorite inventions, the hybrid career. Hers is called ethnobiology, and her particular area of interest is inheritance, specifically the interplay between individual inheritance and group inheritance, between genetic and non-genetic modes of transmission of human information and behavior. The dance, as she likes to say, between molecules and memes. She teaches and does research at the local university, and unlike her formidable husband has no trouble fitting in and getting along.

On the contrary, the job is nearly a perfect match. She likes being part of an institution, likes the stability, the structure, the hierarchy, the clear expectations and tiered chain of command. Having rules frees her from having to waste time ruling herself, and knowing her role frees her to inhabit that role fully. She's a star on the rise and has been steadily climbing the academic ladder. Her sights are set on tenure, and a decision on whether or not she receives it will be made before the year is out.

The chances are good, but there's no guarantee. The field is small and highly competitive, and budgets everywhere are tight. What she needs is another publication. And not just any publication, but something exceptional, to put her name squarely on the map.

She has no dearth of ideas and has made a list of the seven that excite her most. She has put in countless hours of preliminary research, drawn up detailed outlines, including a meticulous inventory of the pros and cons of each. She is nothing if not conscientious, which for her is merely another word for doing the job.

She has set herself a deadline of December 1st, so she'll have the winter break to get a jump start. By the end of November she has whittled the list to three topics. She saves then emails the list to herself, intending to have a final look at it that night. If necessary, she'll sleep on it and come to a decision in the morning.

Arriving home, she finds her husband hard at work, and she takes a moment to watch him unobserved. The piece is growing, in both size and strangeness. No surprise there. Nor is she surprised by her reaction to it: amazement and indigestion. The thing has not yet reached above the fence, and they have an agreement that he will stop before it does. The question is, will he honor the agreement? And how far is she willing to go to enforce it if he doesn't? A clash seems inevitable, which she'd prefer to avoid, not for fear of conflict so much as for the chaos of emotion that is sure to follow in its wake. As a preemptive measure, a sort of prophylactic antidote, she goes inside and straightens up the house. Afterward, she feels better, and better still after swigging down a healthy helping of antacid, its viscousy chalkiness dulling the burn like a protective coat of paint.

Fortified, she's able to turn a calmer and less partisan eye on the mad chimera of her husband's fevered brain. She asks herself if good science can truly come of bad, or at least undisciplined, art. She herself could never work this way, but she herself is not the subject.

The man who is has his own trippy way of thinking when he's doing science (conceiving and designing experiments, for example), or when, like now, he's doing science once removed. He appears to work at random, but she knows this isn't the case. He has a plan, even if he can't articulate it. He'll execute it, and once it's done, he'll know what it was to begin with. (This would be like working backwards for her.) His eccentricity looks eruptive, even slapdash, but it bears the stamp of an interior design.

She can kind of see what he's getting at, the spiraling core of pipes and tubes, which must represent strands of DNA, the chunkier lattice of wood and metal surrounding it, like a supporting structure, each section moving and bending through hinge and ball-and-socket joints and rotating gears, smoothly at times but mostly not. Herky-jerky and spastic, like a newborn's twitchy limbs, but less every day, also like a newborn. Self-corrective and decidedly interactive. It's his vision of the epigene, which they've talked about, and which, in fact, is on her final list of topics. Not his vision of it, but hers.

The epigene, so her thinking goes, is not simply a biological phenomenon, it's a model for how change of any sort—on an individual level and on a larger scale, a societal scale—occurs. And how the different levels of change influence one another and interact. It can be used to describe and predict political, cultural, biological, psychological, anthropological and sociological transformations (any and all of which, she suspects, can be given eigenvalues). Potentially, a powerful tool. And it hasn't been written about, not in the ethnobiology literature, which means the field is wide open.

She sleeps a dreamless night, which is how she likes them, wakes early, and intercepts her husband before he disappears downstairs. This is critical, because once he does that, any meaningful conversation is pretty much a lost cause.

"Can we talk for a minute?" she asks.

He steals a glance at the basement door, gives a curt nod.

"It's about me," she adds in the interest of full disclosure.

What he wants most is to get to work. Second-most is for his Carol to be happy.

"You know what I was before a scientist?" he asks.

It's not the best beginning, but she plays along. "What's that?"

"I collected beetles. Studied them, labeled them. Like Darwin. Raised some, too. Left the collection to my science teacher when I graduated high school."

"And you tell me this because…."

"There're three skills you need to be a successful collector. One, you need to be curious. Two, you need to be patient. Three, you need to be able to pay attention."

She gives him a look, like "are you kidding me?" Then one of her eyebrows rises, just the one, which she can do only if she doesn't try. If she does try…nothing. It's controlled from somewhere beyond her control, like a tic but with a beautiful, arching purpose, and it happens once in a blue moon, when curiosity, skepticism, and annoyance intersect.

"So this is what? Yes, you'll listen to me? Or yes, you'll observe me and take notes?"

"I'll give you my thorough and undivided attention."

She knows he's capable of this. For how long is always the question.

"Thank you. I could use your help."

She leads him to the living room, which has a pair of windows, one facing the street; the other, the yard. The latter is a potential distraction for him, but less of one than the door and stairway to the basement, which are like the siren's call. He can only resist them for a certain amount of time, mainly, she assumes, because he doesn't want to resist. If he did want to but couldn't, she would worry that something was seriously wrong.

He takes the sofa, placing his back to the window overlooking the yard, and makes eye contact with her.

It's a gesture of sincerity on his part, and feeling bullish— provisionally—about the upcoming conversation, she lowers herself into an armchair. "I'm coming up for tenure soon." Pauses, can't tell if his look is expectant or blank. "You know that, right?"

"Yes. Of course."

"I've decided to write a paper on the epigene. My side of it, my version. A view through the ethnobiological lens."

"Interesting."

"I'd like to pick your brain."

He half-turns his head toward the window and makes a flourish with his hand. "There it is."

"Will it bother you? My writing about it?" She means before he does.

"Not at all. Pick away."

She summarizes what she's read: the epigene is a dynamic system. It's in a state of continual flux, but every so often something gets fixed in place. A molecule is attached at a certain spot, and this causes a permanent change.

"Correct," he says. "Relatively permanent."

"And this is different and distinct from a change in the sequence—a mutation, say—of the DNA. Which is what people usually think of when they think of permanent genetic change."

"Not molecular biologists."

"Normal people," she says.

"A benighted bunch."

She pushes on. "And the reason this molecule is formed, then attached, can be due to a number of factors. Hormones, for example. The environment. Stress."

"Yes. The engine of progress, fortunately, has many triggers."

"And this change can be inherited."

"For a generation or two. In certain cases more."

"So evolution can be fast, not slow. It doesn't need eons to manifest itself." The idea is as exciting now as when she first heard of it.

"It's always fast, when it happens."

"What I mean is, it doesn't have to be random. It can be responsive and even purposeful."

Purpose, he would say, is a human concept. Evolution of whatever stripe conforms to the laws of chemistry and physics, not the laws and needs of man. But that's a discussion for a different time and place. Fundamentally—biologically, that is—she is right.

"Expression is the key," he says. "Everything else is just wishful thinking. A change in the epigene or even the DNA sequence does nothing if it doesn't result in other changes: transcriptional or translational changes, in RNA expression and protein synthesis. Otherwise it just sits there, like a train in the station. Only when the train starts moving does it actually become what it is. Only then does it deserve the name 'train.'"

"I like this," she says. "Random mutation is so...so...random. So passive. So gloomy. It cheers me up to know we can do something. We can adjust. We *do* adjust."

"Constantly."

"I like the idea that we're in active conversation with everyone and everything, whether we know it or not. We're participants, not bystanders. We can control who we are and who we become."

"To a degree," he says, then adds, "Control appeals to you."

"Self-control, yes. And I like that we're not complete pawns in the game. That we have something to say about our destiny. I like it because I like it, and I like it even more because it's true."

"You're an idealist."

"I'm an optimist," she offers as an alternative.

"I'm one, too. But realistically, there's only so much we can do."

"Of course. We're only human."

He grins. "Will you mention Lamarck?"

"I will. How could I not? Epigenetics should have a footnote with his name attached."

On this they agree. It wasn't called epigenetics back in those explosive eighteenth- and nineteenth-century days of observational science, but rather the inheritance of acquired traits, a controversial theory, the most famous example of which was the progressive lengthening of a giraffe's neck so that it could reach higher leaves and thus out-compete its fellow giraffes. Such a trait, so the thinking went, was passed on to its progeny. A fair number of scientists held this opinion in an often heated and partisan debate, but it was only one arrow in Lamarck's remarkable quiver. His observations and conclusions about the natural sphere were seminal. He was among the first to believe—and demonstrate—that the world was an orderly place, built and governed according to immutable natural laws. This was before Darwin, who later paid homage to him.

As Dr. Jim does now. "A towering figure, Jean-Baptiste. A gifted scientist."

"He deserved better than he got."

"He bore the cross, it's true. You'll point this out?"

"I'll state the case. It's not total chaos down here. We're not doomed to some predetermined fate. If people want to believe otherwise, there's not much I can do. But if it was me, I'd take heart."

"Lamarck did. It pleased him to know there was structure. Structure and purpose. He liked a world like that."

Who wouldn't? she thinks. It seems the most human of desires and beliefs. How could anyone live with the inevitable highs and lows of life, the swings and shifts of fortune, not to mention mood, without stable ground to stand on and without purpose?

"He liked his giraffes getting taller to reach those leaves," Dr. Jim adds. "His waterbirds developing webbed feet to improve their swimming. These were useful adaptations, and usefulness was rewarded."

"In Heaven and on Earth," she replies, a reference to the world in which he and everyone else of his time lived, the world of religion and the tug-of-war between religion and science.

"Heaven?" Dr. Jim cocks his head. "Is there such a place?"

"He was Catholic. I'm sure it was useful not to antagonize the Church."

"Antagonism is who we are. Rise and fall, push and pull, positive and negative feedback. Contradiction defines us." His eyes drift toward the kitchen, and his attention wavers, then shifts. "We'd be nothing without it," he adds in a trailing voice.

It's a reference, she assumes, to his visits downstairs, and it's as close as he'll come to mentioning them. Although, when she thinks about it, it could be a reference to almost anything, and in fact, his attention has veered again, this time back to the yard, where his gaze is now fixed. In profile the changes in his face are more pronounced, the thickening of the muscles along his jaw, the roughening of his cheeks with their now ubiquitous stubble, the deepening of his eye sockets and paradoxical prominence of his eyes. He looks, oxymoronically, both nourished and underfed, replete and hollowed out, a man of wealth and of hunger, sybarite and victim of his own fanaticism, at this particular moment in intense communion with what he's built.

The look is not deceiving. He's enchanted by what he sees, especially his latest addition: a tetrad of pulleys fused together, a kind of block and tackle, which represents the four-pronged histone unit of the epigene. Through one of the pulleys he's threaded a cable, which represents a strand of DNA. The histone both protects and holds the DNA firmly in place, but below it, between it and a second tetrad of pulleys, the cable is more open and exposed, more accessible and also freer to move, like a running loop of rope. DNA-wise, this is where the action is. Where genes transcribe themselves, communicate with other genes, make RNA and proteins.

He's built, in short, an epigene within the epigene, a microcosm of the whole, a kind of fractal. His paltry skills as an engineer and sculptor don't come close to capturing what the real McCoy represents and does, what it's capable of. Such a cunning design, the epigene. Such a beautiful, pliant system. But what next? What next?

The question casts a shadow on his lofty thoughts and sunny state of mind. He doesn't have the answer, and his love affair with what he's done is pierced by uncertainty. He feels a heaving in his chest, and all at once he's drowning in a sea of negativity and doubt. It happens like that: full of himself one moment, fighting for air the next. Presto chango. Snappety-snap. It's a cold, dark place he's fallen into. A bottomless, watery prison if he doesn't get out. It takes every ounce of will to resist the descent. He has to get downstairs, throws a glance toward the kitchen, struggles to his feet.

A hand stops him.

"Stay," says Carol. "Please. Just a few minutes more. Then I'll let you go. This is really helpful."

Her hand is manacled around his wrist, and he glances at it, then bares his teeth. Immediately, she lets go and quickly threads her fingers through his. He's trembling, and she steadies him with a firm, reassuring grip. She's iron to his quicksilver, ground to his jagged downward burst. At the moment she's also a force greater than the siren call. But not for long.

A minute or two. Max.

"What were we talking about?" he asks in a gravelly voice.

"Lamarck."

He nods, waits, searches her face.

"Will you sit?" she asks.

He sits.

"You said he was a gifted scientist," she prompts.

"A true scientist," he replies after a lengthy silence.

"True? In what way?"

"Not everything he did or said was right. But his effort was right. His passion. I count him as a colleague."

The similarities between Lamarck and her husband have not escaped her. She has certain concerns about this, which must be handled delicately, and she asks herself if now is the time.

"He had a passion for truth. Is that what you mean?"

"For reason, I would say."

She accepts his correction, though it makes her just a tad uneasy. Passion can submarine reason, just as certainty can masquerade as truth.

"Do you know he had no money when he died? His family had to beg for the funds to bury him. Couldn't afford a private grave and had to put him in a rented one."

"He was dead."

"Still."

"Private. Rented. What's the difference?"

"I'm sure it felt different to his survivors. Especially when he was kicked out after the lease expired."

"Great men suffer. It's the same old story. He was brilliant but ahead of his time. His views were not accepted."

"Are yours?"

He doesn't miss a beat. "They will be, when I make them known."

She doesn't doubt it, though she does wonder how long this might take. Two hundred years, as it took for Lamarck, would be on the long side for her.

Not that she's impatient, though she does worry a little about money, because her husband at the moment is making absolutely none. Her income supports them both. A non-issue if she gains tenure. If she fails, they will have to cut their expenses drastically, maybe even sell the house. Live in a trailer, not the worst thing. Revert further and live in the woods.

She could make it. That said, she'd rather have money than not. She likes what it does. Likes having what she needs when she needs it. Likes being able to support Dr. Jim in his quest. She'd prefer not having less of the stuff, though if it came to that, she'd survive.

She's been poor before. She grew up poor. Nothing was ever handed to her on a platter. All that she's gained has been the result of her own hard work.

It's because of this that she values hard work, and it's one of the reasons she values and respects her husband. No one could work harder than he does. And if it comes to pass that he finishes what he's building and goes on to publish his epic book, and it makes no money, she'll be disappointed because he will be, but otherwise she'll be okay. She understands that poverty for some men and for many women is the price of eccentricity. It's the cost of being different, the joy and sorrow of being ahead of one's time. It's not financial poverty that concerns her. It's not poverty of spirit: her husband has spirit to burn.

"Did Lamarck have friends?"

"I have no idea," he replies.

"He had a family."

"Yes."

"A wife. Children. They lived together in a house."

"I assume. You know as much about this as I do."

"I wonder how he felt when he couldn't provide for them. I wonder if he doubted himself. I wonder if he got depressed."

He drums his fingers on his knee, glances toward the kitchen. He really needs to get to work.

"Your point?"

"You've never talked to me about what happened before we met. After you were fired by the university."

"I was never depressed."

"You were hospitalized."

"That was a different man. That wasn't me."

She takes a moment to process this claim. Her husband is many things, and he operates according to his own set of rules and values, but dishonesty has never been one of them. And from the look in his eyes, he's not being dishonest now.

"Aren't there sometimes recurrences?"

Her questions are driving him further from where he needs to be, which right now is down in the basement. He fidgets, shifts, drums, then gets to his feet.

"Is that what this is about?"

Is it? She isn't sure. She began the conversation talking about herself.

"I may not get it."

"Get it?"

"Tenure."

"You don't need tenure."

"I want it."

"Lamarck had it, and look where he ended up."

"You had it, too, and look at you."

He doesn't answer, as if to say what possible difference does it make, and instead begins to pace. He has a powerful urge to flee, when something out the window catches his eye and stops him. The epigene-in-miniature atop his creation is glowing like an ember, as though the rising sun has singled it out and set it on fire. It goes from liquid red to liquid gold, then all at once the light appears to gather and condense. He can barely look, it's so intense.

He hears a hum, then feels a vibration.

"It's powering up," he mutters.

"What?"

He points, spellbound.

She follows his finger.

"It's opening," he whispers.

"What's opening?"

"The door. The path."

"Look at me," she says.

He doesn't respond, forcing her to repeat herself. "I said look at me. I'm talking to you."

Of anything on Earth, her voice, at that moment and in that way, is perhaps the only thing that could reach him. It combines concern with authority, solicitude with resolve, the verbal equivalent of a one-two punch, and the woman, make no mistake, is a force to reckon with. With a shudder he wrenches himself free of his vision, as free as he can be, and makes eye contact with her. Knows that he needs to reestablish a connection. Desperately tries to recall what they were talking about.

"You would have liked him," he says.

"What?"

"You would have liked him."

"Who? Lamarck?"

He nods.

For a moment she's bewildered, as if he's pulled a fast one on her, a rope-a-dope trick. She can't believe the man, but of course she can. He's done his best to give her his undivided attention. It's been heroic, really, how well he's done. But there are some things a man like Dr. Jim cannot resist. Some things a woman like Carol, née Schneeman, now James, cannot resist, either.

Pedagogy, for example. That, and a parting shot.

"Did she?" she asks.

"Did who?"

"Did Mrs. Lamarck?"

〰〰

Energized by the conversation and her husband's interest and support, Carol dives headlong into her subject, tentatively titling her paper "Toward an Epigenetic Future: Beyond Randomness." To her the epigene represents hope: for the future of her species (possibly for all species, though this is beyond the scope of her piece) and for the future of the planet. People change in response to what's going on around them. That's the message and the fact. They change not merely on the surface but inside, intrinsically: as the environment changes, as the culture changes, as the world changes. This has always been the case, but the new idea (or not so new but new to her) is that this doesn't have to rely on random chance. It doesn't have to be glacially slow. It doesn't have to be passive. Quite the opposite: it's an interactive and highly participatory act.

Most exciting of all, the change can be passed on to future generations and built upon. Little by little or quickly, in great bold leaps. It's the answer, if not the antidote, to cynicism, complacency, and helplessness, which infest and plague so many in the world. Another nail in the coffin of the Luddites and the fatalists who fear and despise progress. People adapt, adapt positively, adapt swiftly. This is what the epigene means to her. It's a metaphor, of course, but it's more than a metaphor. She can feel this in herself. She's changing—on the deepest levels—and it seems to be happening, in part, in response to her grasping and grappling with this new idea, working it, following its threads, making intuitive leaps, doubling back, finding ways around apparent dead ends. She feels as if she's tussling with some wild and beautiful animal, making it more beautiful and useful by taming and disciplining it.

She is changing in other ways, too. In response to her environment, for example, her work environment, where the pressure is mounting to get tenure and get it now, while it's within her grasp, and while she's at it, do all the ancillary stuff: publish, teach, administer, procure grants, be exceptional, be more than exceptional, be a star, and if not a star then a pretty damn bright planet. Pressure translates to stress, which has well-known biological effects. Some are epigenetic, and not all of these by any means are deleterious. Being the optimist she is, she has every reason to believe that the positive changes she's undergoing will benefit any future offspring she may choose to produce (currently an open question). It's not just optimism: there's growing evidence that the stress responses of the current generation of children in the nation are blunted, a splendid adaptation, given the exponential growth of sensory and immunologic assaults on their beleaguered defense systems, and proof once again that you can only pound the tip of a nail so much before it becomes dull.

Her home environment is affecting her as well. Being with her husband, listening to what he has to say, watching him change physically and emotionally as his strange—and strangely compelling—sculpture takes shape, wondering where it will all lead and who or what is doing the leading. Is he in control, or is this, as she sometimes fears, a wild-goose chase? How she thinks and feels about him is changing, and this, of course, is changing how she thinks and feels about herself. If she had to guess, she'd say the same is true of him. Change begets change.

A marriage, she decides (independently of him), is epigenetic. Structured, orderly, fluid at times, unpredictable at other times, and at all times interactive: it's like the very thing that's growing in their yard.

Which, by the way, has risen above the fence line. Not by a lot, but enough to get her attention. She's been so absorbed in her paper that it's been weeks since she's given it more than a cursory look. She and her husband have been immersed in their respective projects to the exclusion of all else, like two children at parallel play, the difference, of course, being that these two children are married. How perfect, she thinks, to be as childishly self-absorbed as her husband. How much this helps her understand him. And how much this understanding will help him, in turn, to see the light when she reminds him of his promise.

≈

*From Dr. Jim's Diary:*

*Friday, November 27th. Wake up, head hurts. Take a leak, catch a glimpse of myself in the bathroom mirror. Can that be me? Is this Halloween? A circus? Who let that guy in the house?*

*The effort of trying to figure that one out only makes my head hurt worse, and I throw a couple of aspirin down my throat, then take one of those other, blue-green pills, which I shouldn't, but who's going to stop me? Down in the basement the cage door is unlocked. No worry about his escaping: a beaten animal knows its place.*

*He's sitting on the bench when I enter. I don't have to tell him to get up.*

*We face each other. We're the same height now. I've grown (success adds inches) and he's shrunk. You could say I've cut him down to size.*

*We fight. I beat his pathetic self. Afterward he seems even smaller than before. He also appears more naked, which is odd, because he doesn't wear clothes, hasn't from the get-go. Maybe it's his hair, which used to cover every inch of his body. Now it's patchy and thinned out, like a sick and mangy dog's.*

*Carol's in the kitchen when I come up, a cup of steaming coffee in her hand. She smiles when she sees me, but then a shadow crosses her face.*

*"Something wrong?" I ask.*

*"You look like hell."*

*"I feel great."*

*"Is that right?" She wrinkles her nose.*

*"Got a problem?"*

*She fans the air in front of her face. "You smell."*

"*Of course I smell. It's the smell of human. You no like?*"

"*The human, yes. The smell, no.*"

"*Too bad.*"

She compresses her lips. "*What you mean is, 'You'll get used to it,' delivered in a helpful and encouraging, which is to say, a warm and affectionate voice. 'Too bad' is so cold and antagonistic.*"

"*I'm sorry you're not happy.*"

She considers this, first with an inward look, then an outward one at me, as if trying to see past some particularly ugly packaging to the gift underneath.

"*You're changing,*" she says at length. "*Sometimes I'm happy about it. Sometimes not.*"

"*Be happy.*"

"*Like you.*"

"*Like me. That's right.*"

"*Until you're not.*"

It may be the truth, but it feels like an accusation. "*I don't see that happening. I'm not a guy that gets depressed. What's to be depressed about?*"

"*You make it sound like it's a choice.*"

"*Why would anyone choose to be depressed?*"

"*The point, I think, is why wouldn't they choose not to be?*"

Talk talk talk. Choice is overrated. Things exist or they don't. I have a smell? Damn right I have a smell. It's called the smell of success.

"*I couldn't be happier. You know why? I'm firing on all cylinders. In here,*" I pound my chest. "*Upstairs,*" I pound my head.

"*I'm glad to hear it.*"

"*You should be glad. It's a beautiful thing. We live in a beautiful time. Beautiful minds, beautiful ideas, beautiful place. It's a miracle to be alive. I'm more than happy. I'm ecstatic.*"

"*You're in a zone.*"

A zone, is it? As in something with limits? That has a finite end? I shake my shaggy head.

"*I'm not. The zone is me. It's not going away. Like the smell. It's who I am. Same goes for what I'm building and discovering, and all the good that's going to come of it, how much it's going to change how people think, how much smarter and better they'll become, how much better off and happier, and how it's going to usher in a new age, a golden age, new, improved, and constantly improving—*"

"*The Golden Age of Dr. Jim?*"

"*Why not?*"

*She's checking out my hands, which are down at my sides and, strangely, still bunched into fists, like the residue of something, an indelible mark, perhaps. She's got a curious look on her face, as though puzzling through what this means, which is one of the reasons I love her. She's interested in the what and the why of things, she's observant, and she doesn't jump to conclusions.*

*Not that any conclusion she or anyone might draw would have an effect on me. I'm above and beyond—immune to, you could say—the tyranny of opinion.*

"*The sky's the limit,*" *I tell her.*

"*In the Age of Dr. Jim.*"

"*That's right.*"

"*Where fists rule.*"

"*Fists are good.*"

*She makes a pair of her own, turns them one way then another, regarding them with the same curious and observant expression. After a while she unfurls her fingers, then clenches them into claws. She studies these as well, then pulls them back as far as they'll go, fingertips and nails slightly raised, tendons on the backs of her hands in sharp and tense relief, as though readying for action.*

"*Grrrr,*" *she says.*

"*That's the spirit.*"

*She swipes at the air, left-right-left, makes a hissing sound, bares her teeth. Her eyes flash, then settle on my face.*

"*Got a sec?*" *she asks.*

"*Got a lifetime. What's up?*"

*She turns to the window and points with her chin. "That."*

"*You like?*"

"*We had an agreement.*"

"*It's nearly done.*"

"*I'm willing to talk. I can be flexible. I'll listen to reason.*"

"*Do you like it?*" *I repeat.*

*The question hangs in the air like a coin toss suspended in glass.*

"*Does it matter?*" *she answers at length.*

"*Of course it does.*"

"*Why? Are you building it for me?*"

"*I wouldn't be building it without you, that's for sure.*"

*She looks shocked. Then skeptical.*

*This wounds me, as it should. Skepticism is a dagger to the pure of heart. The innocent, for some reason, are always the first to be accused.*

*"Why are you looking at me that way?" I ask. "Have I done something wrong? Without knowing? Again?"*

*Rhetorical questions, of course, and we both know she'd be better off not answering. She could change the subject—to the weather, the neighbors, the news—to anything else, but she's smarter than that.*

*She apologizes.*

*Then she rubs it in by kissing me. "That's so nice to hear. You know I wouldn't be writing what I'm writing without you, so it goes both ways. And the answer's yes—I do like it."*

*Being immune to opinion does not, apparently, mean being immune to praise. I feel a wave of happiness, then pride, and I take her in my arms, pressing her hard against me. I want to crush her, I love her so much.*

*"Easy," she says. And then, "I have a favor to ask."*

*"Don't tell me. You want to be there when I finish. On the day. The hour. You want to be part of it. You want to celebrate my victory."*

*"Okay," she drawls, as though taken up short and trying her best not to disappoint me. "Now you want to hear the one I was going to ask? Don't go up any higher. Go out if you want to, fill the whole yard if you like, just don't go up."*

*"You're saying size doesn't matter. It's not what's important."*

*"I'm saying control yourself."*

*"You're right. It's not. I don't have to go up. I can go out. I can go in. In is up." The meaning of this—the full, ecstatic meaning—explodes on me with the force of revelation. "Up is up, too. Up and up. And up. And away. Up and away." What a hoot! What a miracle! Another explosion, this time of laughter. "Grab your hat, there's a storm coming, it's going to blow us to smithereens, but the coast is clear. Clear sailing ahead if you don't go up. Go out. Go in. In is up, and up is in—"*

*"Stop."*

*I hoist her in my arms and twirl her around.*

*"I said stop!"*

*Her voice is like the crack of a whip, and I cut my celebration short.*

*Once she's down, feet planted firmly on the floor, she crosses her arms over her chest and squares herself to me. "I need you to promise."*

*"Your will is my command."*

*"I also need you to be serious."*

*I raise my hand and pledge to her. "Not an inch higher. Not an angstrom. Not a snowflake. I swear to you. I promise."*

# Success

〰

Carol has her work cut out for her, trusting him to keep his word. She'll believe it when she sees it, or rather when she doesn't see it, doesn't see the piece get higher, and she learns how much harder it is and how much longer it takes to be convinced by the absence of something than by its presence, in this case the absence of something happening rather than by its occurrence. It's the difference between not and not not, similar to the task of carving out and then maintaining silence in a world defined by noise. But as the weeks go by and he's true to his word, she begins to relax. This, in turn, allows her to devote her full energy to her paper, a good thing, seeing as how she's scheduled to deliver a preview of it at an important conference in two weeks.

She has it well mapped out, all save one new idea she's been wrestling with. It's a bit beyond what's known and established on the subject, right on the cusp of the plausible. It's sure to be controversial, which is precisely what she's aiming for. Academics love a good debate, and an aspiring academic could hope for nothing better than to be the center of one.

What she doesn't want is to be laughed off the floor. She needs to run it by someone first, and the someone she has in mind is her husband. Who knows more than he does about the epigene? Who, when he chooses, can listen with more intelligence? Who won't pull any punches and be sure to speak his mind? When it comes down to it, there's no one she trusts more.

Rising early one morning, she whips up a batch of pancakes, which will slow if not stop him, and has them ready when he comes downstairs.

He's barely awake. His hair is matted and snarled, as it has been for weeks. His beard is becoming a bush. He half-shuffles, half-lurches into the kitchen, where he stops, raises his head, and sniffs.

"Pancakes," she announces.

Half a minute passes before he eyes the basement door. It's a record, and yet another instance of the deep, mind-altering power of scent.

She pulls out a chair. "Have a seat."

He doesn't move, and she doesn't insist.

"I'm going away next week," she reminds him. "For my conference. To deliver my paper."

He shifts on his feet.

"I've been toying with something. Can I run it by you?"

"Can it wait?" He edges toward the door.

She opens her mouth to say no, but his hand is already turning the knob. The door opens, then he disappears, as if falling into a dream, she thinks.

〰

*From Dr. Jim's Diary:*

*Wednesday, Jan 4th. The darkness at first is thick, but my eyes like darkness, they're at home in it, and they adjust quick. The smell of the cellar is abrasive and sharp, and in seconds I'm fully alert. I take the last stairs in a single leap, land like a cat, straighten, look. He's cowering in a corner. What a pitiful excuse for a man. No threat to me or to anyone, and yet at the sight of him my blood boils. Why this is I can't say. But I can say this: he won't fight anymore, not unless I make him.*

*Which I do.*

*Boom boom, and it's over.*

*I almost feel sorry for him.*

*But I don't. Why should I? Does the cherry feel sorry for the pit?*

*Fact is, as he crumples to the floor, I'm elated.*

〰

"I'm going out on a limb," says Carol, after her husband has surfaced. He's sucking down the cakes as if he hasn't eaten in weeks. "I'm speculating that an identical epigenetic change can happen to many individuals in a narrow window of time, possibly simultaneously. And this can cause a recognizable change in culture and society in their lifetimes. It doesn't have to wait for the next generation to manifest itself. It can happen now, as we speak. In real time. Real-time evolution. Not engineered, but natural."

He gulps down a mouthful, goes for another. "Why are you saying that?"

"I believe it, that's why. Or I'd like to."

It's part instinct, part intuition, part hope. It's also part giving her esteemed colleagues something to chew on, and part poking said colleagues in the ribs. "The question is, am I going to sound ridiculous?"

He doesn't answer, leading her to suspect the worst.

"I could leave it out. Stick to what we know."

"And what is that?"

"The epigene is a blueprint for change. It's a paradigm for both stability and adaptation, most notably for individuals, possibly for larger groups. It's biologically based, but it has much broader implications. One of the best and most powerful is that it's future-oriented."

She stops, fearing from his wandering expression that she's lost him. Or lost his support. So she brings it back home, using his own words so there can be no doubt or misunderstanding.

"The epigene is key."

More seconds pass without his responding, enough of them for her to realize how important this is to her, how much his opinion matters. At the moment, however, he's focused on what's in front of him, a fine thick cake from the pan, which he folds in half, then in quarters, smothering it in syrup, then stuffing the fat, dripping wedge in his mouth, chewing and swallowing it, it seems, in a single act, then wiping his chin and lips with the back of his hand, then licking the hand clean. With a belch he settles back in his chair, and finally, at long last, turns his attention to her.

Their eyes meet. She feels a jolt, then a quiver. He gets it. Yes. He understands what she's saying. He understands, and he agrees. She couldn't be happier.

But then he speaks.

"The epigene is nothing. It's dogmeat. It's yesterday's news. The perigene is everything. It's all-encompassing. All change that has or will occur derives from and is contained in it. All being and all possibility. It and it alone is key."

She gapes at him. "The epigene is dogmeat?"

"Don't talk to me about the epigene. It pollutes my ears. All eyes should be on the perigene. It's the source, the nexus, and the crux of existence. It's Heaven's Guiding Hand. Heaven's Crucible. Heaven's Heaven."

"You don't believe in Heaven."

"I'm building Heaven."

His eyes gleam, demonically one might think, and she feels what can only be described as an epigenetic shift, which pricks her like a pin as she glimpses a future that may not include the man she adores.

She's too shaken at first to reply, but then she gathers herself and

finds her voice. It's not the steadiest, but it's steady enough.
"Fine then. Be my guest. Build it."

~~~

Easy to say, he thinks as he hurries into the yard, and not, in fact,
that hard to achieve, not when the fire is raging. It helps that he's had
more than a mere glimpse of his celestial wonder, that he knows,
for example, that the perigene occupies another plane of existence.
Another dimension? Another universe? The jury's still out on exactly
what and where, but here on Earth, in his representation of it, it exists
above and beyond what he's already built. Obviously, then, to depict it
properly requires that he build more, and to this end he's constructed
an ingenious internal ladder that spirals as it rises, nicely echoing the
spiraling DNA portrayed by his cables, pipes, and ropes. The ladder
projects well above the current peak of the project, which means it
is well above the fence. From the top rung, were he so inclined, he
could enjoy a fine view of the neighborhood, not to mention the
neighbors, all of whom have fenced-in yards of their own. But he has
no interest in them. All his attention is focused on the task at hand.
Currently this involves welding ten-foot lengths of copper pipe on
end and in parallel to a steel plate base, then welding the base to the
quartet of pulleys at the top of the structure...in effect, projecting
the parallel pipes into space. At the topmost end of each pipe he's
bolted a swiveling, laptop-sized screen, remotely programmed and
controlled. Rising together, the pipes resemble a line of stout reeds
and also a cross-section of the Golgi apparatus, which is to say, a
system of transport tubes. Two way transport in Dr. Jim's fervid and
frothy imagination: from the epigene upward, carrying information
to the perigene, which is yet to be built, and to the epigene downward
from the heavenly p, which lies somewhere in the ether above, and
from which vantage it conceives, conducts, and conveys its divine and
masterful plan to its genetic and epigenetic underlings. The screens
have been partially covered with duct tape (the stickum and glue
of impatient inventors and freethinkers) in the shape of an ellipse,
leaving a narrow slit exposed. When they light up, they look like
eyes, and once the program starts, they're always going on and off,
always blinking, for what self-respecting perigene would ever sleep?
What man, for that matter, who every day is drawing closer to the
realization of his dream, every day inhabiting it more, would sleep?

# *Success*

Not Dr. Jim. Sleep is the furthest thing from his mind. Not that he could if he wanted to: the need, it appears, has been blasted from his brain. And thank goodness for that. To close his eyes now, on the cusp of his epiphany, with his perigene a heartbeat away, would be insane.

~~~

For altogether different reasons, Carol isn't sleeping either. Her husband is unraveling, and their marriage is hanging by a thread. Couldn't he have waited? she asks herself. Couldn't he have chosen his words with more care? Her confidence is shaken, and the conference is now less than a week away.

She moves to a separate room, which helps. This suggests to her that distance is a good thing, and she takes a room in a motel, which helps more. During the day she's in her office, honing and polishing her presentation, defending it against attack, both expected and outrageous, such as his, so that by the time of the conference she feels prepared for just about anything.

The hour arrives. Her paper is met warmly enough, and in one quarter—the activist, anti-social Darwinism bunch—she brings down the house. That evening, at one of the myriad parties spawned by such conferences, she's approached by a colleague who had the pleasure of hearing her speak. A good-looking guy with all the right moves and a tongue that could charm a dead fish, it's clear within minutes what he's after.

And why not? She's a prize. She's a catch. It's the biological imperative at work.

Her pants feel suddenly too tight around her hips: biology.

The heat rises to her face: biology.

Riot and rebellion lift their lecherous heads. There's a creature that wants out.

Law and order respond.

It's a bad career move for her.

She has a husband.

That husband is a jerk.

Infidelity is no sin, but recklessness, in her book, is. Not so much because it hurts people, which it does, but because it makes a mess of things. That's the heart of the crime. It opens the door to chaos, mayhem, and unnecessary complications. Not to mention uncertainty, which is never a good thing.

So she tells the guy thanks, but no thanks, and excuses herself.

Later, in her room as she's readying for bed, still buzzing from what might have been, she takes a moment to study her face in the bathroom mirror. She's a natural blonde and has never thought to be anything but. Blond and short-haired—for her entire adult life she's always worn it short. She likes the compact, helmeted look, likes being tidy and meticulous, likes knowing that not one hair will stray from its place from the time she wakes up to the time she lies down at night. Not a hair or a thought. So the idea that she could grow her hair out, that she *should* grow it out, and not only that, she should dye it, comes as something of a shock.

She has a glimpse of how she might look. Suppresses a giggle. Stretches her arms. Arches her back. Thinks of her mother. Husbandless and as poor as Mrs. Lamarck. What traits did Mom acquire in her life? What traits did she pass on? Can an inherited trait be gotten rid of, short of being engineered out or waiting for eons until it rids itself on its own? Is she right when she postulates, as she has, that its expression can be willfully, mindfully, purposefully controlled?

It's the subject for more than a single paper. A book, perhaps, but it won't be written tonight. Her bed is waiting, neatly made, and she slides in, appreciating the starched, crisp covers. She's a neat, crisp package herself, no loose ends, nothing wasted, and she's had a productive and rewarding day. And there's more to come.

She, too, keeps a diary, of a different sort from her husband's, a kind of counterpoint to her language-heavy, idea-dominated, scrupulously governed life. She doesn't use pencil or pen. Her entries, you could say, are more like dances, storms, music, free-form collages. Her current volume (and there's a box full of others) is sitting on her bedside table. Propping herself on a pillow and pulling her knees to her chest, she rests it against her thighs and opens it to a fresh page. She stares at the pure white rectangle, letting her mind empty, waiting for the moment of inspiration to make itself known. Tonight it comes quicker than usual, primed, perhaps, by the evening's events, but it's no less delicious for that, no less ecstatic, revealing, or fun. Nor is she less herself as she utters a deep-throated moan, then rakes the page with her nails and rips it to shreds.

The conference is in every way a success for her. By week's end, after being wined, dined, and courted by no fewer than three eminent deans, followed by a hastily arranged meeting with her own departmental chair, who had not failed to notice the roosters circling what he considers his own personal hen, she feels high as the moon, confident that her dream of tenure is all but assured. Her thoughts turn homeward, to her husband. After a week of separation, her feelings toward him have softened. She can live with their intellectual disagreements. The question is, can she live with him?

She recalls what attracted her to him in the beginning, the very eccentricity, self-absorption, and independence of thought that feels so petty and selfish to her now. But she doesn't have to feel this way. As far as self-absorption goes, he's no worse than she is. Or not much worse. He's only being himself, just himself, and when all is said and done, who else could he be?

He's a man, and men are meant to build...how many times has she heard this said? How many times has she written it off as myth, nonsense, bromide, self-aggrandizing, self-perpetuating, male chauvinist, testosterone-induced, delusional crap? But why? There *are* lines of distinction. She can personally attest to this. Women are meant to bear children, tell stories and, if all goes according to plan, get tenure. (Although the child-bearing part, she's been told, appears to be changing. This, according to a fellow ethnobiologist she met at the conference. There seems to be an uptick in the number of women worldwide who no longer have an interest in bearing young, or whose interest is muted by other, stronger desires and plans. This, in response to environmental pressures, demographic changes, and a rising tide of prosperity and feminism. From Europe to Japan to Singapore to Taiwan, the birthrate has fallen below the death rate for the first time in a century. Not a bad thing, necessarily, and certainly not bad for her thesis.)

She decides she can live with his precious perigene. More precisely, she decides she would rather live with it than not live with him. The decision relieves her of a great weight, and she returns home on a wave of optimism, eager to see him, only to find that his creation has grown substantially in her absence and is now visible a block away.

Not only has it grown in size, there are now pieces of paper attached to it in a variety of shapes, colors and sizes, some of them quite large. There must be thirty in all, and he's attached them in such a way that they move freely in the breeze, fluttering like flags. But ridiculous-looking flags, stiff and slapdash, like something coughed up by a demented Betsy Ross, making the whole thing, which once had a certain integrity, if not beauty, look ridiculous.

She pulls into the driveway, climbs out, and as she nears the front door, she gets her first hint, not of the meaning of this new addition of his, which would be too much to expect, but of its effect. Nailed to the door is a rather large piece of butcher paper with a rather explicit message to her and her husband signed by a neighbor.

The idea that someone, without her permission, would drive a nail into her house is offensive. The idea that the message is directed at both her and husband, i.e., that there's no distinction made between the two of them, is embarrassing. The idea that her husband is provoking such an attack is a test.

She tears the paper from the nail and enters the house. The place is a mess, which only reinforces what she already knows, that her husband is besieged by the forces of chaos and needs help. Order needs to be restored, and who better to restore it than herself?

〰

*From Dr. Jim's Diary:*

*Sunday, January 15th. He's standing when I enter, head up, shoulders thrown back, a steady light of intelligence in his eyes. The cage door is open, but he's making no attempt to escape.*

*"Going somewhere?" I ask.*

*He smiles, then opens his arms as if to invite me in and embrace what we both know comes next.*

*Trying to disarm me, the little shit. And for a second he does. Then I get a grip on myself, and we fight, although to call it that is a joke. I punch and he receives, not bothering to punch back or defend himself. Afterwards, though, I feel like I've gone twenty rounds. My legs and arms are heavy, as if I've been leeched of my vital fluids. It's all I can do to drag my sorry ass upstairs.*

*Carol's in the kitchen. The shock of seeing her revives me. "Where did you come from?"*

*"I live here."*

*"You left."*

*"That's right. For my conference." She frowns. "You didn't think I'd walked out on you, did you?"*

*The truth—that I haven't thought about her at all—would doubtlessly upset her. To tell the truth, she already looks upset.*

# Success

"I'm glad you're back," I tell her honestly.

"I'm glad, too."

"I've been busy."

"So I see. Too busy to shower. Too busy to shave. Too busy to change your clothes. Too busy to clean up after yourself."

"I've been working."

"I see that, too." She glances out the window. "It's getting bigger."

"Bigger and better."

"No. Not better. Not even close to better. It's an eyesore. This has to stop."

Her voice is like a cage; her expression, the day of judgment.

"Take it down," she says. "Do what you intended to do. Write the damn book. Or don't. Just stop."

"What book?"

"We had an agreement. Nothing above the fence."

"I'll raise the fence. I'll levitate it."

"You're offending people." She thrusts a ragged piece of paper in my face. It's from the guy next door.

What he has to say makes me laugh. "He's a moron."

"He's our neighbor."

"Fuck him."

"That's one way to handle it."

"It's none of his business."

"I disagree."

"It's none of your business, either."

She gives me a long look, then nods, as if this settles something. "I was afraid you'd say that."

〜

They start the night in the same bed, but once Carol's asleep, Dr. Jim slips out and heads to the patch of grass in the yard beside the ladder at the center of his creation. This has been his bed for several days. It's where he feels most himself, which is not to say most at ease, because he's far from that. He's too driven and excited to be at ease, as if someone has a foot on the gas, and not only that, they're doing the steering. It's a high-octane, exhilarating ride, and even though there's a cliff ahead, and after the cliff a field of razor-sharp rocks, and after the rocks a team of horses just dying to tear him limb from limb, he wouldn't trade it for anything. A few more days, a few more visits to the basement, and the mighty perigene will be his. Besides, cliffs and rocks are for mortals, and horses, especially wild ones, are kin.

Needless to say, this is no time for sleep. All systems are on full alert, antennae tuned to maximum reception, and he spends the night conversing with the moon and stars, absorbing all he can and channeling what he learns to the task at hand. When not in conversation, he's pacing the yard like an expectant father. Carol's reappearance couldn't have come at a better time: she has stuck with him for the long gestation and now she'll be present for the birth. He faces east, exhorting the night to end so that he can get to work.

Daylight comes at last and he rushes inside, only to find a lock on the door to the basement. A shiny new hasp, mocking him like a smiley face with its rictus of false goodwill. He's sickened, wounded even, but hardly deterred. The only real question is how to remove it: slowly and carefully with a screwdriver, sparing the door and the trim, or instantly, with a hammer and crowbar, using brute force? It's another one of those questions that answers itself.

Carol's waiting when he emerges from his lair. It's no time to talk. His business is outside. But when he attempts to brush past her, she blocks his way.

"You going to clean that up?"

Islands and splinters of wood litter the floor. He could care less, but to avoid a quarrel he kicks them downstairs.

"That's not cleaning," she says.

He locates the lock on the floor, hanging limply from its hasp, picks it up, and thrusts it in her face. "Since when did the Nazis arrive?"

Her face curdles.

"The Enemy is here," he spits.

"No. The Enemy is *not* here. Reason, however, is."

It's sad almost. How little she understands and how out of touch she is. With him and with reality.

"Reason? You want reason?" He hurls the lock at the window, somehow missing it and hitting the wall instead.

She doesn't flinch. "Having a tantrum, are we?"

"I won't be squelched."

"And I won't live like this. I can't. Enough is enough."

This, he feels, couldn't be less true. Enough is never enough.

"I'll leave," she adds.

"You did leave."

"For good."

For good? What could this possibly mean? he wonders. His good? Hers? Fleetingly, he feels as if he can breathe freely again. The next moment, though, he's consumed with rage at being dictated to. He wants to grab her, shake her, teach her, make her one with him and his just fury, until she understands and retracts what she said. He so wants her to understand. He loves her that much, he aches with love, and she loves him, and lovers don't leave each other, they don't, lovers are inseparable.

The rising sun catches his eye, interrupting his train of thought. A shaft of light shatters the pale morning sky like a bell ending the round. He hears a call, and instantly, the quarrel is forgotten. He's being summoned, and his terrible rage at his wife becomes an ecstatic rage to get outside. He can no more resist it than the flimsy lock could resist him. He has no reason to resist and every reason to consent, every possible reason to surrender and embrace the promise that lies ahead.

♒

The sun circles.
    The sun sets.
    The sun rises.
    The sun sets.
    The slippery moon appears.
From his grassy bed, Dr. Jim gazes upward through the lattice of his creation. Beyond the winking eyes and eye stalks, the spiraling tubes and strands of metal, the phalanxes of pipes, and the knobby, nodal block and tackle, he spies a tufted, popcorn cloud, drifting past the moon like an exploded ribosome. The speed of its drift is a fraction of the speed of his minnow mind, which darts about quick quick quick. He senses the approach of something vast, not a predator but a storm of some sort, and, leaping to his feet, he races to his ladder. He climbs rapidly, through the forest of copper Golgi tubes and their caps of cyclopic screens, swiveling like searchlights on their mounts. As he passes, one points at him, seemingly at random, then another points, and another, until all ten are fixed on his face, ten eyes trained on him, ten adoring, hungry, acolytic eyes, urging him higher. He hurries upward, until he's standing on the topmost rung, which coincides with the topmost addition, the sum and crown of

his creation: another burnished coil of pipe, shoulder-wide, speaking for all three elements of the grand design—the spiraling gene, the resilient, spring-like epigene, and the angelic perigene, rising and expanding like a whorling halo.

He thrusts his head and shoulders through it. The nighttime sky is dazzling and takes his breath away. The air is charged. The stars feel it and chatter in excitement. The moon feels it and grins. Ribbons of energy burst and sizzle across the sky.

He raises his arms in delight. Laughing, he welcomes the storm, invites it to channel itself through him. As he fills with it and as the force of it grows, he has an epiphany. He's not merely channeling, he's the channel, too. The linker and the link. There is no distinction between creator and creation, between do and is.

From nowhere and from everywhere he hears a crack, then a splintering sound. The air above him quivers, then rips in half. A slit appears, like the pupil of a cat's eye, but a cosmic cat. He has a glimpse of what lies beyond, and his mind soars.

The glimpse lasts a mere fraction of a second. But a fraction of a second, a fraction of a fraction, is more than enough time to know the perigene in all its splendor. More than enough time to feel the glory and perceive the universal web connecting all things. More than enough for absolute and total bliss.

For one life-affirming fraction of a second, Dr. Jim is fully informed, and then reality sets in. The force sustaining him, suspending him, as it were, on a cloud, cannot, it seems, overcome an insistent downward pull. This, he dimly understands, is the pull of gravity, to which, had he been asked just moments before, he would have said he was immune. As he accelerates past the broken rung of the ladder on which he was standing, he has no time to be disappointed in its failure to do its job. If he's going down, which he certainly appears to be—down, as in free-falling—he should make the most of the time he has left. Why fear the ground that's hurtling like a rocket toward him? Why fear injury, pain, death, the unknown? He's just had a glimpse of the unknown, and with the speed of light he has another, and suddenly he's in hysterics. His throat and mouth are like brass. He could be a trumpeter, splitting the air with raucous noise, braying and shrieking the final, wild, delirious notes of his last and greatest song.

# Success

*From Dr. Jim's Diary:*

*Thursday, January 19th. Sleep, or something like it. Wake to gray light, shivering and wet. Head pounds like a drum. Stumble through maze of pillar, pipe, and post to a door. Door leads to another door, which leads downstairs. Gate of bars at the bottom, open as a trap. A man inside, waiting. We face each other. No fight left.*

*He helps me sit.*

*"You've had a tumble," he says gently. "I'm Dr. Jim. You are..." He hesitates. "My guest."*

*He strokes my head, then retreats beyond the swinging gate, shutting it behind him. The clang and clank of the bolt are like a wake-up call, a helping hand of a sort.*

*He gazes at me through the bars. His eyes are misty. His expression is raw with pity, gratitude, and relief.*

*If I could speak, I would, but I'm hollow inside. The days ahead are dark. I churn no more.*

♒

The first order of business is to get his feet back under him; next, to survey and explore. Damage has been done, but then there's always damage. The question is what to do about it.

This depends, principally, on how bad it is and whether or not it can be fixed. Some things are too broken to be fixed. Some broken things, once fixed, are as good as new. Or nearly as good. Some, depending on what material you started with, are better.

Dr. Jim has never been what anyone would call a fixer. He's more a slash and burn, leave the past behind, the best is yet to come kind of guy. So it's no surprise, as he stands beside his midden heap of a masterpiece, his tour de force of bric-a-brac and dream, that he decides, with scarcely a moment's hesitation, to tear it down. The surprise is why. He misses Carol, and when something is broken—a plate, say—and one half not only needs the other half for completion but fits it perfectly, it's senseless not to glue them together, a disservice to both halves not to recreate the whole.

The decision made, he throws himself into the task like a man possessed. In a week the thing is lying in a pile on the ground. The last bolt is barely out of its socket when he calls Carol with the good news.

Her reply to him is short and sweet. She meant what she said. She's not coming back. She wishes him the best. Case closed.

He waits a few days, then calls again. And again in a month. In so many of life's pursuits—from research to weight loss to treasure hunts—doggedness is rewarded, but in this—his pursuit of Carol—it is not. She doesn't answer his calls and doesn't reply to his messages. Undiscouraged, he continues to reach out, if for no other reason than to hear her voice. It's a beautiful voice, and while the recording never changes, each time he calls he hears something new and special in it. Up until the day there's a different voice, informing him with cold proficiency that the number has been disconnected.

〰

Time plods on. At length he has the debris in the yard hauled away. Then he brings a chair outside and sits. It's early spring, and then, seemingly overnight, it's summer. The outline of his sculpture has disappeared: the grass that was crushed by it has regrown and filled in, joined by the stalks and heads of dandelions and other weeds. Ants troop along the ground. He identifies two species, as well as several kinds of beetles, including old friends *Polyphylla decemlineata*, *Stictotarsus eximius*, and *Loricaster rotundus*. He remembers his collection, idly wonders if it has survived, and if so, if its spirit has survived with it, the spirit of observing and collecting, and by doing so, honoring the greatness and the miracle of life's diversity on Earth.

He sits and he sits, watching, listening, observing himself as the emptiness slowly but surely fills, until the day finally comes when he's sat long enough, and that's the day he begins.

〰

A year later he puts the final touches on his opus, the crowning achievement (so far) of his career. On a whim he googles Carol, thinking what the hell, she might want to know. He finds her at a nearby university, a place known far and wide for its hallowed halls, distinguished faculty, and otherworldly endowment, and shoots her an email with a tracer attached.

She deletes it within the hour, probably the minute she saw it. At noon a week later he sends her another, which she deletes at 4 p.m. Probably after coming back from an afternoon lecture. Probably—

once again—as soon as she laid eyes on it.

Still. Four hours compared to one.

He knows he's a fool. The question is, how much of a fool, to consider this progress?

≋

*Carol's Diary:*

Carol thumbs through her diary, surveying the torn, slashed, shredded, mangled, hanging-by-a-thread, pages. What a pleasure, after a long day like today, to make a new entry. Afterward, though, she feels an unexpected emptiness, as though something is missing that shouldn't be. She can't quite put her finger on it, other than to call it "peace of mind," which is far too vague to be helpful.

This happens on a succession of nights, and on each of them she falls asleep, fully expecting she'll wake in the morning with a workable answer. But she doesn't, and finally, after a particularly restless night, she wakes with a new feeling. Or rather the same feeling, subtly amended: it's not, to be precise, that she's missing something she had, but rather that she's missing something that, prior to getting those stupid emails from her ex, she didn't have. Something, in other words, that previously didn't exist and now does.

How fascinating, she thinks...to an ontologist. How infuriating to her.

It's the news of his book and his offer to give her a sneak preview. Dangling the bait. She wouldn't be much of a scientist, not to mention an epigeneticist, if she weren't curious. Say what you will about the man, he's always been an exceptionally deep and original thinker. It would be a feather in her cap, professionally speaking, to get a first peek. Who knows—if he's true to his word about her being an inspiration (she remembers this clearly), she might find her name in the list of acknowledgements.

The more she considers, the more she thinks, *Why not?* It's not as if he's asking for anything. It's no slight on her character, no affront to her dignity, no encroachment on her sovereignty or disrespect to her person that he wants to share the news. If anything, it's an opportunity.

From irritation to interest. From annoyance to cautious optimism. How the mind enlarges. Some say it's a pendulum that swings equally forward and back. Rubbish, says Carol. The mind either shrinks or grows, regresses or advances.

Only a fool would not consider this progress.

∾

As the day of their meeting approaches and finally arrives, Dr. Jim is beside himself with excitement. A normal excitement, he feels. He checks himself in the mirror, checks the time, the mirror, the time, a non-sustainable activity that he interrupts with nervous glances out the window. She said two o'clock, and it's ten minutes past. So many possible reasons for this, but unlike her. Her voice sounded different, too, throatier, more muscular, as if fashioned by a hitherto unknown and unplumbed force. After hanging up, he found himself wondering if there was someone new in her life. He searched the Internet, which didn't have the answer but did have an alternate one. Two separate papers described anatomic changes to the female larynx (and a subsequent deepening of speech) as said females ascended various corporate and non-corporate ladders. So the voice thing could be due to that and not a new lover, which relieved him somewhat.

At eighteen past the hour, an SUV pulls into the driveway. He rushes to the front hall, and when the doorbell rings, flings the door open.

Perched on the threshold is a woman who, at first glance, he barely recognizes. She has long black hair that flies from her head in an explosion of curls. Deep-red lipstick and deep-red, miter-shaped nails. A long-sleeved black knit dress. Bracelets on both wrists. A silver barbell eyebrow ring. Eye shadow the color of smoke.

She's grown, it appears, both in size and in stature. An imposing package.

He invites her in and escorts her to the living room, which he has swept, vacuumed, dusted, and straightened within an inch of its life. Thinking this will please her, as it used to.

Without comment, she sits.

"You look well," he says.

"Different, you mean."

"Different, yes. But also well."

She inclines her head. "I am. Very."

"Your work agrees with you."

She assumes he knows what it is from having reached her online and seen her various postings. "I love my work. I love being tenured. I love being able to do what I choose. Within limits, of course."

"Limits agree with you, too."

"If you say so." She pushes a bracelet up until it's tight on her forearm, like a bridle choking a snake. "I love being able to call the shots. Not all of them, obviously. There're plenty of hungry fish above me in the chain, but in my little school, my fiefdom, I'm boss."

"As you should be."

"I completely agree."

"You're secure."

"I've always been secure. Now I have security."

He wants to ask if she's happy, knows it would be a mistake. "Have you been writing?"

"I have. It's what I was hired to do. Among other things."

"About what?"

"You don't know?"

"I saw you've written a book."

It sounds like he hasn't read it. She didn't expect that he would and in fact has prepared herself not to be bothered by this. Which is not to say she isn't.

"Yes. It's the one I was working on when you were...." She stops, rephrases. "Before you started on yours."

"How has it done?"

"It's gotten some play in the press. Mostly the academic press, but not exclusively."

"Has it been well received?"

"Very well. I've become something of a celebrity. The high priestess of cultural epigenetics. A lightning rod for visionaries, idealists, crackpots, and the suppressed."

"The suppressed?"

"Yes. I tell them to express themselves. That's something I learned from you."

"Do they listen?"

"Actually, I tell them they're expressing themselves all the time, whether they know it or not. The epigene, it turns out, *is* key. That's where expression begins. I know you don't agree, but there it is."

She's right: he doesn't. Her statement is not only true but prescient. His own book contains a long and detailed argument against this very point of view. It stops short of being a diatribe, though she might not agree, especially given what he's titled the epigene section—"High Hopes, Diminishing Returns"—which she won't possibly miss if she has even a cursory look. Now has to be the worst conceivable time to give her the opportunity. A quarrel is the last thing he wants.

So what is it with him? Pride? Boastfulness? Ingenuousness? The desire to share something precious with her? His natural and troublesome impulsivity, aka the uncanny ability to shoot himself in the foot? What is it that makes him blurt, "I've written a book, too."

"Yes. You said."

"Would you like to see it?"

"Now?"

"Why not?"

He leaves and returns with a tome as thick and heavy as a brick. It's got a clear plastic cover, beneath which is the title page. She reads it aloud:

"'The Halo, Not the Helix: The Science and Promise of Perigenetics.'" She raises an eyebrow. "It's a science, is it?"

"An evolving science. Feel free to have a look."

She riffles through the pages, pausing every now and then—at section and chapter titles, or at one of his winsome little hand-drawings that are sprinkled throughout the work.

"Take it home if you'd like."

"You're not serious."

"I'd welcome your opinion."

"You want me to read it?"

"I insist. I'd love to hear what you think."

She hides her pleasure at this. "I'm extremely busy these days— you know how it is. I may not get to it for a while." She pauses. "Quite a while. I'm really up to my ears with work."

This is payback, pure and simple, for his not reading hers. In truth, she'd like nothing better than to dive into it at once. She can't wait to see where his prodigious intelligence has taken him. Knows there'll be plenty to chew on. Expects to be inspired, challenged, irritated, and galvanized.

"Take your time," he replies with equanimity. "It's good to have a full plate. I'm always happiest when I'm busy."

He's so different from how she remembers. Patient, attentive, engaging.

"What's up next for you?" she asks, warming to him.

"Next?"

"Yes. What's your next project? I assume you have a next project. Actually, I assume you've already begun."

He smiles.

She laughs. "I'm right, aren't I? Want to tell me what it is?"

He won't meet her eyes.

"C'mon. Tell."

"It's hard to put into words."

"Shall I guess?"

"If you like."

She rattles off a series of ideas and projects, each one a little more provocative and outrageous than the next. When she's done, he shakes his head.

"None of those."

She leans forward to study him more closely, as though to read his mind. The light from the street catches his face in such a way as to make him look young, boyish even. All the boys she's ever known have had double, or triple, lives. It feels pointless to continue guessing.

"I give up."

"It's not an easy thing for me to say."

She gets a tightness in her chest, as though something hurtful is on the way. This infuriates her, to fall prey like this, and she rises quickly, weight on the balls of her feet, prepared in an instant to walk out. At the same time, unconsciously, she claws her hands at her sides.

"Spit it out," she says.

He nods decisively. But as the seconds tick away without his uttering so much as a peep, the tension mounts.

Finally, he summons his courage and breaks the silence. "Would you ever think of trying again?"

Her eyes widen. Her ears, she decides, are playing tricks on her.

"Trying again?"

"Coming back."

"And doing what? Getting remarried?"

They've been divorced a year. Swiftly, he responds. "Not necessarily that. Just trying again. Trying to do better."

Shock gives way to a peal of laughter. "You want me to come back? To you? To a man who works every minute of every day? Yet somehow, at the same time, defines the word 'unsteady'? A man with more moods than a mood ring. A man not merely divided in his attention but divided against himself."

She's spoken the unspeakable. He would never have allowed this before, but he's hardly in a position to tell her to shut up.

And now that the gates are open, she's not about to hold back.

"Do you know what it's like? I'll tell you. It's like living with three people in the house. Someone is always the odd person out. Always. If you live alone, you get lonely sometimes. If you're a couple, you fight and make up. If there're three of you, there's always a third wheel. Someone's always out in the cold. Three is the absolute worst."

"I take it that's a no."

She begins to reply, pauses, purses her lips. "To a threesome, yes."

At first he doesn't understand. Then it hits him. It's an impossible request. Yet she's such a commanding presence. Maybe he can do it. Maybe, with her help.

"I can't promise," he says.

"Can't promise what?"

He makes a gesture to include the two of them. "You and me. Just us."

She frowns, then pulls out her phone and types in a message. Moments later, the side door of the van slides open and a woman steps out. She has short blond hair, a pale complexion, and a stiffish, self-conscious gait, as though balancing something breakable on her head that could, with the slightest misstep, fall and shatter.

"Recognize her?" Carol asks.

She does look familiar. The hair at the back of his neck must think so, too, because it stands at attention.

"A friend of yours?" he asks.

"More than a friend."

"Should I be jealous?"

"I can't answer that. I will say it's not why she's here."

"Are you trying to teach me a lesson? Is that it?"

"Why don't you meet her and then decide."

"Decide?"

Is he that obtuse? She has the urge to order the woman back into the van and slap Dr. Jim across the face. Not without affection. She would never slap a man she didn't like or respect.

She glances around the room, then up toward the ceiling, imagining the upper floor. In her mind she's measuring the house. She has to decide, too.

She turns her eye on Dr. Jim. "We're not that different, you know."

"Decide what?" he asks.

Measuring him, measuring herself. "If there's room for all of us."

# Karin Tidbeck

## Moonstruck

**Karin Tidbeck** *works as a freelance writer, teacher and translator in Malmö, Sweden. Her short fiction has appeared in* Weird Tales, Tor. com, Lightspeed Magazine *and* Strange Horizons *and numerous anthologies including* The Time-Travelers Almanac *and* Steampunk Revolution. *Her work has received the Campbell Award, the SF & Fantasy Translation Award, as well as a World Fantasy Award nomination. "Moonstruck" was nominated for the British Fantasy Award 2014.*

They lived on the top floor in a building on the city's outskirts. If the stars were out, visitors would come, usually an adult with a child in tow. Alia would open the door and drop a curtsy to the visitors, who bade her good evening and asked for Doctor Kazakoff. Alia would run halfway up the stairs to the attic and call for the Doctor. At the same time, Father would emerge from the kitchen in a gentle blast of tea-scented air. Sometimes he had his apron on, and brought a whiff of baking bread. He would extend a knobby hand to pat the child's head, and then shake hands with the adult, whom he'd invite into the kitchen. While the parent (or grandparent, or guardian) hung their coat on a peg and sat down by the kitchen table, Father poured tea and wound up the gramophone. Then Mother, Doctor Kazakoff, would arrive, descending the spiral staircase in her blue frock and dark hair in a messy bun. She'd smile vaguely at the visiting child without making eye contact, and wave him or her over. They'd ascend the stairs to the darkened attic and out onto the little balcony, where the telescope stood. A stool sat below it, at just the right height for a child to climb up and look into the eyepiece.

Alia would crawl into an armchair in the shadows of the attic and watch the silhouettes of Mother and the visiting child, outlined against the faint starlight. Mother aimed the telescope toward some planet or constellation she found interesting, and stood aside so that the child could look. If it was a planet, Mother would rattle off facts. Alia preferred when she talked about constellations. She would pronounce each star's name slowly, as if tasting them: *Betelgeuse. Rigel. Bellatrix. Mintaka. Alnilam. Alnitak.* Alia saw them in her mind's eye, burning spheres rolling through the darkness with an inaudible thunder that resonated in her chest.

After a while, Mother would abruptly shoo the child away and take his or her place at the telescope. It was Alia's task to take the child by the hand and explain that Doctor Kazakoff meant no harm, but that telescope time was over now. Sometimes the child said goodbye to Mother's back. Sometimes they got a hum in reply. More often not. Mother was busy recalibrating the telescope.

When the moon was full, Mother wouldn't receive visitors. She would sit alone at the ocular and mumble to herself: the names of the seas, the highlands, the craters. Those nights (or days) she stayed up until the moon set.

〰〰

On the day it happened, Alia was twelve years old and home from school with a cold. That morning she found a brown stain in her underwear. It took a moment to realize what had really happened. She rifled through the cabinet under the sink for Mother's box of napkins, and found a pad that she awkwardly fastened to her panties. It rustled as she pulled them back up. She went back into the living room. The grandfather clock next to the display case showed a quarter past eleven.

"Today, at a quarter past eleven," she told the display case, "I became a woman."

Alia looked at her image in the glass. The person standing there, with pigtails and round cheeks and dressed in a pair of striped pyjamas, didn't look much like a woman. She sighed and crawled into the sofa with a blanket, rehearsing what to tell Mother when she came home.

~

When the front door slammed a little later, Alia walked into the hallway. Mother stood there in a puff of cold air. She was home much too early.

"Mother," Alia began.

"Hello," said Mother. Her face was rigid, her eyes large and feverish. Without giving Alia so much as a glance, she took her coat off, dropped it on the floor and stalked up the attic stairs. Alia went after her out onto the balcony. Mother said nothing, merely stared upward. She wore a broad grin that looked misplaced in her stern face. Alia followed her gaze.

The moon hung in the zenith of the washed-out autumn sky, white and full in the afternoon light. It was much too large, and in the wrong place. Alia held out a hand at arm's length; the moon's edges circled her palm. She remained on the balcony, dumbfounded, until Father's thin voice called up to them from the hallway.

~

Mother had once said that when Alia had her first period, they would celebrate and she would get to pick out her first ladies' dress. When Alia caught her attention long enough to tell her what happened, Mother just nodded. She showed Alia where the napkins were and told her to put stained clothes and sheets in cold water. Then she returned to the attic. Father walked around the flat, cleaning and fiddling in quick movements. He baked bread, loaf after loaf. Every now and then he came into the living room where Alia sat curled up in the sofa, and gave her a wordless hug.

~

The radio blared all night. All the transmissions were about what had happened that morning at quarter past eleven. The president spoke to the nation: *We urge everyone to live their lives as usual. Go to work, go to school, but don't stay outside for longer than necessary. We don't yet know exactly what has happened, but our experts are investigating the issue. For your peace of mind, avoid looking up.*

Out in the street, people were looking up. The balconies were full of people looking up. When Alia went to bed, Mother was still outside with her eye to the ocular. Father came to tuck Alia in. She pressed her face into his aproned chest, drawing in the smell of yeasty dough and after-shave.

"What if it's my fault?" she whispered.

Father patted her back. "How could it possibly be your fault?"

Alia sighed. "Forget it."

"Go on, tell me."

"I got my period at a quarter past eleven," she finally said. "Just when the moon came."

"Oh, darling," said Father. "Things like that don't happen just because you had your period."

"Are you sure?"

Father let out a short laugh. "Of course." He sighed, his breath stirring Alia's hair. "I have no idea what's going on up there, but of this I'm sure."

"I wish I was brave," said Alia. "I wish I wasn't so afraid all the time."

"Bravery isn't not being afraid, love. Bravery is perseverance through fear."

"What?"

"Fancy words," said Father. "It means doing something even though you're afraid. That's what brave is. And you are."

He kissed her forehead and turned out the light. Falling asleep took a long time.

♒

Master Bobek stood behind the lectern, his face grey.

"We must remain calm," he said. "You mustn't worry too much. Try to go about your lives as usual. And you are absolutely not allowed to miss school. You have no excuse to stay at home. Everyone will feel better if they carry on as usual. Itti?" He nodded to the boy in the chair next to Alia.

Itti stood, not much taller than when he had been sitting down. "Master Bobek, do you know what really happened?"

The teacher cleared his throat. "We must remain calm," he repeated.

He turned around and pulled down one of the maps from above

the blackboard. "Now for today's lesson: bodies of water."

Itti sat down and leaned over. "Your mum," he whispered. "Does she know anything?"

Alia shrugged. "Don't know."

"Can you ask? My parents are moving all our things to the cellar."

She nodded. Itti gave her a quick smile. If Master Bobek had seen the exchange, he said nothing of it, which was unusual for him. Master Bobek concentrated very hard on talking about bodies of water. The children all looked out the windows until Master Bobek swore and drew the curtains.

≈

When Alia came home from school, she found the door unlocked. Mother's coat hung on its peg in the hallway.

"Home!" Alia shouted, and took off jacket and shoes and climbed the stairs to the attic.

Mother sat on the balcony, hunched over the telescope's ocular. She was still in her dressing gown, her hair tousled on one side and flat on the other.

Alia forced herself not to look up, but the impossible Moon's cold glow spilled into the upper edge of her vision. "Mother?"

"The level of detail is incredible," Mother mumbled.

Her neck looked dusty, as if she'd been shaking out carpets or going through things in the attic. Alia blew at it and sneezed.

"Have you been out here all day?" Alia wiped her nose on her shirt sleeve.

Mother lifted her gaze from the telescope and turned it to somewhere beyond Alia's shoulder, the same look that Doctor Kazakoff gave visiting children. Grey dust veiled her face; the rings under her eyes were the colour of graphite. Her cheekbones glimmered faintly.

"I suppose I have," she said. "Now off with you, dear. I'm working."

≈

The kitchen still smelled of freshly baked bread. On the counter lay a loaf of bread rolled up in a tea towel, next to a bread knife and a jar of honey. Alia unfolded the towel, cut a heel off the loaf and stuffed it in her mouth. It did nothing to ease the burning in her stomach. She turned the loaf over and cut the other heel off. The crust was crunchy and chewy at the same time.

She had eaten her way through most of the loaf when Father spoke behind her. He said her name and put a hand on her shoulder. The other hand gently pried the bread knife from her grip. Then her cheek was pressed against his shirt. Over the slow beat of his heart, Alia could hear the air rushing in and out of his lungs, the faint whistle of breath through his nose. The fire in her belly flickered and died.

"Something's wrong with Mother," she whispered into the shirt.

Father's voice vibrated against her cheek as he spoke. "She's resting now."

〰〰

Alia and her father went about their lives as the President had told them to: going to work, going to school. The classroom emptied as the days went by. Alia's remaining classmates brought rumours of families moving to cellars and caves under the city. The streets were almost deserted. Those who ventured outside did so at a jog, heads bowed between their shoulders. There were no displays of panic or violence. Someone would occasionally burst into tears in the market or on the bus, quickly comforted by bystanders who drew together in a huddle around him.

The radio broadcasts were mostly about nothing, because there was nothing to report. All the scientists and knowledgeable people had established was that the moon didn't seem to affect the earth more than before. It no longer went through phases, staying full and fixed in its position above the city. A respected scientist claimed it was a mirage, and had the city's defence shoot a rocket at it. The rocket hit the moon right where it seemed to be positioned. Burning debris rained back down through the atmosphere for half a day.

As the moon drew closer, it blotted out the midday sun and drowned the city in a ghostly white light, day and night. At sunrise and sundown, the light from the two spheres mixed in a blinding and sickly glare.

Mother stayed on the balcony in her dressing gown, eye to the ocular. Alia heard Father argue with her at night, Father's voice rising and Mother's voice replying in monotone.

Once, a woman in an official-looking suit came to ask Doctor Kazakoff for help. Mother answered the door herself before Father could intercept her. The official-looking woman departed and didn't return.

Alia was still bleeding. She knew you were only supposed to bleed for a few days, but it had been two weeks now. What had started as brownish spotting was now a steady, bright red runnel. It was as if it grew heavier the closer the moon came.

︫

Late one night, she heard shouts and the sound of furniture scraping across the floor. Then footsteps came down the stairs; something metallic clattered. Peeking out from her room, Alia saw Father in the hallway with the telescope under one arm.

"This goes out!" he yelled up the stairs. "It's driven you insane!"

Mother came rushing down the stairs, naked feet slapping on the steps. "Pavel Kazakoff, you swine, give it to me." She lunged for the telescope.

Father was heavy and strong, but Mother was furious. She tore the telescope from him so violently that he abruptly let go, and when the telescope crashed into the wall she lost her grip. The floor shook with the telescope's impact. In the silence that followed, Father slowly raised a hand. The front of Mother's dressing gown had opened. He drew it aside.

"Vera." His voice was almost a whisper. "What happened to you?"

In the light from the hallway sconce, Mother's skin was patterned in shades of grey. Uneven rings overlapped each other over her shoulders and arms. The lighter areas glowed with reflected light.

Mother glanced at Father, and then at Alia where she stood gripping the frame of her bedroom door.

"It's regolith," Mother said in a matter-of-fact voice.

She returned upstairs. She left the telescope where it lay.

︫

A doctor arrived the morning after. Father gave Alia the choice of staying in her room or going over to Itti's. She chose the latter, hurrying over the courtyard and up the stairs to where Itti lived with his parents.

Itti let her into a flat that was almost completely empty. They passed the kitchen, where Mrs Botkin was canning vegetables, and shut themselves in Itti's room. He only had a bed and his box of comics. They sat down on the bed with the box between them.

"Mother's been making preserves for days now," said Itti.

Alia leafed through the topmost magazine without really looking at the pictures. "What about your father?"

Itti shrugged. "He's digging. He says the cellar doesn't go deep enough."

"Deep enough for what?"

"For, you know." Itti's voice became small. "For when it hits."

Alia shuddered and put the magazine down. She walked over to the window. The Botkins's apartment was on the top floor, and Alia could see right into her own kitchen window across the yard. Her parents were at the dinner table, across from a stranger who must be the doctor. They were discussing something. The doctor leaned forward over the table, making slow gestures with his hands. Mother sat back in her chair, chin thrust out in her Doctor Kazakoff stance. After a while, the physician rose from his chair and left. He emerged from the door to the yard moments later; Alia could see the large bald patch on his head. The physician tilted his head backward and gave the sky a look that seemed almost annoyed. He turned around and hurried out the front gate.

〰〰

Father was still in the kitchen when Alia came home. He blew his nose in a tea towel when he noticed Alia in the doorway.

"Vera is ill," he said. "But we have to take care of her here at home. There's no room at the hospital."

Alia scratched at an uneven spot in the doorjamb. "Is she crazy?"

Father sighed. "The doctor says it's a nervous breakdown, and that it's brought on some sort of skin condition." He cleared his throat and crumpled the tea towel in his hands. "We need to make sure she eats and drinks properly. And that she gets some rest."

Alia looked at her hand, which was gripping the doorjamb so hard the nails were white and red. A sudden warmth spread between her legs as a new trickle of blood emerged.

Father turned the radio on. The announcer was incoherent, but managed to convey that the moon was approaching with increasing speed.

〰〰

# Moonstruck

Mother's dressing gown lay in a heap on the chair next to the balcony door. Mother herself lay naked on the balcony, staring into the sky, a faint smile playing across her face. Alia could see the great wide sea across her chest, and the craters making rings around it. All of the moon's scarred face was sculpted in relief over Mother's body. The crater rims had begun to rise up above the surface.

Alia couldn't make herself step out onto the balcony. Instead, she went down to the courtyard and looked up into the sky. The moon covered the whole square of sky visible between the houses, like a shining ceiling. It had taken on a light of its own, a jaundiced shade of silver. More blood trickled down between Alia's legs.

With the burning rekindling in her stomach, Alia saw how obvious it was. It was all her fault, no matter what Father said. Something had happened when she started bleeding, some power had emerged in her that she wasn't aware of, that drew the moon to her like a magnet. And Mother, so sensitive to the skies and the planets, had been driven mad by its presence. There was only one thing to do. She had to save everyone. The thought filled her with a strange mix of terror and anticipation.

〰
〰

Father was on the couch in the living room, leafing through an old photo album. He said nothing when Alia came in and wrapped her arms around him, just leaned his head on her arm and laid his long hand over hers. She detached herself and walked up the stairs to the attic. Mother was as Alia had left her, spread out like a starfish.

Alia crouched beside her still form. "I know why you're ill."

Mother's bright eyes rolled to the side and met Alia's gaze.

"I'll make you well again," Alia continued. "But you won't see me again." Moisture dripped from her eyes into the crater on Mother's left shoulder, and pooled there.

Mother's eyes narrowed.

"Goodbye." Alia bent down and kissed her cheek. It tasted of dust and sour ashes.

〰
〰

The plain spread out beyond the city, dotted here and there by clumps of trees. The autumn wind coming in from the countryside was laden with the smell of windfallen fruit and bit at Alia's face. The moonlight leached out the colour from the grass. The birds, if any birds remained here, were quiet. There was only the whisper of grass on Alia's trouser legs, and an underlying noise like thunder. And the moon was really approaching fast, just like the radio man had said: a glowing plain above pressed down like a stony cloud cover. The sight made Alia's face hot with a shock that spread to her ears and down her chest and back, pushing the air out of her lungs. She had a sudden urge to crouch down and dig herself into the ground. The memory of her mother on the balcony flashed by: her body immobile under the regolith, her despairing eyes. Bravery was perseverance through fear. Alia took another step, and her legs, though shaking, held. She could still breathe somehow.

〰

When Alia could no longer see the city behind her, a lone hill rose from the plain. It was the perfect place. She climbed the hill step by slow step. The inside of her trousers had soaked through with blood that had begun to cool against her skin, the fabric rasping wetly as she walked. At the top of the hill, she lay down and made herself stare straight up. Why did they always describe fear as cold? Fear was searing hot, burning a hole through her stomach, eating through her lungs.

She forced out a whisper. "Here I am," she told the moon. "I did this. Take me now, do what you're supposed to."

Alia closed her eyes and fought to breathe. The muscles in her thighs tingled and twitched. The vibration in her chest rose in volume, and she understood what it was: the sound of the moon moving through space, the music of the spheres.

〰

She had no sensation of time passing. Maybe she'd fainted from fear or bleeding; the sound of footsteps up the hillside woke her. She opened her eyes. Mother stood over her, the terrain across her body in sharp relief against the glowing surface above. The whites of her eyes glistened in twin craters. She held the broken telescope in one hand.

"Go home." Mother's voice was dull and raspy.

Alia shook her head. "It's my fault. I have to make everything okay again."

Mother cocked her head. "Go home, child. This isn't about you. It was never about you. It's my moon."

She grabbed Alia's arm so hard it hurt, and dragged her to her feet. "It was always my moon. Go home."

Mother didn't stink anymore. She smelled like dust and rocks. Her collarbones had become miniature mountain ranges.

Alia pulled her arm out of her mother's grasp. "No."

Mother swung the telescope at her head.

〜〜〜

The second round of waking was to a world that somehow tilted. Alia opened her eyes to a mess of bright light. Vomit rose up through her throat. She rolled over on her side and retched. When her stomach finally stopped cramping, she slowly sat up. Her brain seemed to slide around a little in her skull.

She was sitting at the foot of the hill. Over her, just a few metres it seemed, an incandescent desert covered the sky.

The moon had finally arrived.

〜〜〜

Afterward, when Father found her, and the moon had returned to its orbit, and the hill was empty, and everyone pretended that the city had been in the grip of some kind of temporary collective madness, Alia refused to talk about what happened, where Mother had gone. About Mother on the top of the hill, where she stood naked and laughing with her hands outstretched toward the moon's surface. About how she was still laughing as it lowered itself toward the ground, as it pushed her to her knees, as she finally lay flat under its monstrous weight. How she quieted only when the moon landed, and the earth rang like a bell.

# John R. Fultz

## The Key to Your Heart is Made of Brass

**John R. Fultz** *lives in the North Bay Area of California but is originally from Kentucky. His "Books of the Shaper" trilogy includes* Seven Princes, Seven Kings, *and* Seven Sorcerers, *available everywhere from Orbit Books. His story collection* The Revelations of Zang *features the adventures of Artifice the Quill and Taizo of Narr in a series of interrelated tales. John's work has appeared in the magazines* Weird Tales, Black Gate, Space & Time, Lightspeed, *and in the anthologies* Shattered Shields, Way of the Wizard, Cthulhu's Reign, The Book of Cthulhu II, *and* Deepest, Darkest Eden: New Tales of Hyperborea. *John keeps a blog at johnrfultz.com*

Wake up. Something is wrong.

Greasy orange light smears the dark. Only one of your optical lenses is functional. The walls are slabs of corroded metal with rust patterns like dumb staring phantoms. You lie awkwardly across the oily flagstones of an alley where curtains of black chains obscure the night. Bronze lanterns hang from those chains, but most of them are dead. Lightless. Like your left optical.

Struggling to hands and knees, you realize your porcelain face has been shattered. White shards gleam on the alley floor between puddles of greenish scum. You lift a gloved hand to explore your ruined visage; the upper left side took the brunt of the blow. Your fingers brush across the silver skull beneath the missing porcelain.

This won't do at all. To be seen without one's face. It could damage your reputation.

It might even be illegal.

That same blow—the one you don't quite remember—must have dislodged your left optical. There it is now, lying among the porcelain fragments, a thumb-sized orb of blue glass. Removing your gloves, you wipe the scum from its glistening surface and carefully reattach it to the vitreous filaments inside your left socket. Much better. Your depth perception is restored. Inside its silver casement, your tender brain begins processing images from the repaired optical. You slide the blue orb carefully back into place, grateful it wasn't damaged.

Now at least you can see. And perhaps remember...

The girl...the Doxie...you remember her ceramic face, exquisitely formed with tiny lips painted crimson. The gentle amber of her opticals peeking through the beautiful mask. Her gown, a flowing affair of scarlet satin and black lace. The red fabric hugs the supple curves of her torso before spreading out to engulf her lower body. You met her in the alley, beneath the dead lanterns. By that fact alone, you know what she must be.

She is a Beatific, like you...but not like you at all. She's a prostitute.

Your bodies are sculpted to the same degree of slim perfection, your faces designed for maximum aesthetic value. Yet she is a creature of the streets, the gutters, a plaything of her nameless clients. It dawns on you with a sick familiarity that *you* are one of those clients.

You snap out of the vision, frightened by rushing memories. Your waistcoat is stained by the filth of the alley, but you brush off the grit as best you can. Near a receptacle of eroded copper tubing you find your top hat. Your expensive walking stick appears to be gone...stolen. Perhaps it was the bludgeon that shattered your face; the pommel was a bronze orb sculpted in the likeness of a grinning toad. A formidable weapon, but it had done you no good. Your attacker, however, had found it a useful tool.

The purple neon glow of the street is a watery vision at the end of the alley. Before you can go out there and find another face to wear, you must look presentable. There are certain rules of Beatific conduct, and you must adhere. Reputation is everything in the Urbille.

Checking your neck kerchief, you discover the emptiness in your breast pocket. A shock of panic runs through your lean limbs, and the gears of your joints grind like creaking doors. Your fingers invade the pocket, searching but finding nothing. The key to your heart is gone. Horror rushes down your throat like a bitter oil. The gentle whirring and clicking in your chest cavity is now the sound of ticking dread.

You sink to your knees, searching the alley. Where is the key? You remember inserting it into the narrow slot in your bare chest last morning, turning it full round ninety-nine times, enough to power the gears and cogs and wheels and springs of your Beatific body for another twenty-four hours. Winding the clockwork mechanism that is your living core. The key is made of shining yellow brass, and like all Beatific heart-keys it is one-of-a-kind, a customized symbol of your status.

*It's not here!*

You paw at your trousers and find that ironically your pocket watch has not been stolen. It is almost three a.m. You have six hours to get a replacement key made. The alternative is unthinkable...winding down to an inanimate collection of useless parts while your brain rapidly dies inside its silver casement.

The Doxie...she must have taken the key. But that makes no sense. She...or someone with her...clubbed you over the head with your own walking stick and stole your heart key. Why would anyone else want it? It will not wind the heart of any other Beatific. Its only value is the daily function it plays in keeping you, and only you, alive. This is the course of your existence: Wake, wind the heart-key, get dressed, and go about the business of your day.

You had never considered the possibility of a day without your key.

You have never considered what that would mean.

Duplicating one's heart-key is a High Crime. Beatifics have been dragged off to prison for contemplating it aloud. The Potentates' decree was *One Key for One Heart*. "We must preserve our individuality or risk becoming soulless copies of one another." The words of Tribune Anteus, as broadcast on high-frequency transistor during the last key duplication scandal.

Fear breaks the icy stillness of your reverie.

The key isn't here, so there is only one option.

You must solicit the Keymaker.

And you have six hours.

〰

You pull the top hat down low to disguise your shattered cheek. At this late hour no one of any consequence is likely to be about. At least not in this quarter of the Urbille, where Beatifics seldom wander. Here among the decaying spires of ancient metal, the bulwarks of rust and corrosion, the moldering and brittle bones of bygone industrialism. Decrepit factories have become squatter's kingdoms, and iron bridges span brackish waterways where finned, scaly things slither and swim.

Lanterns gleam atop iron posts, the flames of viridian gas dancing in their soiled globes. This is the Rusted Zone, where the metals of previous ages have gathered like flotsam washed upon a dirty beach. You would never come here in the light of day. But you have needs, and your wife has been dead thirty years. A man…even a Beatific man…can only hold out so long.

As you shuffle into the deserted street your elastic skin tightens. The sign of a brewing rabidity in the atmosphere. A storm will break soon.

Your time with the Doxie comes back to you now. A shameful memory of fulfilling base desires. This isn't the first time you've crawled among the rust to seek the company of whores. You always feel pity for them, even as you enjoy the pleasures of their trade. You remember this one well…your gloved fingers against the base of her skull, the golden glow of her opticals behind the porcelain facade. Revulsion intrudes as you remember the slick softness of her thoughts…the way your consciousness slid hungrily into hers. You almost feel sorry for her, and all her kind, those who open their minds to the nearest paying stranger. Until you remember what she did to you…broke your face and stole the key to your heart.

Her psyche was a red and pulsing universe. You soared there like some winged beast, looking down upon the nooks and crannies of intellect from the lofty cloud-realm of her thoughtsphere. You did not consider the countless number of other men who had invaded her mentality. Somehow this never matters in the throes of psychic ecstasy.

You played with stray impulses, gnawed on the raw assumptions of her personal reality, dominated her cognition. Such a satisfying conquest of the female mind by the lusty intelligence of the male. She was sweet, this one…yet something untouchable lingered beyond the curtains of her memory…something she refused to share with any client, including you. Your thoughts slammed against those gates like battering rams…you wanted to know her every secret. You wanted to claim her utterly, never caring that you might discover what caused her to fall from grace, why this Beatific maiden became a Doxie trollop. In the heady grip of your blind need, you strove to penetrate deeper.

That's when it must have happened…someone in that dingy alley grabbed your bronze-topped cane and brought it down against your forehead with all force. The mental link was broken immediately as you lost consciousness. Your mind yanked from hers as your body fell to the filthy flagstones. She must have had a partner. But why? What could she...they... possibly gain by stealing your heart-key? If they wanted you dead, they could have killed you right there.

The wind picks up, pelting you with clouds of sandy rust. The twisting street (you never caught the name) is narrow, and few other figures move in the pre-rabid gloom. Outside the doorway of a ramshackle saloon a pair of Clatterpox ramble noisily. The neon placard above the door reads THE DISTENDED BLADDER. Three more Clatterpox lumber across the street ahead of you, heading for the tavern. Their cylindrical bodies rumble and clang, supported by thin iron legs and metal-slab feet. Their chest furnaces burn hot, exuding foul vapors and smokes from the various holes, tubes, and vents placed about their grotesque frames. They turn oval heads toward you as you walk past, staring with flat optical lenses of grey glass.

Poor souls. You do not envy their mean existence, hearts fueled by chunks of burning anthracite, their days spent working mindless jobs just to afford the black rocks that keep them ambulatory. They are the poor of the Urbille, the wretched working class. If they recognize you as a Beatific, they may assault you. Class distinctions are dangerous among the rust. If they knew you were the head of House Honore, what would they do? Tear you apart and sell your gears for scrap?

Now it comes to you: Could the Doxie have known? She might have been someone important at one time. She might even be an ancestral enemy. Someone your father or grandfather ruined in some forgotten business dealing. Could the theft of your heart-key be some form of belated revenge?

One of the Clatterpox shouts something as you hurry past, but you turn the corner without looking back. The sound of their rattling bodies follows you down the street, but you turn and turn again, finally losing them in the shadows of a lightless thoroughfare. Here the sky is clear, and you see the swirling constellations of night. Unfortunately, this welcome sight does you no good because the rabidity has arrived.

It swoops down upon the dark streets like some predatory bird of legend. A tightening of the air itself, a freezing and cracking of atmospheric forces. It keens in your ears like a wailing tea pot, and the wind takes your hat into the night. Fissures in the fabric of space/time erupt along the street. You've walked right into the heart of this one. The air splits open not six yards away, and you see another world revealed beyond the throbbing gash.

It's green and steaming…a jungle like the ones from ancient botanical texts. Colossal lizards feast on one another, tearing flesh, skin, and tendon with terrible fangs. The sounds of their shrieking flows from the vacuity. The gravity of that primeval world pulls at your lapels. If you let it, it will pull you through and your life will wind down in that nameless wilderness. The gears of your legs grind as you pull away from the hovering fissure. The wind screams. You walk against it and pass another vacuity, a rip in existence that pulses and expands, bleeding gravity. Beyond this one you see a night-dark sea and a distant shore lined with luminous towers. Golden-skinned beings sail the waters in skiffs of pale wood. They must see the vacuity from their side as well because their glowing emerald opticals turn toward you as you walk past. The vision dies as the vacuity begins to shrink.

You stumble into the dying wind as the storm subsides. A dozen more vacuities glimmer in your vicinity. You ignore them. At a meeting of four streets ahead, you see a Clatterpox staring at one of the fissures as it closes completely. Then his round head turns toward you with a fresh burst of vapor and a hissing sound. Is it the same one, who called after you? He stares uncertainly in the post-rabidity calm. You step toward the windows of an all-night merchant on the corner.

Above the doorway the name HOFFSTEIN'S gleams in torrid blue neon. You walk inside and find yourself hemmed by rows of crowded shelves. The proprietor is a handsome Beatific, but he greets you with a suspicious glare as you approach the display of porcelains. No time to be choosy. You pick the first masculine face on the stand and carry it to the counter.

"You're out late, Sir Honore," says the proprietor. "Some wild party, eh?"

"Something like that," you say.

"Must have gotten a bit rough…" He nods toward your busted face.

You say nothing, avoiding his glare.

"Anything else?"

"No," you say. "Yes…a hat. That one." You pick a simple black topper. It's been nearly an hour since you awoke in the alley. You must move quicker.

"Seventeen brilliants," says the merchant.

"Put it on my account," you say. Earlier tonight you emptied your pockets to pay the Doxie.

"Very well. Have a good morning, Sir Honore."

You cast your old face into the store's dustbin and replace it with this splendid new one.

New hat sitting firmly on your head, you head back into the street.

Making for the Steeple Road, you notice a shadowy figure trailing a block behind you. You stop near a pile of metal sculpted into a hideous beast and stare back at the pursuer. A Clatterpox, of course. Now you can hear his hissing, rattling locomotion as he draws nearer. He carries a club or a dark blade in one of his metal fists…you cannot tell which.

Now you run. The Rusted Zone becomes a blur of grey, brown, and dirty neon, and you ache to put it all behind you. The Clatterpox could never move as fast as you. Soon you see the Steeple Gate, and the faces of its stone gargoyles glare at you like old friends. You speak the word of command and the gate opens. On its other side the streets are well-lit with spherical lanterns kept shiny and clean. As the iron gate closes behind you, you realize the Clatterpox might know the command word as well. So you hurry, shuffling between the houses of ornate stone and their lawns of crushed glass until you see the spiked fence of the Keymaker's estate.

A great brass bell hangs at the gate, and you hate to ring it so late. Your pocket watch says 4:03 a.m. But it can't be helped. You ring the bell once. Wait. Again. No lights go on inside the stone mansion. You ring it a third time and notice the front gate is ajar. You pull it open just enough to creep inside. The lawn is immaculate, filled with sculptures of glass and stone in the shapes of skulls, fantastic machinery, and abstract forms recalling the Organic Age. Your shoes sound far too loud as you walk across the crushed glass toward the Keymaker's door. He will be annoyed to be awakened so late (or so early), but you will offer him whatever price he demands to cast a mold of your chest lock and make a new key before 9:00 a.m. You have little choice. His workshop is attached to the mansion, a domed miniature factory of green stone, possibly jade. Certainly you cannot be the first panicked Beatific who has come to him after hours with a lost key emergency.

The front doors are hanging open and a single lantern burns somewhere inside. Something is not quite right here. The estate is not large, but the nearest neighbor is several hundred yards away. Perhaps someone out there heard you ring the gate-bell, or perhaps not. But the front door should not be open.

You almost stumble over a lump of metal at your feet. A two-headed canine lying on its side. A lean body of iron and bronze covered in fuzzy, elastic skin. Both its necks have been broken, and the inner workings of its guts have been torn out. A scattered mess of cogs and gears litters the foyer.

You walk cautiously toward the dim light, already knowing what you will find. Ahead lies the parlor where the Keymaker keeps his bookshelves. You were here twelve years ago for a party honoring his fourteenth decade of service. You remember his great easy chair, where he sat and entertained his guests with stories of his youth. Now you slip into that curtained room and see him sitting in the same chair, dressed in a satin night-robe. The lantern flickers unsteadily on the table beside him. He is headless, his body reclining on the cushioned velvet, gloved hands resting on his lap. His head lies a few feet away, fractured porcelain cheek against the burgundy carpet. Scattered bits of copper and wire spill across his chest and lap. Once again fear steals your ability to move.

The Keymaker is dead.

You press your ear to his breast, but you hear no mechanized whirring, no clicking of cogs or sighing springs. The lantern oil burns low; this happened hours ago. You know his brain has died inside that severed skull. He is gone.

You stumble backwards until you fall into the soft embrace of a couch.

The Keymaker was not a true Beatific...he did not inherit his title...he worked to earn it. He was a laborer, basically. He had no fortune or noble lineage. But he was a man of honor. And he was the only man who could save your life.

A noise breaks the silence of the dead man's study. Something heavy, moving on the terrace. No, in the foyer. You glance around for a weapon, an exit, something, anything...an ancient cutlass hangs on the wall, blade eaten by rust. You pull it down and brandish it, fists wrapped around the hilt. You have no idea how to fight with blade or pistol.

The sound moves nearer. Heavy footsteps. Now the hissing of steam through a vent.

You remember the sound of the Clatterpox following you, and sure enough he stands in the doorway of the parlor. A terrible thing of corroded iron, leaking pistons, purple vapors, and swiveling joints.

He stares at you with his flat grey opticals. His mouth is a horizontal slit, dividing round chin from oval head. He sighs at you...no, it's the sound of hot air leaking from his heart-furnace. The grill of his chest emits orange light where the anthracite burns hot.

"Honore," he says, voice flat like the ringing of tin. "We have something you want."

Now you recognize the weapon he carries in his left hand.

It is your walking stick with the bronze toad head.

∽

"Who are you?" You wave the useless cutlass at the Clatterpox like some protective talisman. But you know it offers no protection.

"My name is Flux."

"You're with the Doxie."

"Yes."

"You assaulted me and stole the key to my heart."

"Yes."

"Why?"

The Clatterpox shrugs its rusted shoulders. Something *pings* inside its whirring guts.

"Because you have wealth. We need it."

"Extortion...the device of cowards." Your words sound brave. But terror swims in your chest cavity, runs along your plastic skin like spilled oil.

"That may be..but we have your brass key. We want a hundred-thousand brilliants. Bring them to the Well of Bones at sunrise. Or we will drop your key in the well and you will never find it. You'll wind down. Your brain will rot and die."

You consider this. Your ancestral fortune is vast. You won't miss a hundred thousand brilliants. Besides, there are no other options.

"You...you killed the Keymaker."

"Of course," says the Clatterpox. "Don't be late." He thumps across the foyer and out into the courtyard, then beyond the gate and down the road into the Rusted Zone.

You lay the ancient sword down at the Keymaker's feet. There is no time to mourn for him. The sun will rise in less than two hours.

You run along the winding avenues of the Good Hills, ignoring the stone domiciles of your fellow Beatifics. Rarely do any lights glow in the oval windows at this rude hour. You dash north, heading toward your manor house, and the fractured moon rises above the palace of the Potentates at the top of the great hill. Its crumbling walls and crenellated towers are older than the Urbille itself, and large enough to house a second city, which according to rumor, it does. The Potentates live inside its walls of mossy stone, and not even Beatifics are allowed to sully its precincts with their presence. Once per year the Potentates emerge for the Parade of Iniquities, carried by clockwork horses through the streets of the Urbille, wrapped in their dark robes and chains of gold, their bulbous heads veiled, the dark shadows of their opticals scanning the populace in silent judgment. They are terribly tall, the Potentates, hence the immensity of their stone citadel. Rumors speak also of the labyrinth below that towering fortress…a dungeon into which only the most evil and unrepentant of lawbreakers are cast. You imagine the Doxie and her murderous Clatterpox cast into that dark maze, pursued by terrible ancient things.

The Honore Estate lies three miles from the outer wall of the great palace. You reach it an hour before sunrise and race through your front doors toward the sealed portal that guards the lower vaults. Once the house was full of servants, semi-organic toadlings imported from stabilized vacuities. They kept the manse from disintegrating and the cobwebs from accumulating. Now, many years after Siormah wound down and left you, your outer garden is a hideous collection of weeds and vine. Your walls are clammy and the stone crumbles a bit more each year. You often sit here, in the heart of your inherited power, and contemplate the transitory nature of things. At times you can almost feel the pillars and the stone slabs of your walls decaying slowly into blackened sand. Stone is no more permanent than metal. You realized this long ago. Your stone mansion will one day collapse, as will all the Beatific dwellings, and eventually the stone palace itself will tumble down upon the bloated skulls of the Potentates. Will anyone still be alive when that day comes?

At the bottom of the spiral stair you speak the Word of Lineage and the round vault door swings open. Inside a hung lantern lights itself automatically and a world of clashing colors fills the chamber. The floor is hidden under pile after pile of brilliants, precious stones in all the shades of ruby, amber, emerald, topaz, sapphire, violet, opal, and diamond. Here is the great fortune that your ancestors built. And on the four walls of this chamber, emerging from the grey stone in bas-relief, are the faces of those ancestors.

Your father, your grandfather, your great-grandfather, and a dozen more, going back a thousand years to the last Organic Age. Their opticals open and stare at you with flame-bright lenses. Somehow, as you wade into the room and begin scooping brilliants into an iron chest, their stone lips move and they speak in whispering voices. You try to ignore them, you know their cruel wisdom. You've long passed the days when you would come down here for advice. You learned eventually that your ancestors were just as ignorant of the world as you. Their accumulation of wealth and title was their only virtue.

"What are you doing, René?" asks the stone face of your father.

"You fool!" seethes your grandfather's visage. "Wasting our wealth again!"

"I need this…all of it," you say, not bothering to meet their radiant opticals. "Leave me alone."

"Leave him alone, he says!" Your father again. "Still haven't learned to respect your elders?"

"What are you doing?" asks another face, some older predecessor. Each succeeding member of the family lived longer than the one who came before. "What could be so costly?"

"I've lost the key to my heart!" you shout, overcome by strange emotions. "I have to buy it back."

"By all the Gods That Never Were," swears your grandfather's face. "That old scam again. You are being taken for a rube, boy."

Another stone face speaks, someone from terribly far down the line of ages.

"All of these stones are worthless, you know," says the face. "Bits of worthless glass. The Potentates manufacture these by the million."

"Nonsense!" says your father's visage. "Their worth is what made us a great family."

"No, he is right," says another ancient face. "The last true jewels were lost ages ago. This is all fakery. Our wealth is an illusion."

You scrape more armloads of the brilliants into the chest, hurrying. To stay in this chamber too long will drive you mad. Don't listen to their babble. They are liars and fools. And they are dead.

"René," says another nameless face of stone. "*All* wealth is an illusion. When you join us you will understand."

"Join us," says another face. "You are so close already."

"Join us," says another, through stone lips.

"Shut up!" you shout.

The faces grow still, but their fiery opticals stare at you.

You close the chest of brilliants, heft it to your shoulder, and leave the vault. The door slams closed behind you like the thunder of a collapsing empire.

You race up the stairs and check your pocket watch.

Less than an hour until sunrise.

You run out the front door, cross the overgrown courtyard, and head down the hillside.

Early risers are lighting their lanterns as you pass the gates of Beatific mansions.

Once through the Steeple Gate you head into the Rusted Zone, directly toward the Well of Bones, clutching the chest in your tireless arms, a precious ransom of a hundred-thousand worthless brilliants.

$$\approx$$

Along the Avenue of Copper Lungs you nearly stumble into a fizzleshade as it manifests in a haze of wispy hair and antique clothing. It stares at you with transparent opticals, pleading for help. They always want the same thing…the completion of unfinished business. Something left undone before they perished.

*Please*…this one moans…*my name is Enri…I left two children behind when I died. Will you find them and tell them about my hidden gold?*

"You died three-thousand years ago," you mutter, shuffling along under the weight of your burden. "Your children are long dead, too."

The phantom follows you, blinking in and out of existence, losing its purchase in the living world.

*Pleeaaaasssse*…it wails. *The children will starve! You must help me. I bled to death in this gutter…don't leave them alone.*

"Piss off!" you shout, a stab of guilt in your clicking chest.

Behind you the fizzleshade blinks into nothingness.

The light of pre-dawn limns the corroded skyline with an amber glow. The exact shade of the Doxie's opticals. You scurry along the streets of twisted metal, avoiding crowds of Clatterpox on their way to the factories. Gendarmes in black trenchcoats and stove-pipe hats patrol the streets now. Their faces are clusters of optical lenses, swiveling in multiple directions at once, observing the early morning activity, always alert for anything out of the ordinary.

Suddenly you realize that *you* are out of the ordinary. You are exactly the kind of anomaly the gendarmes look for as they enforce the laws of the Urbille: a lone Beatific carrying a heavy chest through the pre-dawn rust. And if that chest were to be inspected, a fortune in brilliants. You walk quietly now, hoping to avoid their attention. If there were time, you might tell them of your blackmailers' plot and let the Potentates' justice fall upon the Doxie and her confederate. But by the time they investigated your claims the sun would rise, your heart-key would be lost forever, and you would be dead.

No other course now but the Well of Bones.

You rush past steaming grates, the crooked frames of aluminum huts, and cross a bridge painted with the sigils of feuding Clatterpox gangs. Luckily, at this hour only working citizens will be up and about.

There it is. The walled plaza containing the Well of Bones. You walk through the open gate, glad there are no guards here. Who would care to guard a worthless pit of bones? This place is haunted by the lowest of scavengers, those who climb the sheer walls of the pit for miles deep and crawl back up with a bag of bones to sell for a few copper bits, or trade for drugs. Bone used to be highly valued in the Urbille, but nobody wants it anymore. It is a relic of the organic times.

Now you stand before the great pit, among the piles of scrap metal and the crude huts of bone-divers. There is no time to think about how completely vulnerable you are in this place because the sun has broken the jagged horizon, and you see the Doxie and her Clatterpox enter the plaza.

She moves gracefully across the muddy scrapyard, as out of place as yourself. Today her fine gown is green, the color of damp moss. Her black hair is a tall oval, secured with a spiral of copper wires. Her face is the one you remember: superb with its tiny red lips, arcing painted eyebrows, and the delicate curve of perfect cheeks. Her opticals glimmer at you, although with malice or amusement you cannot say. The Clatterpox named Flux shambles beside her, filling the air with his noxious exhalations.

"Sir Honore," she greets you, her voice that of a high-bred Beatific. You would never guess she was a mind harlot if you met her on an avenue in the Good Hills. "So glad you could make it."

You sit the chest of brilliants at her feet. You don't bother to return her greeting, or to remove your hat. She deserves no respect from you.

The Clatterpox opens the lid of the chest and looks inside. He nods his bulky head, and the Doxie reaches inside her cleavage. She produces the brass key that means your life. She offers it to you in the palm of one white-gloved hand.

"Why?" you ask, taking the key from her. You need to wind your

gears soon, but you have about two hours left. And you must know…
if she will tell you.

As the Clatterpox lifts the chest in its metal arms, she reaches to
caress its grimy cheek.

"You would not understand, Honore."

"I doubt that I will," you say. "But I've paid a heavy price. I deserve
an explanation."

The Doxie smiles and turns her amber lenses toward you again. "I
did it for my lover," she says.

Your neck gears nearly slip. "You love this Clatterpox?"

"Yes," she says. "So you *do* know the concept of love…"

"I am well versed in matters historical, Madame. As well as the
poetic arts."

She nods, the morning light glinting off her delicate nose. "But do
you know that love is real? Have you ever felt it?"

"You mock me."

"No, Honore," she says. "Not at all. Extort yes, but never mock. I,
too, am a Beatific."

"Your behavior suggests otherwise."

"We are this way, you and I, only because we could afford the
process."

The process. Beatification. You recall it, three centuries past. A *rite
of passage*, your father called it. The shedding of useless organic bulk,
everything but the all-important brain, center of the living intellect.

"Beatification is open to anyone," she reminds you. "Anyone who
can pay a Surgeon's fees."

She looks at the Clatterpox Flux again, and he seems to smile,
though his iron jaw will not permit such an action.

"You did this for *him*…" you say it for her, accepting the
preposterousness of it. "You wish to Beatify him…so you two can be
together."

"You are wise, Honore," she says.

"It is…abominable," you say.

"According to whom?" she asks. "Once Flux's living brain rests
inside a Beatific body, he will be no different than you or I. We really
cannot thank you enough, Sir Honore."

She turns to walk away with her Clatterpox lover and your
stolen brilliants, and you want to say something. A last comment or
condemnation…but your mind is blank. You squeeze the brass key in
your hand, taking comfort from its firmness.

The Doxie's head erupts like a burst lantern. A shower of porcelain shards, silver fragments, and brain tissue assaults your waistcoat and shirt. The Clatterpox drops the chest and it cracks open, spilling brilliants across the muddy ground.

You stand there numb, paralyzed by shock and confusion, as the black-coated gendarmes rush into the plaza, leaping from walls and gates. Bone-divers scamper from their illegal habitations and climb the walls like pale spiders. The gendarmes carry pistols and rifles, one of which has ended the Doxie's life.

The enforcers turn their clustered opticals toward the Clatterpox. The rusted monstrosity falls to its knees before the dead Doxie, cradling her headless corpse. Inside the open hollow of her neck, gears and springs pop and grind into stillness. The Clatterpox pulls something from his side...a key that he inserts between her sculpted breasts. The gendarmes believe it a weapon and begin firing. You leap to the ground to avoid the hail of bullets. Lying there, so close to the Doxie and her lover, you watch him turning her heart-key, trying to restart her life. But her head is ruined, her brain—the center of all life functions—spread across the ground, a litter of shredded blue flesh. Yet why is there is no blood or cranial fluid? Her Beatific brain wasn't alive at all. The organ was dried...congealed...preserved.

Is every Beatific brain like hers—nothing but dead, decayed flesh?

The implications of this question run through your mind yet refuse to take root.

The gendarmes' bullets bounce off the Clatterpox's iron body, or create holes like ruptured pustules. He turns the heart-key again and again, heedless of their assault. Eventually, they stop shooting and approach him on foot. The vapors from his vents and exhaust pipes flow black and heavy now. They tear him away from the Doxie's corpse and secure his arms with titanium shackles.

You start to rise, but two tall gendarmes lift you sharply to your feet. One of them stares at you with his cluster of opticals, nine blue-green lenses bright with the caress of dawn.

"Sir René Honore?" the gendarme asks through some mouth aperture hidden below his high collar.

You nod, still too stunned to speak.

"By order of the Tribune, you are under arrest."

"What? I have done nothing. I was blackmailed..."

"We understand," says the gendarme, his anterior opticals already scouring the rest of the plaza. "To blackmail a Beatific is a High Crime.

As is the paying of any funds to blackmailers. You broke the law. You will face justice."

You watch as they gather up the body and assorted remains of the Doxie and cast her into the Well of Bones. You know she will fall for several minutes before she reaches the bottom. There she will lie among the antediluvian bones, until perhaps some bone-diver gathers up her parts to sell as scrap. All that is left of her are the shards of an exquisite face, a few slivers of porcelain lying in the mud.

The Clatterpox Flux wheezes and coughs as they drag him away.

The gendarmes leave the brilliants lying trampled in the muck. Mere bits of colored glass beneath their notice.

You remember what the elder stone face said about the jewels, and you laugh as they lead you out of the plaza and into the rust.

〜〜〜

You're still laughing when they haul you before the veiled Tribune on his high bench, and later when they drag you across the stone bridge and deep beneath the walls of the crumbling palace. In the endless dark of the labyrinth, your laughter draws nameless things closer.

Soon you will join your ancestors on the wall of the sunken vault.

A laughing face of stone.

# Jeff VanderMeer

## No Breather in the World But Thee

**Jeff VanderMeer's** *most recent fiction is the NYT-bestselling Southern Reach trilogy (*Annihilation, Authority, *and* Acceptance*), all released in 2014. The series has been acquired by publishers in 16 other countries and Paramount Pictures/Scott Rudin Productions have acquired the movie rights. His* Wonderbook *(Abrams Image), the world's first fully illustrated, full-color creative writing guide, won the BSFA Award for best nonfiction and has been nominated for a Hugo Award and a Locus Award. A three-time World Fantasy Award winner and 13-time nominee, VanderMeer has been a finalist for the Nebula, Philip K. Dick, and Shirley Jackson Awards, among others. His nonfiction appears in the New York Times Book Review, the Guardian, the Washington Post, and the Los Angeles Times. VanderMeer has edited or coedited twelve fiction anthologies and serves as the co-director of* Shared Worlds, *a unique teen SF/fantasy writing camp located at Wofford College. Previous novels include the Ambergris Cycle, with nonfiction titles including* Booklife *and* The Steampunk Bible. *He lives in Tallahassee, Florida, with his wife, the noted editor Ann VanderMeer.*

The cook didn't like that the eyes of the dead fish shifted to stare at him as he cut their heads off. The cook's assistant, who was also his lover, didn't like that he woke to find just a sack of bloody bones on the bed beside him. "It's starting again," he gasped, just moments before a huge black birdlike creature carried him off, screaming. The child playing on the grounds outside the mansion did not at first know what she was seeing, but realized it was awful. "It's just like last year," she said to her imaginary friend, but her imaginary friend was dead. She ran for the front door, but the ghost of her imaginary friend, now large and ravenous and wormlike, swallowed her up before she had taken ten steps across the writhing grass.

From a third floor window, the lady of the house watched the girl vanish into the ground, the struggling man become an indecipherable dot in the sky. Then nothing happened for a time, and she said to the dust, to her long-dead husband, to the disappeared daughter, to the doctor who now lived somewhere in the walls: "Perhaps it's not happening again. Perhaps it's not like last year." Then she spied the disjointed red crocodile walking backwards across the lawn: a smear of wet crimson against the unbearable green of the finger-like grass. The creature's oddly bent legs spasmed and trembled as it lurched ahead. No, not a crocodile but a bloody sack of human flesh and bones crawling toward the river at the edge of the property. Was it someone she knew? Of course it was someone she knew.

An immense shadow began to grow around the unfortunate person like a black pool of blood. This puzzled her, until she realized some vast creature was plummeting down from an immense height toward the lawn. Raw misshapen pieces of the behemoth began to rain down, outliers of the body itself. Within seconds, it would descend, whole. The crawling bag of bones redoubled its efforts, seeming aware of the danger, frantic to avoid being caught in that impact. Now the lady of the house could not contain her fear any longer. She turned and ran, intending to flee down the stairs and seek shelter in basement. But something wide and white and cut through with teeth reared up out of the darkness and bit her in half, and then quarters, and then eighths, before she could do more than blink, blink rapidly, and then lie still, the image of the crawling man still with her. For awhile.

In the basement, waiting for the lady's return, a furiously scribbling man sat at a desk. He did not look up once; beyond the candlelight things lurked. As his mistress fell to pieces above him, the man was writing:

> Time is passing oddly. I feel as if I am sharing my shadow with many other people. If I look too closely at the cracks in the wall, I fear I will discover they are actually doors or mouths. There's something continually flitting beyond the corner of my eye. Something she tells me that I don't want to remember. Flit. Flit….No. *Tilt*. Tilt, not flit. *Tilt*.

He stopped for a moment to restore his nerve because a certain mania had entered his pen…and he didn't know who he was writing to. The child? The doctor? God? Something white and terrible waited in the shadows, its movements like the fevered wing-beats of a hundred panicked thrushes crushed into the semblance of a body. With an effort, he continued:

> The tilt is a gap. The gap is the cracks becoming corridors when I look away, and yet there no way out. This ends well only if I can be in two places at once. But if other people are using my shadow, isn't that a kind of door as well? Can I use my own shadow as a window? Can I escape?

A mighty crash and thud shook the mansion, as if something enormous had landed on the lawn. Dust and debris cascaded down on the man writing. A distant rattling cry came that did not bear thinking about. He looked up from his work for a second, thought, *It's happening again, just like the doctor warned*, but continued writing, as if the words might be the spell to undo it all.

…or is it just an inkling? Inklings are like questions that haven't been answered yet: by the time we ask them, we're being swallowed by the doors they open. And all that's left at the end, after the question's answered, is the shadow, haunting us. The man looked up one more time, and now his own pale shadow leered up and curled monstrous across the wall, the desk, the candle, and the rictus of his face.

"It's just an inkling, an inkling!" he screamed, but still his own pale shadow took him, teeth glittering cold in the chilly room in the bowels of the mansion where no other thing stirred, or should have stirred, and yet sometimes did. No words, soothed the shadow, as if it made a difference. *No words. I'm happening again. I'll always happen again.* But the shadow was him, and he could not tell where his writing ended and the shadow began.

On the first floor, the maid had fallen to her knees at the impact of the monster from above hitting the lawn. Now it tore into the grass as it bounded forward. It hit the side of the mansion like a battering ram so that the chandeliers cascaded and crashed all around like brittle glass wedding cakes, shards splintering across the floor and beads rolling with a heavy clunk under chairs and sofas. The thing shrieked out words in a language that sounded like dead leaves being stuffed into a gurgling fresh-cut throat. But she kept her grip on the shotgun she had taken from the study cabinet. "It won't be like last year," she shouted, although "last year" was something horribly vague in her memory. "It's too soon!" She shouted it to the house, to the lady of the house, to the man in the basement who had come to document everything the doctor had wanted to do, a very long time ago. *I will not blame the child.*

Again the monster smashed up against the mansion. Unpleasant chortles and meaty sounds smashed down through her ears, tightened around her heart, her lungs. She stood with an effort and headed back to the study. The study window was occluded by a huge, misshapen blue-green eye ridged with dark red. The monster. She brought the shotgun to her shoulder, braced for the recoil, and fired. The monster blinked and bellowed but the shots did not fall hot into its corona. Instead, the shotgun barrel curled around to sneer at her. A flash of white. From behind something wet and unpleasant slapped her head from her neck. For longer than she would have thought, as her head rolled across the suddenly slippery floor, the maid saw the eye and the great bulk behind it withdraw from the window, and then, for a moment, the searing blue sky beyond and a black tower around which flew hideous bird-like shapes. "It's *different* than before," she wanted to say—to the butler, to the lady of the house, to the young writer in the basement who had become her lover—but that impulse soon faded, along with everything else.

Earlier that day, the maid had argued with the butler, for the butler had seen the eyes of the dead fish move while in the kitchen and knew better than to fight. He had retreated to the huge coffin abandoned near the huge back doors to the mansion when the lady of the house had decided on the mercy of cremation for her husband instead. To either side lay the twin cousins, age twelve, all three waiting for it to be over. "Surely it will be over soon," one twin whispered into the watchful silence. "It was over last year very quickly," the other twin said in a hopeful tone. But neither twin could tell the butler exactly what they thought had happened last year. The butler knew, and had avoided the doctor ever since, but it made no difference now.

As they lay there, the coffin expanded into a limitless night, and at the edges grew terrifying fangs until the coffin was a gigantic mouth, forever contracting until the fangs were too sharply close. The butler lost his nerve and though he told the twins to close their tear-streaked eyes as he prepared to escape, still they saw all that happened next. As one they burst from the coffin—and through the back doors of the mansion, seeking the grass, the limitless sky, the verdant forest beyond. But the monster lay in wait, had opened its huge mouth to cover the door, and they in their headlong rush were crunched down, heads pulped, before even one of them could do more than think, "It's much, much *worse* than before."

The doctor received tell-tale glimmers of the butler's demise from his secret compartment in the walls at the heart of the mansion. Skilled in both medicine and the arcane arts, he had spent a year of disturbing visions, secret guilt, and hysterical mania building a place of mirrors meant to repel the uncanny, breaking almost every piece of glass in the house to capture the shards and position them with glue and nail. Each mirror piece reflected some fragment of another, so that from all sides, using cunning angles, he could glimpse moments of what was happening elsewhere. The doctor saw a hint of the cook turned to quivering meat, a scintilla of the cook's lover carried off, a suggestion of the girl betrayed on the lawn, and all of the rest. Now he stood quite silent and still in his narrow chamber of bright fragments, lit by a lantern, sweat dribbling down his face, arms, and chest.

Many quick-darting thoughts passed through the doctor's mind, reflected in the rapid blinking of his eyes. The flow of these thoughts was interrupted only by the continued siege of the mansion by the monster outside. Each *lurch* changed his focus.

> Did I make the pieces small enough? Did I make it impossible for them to see me, or do they see *all* of me now? Why would this happen to me who did nothing out of sequence or step? No one should endure this, and yet almost all of them are dead and they did nothing except the writer who carried on with both the maid and the lady of the house, but how would this concern *it*? How I wish I had never used a bone saw or performed surgery. It makes this all so much worse because [*lurch*]

> She was kinder than anyone I knew to tell me what to expect, that poor child, and perhaps I should have indulged her about her *friend* but I am a man of science too and how could I and now I wonder if her friend was indeed a manifestation or simply a terror in her mind and that I should have ergo ego ego…should have conducted an exorcism while I could rather than recommend a psychiatrist a séance to her mother

but her mother was so nice to me and so concerned and there was no way to tell that creating a circle might [*lurch*]

Was that a sound? Was that a noise other than whatever is outside? How can I tell? I cannot tell a sound beyond that sound. How hellish it is to be trapped within one's mind for even an instant without recourse to another person. How like a hell and all the thoughts that come pouring out and [*lurch*]

Be composed. Be composed. You have planned well. The glass will hold. The glass is good. Oh how now I would give for just a glimpse or touch of my beloved, thigh, face, feet. To be in her embrace, and yet this is selfish selfish selfish. [*lurch*]

Is the beast closer? A surgical cut, across the throat, from any of these shards, would be quick, painless, without guilt. No one would blame me for that. No one would blame me for that. No one left to. Oh that day we all spent on the lawn, that day glorious and sun-soaked before it began, and how could I ever give up hope of that again. Let that be what makes me strong. Do I deserve to? Do I deserve? Did I feed it? Did encourage it? [*lurch*]

Fear that brings sickness.
Fear that brings sorrow.
Fear that inhabits the smallest places.
Fear that undoes me.
Fear that makes me ill. Oh my chest. Oh my stomach.

No lurch disrupted the doctor's thoughts next. Instead, the white worm of a creature embedded inside of him so many months ago while he slept had awakened, drawn by the cries of the monster outside. As it crunched through tissue and organs, soon there was nothing larger than a fragment of the doctor left, and every single fragment of mirror covered in its entirety with blood so that his once blazing light chamber was now the darkest place in the mansion. Early in the process, the doctor felt a fierce and annihilating joy that made him shout his ecstasy to the heavens. *Is that you, my imaginary friend?* Late in the process, he managed to whisper, "Where am I?" But he knew where he was, and then he knew no more.

The doctor's screams—amplified from his hiding place by the vents, the dumbwaiter, the floorboards, the very pores of the walls— seemed to the lady's older daughter, kneeling beside a chimney on the roof, to emanate from a mansion in agony. She had chosen this vantage to observe the monster and the growth of the tower. Long ago she had been an amateur biologist familiar with certain types of animal mimicry. Now she crouched with a small telescope aimed at the tower. She could no longer force herself to observe the monster. The stench of it wafted up and made her feel as if she were being smothered in maggot-covered meat no matter how she tried to *unsee* the atrocity of its form.

Using the telescope was akin to using the microscope in her make- shift laboratory to examine cells from the strange grass of the lawn: a way to know the truth of things, no matter how uncomfortable. The telescope confirmed that it was all happening again, although only the accounts of others from that time told her anything, really. She had avoided thinking about the implications of her own notes from last year, which were incomprehensible and toward the end written in blood:

> center of the shadow near the marrow might be a door a door a door that in the white shadow there comes a presence that is made of the center of the door that in the window reflects mimics a wall a room but if we were to touch would recoil would we recoil from that the tiny white worm inches and inches cross the floor watch it carefully resurrecting, this extraction is extracted.

At the far edge of the lawn, the tower had grown pendulous and resembled less a tower now than the upper half of some thick serpent or centipede. It had been birthed by the monster, which had planted a huge, glistening white egg in the crater created by its impact. The tower curved and shook from side to side now while the ragged bird- things circled it, cawing.

The scientist also followed the cook's efforts to reach the stream; with the telescope his blunt visage was still recognizable despite the awful softness of his skull. Coming from the tower on his left, the bird-things swooped down at times to tear flesh and gristle from him, returning to toss it onto the top of the tower. Somehow, his excruciating journey seemed important, but the scientist did not know why. She knew only what the writer and doctor had speculated, for she had not been part of the circle. "You did this while I slept?" she had said, enraged that they had taken such a risk. Then retreated to her experiments to keep at bay the feelings of depression and helplessness that ever since threatened to engulf her.

Below, the monster attacked the mansion again and the mansion screamed and she made observations of a scientific nature to calm her nerves. She dispassionately noted, too, the way the forest to all sides seemed thicker, more impenetrable, and the sky brighter than ever before, and took grim delight in her detachment in recording that "long, fleshy arms have begun to sprout from the sides of the tower." As she watched, these arms began to snatch the bird-things from the sky and toss them into a gaping pink opening near the top of the tower. "It is feeding itself to grow even larger," she observed. "And it is now obvious that it is not a tower. I do not believe it is a tower. I do not believe it is a tower." She had to say it three times to truly believe it. She had no notepad to record these thoughts, and even when she braced her arm against her knee, the telescope shook a little.

Now the tower sang to the monster battering the mansion, and the monster seemed unable to resist the melody. The singing intensified and the scientist wished she had cotton to stuff in her ears, for the song was so sweet and light and uplifting that it was like an atrocity in that place, at that time. And especially now against the extreme quiet of the mansion, for the screams had stopped. Finally. "It's *nothing* like last year."

The monster, swaying in a drunken fashion, came closer and closer to the tower, trying to break away, unable to break away from its song. Until, finally, within the unbroken circle of fact that was the telescope's lens, the indescribable beast curled up at the base of the tower. The tower was cooing now, almost as if in reassurance, and the scientist's fascination at this muffled her terror…even though she could hear wet, thick sounds on the stairwell that led to the roof…and a snuffling at the locked door directly behind her.

The tower, still cooing, stretched impossibly tall, lunging up into a sky beginning to bruise in anticipation of dusk. It leaned over to contemplate the monster below with something the scientist thought might be affection. With incredible speed and velocity, it dove down to pierce the monster's brain. The monster flailed and brought its legs up to struggle, to push out the dagger of the tower, but soon this effort became half-hearted, then ceased altogether. A flow of gold-

and-emerald globules rose up through the tower's darkness from the monster. The farther these globules rose, the more transparent they became, until the tower had assimilated them entirely and was as dark as before.

The monster lay husked. The tower grew taller and wider. The mansion beneath the scientist grew spongy and porous, and a kind of heartbeat began to pulse through its many chambers. But the scientist observed none of the things. The tower's song and the piercing of the monster's brain had pierced the telescope, too. The telescope, grown strange and feral and querulous, had punctured her eye on its way to her brain, and as she lay there and the tower ate the monster, so too the telescope made a meal of her. Satisfied, the white worm behind the door retreated.

Dusk came over the land. An impossibly large, impossibly purple-tinged moon sent out a blinding half-light across the wandering grass, the mansion, and the tower. The cook had finally reached the lip of the river bank, and in some instinctual way recognized this small victory, even though the remains of his head were twisted above by happenstance to look back across the lawn.

The mansion had become watchful and its upper windows gleamed like eyes. The corners of the mansion had become rounded so that it squatted on powerful haunches, poised to spring forward on four thick legs. The cook was unsurprised: he had argued for months that the mansion had been colonized by something *below* it, rising up, and the walls had begun to even seem to *breathe* a little. But they had laughed at him. "It's like last year," he said, although he could not really remember last year...or why the fish had looked so strange.

At a certain hour, the tower began to stride toward the mansion, and the two joined in a titanic battle that split the air with unearthly shrieks: solid bulk against twisty strength. Around the two combatants, their tread shaking the ground, the grass rippled with phosphorescence and from the forests beyond came the distant calls of other mighty beasts.

The remains of the cook found no horror in the scene. The cook was beyond horror, all fast-evaporating thought focused on the river that had been the site of his happiest memory—a nighttime rendezvous with his lover. As they lay beside each other afterwards, the contented murmur in his ear of a line of a poem. "*No other breather....*" This memory tainted only by the pain of remembering his lover's reaction when he had slid into bed that last time, after having been so reduced by the white worm that had sprung at him from the walls of the kitchen.

So he slid and pushed, still hopeful, losing more flesh and tissue and bone fragments, down the bank of the river, and by an effort of will he managed to whip his head around to face the water. There, through his one good eye, the cook saw his lover and the little girl and the lady of the house and the doctor and the maid and the butler, the lady's two young cousins, and the scientist...they lay at rest at the bottom of the river. Waiting with open, sightless eyes. He had a sudden recollection of them all sitting around a table, holding hands, and what came after, but then it was gone gone gone gone, and he was sliding down into his lover's embrace. The feel of the water was such a balm, such a release that it felt like the most blissful moment of his entire life, and any thought of returning home, of reaching home, vanished into the water with him.

Behind him, under stars forever strange, the tower and the mansion fought on.

# Other Notable Works of Weird Fiction

"Vivian Guppy and the Brighton Belle," Nina Allan, *Rustblind & Starbright*

"Americca," Aimee Bender, *Slate*

"The Sweet Virgin Meat," Kola Boof, *Exotic Gothic 5*

"The Vast Impatience Of The Night," Mark Fuller Dillon, *In a Season of Dead Weather*

"Oubliette," Gemma Files, *The Grimscribe's Puppets*

"Rocket to Hell," Jeffrey Ford, *Tor.com*

"The Man Who Escaped His Story," Cody Goodfellow, *The Grimscribe's Puppets*

"Diamond Dust," Michael Griffin, *The Grimscribe's Puppets*

"Baba Makosh," M.K. Hobson, *The Magazine of Fantasy & Science Fiction*

"Interstate Love Affair," Stephen Graham Jones, *Three Miles Past*

"Mother of Stone," John Langan, *The Wide Carnivorous Sky & Other Monstrous Geographies*

"The Cave," Sean F. Lynch, *The Magazine of Fantasy & Science Fiction*

"Hideous Interview with Brief Man," Nick Mamatas, *Fiddleblack*

"In the Darkest Room in the Darkest House on the Darkest Part of the Street," Gary McMahon, *For the Night is Dark*

"The Design," China Mieville, *McSweeney's 45*

"All Your Faces Drown in My Syringe," Ralph Robert Moore, *Black Static 37*

"Black Hen a La Ford," David Nickle, *In Words, Alas, Drown I*

"The Last Hour of the Bengal Tiger," Yoko Ogawa, *Revenge*

"The House on Cobb Street," Lynda Rucker *Nightmare Magazine*

"How I Met the Ghoul," Sofia Samatar, *Eleven, Eleven*

"The Painted Bones," Kelly Simmons *Unlikely Story Issue 6*

"Touch Me With Your Cold, Hard Fingers," Elizabeth Stott, *Nightjar Press*

"Abyssus Abyssum Invocat," Genevieve Valentine, *Lightspeed Magazine*

"The Fox," Conrad Williams, *This is Horror*

"On Murder Island," Matt Williamson, *Nightmare Magazine*

## COPYRIGHT ACKNOWLEDGEMENTS

Foreword by Michael Kelly. Copyright © 2014 by Michael Kelly.

"Introduction: We Are For the Weird" by Laird Barron. Copyright © 2014 by Laird Barron.

"The Nineteenth Step" by Simon Strantzas. Copyright © 2013 by Simon Strantzas. First published in *Shadows Edge*, edited by Simon Strantzas, Gray Friar Press.

"Swim Wants to Know If It's As Bad As Swim Thinks" by Paul Tremblay. Copyright © 2013 by Tremblay. First published in *Bourbon Penn #8*.

"Dr. Blood and the Ultra Fabulous Glitter Squadron" by A.C. Wise. Copyright © 2013 by A.C. Wise. First published in *Ideomancer* Vol. 12, Issue 2.

"Year of the Rat" by Chen Qiufan, translated by Ken Liu. Copyright © 2013 by Chen Qiufan. Translation copyright © 2013 by Ken Liu. First published in *The Magazine of Fantasy & Science Fiction*, July/August 2013.

"Olimpia's Ghost" by Sofia Samatar. Copyright © 2013 by Sofia Samatar. First published in *Phantom Drift #3*.

"Furnace" by Livia Llewellyn. Copyright © 2013 by Livia Llewellyn. First published in *The Grimscribe's Puppets*, edited by Joseph S. Pulver Sr., Miskatonic River Pres..

"Shall I Whisper to You of Moonlight, of Sorrow, of Pieces of Us?" by Damien Angelica Walters. Copyright © 2013 by Damien Angelic Walters. First published in *Shock Totem #7*.

"Bor Urus" by John Langan. Copyright © 2013 by John Langan. First published in *Shadows Edge*, edited by Simon Strantzas.

"A Quest of Dream" by W.H. Pugmire. Copyright © 2013 by W.H. Pugmire. First published in *Bohemians of Sesqua Valley*.

"The Krakatoan" by Maria Dahvana Headley. Copyright © 2013 by Maria Dahvana Headley. First published simultaneously in *The Lowest Heaven*, edited by Anne C. Perry and Jared Shurin, and *Nightmare Magazine*, July 2013.

"The Girl in the Blue Coat" by Anna Taborska. Copyright © 2013 by Anna Taborska. First published in *Exotic Gothic 5, Vol. 1*, edited by Danel Olson.

"(he) Dreams of Lovecraftian Horror" by Joseph S. Pulver Sr. Copyright ©
2013 by Joseph S. Pulver Sr. First published in *Lovecraft eZine #28*.

"In Limbo" by Jeffrey Thomas. Copyright © 2013 by Jeffrey Thomas. First
published in *Worship the Night*.

"A Cavern of Redbrick" by Richard Gavin. Copyright © 2013 by Richard
Gavin. First published in *Shadows & Tall Trees #5*.

"Eyes Exchange Bank" by Scott Nicolay. Copyright © 2013 by Scott Nicolay.
First published in *The Grimscribe's Puppets*, edited by Joseph S. Pulver Sr.

"Fox into Lady" by Anne-Sylvie Salzman. Copyright © 2013 by Anne-Sylvie
Salzman. First English-language publication in *Darkscapes*.

"Like Feather, Like Bone" by Kristi DeMeester. Copyright © 2013 by Kristi
DeMeester. First published in *Shimmer #17*.

"A Terror" by Jeffrey Ford. Copyright © 2013 by Jeffrey Ford. First published
at *Tor.com, July 2013*.

"Success" by Michael Blumlein. Copyright © 2013 by Michael Blumlein. First
published in *The Magazine of Fantasy & Science Fiction, Nov./Dec. 2013*.

"Moonstruck" by Karin Tidbeck. Copyright © 2013 by Karin Tidbeck. First
published in *Shadows & Tall Trees #5*.

"The Key to Your Heart Is Made of Brass" by John R. Fultz. Copyright © 2013
by John R. Fultz. First published in *Fungi #21*.

"No Breather in the World But Thee" by Jeff VanderMeer. Copyright © 2013
by Jeff VanderMeer. First published in *Nightmare Magazine, March 2013*.

UNDERTOW
PUBLICATIONS